Praise for Mary Freeman's
GARDENING MYSTERIES

"An appealing new detective with a green thumb . . . and a sharp eye for clues."　　　　—Susan Wittig Albert

"Mary Freeman evokes for us the dark goings-on in and around the charming gardens of the mythical town of Blossom, Oregon. We can't relax until the landscaper heroine, Rachel O'Connor, unearths the solution to some very nasty murders."　　　　—Ann Ripley

"Fans who enjoy a warm tale about small-town living will gain much pleasure from Mary Freeman's novel."
　　　　—Harriet Klausner

"Interesting characters, a sharp puzzle, gardening details, and not one, but two romances make *Devil's Trumpet* a scintillating mystery debut. Rachel O'Connor is an engaging character, definitely worthy of a series. The pace is lively and the story intriguing. What more could anyone ask for in a mystery?"　　　　—*Romantic Times*

"Mary Freeman writes as though she has known these townspeople all their lives. . . . [*Devil's Trumpet*] kept me guessing till the end. I would love this story to become a series. [She] has created a whole new world for mystery lovers to roam! Stimulating plots, intriguing characters, and author with a talent for both."　　　　—*Literary Times*

"Music, gardening, herbs, and old hurts combine perfectly in this enjoyable debut novel."—*Mystery Time & Rhyme*

"A very good amateur sleuth mystery. Readers will like the characters and the serpentine plot filled . . . with red herrings."　　　　—*Midwest Book Review*

MORE MYSTERIES FROM THE
BERKLEY PUBLISHING GROUP . . .

SISTER FREVISSE MYSTERIES: Medieval mystery in the tradition of
Ellis Peters . . .

by Margaret Frazer

THE NOVICE'S TALE	THE BISHOP'S TALE
THE OUTLAW'S TALE	THE BOY'S TALE
THE PRIORESS' TALE	THE MURDERER'S TALE
THE SERVANT'S TALE	THE REEVE'S TALE
THE MAIDEN'S TALE	THE SQUIRE'S TALE
	THE CLERK'S TALE

PENNYFOOT HOTEL MYSTERIES: In Edwardian England, death takes
a seaside holiday . . .

by Kate Kingsbury

ROOM WITH A CLUE	GROUNDS FOR MURDER
SERVICE FOR TWO	PAY THE PIPER
CHECK-OUT TIME	CHIVALRY IS DEAD
DO NOT DISTURB	RING FOR TOMB SERVICE
EAT, DRINK, AND BE BURIED	MAID TO MURDER
DEATH WITH RESERVATIONS	DYING ROOM ONLY

GLYNIS TRYON MYSTERIES: The highly acclaimed series set in the
early days of the women's rights movement . . .
"Historically accurate and telling." —Sara Paretsky

by Miriam Grace Monfredo

SENECA FALLS INHERITANCE	THROUGH A GOLD EAGLE
BLACKWATER SPIRITS	THE STALKING HORSE
MUST THE MAIDEN DIE?	SISTERS OF CAIN
NORTH STAR CONSPIRACY	BROTHERS OF CAIN

MARK TWAIN MYSTERIES: "Adventurous . . . Replete with genuine
tall tales from the great man himself." —*Mostly Murder*

by Peter J. Heck

DEATH ON THE MISSISSIPPI	A CONNECTICUT YANKEE IN CRIMINAL COURT
GUILTY ABROAD	THE PRINCE AND THE PROSECUTOR
	TOM'S LAWYER

GARDEN
VIEW

Mary Freeman

BERKLEY PRIME CRIME, NEW YORK

GARDEN VIEW

A Berkley Prime Crime Book / published by arrangement with the author

PRINTING HISTORY
Berkley Prime Crime mass-market edition / May 2002

6084 5970
4/16

Visit our website at
www.penguinputnam.com

ISBN: 0-425-18454-4

Berkley Prime Crime books are published
by The Berkley Publishing Group,
a division of Penguin Putnam Inc.,
375 Hudson Street, New York, New York 10014.
The name BERKLEY PRIME CRIME and the BERKLEY PRIME CRIME
design are trademarks belonging to Penguin Putnam Inc.

PRINTED IN THE UNITED STATES OF AMERICA

10 9 8 7 6 5 4 3 2 1

For Dick Morris

I'd like to thank Jake Rosenblum for the Search and Rescue details, Debbie Cross for her as-always great critique, Marti Dell for legal details, and Hank and Joyce for their eternal support.

PROLOGUE

The old woman knelt. Slowly, stiffly, her knee joints flexing reluctantly, as if unwilling to give in to the pull of gravity, she lowered herself to the floor. The ivory satin bathrobe pooled around her in shimmering folds and her white hair wisped around her face, haloing the withered crepe-like skin. The woman raised her clasped hands as if in prayer. Hands, satin robe, and the nimbus of white hair gave her the appearance of a religious icon—perhaps the image on the cover of a religious card.

But her eyes were fixed on a gold-framed photograph placed carefully on a small table beneath a brass table lamp. The yellow light from the lamp warmed the woman's pale skin, and the satin rustled slightly as she sighed. "I am sorry." Her whispered words barely stirred the air. "I know it's too late to make anything right, but . . . forgive me. Please. Forgive me."

The woman and the two young children in the photograph smiled for the camera, their faces bright and full of life. On the rug, the old woman buried her face in her hands and gave a single dry sob.

A gentle tap sounded on the white-painted door. The old woman's head jerked up and she lurched to her feet. "Who's there?" She licked her dry lips and crossed to the door, head tilted as if to listen at the crack.

"It's just me."

"Oh, I thought you'd already gone home." Her face relaxing into a smile, the woman turned the bolt and opened the door. She looked out into the carpeted hall, still smiling. "What are you doing here at this hour? Come in, come in before someone sees you."

She stepped back, ushering her guest into the room.

CHAPTER

1

Perspiration trickled down Rachel O'Connor's face as she drove the sharp blade of her trenching spade into the dry summer soil. A hot wind blew down the Columbia Gorge, scorching the roadside grass to tinder-dry gold and crisping tender leaves. In the orchards of Hood River, the Gravenstein apples were ripening early, their red-streaked sides plump and sweet with the extra sun and heat this summer. Rachel dumped clods of hard dry dirt onto the tarp she had laid out beside the narrow trench, then straightened up to wipe her face on her sleeve.

This job at the Garden View Retirement Village was a triumph for her young landscaping business—a tempting promise of bigger jobs to come. The facility sat on five gently sloping acres above the river with a nice view of the water and five acres of young pears. The original landscaper had gouged a pond into the front lawn, had ringed it with young willows that had mostly died, seeded the lawn, and had apparently called it good. Without a water system, the young lawn had quickly dried up and mostly died in the first summer's sun, to be replaced by dandelions, hawk-weed, plantain, and a few of the tougher members of the grass family. Two of the willows had survived, providing a bit of shade for a path that followed the pond's edge. The bank had dried and cracked in the sun, and the water had transformed into green soup in the summer heat.

Above it, the long pale pink wings of the sprawling complex of apartments and condominiums that made up the Village baked in the sun, sheltered by nothing more than a rank of sulky *arbor vitae* that had been planted to hide the foundation. Bark covered nearly everything that wasn't sidewalk, eroding to reveal the heavy landscape fabric beneath. A jumble of boulders in a couple of strategic locations barely suggested ornament. Lawnmower landscape, Rachel thought as she surveyed it once more. Boring. She ran a hand through her short, black curls. No, worse than that, the landscape was *bleak*. She wrinkled her nose, letting the scene blur into a vista of curving beds filled with interesting foliage and washes of bright flowers. Trees and drought-tolerant vines would shade the walkways between the wings, offering private nooks for chatting or reading. Birds would sing in the shrubbery and the pond would be an oasis of cool water aerated by a fountain and flanked by shaded benches. The barren slope above would become a rock garden threaded with accessible paths and filled with the bright clusters of hens-and-chicks and sempervivens. Lewisias, she thought dreamily. Small penstemons. She might try a couple of ceanothus for their lilac flowers, although the Gorge winter might be too cold for them. Still, she could shelter them from the wind with some strategic boulders. It was worth a try. Rock cress and some creeping chamomile . . .

She had been excited when the new administrator had asked her for a bid. She had been ecstatic when she had won the bid. The director had been enthusiastic about her proposal to use edible plants that would pose no threat to confused elderly residents, and to use drought-tolerant natives as much as possible. A magazine was going to do a story on the renovation of the long-neglected Village, and the landscaping would feature in it, she had assured Rachel. Rachel sighed and shook her head, banishing her visions and hefting her spade again.

She wasn't so ecstatic anymore. To put it mildly.

With another head shake, Rachel went back to shoveling, hacking out more soil, extending the trench another few inches. Pipe for the irrigation system would lie here, joining the old pond-side beds to the main water line that would supply the new beds. Drip watering and low-flow sprinklers would water the beds and individual plants. Already she had had to alter her original design. Of course, the director had forgotten to mention the new fence that would surround the facility—six feet of chain link so that no resident could wander off and get lost, she had explained. But, the beds would hide it, wouldn't they?

They wouldn't, since Rachel hadn't known that the fence existed. She had kept the plantings low so as not to block the view of the Columbia. So she had redesigned— and had to increase her estimate, because the plants that would hide the fence added considerably to her plant budget. Since she was choosing only nonpoisonous species, her choices were limited.

The director had not been happy.

Across the sunburned lawn, Eduardo straightened suddenly, leaning on the handle of his spade. The man working with him—a short, thick-shouldered man with a gold tooth that flashed when he grinned—stopped digging, too. Eduardo shrugged as Rachel looked his way, let one shoulder droop in a fatalistic gesture that sent chills down Rachel's spine.

"No." She closed her eyes briefly. "Not again. Don't tell me."

Eduardo shrugged impassively and tapped his shovel blade on the bottom of the trench that had been creeping toward her own. The ring of metal on stone wrung a groan from Rachel.

"More lava." She didn't bother to make it a question.

The Columbia Plateau was called the Columbia Lava Shield for a reason. Back in prehistoric times the Cascade Range had been born, rising in thick layers of molten rock from that ancient plane. That molten birthing had piled up to form the Cascade Mountain Range and lurked always beneath the thin layer of soil that had formed on top of it. It was a *very* thin layer in places but thicker here in the Hood River Valley. Still, the odd rib or ridge of old basalt occasionally jutted up through that thin flesh of soil.

You couldn't dig an irrigation trench through solid basalt.

Blasting was a bit extreme. Or maybe not. Rachel clenched teeth and fists. The main line needed to be buried, although the quarter-inch drip lines could trail on the surface. "Well, I guess I'll have to redraw the system." She managed an admirably calm tone of voice that fooled no one. She did not add "again." This would be the third time she had had to reroute the plumbing. "You know, I walked over every square foot of this damn place. With a probe. There are no lava ridges here. None."

Eduardo gave her one of his glazed, *no comprendo* looks, which meant either that he really didn't understand what she was saying, or that she was acting like a crazy-Anglo-boss-lady again and he wasn't going to be rude enough to acknowledge it. Probably the latter, Rachel thought grimly. She was feeling a little crazy right now. "Take a break," she said wearily. "Get me the probe first." She stabbed her spade into the unfinished trench. "Let me see if we can work around this."

"What are you doing, taking a break? You just started." Director Jennifer Bellington's clear, carrying voice rang out behind Rachel. "I assume this means you are back on schedule again?"

Drawing a deep breath, struggling to hang on to the Irish temper she'd inherited from her father, Rachel turned around. "Actually, we started several hours ago." She managed a smile although it felt as if someone had applied it to her face with a butter knife. "We were working before you arrived. And we were making up time." Were. "But we hit another vein of basalt. I'll need to redraw the water system."

"Again?" Director Bellington's neat eyebrows rose into twin arches of disbelief as she stared down at Rachel from her six-foot-plus height. "I thought I understood at our last setback that we would have no more trouble with rock." Her precisely lipsticked lips curved into a very chilly red smile. "You do remember that we are facing a deadline here?"

"Yes, I do." Rachel cursed her burning cheeks, wishing she didn't blush at the drop of a hat. "I thought I had checked this slope thoroughly. Apparently this is a narrow ridge and I missed it. We should be able to get around it easily," she said with a confidence she wished she could feel.

"I hope so." The director's gray eyes gleamed like steel. "The article about Garden View village is scheduled for next fall, and that means that we need to have the photography done this fall, before the winter. I hope you're keeping our magazine debut in mind?" She glanced around at the sunburned patches of grass and seeding dandelion. "We have a long way to go, don't we?"

We? Rachel resisted the temptation to hand her boss a spade. "I'll have it looking nice for the cameras," she said instead.

"I would certainly hope so." The red smile came and went again, like a glimpse of next winter's ice, echoing the chilly hint of threat in her tone. With a final nod, the director turned on her heel and marched back across the lawn toward the west wing of the Village, where her office was located. Even in the heat of the late morning, her crisp linen suit looked freshly ironed and not a hair dared stir out of its neat French roll. Rachel grabbed her spade, feeling sweaty, grubby, chunky as a draft horse—and incompetent. One thing after another had gone wrong with this job.

Eduardo and his crewman, looking after the director, gave each other knowing looks, and Eduardo said something in a low tone that made the other man grin. Then they both shrugged and looked at Rachel.

"Get me the probe and go take a break," she said wearily. "This won't take long."

It didn't. It took her less than twenty minutes to discover that the ridge—narrow as a roadside curb in places—neatly bisected the north-facing slope. It was as if a prehistoric mole had burrowed across the lawn, leaving basalt in its wake. She threw down the probe with a comment that made both men grin. She was going to have to route the water line clear around the perimeter of the property and come up to the beds around the pond from the north boundary. This was just about going to double the amount of pipe needed to feed the irrigation zones she had already planned. She'd already had to increase the cost of the irrigation to cover the new watering zones created by the increase in plantings to screen the fence. This new addition was going to take her into the red, Rachel thought gloomily. She was going to have to talk to the director.

Not today. "First we make amazing progress," she told the two men as she sketched in the new water lines on her working plan. "Then we tell her about the increase in cost." She grabbed up a handful of flagged stakes and marched out, sweating, to lay out the new course for the pipe. All that digging this morning for nothing. Grimly she began to plant stakes. Expensive way to aerate the soil, those trenches. As she stabbed the last of the flagged stakes into the rock-hard soil, she noticed a small, spry man waving to her from the parking lot by the main building. As he descended the slope the sun gleamed on his bushy white hair and Rachel recognized Dr. Cory Welsh, longtime and only resident doctor for the nearby city of Blossom, dressed in the light gray suit he always wore when he was "on duty." Dr. Cory was an avid fisherman. If you needed him and he wasn't dressed in his suit and at home or at his office on Main, you asked Roth Glover, who ran the hardware store, where Doc would most likely be fishing that day.

"My dear, you don't look like you're having a good time," he called out as he reached her. "I was so pleased to hear that they hired you for this job. You have such a nice eye for the natural."

"Thank you." Rachel smiled, some of her dark mood lifting. Doc was like that—his cheerful mood was contagious. "I'm just having trouble with lava." She wrinkled her nose. "It keeps sneaking up behind me and making my life difficult."

"Lively stuff, eh?" The old man's blue eyes twinkled beneath his unruly mop of snow-white hair. "And kind of hard to dig through, I'd say. It's noon." He pulled a genuine pocket watch on a chain from his pocket and flipped open the filigreed lid. "I bet a glass of iced tea and a chicken salad would improve things. Would you honor an old man with a lunch date?" He twinkled at her again, offering his arm with an old-world courtly charm. "You're way too healthy. I rejoice for that, but I never get to visit with you."

"You should teach me how to fish then." Rachel laughed. "I didn't know it was that late. I'm supposed to be meeting Madame DeRochers and Harris McLoughlin for lunch," she said. "Can you join us? You know them both, don't you?"

"Oh, of course I know Anne-Marie. She is such a vital woman. She'll outlive us all." The doctor laughed. "And I've met Harris before. He was a policeman, wasn't he?"

"A detective. Just a moment. I need to give my crew some directions." She hurried over to Eduardo, telling him to go ahead and have his lunch, then to begin the new ditch if she wasn't back when they'd finished. "And please don't hit any more rock," she muttered under her breath as she rejoined the doctor. "I was going to change." She eyed her jeans and T-shirt ruefully. "But I don't have time. Hope they don't throw me out of the dining room."

"You look fine, dear." Dr. Welsh patted her hand. "How is your mother doing? I haven't seen her zooming about in her little car lately."

"She's doing a lot better since she finished the chemotherapy." Rachel stopped at her truck to wash her hands and change her dirt-crusted work boots for sneakers. The irrigation pipe loaded onto the bed rack mocked her. More money to spend . . . "Her hair has started to grow back." Rachel smiled. "She says she's disappointed. She hoped it would come back blond."

"She's much too feisty a lady to be a blonde." Dr. Welsh laughed. "I'm glad she's doing well."

"What brings you here?" Rachel accompanied him along the unadorned concrete walk that led from the parking lot to the main entrance. "Is someone sick?"

"Oh, no, not really." A dimple dented the doctor's weathered cheek when he smiled. "I drop in every afternoon just to listen, you know? Sometimes that's enough. Sometimes I hand out a few vitamins or some of the herbal remedies—nothing wrong with a dose of Saint John's wort or echinacea, you know. A few folk here worry a lot about their health." He smiled wryly. "Helps to keep your ear to the ground. Separate fact from fancy, if you get what I mean. Emily Barnhart has been having some bouts with a stomach flu this summer." He clucked his tongue. "She's sure she's got stomach cancer, but I suspect she just needs to go easy on the fresh fruit. She's a bit . . . ah . . . overindulgent at times. Although she really did pick up one of those late flu bugs that made the rounds here near the end of the school year. Grandchildren!" He shook his head. "Infectious creatures." They had reached the double wood and glass doors that led into the main entry of Garden View Retirement Village.

With a slight bow, Dr. Welsh ushered her through the door and into the cool dimness of the interior.

The new director had done a nice job of redecorating, Rachel mused. Glazed earth-toned tiles floored an open space dotted with planters full of bamboo and ferns. Sofas and armchairs stood in cozy groups that invited conversation. There were no rugs to tangle canes or walkers and plenty of space for wheelchairs to thread between the furniture. Colorful quilts and woven hangings hung on the walls, adding warmth. Very upscale, Rachel thought as she eyed the small groups of men and women who chatted here and there. A foursome worked on a jigsaw puzzle at a table in one corner. This might be a resort, rather than an assisted-living facility.

"I was concerned that you might have forgotten our appointment." Anne-Marie Celestine DeRochers, eighty and still handsome in a black dress and pearls, rose from one of the chairs near the dining room door. "How lovely. You have brought the good doctor to eat with us?" She extended one graceful, long-fingered hand to the doctor, who kissed it with a flourish. "Ah, such a fervent man." Madame withdrew her hand and batted her eyelashes coquettishly, but her voice was unusually cool.

"Are you trying to make me jealous, my love?" The lean, steel-haired man seated in a wheelchair beside her held out a hand to Rachel. "You look great. Your job agrees with you. I hear you're doing well at it."

"I don't know about well, but I do know that I look like I've been digging ditches. Which I have." Rachel laughed, but a sudden awkwardness seemed to have descended over the foursome. "You look good yourself," she said with a shade too much enthusiasm as she eyed McLoughlin's muscular shoulders and trim waist, which weren't at all disguised by the light shirt he wore. "You look like you've been working out."

"I jog," Harris said with a straight face.

"Ten miles." Madame rolled her eyes and pouted. "Leaving me to sit all alone in the mornings, without conversation."

"I keep inviting you to come." Harris put his hand on her knee. "I'm never sure I should let you out of my sight, anyway."

"It is too hot." Madame fanned herself languidly. "And I have no need to huff and puff along like these girls in their shiny tights. Do they know how they appear? All this bouncing!"

"You would be lovely in spandex." Harris took her hand and kissed her palm. It was a long kiss.

"You two are impossible." Rachel laughed because Dr. Welsh actually looked the tiniest bit shocked. "You're going to get thrown out of here, you know."

"I suspect our dear director would like that all too well." Madame made no move to free her hand. "But she cannot," she said complacently. "I own my apartment here, and so does Monsieur." She nodded at Harris, who was now merely holding her hand. "Shall we go in?" She nodded at the steady trickle of elderly residents entering the dining room. "I must inform my friend Ricki that we will need a table for *four.*" She stressed the word every so slightly and gave Dr. Welsh the tiniest of glances.

"Oh, there's no need. I need to see the director." Dr. Welsh cleared his throat and gave them a vague smile. "It was nice to see you, Rachel." His smile warmed as he lifted a hand to her, then vanished in the direction of the director's office.

Rachel accompanied Madame and McLoughlin into the dining room. The same pale tile covered the floor, but the north wall had been replaced with a greenhouse wall. Hanging plants—asparagus fern and philodendron— added a garden ambience.

Madame and Harris really did make a rather wonderful pair, Rachel thought, watching them thread their way through the tables hand in hand. Although he was a good twenty years her junior, they both seemed eternally youthful. And eternally lusty. Rachel grinned to herself, hoping that she'd be half that vigorous at their ages. A freckled young woman in the pale blue smock of an aid waved to them from a table near the window in a secluded corner. With surprise, Rachel noticed that she was wearing a white kitchen apron over her smock.

"Ah, Ricki, you have done well." Madame nodded graciously to the young woman as she seated herself. "Thank you."

"I'm glad you got here. Sandra Willis always snatches this table. Good thing she's late coming in today." She smiled at McLoughlin, her hazel eyes dancing. "I saw you wheeling along the road at the crack of dawn this morning. I couldn't keep up with you, running. No wonder you've got those shoulders." She winked at Madame. "Good thing he's taken."

"Indeed," Madame said with enormous complacency. "It is a good thing. This is Rachel O'Connor. She is creating the garden."

"Oh, I wanted to meet you." Ricki filled their glasses with ice water. "My great-uncle came back to Blossom to retire. He lives just up from Main Street, on Second. At Fir. He used to be a private gardener for a couple of really rich families in Portland—oh, years ago. You should meet him someday."

"I'd like to." Rachel looked around, noticing that other aides were filling glasses and carrying plates. "Is the wait staff on strike?"

"You didn't hear?" Ricki tugged at her ginger ponytail. "We're now waiting tables. The Dragon Lady says it's so that we can have more bonding time with the residents. Ha!" She lowered her voice, casting a slightly guilty look around the rapidly filling room. "She's cutting back in all kinds of little ways. We're always short of this and that, and she won't hire any new staff. We barely have enough aids as it is." She wrinkled her nose in exasperation as she scooped up her pitcher. "I'd better get hopping. So you want the special? It's good today—grilled salmon and pasta."

They agreed on it unanimously and Ricki scurried off to fill more glasses. Two women in flowered dresses took the table next to them. "You stole my table." The shorter of the two women, the one with the seriously lavender hair, waved. "I'll let you keep it this time," she called cheerfully. The taller, skinnier one ignored them all. She wore a magnificent necklace of pearls, Rachel noticed with a twinge of envy. They shone like tiny moons against her yellowish, flaccid skin.

"So how can the Village be short of money?" Rachel turned to Madame. "I mean, I just took on a huge contract to landscape the grounds."

"There is much that lurks beneath the surface of our little enterprise." Madame gave her a darkly knowing look. "All shall be beautiful on the outside, you see? It is, how is it said, *trés* upscale, *non*? You come here, you see flowers and expensive tile, you eat salmon, and you say, yes, sign me up! I will buy a condominium in this place! I will live here and enjoy the luxury. But is it so?" She flourished her starched white napkin at Rachel. "Before, it was just an old-folks' home, yes? And now it is transformed. But where is the money to do so? Aha." She looked at McLoughlin, who raised one eyebrow enigmatically. "I think the money is not here yet." Madame leaned forward, lowering her voice. "Or perhaps it is, and it inhabits the wrong pockets."

"What's this? Secrets at the table? Oh, let me in on them. I love a nice bit of juicy gossip." Ricki appeared with an enormous metal tray. Balancing it on the edge of the table, she whisked small plates of salad and large plates of pasta and salmon down in front of each of them. "Bread and butter, and I can't believe I made it in one trip." She set down the wicker basket of rolls and a small dish of skimpy butter curls. "Forgotten skills from working at Fong's after school." She laughed. "Once a waitress, always a waitress."

"My dear, I'm telling you that they are stealing from us." The shrill, angry complaint from the next table silenced even Ricki. As one, they all looked at the two women. The tall skinny one with the pearls was glaring at her lilac-haired companion. "I didn't order extra maid service. And I didn't order any grocery deliveries either. Margaret buys whatever I need and delivers them every Sunday. They just think I'm senile. They think I don't read my bills. A few dollars here, a few dollars there, but after a year or ten it adds up, doesn't it?"

Her companion shot them a brief apologetic glance and leaned forward, murmuring, obviously soothing her upset tablemate.

"You just check your bill next month," the skinny woman said in a slightly lower tone. "You just check. I may be ill, I may be dying, but I am not senile. Not at all."

"That's Emily Barnhart ," Ricki said in a whisper. "Check her bill?" She rolled her eyes and made a face. "She has complained no less than three times now that somebody has broken into her room and used her special tea mug. They didn't put it back just right, she said. I mean, I ask you." Ricki shook her head. "Maybe the same person sneaked into the director's office and doctored her bill, too. If she's not senile, she's crazy." Ricki shook her-head as she vanished with her tray toward the kitchen.

"Life is never dull," McLoughlin said dryly and Madame laughed, but Rachel noticed the brief intense look that passed between them.

"She was the patient Dr. Welsh was coming to see." Rachel poked at her pasta, searching for promised salmon, watching another glance pass between her companions. She gave up on the elusive fish and forked up a bite of pasta and sauce. "She doesn't look awfully sick."

"Many here who seem well are not, it appears," Madame said darkly. She gave McLoughlin another glance as he cleared his throat meaningfully.

"What do you mean?" Rachel asked innocently.

"I mean that people die here who are not ready to die," Madame said. "This is no longer a healthy place. I think our good doctor, he does not have eyes to see."

"I think you need to be careful about what you say, love." Harris shook his head. "People here are old. Dr. Welsh is a good doctor."

"*I* am old, and I am not ready to die." Madame tossed her head. "When someone is ready, you may see it. If you choose to look."

"Anne-Marie!"

Madame pressed her lips together and bowed her head ever so slightly. "I apologize," she said to Rachel. "I spoke out of turn."

Rachel had never heard Harris McLoughlin use Madame's first name in that tone before. The conversation moved on to a lighthearted discussion of the upcoming harvest and the topic of whether Blossom should join Hood River for a joint Harvest Festival in the fall. They finished their salmon-flavored pasta and had coffee. During it all, Rachel found herself wondering just what exactly was going on at the Garden View Retirement Village.

CHAPTER
2

They made good progress that afternoon, but by the time Rachel told the men to clean their tools and quit for the day, they were even more behind schedule than before. After Eduardo and his helper had left in Eduardo's battered car, Rachel walked the site for a while, frowning, adding up the additional materials needed to extend the water system in its new path. A faint scent of smoke in the air made her pause, connectors, bubbler hydrants, and vertical risers forgotten, to scan the slopes around her and the stretch of Interstate 80 visible from where she stood, searching for flames.

This summer had been dry and already careless cigarettes had blackened a half-dozen stretches of bone-dry grass and weeds along the interstate. Everyone was edgy. She eyed the pile of dry scotch broom and debris piled at the bottom of the slope below the Village buildings. That was another sore point between her and the director. It was unsightly. It needed to be dealt with. But dealing with it meant burning it and burning wasn't going to happen until it had rained for a while. Hauling it off would be way too expensive, Rachel had patiently explained. The director did not seem to hear her.

Feeling utterly worn out, Rachel racked the last of the spades in her truck and locked the tool box. A couple of women residents were strolling along the concrete walk-way between wings, dressed in nearly identical pastel-print slack and blouse sets. One of them carried a faded green umbrella that served as a sun shade. Few residents ventured out in the hot afternoon sun, Rachel had noticed. There was nothing to do out here, and no shade. She had spent nearly a week in the Willamette Valley scouring nurseries for the largest shade-tree specimens that she could plant without using expensive heavy equipment. Those she found weren't going to be awfully big, but they were at least a promise of shade to come. Hand on the door of her truck, she paused as a blue-smocked man stopped to speak to the strolling couple, then hurried her way. One of the aids. He smiled as he reached her, tall and athletic, with an open, friendly face and an easy grin. "I noticed that your crew left. I just thought something might be wrong," he said, nodding at her truck. "Won't it start?"

"No, I was just thinking. That's all." Rachel smiled, anxious to get out of there and take a long shower.

"I saw you at lunch. I've been meaning to . . . I just wanted to say . . ." His face reddened and he cleared his throat. "A lot of people here—us aids and the residents— well, we were all at that presentation you made about what you were going to do. We think you're doing a great job and we all can't wait until we have something out here to walk in besides this . . . pasture." He waved at the sunburned and tunneled slope. "And the Dragon Lady is giving you a hard time because she wants you to quit, and we all hope you don't, because if you do, she'll do some-thing cheap and easy, or probably leave it like it is and . . .

well, we all want what you showed us. We're tired of being stuck inside most of the year with nothing to look at but a few pear trees in rows and the river."

"Thank you." Taken aback and a bit moved, Rachel studied his face. "Why do you think she wants me to quit?"

The aid looked around quickly, as if he feared to be overheard, then leaned closer. "Money," he said in a low voice. "She's already gotten the landscaping budget approved by the Board, you see. If she got somebody cheaper, she could slip it by them and pocket the difference. They're not local people. They just come for a meeting once or twice a year and listen to her the rest of the time. I don't think they really know what's going on here. They just read her reports."

"Really." Startled, Rachel frowned. "Somebody told me that the Village might be having financial trouble," she said cautiously

"I don't know why." The young aid shrugged. "I mean, yeah, that's what she said when she cut the kitchen staff and stuck us with waiting tables, but how come?" His blue eyes were guileless. "The Village got bought by this big national company that buys rundown retirement homes and turns them into upscale places with Alzheimer care and all kinds of fancy extras. It's like a chain of restaurants, you know? They're paying all the bills, and they came in and told us all how they're going to really make this place fancy to attract more buy-in residents. Then they can up the monthly service fees. Why should they cut operating money?"

Why indeed? "This is all very interesting," Rachel said slowly. She'd have to ask Madame about this, she decided. Madame knew everything. "Anyway, you can tell people that I'm not going to quit," she said with decision. "When I take on a project, I finish it."

"Oh, good." The aid gave her a wide grin. "Everyone will be glad to hear that, I can tell you. We can't wait." He chuckled. "Folk are already reserving time for card games in that gazebo you're going to build." One of the two women on the walk was waving and calling to him, her words fragmented by the hot afternoon wind. "Coming!" he called back, and made a brief face at Rachel. "That's Roberta. I promised I'd come play poker with them. She flays me every time because I can't bluff for beans. Good thing it's penny-ante. I'd better go. See you around. I'm Jason Marl, by the way." He gave her a jaunty wave and trotted back up the slope to join the two women.

Rachel had a feeling that the handsome aid with his boyish manner was in great demand by many of the female residents here. Her expression thoughtful, Rachel climbed into her truck and left the Village, driving west along the county road above the freeway and into the town of Blossom itself.

She had meant to go straight home and climb into the shower, but instead she slowed, and turned off Main Street, crossing beneath the freeway overpass to the newly built boardwalk along the river. The new shops offered kites and sailboarding gear to the increasing influx of tourists driving down the Gorge. Shorts and L.L. Bean polo shirts dominated the fashion here, and even this late on a weekday afternoon at the beginning of harvest, cars filled the parking spaces in front of the Bread Box Café. Rachel squeezed her truck into the space between a new Ford Explorer with two sailboards on top and a silver gray BMW.

Blossom and Hood River were rapidly changing from orchard towns to tourist centers. It was not a change that sat easily with some residents. One of her cousins had had the audacity to suggest to her uncle that the family orchard should remake itself for the tourist trade—build a petting zoo and a gift shop, sell local wines and fruit products, and put on harvest fests and pumpkin-picking parties in the fall.

Rachel had thought her Uncle Jack would have a stroke on the spot. Too bad. It was working for some of the Hood River orchards. Smiling and shaking her head, she climbed the wooden ramp to the wide plank walk in front of the Bread Box. Inside, couples and small groups sat at the round metal-mesh tables sipping iced tea and eating the savory bruschetta that Joylinn Markham, the owner and baker, had recently added to the menu. The tables out on the deck that overlooked the river were full, but there was still plenty of seating space inside. Joylinn winked at Rachel as she hurried past with a tray full of salads and a pitcher of iced tea, her thick auburn braid bouncing between her shoulder blades. Rachel waved at her and took a seat at her usual table near the kitchen door.

Joylinn did most of her baking very early in the morning, but the scents of cinnamon and yeast from her famous cinnamon rolls lingered all day. Rachel's stomach growled and she scowled down at it, measuring her thick, stocky frame against Joylinn's willowy height. There was no fighting genes. She sighed. But there was no reason to give in to her hips' desire to spread, either. So when Joylinn appeared at the table with two glasses of iced coffee and a platter of those very same cinnamon rolls, Rachel made herself take the smallest one.

"Oh, come on." Joylinn laughed as she took a nice fat one for herself. "Julio stopped in earlier and said you were digging trenches out at the Village. You've used up plenty of calories today." She licked cream cheese icing from her fingers.

"Not enough. You know, I could hate you for being thin." Rachel took a huge and satisfying bite of her roll, noting with regret that there wasn't all that much left. "These just keep getting better," she said with her mouth full. "And I'll need the calorie deficit because Jeff and I are having dinner with Mom and Joshua tonight and you know how Joshua cooks."

"Real cream and olive oil." Joylinn grinned. "Gourmet cooks do not worry about calories, do they? I'm not sure I'd still be thin if I was married to him."

"You forgot real butter, too," Rachel said dreamily. "I have no willpower over there. I don't know how my mother can stay so slim."

"She puts all her energy into driving that sports car of hers fast," Joylinn drawled. "As long as you're here . . ." She gave Rachel a sideways glance. "Did you think about what I suggested yesterday?"

"Jeff and I are not going to have a big wedding." Rachel rolled her eyes. "And no amount of attempted bribery with free catering is going to change our minds, girl. So give it up."

"But you owe it to the town," Joylinn said sweetly. "You're being so selfish. Jeff's the chief of police, after all."

"Until the mayor loses the next election . . ."

"Which he won't."

"He will if my uncle has anything to do with it. I think he may run himself, just so he can rant in front of more people. And then the new, conservative mayor will kick Jeff out in favor of someone older and more to his liking."

"Won't happen." Joylinn waved a hand airily. "You're ignoring your civic duty."

"Darn right." Regretfully, Rachel popped the last fragment into her mouth. "Actually, we were talking about eloping just last night. We could run off like Mom and Josh did, get married in Vegas, and go camping for a couple of weeks."

"Don't you dare." Joylinn glared at her. "And you couldn't pry Jeff away from his job for two weeks."

That was true. Rachel sighed. "Have you visited your grandmother lately?" Time to change the subject.

"Madame?" Joylinn sipped at her tea. "I took her weekly rolls out to her just yesterday. Why?"

"Has she said anything to you about money troubles at the Village?" Rachel leaned forward as she picked up her dewy glass of tea. "The aids are waiting tables now."

"She mentioned that." Joylinn frowned. "Madame doesn't have much good to say about the new director, I know that. I think maybe she's met her match in the woman. Quebecois stubbornness meets immovable American bureaucracy and loses." She smiled, her expression curious. "Why?"

"A couple of people there were complaining about budget cuts." She shrugged. "The company that bought the place is certainly paying me enough."

"They should." Joylinn tossed her head. "They were impressed enough with that proposal you gave them—about using only edible native species for the landscaping, putting in all drip water, and using plantings as natural barriers for wandering residents. They ought to pay you more. I bet you're going to be a big part of their advertising." She sighed. "I just hope they don't raise the fees for all the residents once they fix the place up. Madame owns her own unit, but those service fees eat up a lot of her income. I don't think Madame would be happy living with me on the houseboat." She smiled crookedly. "I love my grandmother dearly, but I only have one bedroom and I think it would feel awfully small awfully fast."

"Besides, you'd have to take Harris in, too," Rachel said with a straight face.

"You think you're kidding?" Joylinn rolled her eyes. "At least this director doesn't seem to be as scandalized by their behavior as that last one. She used to call me once a week to complain. She wanted me to take Madame to a psychiatrist. Honestly. Although I do feel a little sorry for her—getting demoted to assistant director when the new company took over. I'm surprised she didn't quit."

She got to her feet as two couples in shorts and summer shirts came through the door. "Back to work, girl. Talk to you later."

Rachel finished her tea and was about to get up when Julio Peron, her young assistant, came through the door. Rachel recognized the small dark-skinned woman with him. Anita was a recent Guatemalan immigrant who had grown up near Julio's predominantly Mayan village. He had been teaching her English. Rachel waved as they threaded their way among the tables.

Julio's eyes were gleaming and he greeted her enthusiastically. Anita smiled in her shy and slightly wary manner, still unwilling to use her English with Anglos much. Still, she moved with much more confidence than she had displayed when Rachel had first met her.

"Eduardo said you had more trouble with the water today," Julio said in his precise and careful English as he sat down. "He said you dug much more." His dark eyes clouded as she nodded. "This will make the job pay badly?"

"It's not going to help." Rachel sighed, then managed a smile. "But we'll manage." She turned her smile on Anita. "Julio said you are working for him now."

The young woman nodded, smiling, her eyes sliding sideways to Julio's face.

"She is good." Julio beamed at her and then took her hand. "We came to tell you that we will be married."

"How wonderful! Oh, I'm so glad!" And not terribly surprised, either, Rachel reflected. Since she had first introduced Julio to Anita, he had spent most of his free time with her, as far as Rachel could tell. "When is the wedding?"

"Soon." Julio's expression had turned serious, and he glanced at his fiancée, his posture suddenly hesitant. "I have two new clients this week," he said slowly.

"That's great!"

"And the mayor tells me today that you do not want to care for the planters on Main Street anymore, and he wants to put in hanging baskets on the light poles and more flowers, and he asked me if I would be hired to take care of them. Is that right?" He looked positively anxious now. "You do not want this job?"

"Yes, yes." Rachel nodded, because she had not only told the mayor that she didn't have time for the maintenance, she had suggested that he hire Julio. "Maybe you won't have to drive over to Hood River quite so much."

"It is a good contract." He looked down at the table, frowning now. "And with new clients . . ." He shifted in his seat, then raised his head and met Rachel's eyes. "I think I have to work for myself only now. There is enough work. Anita and I can do it all, but only if I do not work for you."

Rachel swallowed, feeling as if the floor had just dropped a couple of inches. Well, she had realized long ago that as his landscape maintenance clientele grew, he would eventually have to stop working for her and concentrate on his own business. And she had referred plenty of clients to him. But Julio had been her assistant from the day she had created Rain Country Landscaping. He knew the job nearly as well as she did. It would be hard to replace him.

Mostly, she would miss his quiet humor and his patience. Never mind the fact that he worked as hard as she did, and seemed to have a nearly equal pride in the business. She managed a wide smile. "Congratulations." She reached across the table to shake his hand. "Two things to celebrate! I hope I can find someone half as good as you to replace you." She wasn't quite able to keep the regret out of her voice. Julio was a gem.

"I will find someone for you," Julio said cheerfully. "I will find someone good." His smile gleamed bright as the summer sun outside.

Anita was watching Rachel's face. Behind her diffident smile, a hint of hard purpose gleamed in her eyes. Rachel had a feeling that Julio's decision had its origins here. For all her quiet manner, Anita was a woman who had survived a lot in her few years—far more than she was willing to talk about, Rachel guessed. She knew what she wanted. And Rachel stifled a small spurt of resentment. Because she paid well—better than Julio could have made in the orchards. Better than she could afford to, to tell the truth.

Well, she had started her business because she had wanted to be her own boss. Why shouldn't Julio feel the same? Rachel let her breath out in a silent sigh as Joylinn approached with glasses of iced tea and a plate piled high with the new bruschetta. She could have worked for Uncle Jack on the family orchard, and would have made better money than she did landscaping.

"I was eavesdropping." Joylinn unloaded the tray. "Congratulations, Julio. You, too, Anita. You're the perfect couple. This is on the house." She set the plate down. "A celebration."

"I have to leave, I'm afraid." Rachel got to her feet. "Can you help me tomorrow, Julio?"

He nodded, his attention on Anita. "Oh, *sí*. I will not stop before there is someone else."

"Thanks." Rachel headed for the door, trying not to feel depressed.

"What's that? I missed something." Joylinn caught up with her. "Julio's quitting?"

"His business is growing." Rachel dredged up a smile. "So I'm in the market for a new assistant."

"Oh, I'm sorry. He was so good. But it's great that his business is taking off," Joylinn said blythely. "He deserves it."

True. And she was being selfish, Rachel thought as she climbed into her truck and crossed Main, turning up the slope to the small side street where she lived. She couldn't help it. Julio had spoiled her. Now she was going to have to start all over, and at the beginning of picking season, experienced workers were going to be scarce. Eduardo was doing her a favor, digging ditches for her. They both knew it.

Rachel had hoped that Jeff might meet her at the apartment, but the narrow parking area beside the house was vacant except for Mrs. Frey's shiny blue Volkswagen. Her landlady had driven home in it without warning one evening a month ago. "It's so cute," she had said, and that was her only explanation for why she had traded in her trusty old Dodge Dart. The evening sun gleamed on the sparkling blue paint as Rachel squeezed her truck carefully between the new car and the hedge. Somehow, the car didn't seem to go with the staid old house and the formal rose garden behind it. Rachel groaned as she spotted Peter, her cat, stretched languorously on the car's shiny hood.

"Get off of there, you idiot feline, before Amelia skins you alive." Rachel hopped out, slamming the truck door, and making shooing motions with her hands. "You'll get us both kicked out of here." She glanced at the lace curtains that covered the downstairs windows, expecting her landlady to come charging out at any moment brandishing a broom and threatening mayhem. She and Peter were already at war over the chickadees who visited Mrs. Frey's bird feeder.

Pouncing on Peter, she scooped the disgruntled cat into her arms and hurried up the steep stairway that led to her second-floor apartment. Peter squirmed in her grasp, yowling his outrage over this treatment, but she hung on to him until she reached the top of the stairs. Shoving the door open, she burst into the apartment, dumping the cat unceremoniously onto the floor and slamming the door in his face as he made a dash for the outside. "No, you don't!"

Peter leaped onto the back of the sofa and glowered at her.

"You stay right there while I take a shower. If Amelia catches you on that car, it'll take me a half hour to calm her down, and I'm going to be late as it is."

Peter yawned, stretching his striped body out along the couch. He couldn't care less if she was late. He made it quite plain.

"See if I feed you tonight," she threatened as she started to strip out of her grimy work clothes. It was stuffy up here, in spite of all the insulation Amelia's son Ralph had added when he built the apartment. Rachel turned on the box fan in the front room, luxuriating in the coolness of the moving air as she turned on the shower. It would feel good to scrub off the layers of sweat and dust. It would feel wonderful. She was just stepping beneath the cool spray when the phone rang.

"No." She answered its shrill demand. "No way. Talk to the machine." Suppressing the merest twinge of guilt, she stepped into the lovely shower of cool water and pulled the curtain closed behind her. But as she scrubbed and rinsed and shampooed her hair, that tooth of guilt nibbled at her. It might have been Jeff. She turned off the water, and stepped out, goose bumps rising as she toweled off in the fan's breeze. Still damp, she wrapped the towel around her and checked her machine. The light winked at her. One call. She hit the button.

"I've been watching you." The sibilant whisper on the tape might belong to either a man or a woman. *"You're a nice girl. You be careful working out here, now. You make sure you get paid. And you be careful. I don't want to see you get hurt, not in any way. Because you're a nice girl. So you be careful, hear? Because I think maybe peo-*

ple are dying." A brief bit of dial tone sounded before the machine message ended.

Rachel stood staring at the black box of the machine. The goose bumps on her skin didn't come from the fan's breath anymore.

CHAPTER

3

It was well after six, so the parking lot behind Blossom's brick cube of a City Hall was nearly empty. Rachel spied Jeff's black Jeep CV and a new dark green Chevy pickup that she hadn't noticed here before. Late business? If so, he probably wouldn't make dinner. Jeff took his job seriously.

Too seriously, she sometimes thought.

Parking her truck beside the other two vehicles, she crossed the parking lot quickly, unable to quite suppress a shiver as she passed the spot where one of her crew had once discovered a body beneath a pile of bark dust. A light shone faintly in an upstairs window. That would be the mayor's office. Phil Ventura took his job seriously, too, and like Jeff, he was young. Too young and too progressive for a lot of Blossom's older residents, her Uncle Jack included. Finding the small staff door around the corner unlocked, she slipped inside.

The building smelled of floor wax and disinfectant, with a faint hint of ancient cigar smoke. The janitor must have just left, because the marble tiles in the main foyer gleamed with a trace of moisture. Rachel tiptoed across the wet floor to the glass and wooden double doors with the word POLICE written in flowing gilt script that was crumbling away particle by particle. Pushing through the doors, she found Jeff and a wide-shouldered stranger with a sandy military cut and the muscled arms of a weight lifter deep in conversation behind the wide wooden counter with its swinging gate.

"Hi," she said. Both men started and looked up with identical scowls. Jeff's altered instantly into a welcoming grin. The stranger merely eyed her with polite reserve.

"Is it that late already?" Jeff glanced at the wall clock above her head. "I guess it is. Sorry," he said with a lop-sided smile. "I meant to show up at your apartment some time ago. Bert, this is my fiancée, Rachel O'Connor. Rachel, meet Bert Stanfield, our new addition to the department."

"Oh, yeah. Jeff told me about you." Rachel pushed through the swinging gate, offering her hand to the new officer. Jeff had been jubilant when the Blossom City Council had grudgingly okayed the new contract. The Blossom Police Department had consisted of three people, and when somebody resided in the tiny two-cell jail, the three of them worked long hours. Jeff had been arguing for some time that the increase in tourist traffic and week-end renters required more people. "I'm so glad to meet you," she said with a smile.

"The pleasure's all mine." He gave her a wide smile, and a handshake that nearly made her wince. Stanfield had a square face and stocky frame without an ounce of fat on it. Even at this time of day, his uniform was as crisp and neat as if he had just donned it.

Former military, Rachel thought. She would bet money on it. He looked as if he was a fit mid-fifties. He had been with the Portland police, Jeff had told her, but had decided to move to a small town for the sake of his family.

"So you don't think we ought to start leaning on the kids who hang around here after school?" Stanfield went back to his interrupted conversation with Jeff. "We really cleaned up Eighty-second and a Hundred-and-twenty-second Avenue in Portland that way. You're a kid, you're on the street with no good reason to be there, and we run you off. Just like that. If you're in a car, you get a ticket. Downtown is off limits to kids, unless they're on legitimate business—shopping, or eating, or seeing a movie. We shut the cruising down and reduced the graffiti and vandalism a lot."

"Most of the kids down here at night aren't doing any harm," Jeff said patiently. "They don't have much else to do except drive over to Hood River or go off and party somewhere. No reason to run them off." And he took Rachel's hand with a subtle wink, because once upon a time, some years back, they had been part of those kids hanging out on the town's main street. Jeff was right. There wasn't much else to do.

"Better they should be down here than off drinking and then driving home."

"You're the boss." Stanfield clearly wasn't impressed with this logic. "But we sure found out that if you let the kids run wild, you got a lot of troubles on your hands." He nodded. "Get tough from the beginning and they respect you."

"Right now I think we've only got one kid to get tough with." Jeff shrugged, obviously ending the conversation. "If it's a kid doing this. Let's deal with this first, and worry about policy later. I'm off," he said and reached for Rachel's hand. "Shall we?"

"What was that all about?" Rachel asked as they crossed the echoing main entry and left by the side door. "Trouble with teens?"

"Maybe." Jeff shook his head, scowling briefly. "We've had a couple of instances of vandalism in the past ten days. A little petty theft. Some graffiti. I think it's the same person or couple of persons, but it's just a feeling. Not enough to go on yet, but I'll hear who it is sooner or later. Somebody will hear them boasting, or see them, and it'll get around." He smiled, but it had a slightly forced feeling. "Bert isn't used to small-town ways yet. He's overreacting, that's all."

Maybe. Rachel gave Jeff a sideways look, admiring his high cheekbones and lean profile, but seeing the worry there in the tight creases at the corners of his mouth. "You'll always take things too seriously," she murmured. "I guess that's what makes you so good at your job."

"Quite an analysis. And did I detect just a hint of criticism?" He made a face. "Well, you're entitled, and you're right." He stopped, grinned down at her, and right there on the steps outside City Hall, he pulled her into his arms and kissed her thoroughly. Very thoroughly indeed.

"What if the mayor's watching?" Smiling, Rachel finally pulled away. She glanced up, realizing that he would have a great view from his window, and groaned because the lights were still on and the blinds open.

"So let him be jealous." Jeff rested his chin on top of her head, his arms still around her. "I guess we'd better get going," he said reluctantly. "Or we'll be late and Joshua will never forgive us."

"Oh, he never cooks anything until the last minute." Rachel twined her fingers through his as they walked across the lot. "Take my truck?"

"Fine by me. Since you don't drive like your mom." He winked. "Good thing she knows the chief of police personally."

Her mother drove a metallic blue MG Mini, and her driving was legend in Blossom. Breast cancer hadn't slowed her down one bit. "She should have become a race car driver." Rachel laughed, watching Jeff's face relax. Sometimes she wished that he had gone into some profession other than law enforcement.

She told him about her lunch with Madame and the rumors that something wasn't right at the Garden View Retirement Village. "She seemed a little miffed at Doc Welsh, too." Rachel carefully negotiated a curve in the narrow county road that climbed the side of the Gorge, thinking that maybe she wouldn't mention that phone call just yet. Jeff worried, and he had enough to worry about, clearly. Besides, it was a prank. Surely. "I wonder what's going on?" Rachel continued quickly. "Madame said something about too many people dying at the Village. Or something like that." So had the caller . . .

"Maybe she's feeling her age." Jeff shrugged. "Although I can't really imagine Madame feeling old, much less worrying about death. She's going to live forever."

"Probably." She gave him a sideways look. He wasn't really paying attention. "What's bothering you? The vandalism?"

"You do the mind-reading thing pretty well." Jeff gave a half-laugh. "Remind me never to play poker with you. It's nothing much." He paused for a moment, his eyes on the road in front of them as it unwound between orderly rows of pear trees. The sinking sun edged the leaves with gold, and stacked wooden boxes, waiting for harvest, cast long dark shadows across the ground.

"I talked to my mother," Jeff said at last. "She can't make it up here for the wedding. She said she can't get away. Like I said—it's nothing much."

"I'm sorry," Rachel said. His mother had been a single parent in Blossom—a reclusive woman who wasn't well liked. She didn't serve on committees or show up for PTA meetings. She didn't serve punch at the grange hall, or show up for community meetings at the high school. She had taken Jeff and moved to Los Angeles in the middle of their junior year in high school. As far as Rachel knew, she and Jeff hadn't had much contact since she had re-married. There didn't seem to be anything else to say.

"Don't worry about it." Jeff leaned across the seat to brush a wisp of hair back from her face. "I'm not. Looks like your folks have company." They had turned onto Joshua's driveway. A pickup camper mounted on a bat-tered Ford was parked next to her mother's bright MG in the circular drive next to the house. "That's Cory Welsh's fishing rig," he said.

"I just saw him today, out at the Village." As Rachel turned off the engine, she ran an automatic cye over the vista of gardens and terrace below the house. This had been her first big job as Rain Country Landscaping. It hadn't been an easy job and she was pleased with it, now that the plantings had had a chance to mature a bit. Her stepfather had hired Julio to maintain it, and Julio was certainly doing a good job. Rachel sighed.

"What?" Jeff touched her arm. "Something wrong?"

"Oh . . . not really." She hesitated, wondering again if she should mention the call. Later, she decided. When Jeff could give it his full attention. "Julio is doing so well with his new business that he's not going to work for me any longer." Rachel gave a jerky shrug as she slid from behind the wheel. "And I'm really glad that he's doing so well." She winced as she slammed the door a little too hard. "But I wish he wasn't quitting."

"You'll find somebody good." Jeff put his arm around her as they climbed the steps that led up to the main entry and the wide deck that fronted the huge kitchen–living area.

"We're out here." Rachel's mother waved from the deck, her fine-boned face framed by masses of very short, dark wavy hair. You would never know that she had been bald from chemotherapy only six months before, Rachel thought as they climbed the broad steps that led to the

deck. Her eyes strayed unavoidably to the front of her
mother's sleeveless cotton shirt. You couldn't tell . . . Rachel couldn't quite suppress a shiver, although the glint
of amusement in her mother's eyes made her blush. Sometimes she thought that the surgery for breast cancer bothered her more than it had ever bothered her mother. "I'm
more than a pair of breasts," her mother had told her.
Which was certainly true. But still. . . .

"Glad you made it." Joshua emerged from the kitchen,
carrying two glasses of wine. The last of the sunlight
gleamed on his silver hair and accentuated his muscular
shoulders. "We've got fresh trout for dinner. Thanks to
Cory."

Dr. Welsh followed him through the doors, a glass of
ice and scotch in his hand. "I got lucky this evening, is
all." Dressed in a faded and well-washed denim shirt and
khaki pants, he gave them a weathered grin. "Too many
fish for one man to eat and they're only good when
they're fresh. Freeze 'em, and you might as well be eating
canned tuna."

"How is the job at the Village?" Joshua handed her one
of the glasses of white wine. "Are you getting lots of
advice from the residents?"

"Oh, they're great." Rachel sipped at the wine, appre-
ciating the crisp dryness. Joshua always served good wine.
"So far, though, the lava is winning hands down."

"What?" Her mother paused as she laid places at the
polished wood table that served for al fresco dining.
"What about lava?"

"Oh, I just keep hitting veins of it that I swear weren't
there when I did the estimate." Rachel couldn't quite con-
tain a sigh. "At this rate, the irrigation lines are going to
look like a maze. Or a spider's web." She paused to sniff
the air as the sound of sizzling and the scent of crisping
trout wafted from the kitchen. "I think I'm about to die
of hunger," she said plaintively. "Can I help?"

"I think Jeff and Cory are taking care of everything."
Rachel's mother nodded toward the kitchen, into which
the men had disappeared. "Let the boys do everything
tonight." She winked. "While we get to enjoy the sunset."

For a moment or two, Rachel managed to admire the
pastel orange glow on the western horizon. It was too dry
this time of year to get a really spectacular sunset. She
glanced over her shoulder, discovered Jeff and Doc in
deep conversation about fish as they carried out plates,
utensils, and salad. Joshua was busy in the kitchen.

"Okay, what's bothering you?" Her mother leaned her
elbows companionably on the railing, her face serene.
"Want to tell me, or should I start digging?"

"Jeff's mother," Rachel blurted and felt a moment of
surprise. *That* wasn't bothering her. It was . . . well . . . it
was . . . "She's not coming to the wedding. I guess . . . I
dunno." She shrugged, feeling awkward and young and
irritable all at once.

"I don't imagine she would." Deborah O'Connor's eyes
were on the deepening hues of peach and orange on the
horizon. "It would be hard."

"Why? It hurts Jeff." And Rachel wondered immediately when she had figured that one out. Seemed as if her
mouth was way ahead of her brain tonight.

"Well, you know, she never really belonged here." Rachel's mother gave her a gentle look. "She arrived with a
new baby and a husband who promptly became the town
good-for-nothing drunk, and then he left her with the kid.
You know, if she'd just let folk help her, it would've been
all right." Deborah's eyes were back on the fading light
of the sunset. "But she didn't. And she hurt some feelings,
saying 'no, thanks' a little too hard. I don't think she
meant to. I think it was just pride. But when you say 'go
away,' after a while people do. People like to help, Rachel." She turned to her daughter, her expression serious.
"It's not always a burden. Sometimes it's a benefit to ask

for help. You give people a chance to be a giver when you ask for help. It makes almost everyone feel good. Don't forget that, all right?"

"I won't." Rachel glanced over her shoulder, saw dinner about to happen. "So what about Jeff's mother? Why won't she come?"

"She thinks people don't like her here." Deborah shrugged. "People thought she didn't like them. Misunderstanding, but that happens a lot."

"I want her to come." Rachel frowned, because this realization rubbed like a new pair of boots. "It matters to Jeff, and I think . . . it matters to me." Which was funny, because as a kid, she had resented Jeff's mom, who grounded him every time they did anything fun, like when Bill's car broke down and they spent the night at the foot of the Cooper's Spur trail, even when nobody else's parent got upset. "I really do," she added, a bit amazed by her own sentiment.

"So ask her."

"Oh yeah, just like that." Rachel gave her a look. "That woman never did like me."

"Why?" Her mother put on her most innocent face. "Just because you were going to take her son away from her?"

"I was not. I . . ." Rachel bit off the rest of the sentence, eyeing her gently smiling mother. "So that's why you weren't happy about Jeff," she said slowly.

"Wait until you're a parent."

"Right!"

"And then you'll understand. That's it for the clichés tonight," her mother said briskly. "Dinner is ready. Cory is on his way to fetch us," she said, looking over Rachel's shoulder. "Let's eat."

Doc Welsh was indeed on his way across the deck with a beckoning look on his face.

They sat down to plates filled with crisp trout, sautéed baby squash, and a neat mound of red-pepper pasta that Rachel guessed Joshua had made with his well-used pasta machine. "You should open a restaurant," she said.

Joshua chuckled at the murmured agreement. For a time, everybody was too busy eating to say much. But finally, the pace slowed down. "Looks like you're making progress on the Village landscape," Dr. Welsh said, reaching for another piece of bread. "I never would have believed you could do anything with that hillside if I hadn't seen your drawings. It's going to be a lovely place," he said with a touch of wistfulness in his tone. "I'll have to drop by and take a look when it's all finished."

"You're not going to quit going out there?" Deborah looked up in surprise. "Who are they going to get to replace you?"

"Oh, a lot of the folk have their own doctors in Hood River. Like I said, I'm just there to listen, mostly." But he kept his eyes on his plate, prodding his half-eaten trout with the tines of his fork. "Time for me to slow down a bit. And I'm burying too many folk I know. I'm looking forward to spending more time fishing."

"You've sure earned yourself some fishing time," Joshua said heartily. "When was the last time you really took some time off, anyway?"

Rachel shifted in her seat, thinking again about that call, remembering Madame's cool manner toward the doctor today. Doc Welsh, as everyone called him, had been a beloved daily visitor to the Village for as long as she could remember.

"Penny for your thoughts?" Her mother was regarding her with raised eyebrows and a quizzical expression.

"I'm just tired." Rachel quickly forked up the last bits of her trout. "We did a lot of digging today."

"So what's this I hear about a rash of vandalism in town?" Joshua asked Jeff as he poured more wine. "Stan

Bellamy told me somebody threw a rock through the Homestyle Café's window the other night." Joshua set the bottle back down as Jeff shook his head. "He said this sort of thing is happening every night."

"Not quite every night." Jeff pushed his fork into his nearly untasted trout. "I think this is one person, not a bunch of kids making trouble. Someone would have seen something if it was a group. Whoever is doing this is fast and quiet and knows Blossom awfully well."

The telltale hints of stress had reappeared at the corners of his mouth. "I met one of the new aids at the Village today." Rachel changed the subject brightly. "Ricki. She told me she has an uncle who was a private gardener for some of Portland's wealthy families."

"That's Gus's niece. Well, she's a grand-niece actually. But he raised her. Gus Van Dorn." Dr. Welsh refilled his glass. "We went to high school together in Hood River." A glaze of memory filmed his eyes. "We were on the football team. He got a scholarship to the University of Oregon, same as I did, but at the last minute his dad got hurt when a tractor rolled over on him. Gus stayed home to take care of the family. Ironic." Dr. Welsh shook his head, the nostalgia in his eyes deepening to sadness.

"What's ironic?" Joshua asked.

"He was the one who always wanted to be a doctor— from the time we were in grade school." Dr. Welsh pushed back his chair. "Me, I didn't have a clue what I wanted to do with my life. Well, I've got to get going," he said to Joshua. "It sure has been fine tonight." He reached for Deborah's hand and kissed it with a courtly bow. "You're looking wonderful, my dear," he murmured with a weary smile. "I don't worry about you at all."

"I worry about you." Rachel's mother rose to slip her arm through the older man's. "I'll walk you out to your car and let Rachel clear the table." She winked at her daughter as they strolled toward the steps.

Rachel and Jeff cleared the table together, although Joshua wouldn't let them do anything but stack the dishes on the counter by the sink. Leaving the two men to argue over baseball, Rachel went outside to find her mother. She was standing at the end of the deck, her fine-boned face tilted toward the starry sky. "Something's eating at Jeff, isn't it?" she asked without turning around. "It isn't the wedding, is it?"

"It's this vandalism, I think." Rachel sighed. "I wish he didn't have to be so perfect all the time."

"Then he wouldn't be Jeff, would he?" Her mother turned and rested her hands lightly on her daughter's shoulders. "He's always going to be hard on himself. He was doing that when you kids were in grade school, don't you remember? That's who he is."

"Yeah, it is." Rachel looked away. "I just wish sometimes that he'd give himself a break."

"I think you help." Her mother's eyes shifted. "So did you boys clean everything up?"

"We sure did, ma'am." Jeff came up behind Rachel, not touching her, but a warm presence behind her.

"We should probably go," Rachel said to her mother. "I think we've both had a long day."

They made their farewells and went hand in hand down the steps to the driveway. It was fully dark now, and a million stars blazed across the sky. "I should let Peter out," she said as they reached the truck. "But then I could give you a ride home. That way you could leave the Jeep at City Hall. Less pollution."

"How environmental of you." Jeff gave her a grin. "Won't Peter feel neglected?"

"He spends the night outside anyway. Haunting Mrs. Frey's rose garden jungle."

"I thought he was only interested in her chickadees."

This reference to her landlady's long-standing feud with Peter made them both laugh, but on the drive back to town, Jeff was quiet. The bright sickle of the new moon gleamed like silver against the star-spangled night.

"Doc wasn't himself tonight." Jeff spoke up finally.

Rachel had opened her mouth to tell him about her anonymous caller, but it was too late, tonight. "Maybe he's not happy with the change to the Village. You and I are officially off duty as worriers tonight," she announced.

"Anything you say," Jeff said meekly.

"Damn right."

CHAPTER

4

Peter leaped down from his casual perch on the back of the sofa as they entered Rachel's apartment. Tail erect, he stalked around them in a tidy circle proclaiming his imminent starvation. His rumpled gray-striped coat bristled in outrage.

"I don't suppose you remember that I fed you when I got home this evening," Rachel said mildly.

He glared.

Giving in to a twinge of guilt for leaving him after all, she opened a can of cat food and took it outside, scooping a generous spoonful into the dish on the landing. "All right. There's your midnight snack," she said as she went back inside to grab a change of clothes. "No more complaints."

Peter was too busy to complain as they went down the steps and got back into her truck. Jeff lived high above the river in an old farmhouse that he was remodeling. They started back through town toward the county road that would take them up away from the river. But as they

reached the cross street that led beneath the freeway and
to the riverside street where the Bread Box was located,
Jeff suddenly leaned forward. "Turn right," he said
sharply. "Quick."

Rachel swung the truck hard into the turn, searching
the shadowy street ahead of them. It ended on the riverbank, beside the new row of boardwalk shops. There! A
dark figure leaped from the boardwalk and darted across
the lot.

"I bet that's our vandal. He's headed to the east end of
the lot."

Rachel sent the truck leaping forward, engine roaring.
They hurtled into the lot and across it, her headlights spotlighting for one fractured second a running figure in dark
jeans, a black sweatshirt, and a ski cap. Then the fugitive
vanished around the corner of the last building. Rachel
hit the brakes, tires squealing, her headlights flooding the
corrugated green wall of a covered Dumpster. Jeff flung
the door open and leaped from the still-rolling truck, racing after the suspect. He disappeared around the corner of
the Dumpster and the slap of his running footsteps faded
almost immediately.

Rachel leaned out the window, leaving the truck running, trying to penetrate the darkness beyond the yellow
flood of her headlights. What if this person had a knife?
Or a gun? She fumbled her cell phone from beneath the
seat and dialed.

"Blossom Police." The male voice on the line wasn't
familiar. The new man? "This is Rachel O'Connor. Jeff
Price is chasing someone toward the Bread Box. Maybe
the vandal."

"I'm on my way." The line went dead.

Night calls went straight through to the cell phone of
the officer on duty. Rachel held her breath, and sure
enough, a moment later the nose of Blossom's single
black-and-white car appeared at the intersection. It pulled

up beside her in a rush, and the new officer got out, his hand on the gun at his belt. Stanfield, Rachel finally remembered his name.

"What happened?" He leaned down to the window, the headlight glow streaking his square face with shadow.

"They ran around behind the building," Rachel said. "Toward the Bread Box."

Stanfield followed, unsnapping his holster as he went. In a moment, the darkness beyond the flood of her headlights swallowed him. Slowly Rachel reached out and turned off the engine. In the sudden silence, she could hear the murmur of the Columbia and the distant yowl of a prowling cat. A gust of wind whispered across the lot, cooling the summer air with the river's breath, sending a scrap of paper tumbling across the pavement. Rachel strained her ears, but heard nothing other than these small sounds of the summer night.

Something moved at the far end of the lot.

She froze, staring out into the darkness, her heart leaping into her throat. Nothing. Her eyes, dazzled by the headlight beam, couldn't penetrate the darkness. There! She saw it again—just a hint of movement, a bit of different darkness. The fugitive had been wearing a dark sweatshirt. Rachel slammed the lock down on the door, rolled the window up. She leaned across the seat to lock the other door, half expecting a dark figure to rush out of the darkness at her.

Nothing. If someone was out there, he was holding very still.

Taking a deep breath, Rachel turned off the headlights. The darkness seemed to rush in like a wave, drowning her in momentary blindness, making her heart pound. Her vision slowly cleared, and she began to make out the faint shapes of the weeds and brush that filled the lot beyond the shops. The ruins of an old fruit warehouse loomed in the background, doors and windows gaping empty. What better place for someone to hide? Jeff must have looked there. Jeff must be there. Surely. Or Stanfield. She stared at the faint silhouettes of weeds and grass, seeing shapes in the darkness, monsters straight from beneath her childhood bed. Nothing more moved.

A dark shape loomed suddenly beside the door and a hand closed on the handle.

Rachel screamed, then gasped with relief as she recognized Jeff's face leaning close to the glass. She fumbled the door open.

"We lost him. We're going to split up and take a look for him. Are you okay?" He leaned down, his expression worried in the yellow glow of the dome light. "Did something happen?"

"I'm fine. I just . . . saw something." She pointed "Over there."

"Turn the truck around," he said tersely. "Turn your headlights on."

She twisted the key and the engine purred to life. Backing the truck, she switched on the headlights so that their yellow glare flooded the abandoned lot. Clumps of tawny sun-scorched grass sprang to life, interspersed with the thick fuzzy stalks of pale green mallows ready to bloom. Bits of thorn-spiked trash decorated the blackberry canes that sprawled across the baked and rutted clay. Beyond, the bleak gray walls of the old warehouse stared with eyes of darkness that the light utterly failed to penetrate.

"There!" Rachel pointed, turning off the engine. "Oh my gosh, what's that?"

A black shape—seemingly as large as a calf—hunched in the tangled net of thorny blackberry canes.

"It's a dog." Jeff laughed. "That's all."

"A dog? It's huge!"

"I'll start at the west end of town. Maybe we'll spot him." Stanfield emerged from the darkness, breathing hard. "Damn, that guy can run."

"Hold on a moment, Bert." Jeff waded into the weeds, picking his way around piles of debris.

"What now?" Stanfield squinted, his thumbs hooked in his leather belt. "We've got that perp to catch. Hey, we're wasting time. What the hell are you up to?"

"It's a dog." Rachel got out of the truck as Jeff squatted beside the dark shape, nearly hidden by the sun-dried weeds. "Watch out it doesn't bite you."

"Go cruise Main, Bert," Jeff said sharply. "That should scare him off. Yell if you see anything."

"Leave the damn dog."

"Get moving," Jeff said flatly. "I'll be there as soon as I can."

Stanfield grunted. "Damn kids." He stalked off and, a moment later, pulled out of the parking lot in a flurry of scattered gravel.

"We're not going to catch him tonight." Jeff spoke conversationally, but there was a flat undercurrent of anger beneath the mild words. "He's played this hide-and-seek game with us for three nights running now. He has a half-dozen bolt holes all picked out."

"Jeff?" Rachel picked her way cautiously into the jungle of weeds, watching for nails and boards. "What's going on?"

"Do you have a piece of rope in your truck box?" Jeff still faced the dog, his back turned to her. "Can you get it? He doesn't even have a collar."

Rachel froze as she got a good look at the animal. It was huge, a hundred pounds at least, with a head that was as big as a basketball. She swallowed, thinking of what would happen if those huge jaws closed on the hand Jeff was offering to it. It was panting, its eyes glazed, tongue lolling over terrifying white fangs. Black fur marked with brown looked rumpled and muddy and its side had been scraped raw. It whined low in its throat and stretched its head suddenly to lick Jeff's hand.

"It's hurt," Rachel said.

"Rope?" Jeff slowly eased forward to scratch beneath one black ear.

"I've got some. Be careful!" She fled back to the truck, waiting for a snarl, the sound of attack.

She found the coil of nylon rope in her box and hurried back to Jeff with it. "You can cut off a piece," she told him. He cut a six-foot length with his clasp knife, made a loop in one end, and gently eased it over the dog's head.

"Let's go, boy." He got to his feet and tugged gently on the makeshift leash. "Let's get you some help. You're too big to carry."

"Jeff, what happened to it?" Rachel backed away in spite of herself as the huge dog lumbered to its feet. Its left side was a mess of matted hair and bleeding hide, and it held its left front leg clear of the ground.

"He went out of a pickup. I'll bet you a hundred bucks." Anger chilled Jeff's tone. "You see 'em all the time—dogs standing in some yahoo's pickup bed. So the idiot swerved, or maybe hit the brakes, and the dog went out. He hit the pavement and slid. I wonder if they even noticed. Some people shouldn't own dogs," he said harshly.

The dog hobbled painfully toward them on three legs as Jeff tugged on the leash. "Poor thing." In spite of her fear of its size, she couldn't help but feel a surge of pity for the injured animal.

"Can we put him in the back of your cab?" Jeff asked as he urged the dog along. "Or I can give you the keys and you can go get my Jeep. He's pretty filthy."

"I've got a plastic tarp in my box. I'll put that down." Rachel ran back to her truck to get the tarp from her box. She spread it out on the floor of the space behind the seats in her extended cab and stood back as Jeff coaxed the dog up to the vehicle. It actually tried to climb in, although he had to boost its hindquarters aboard. The dog gave a hoarse yelp as he put his weight on his injured leg, then settled onto the floor with a thump and a forlorn sigh.

"Let's go wake Dr. Stone up." Jeff climbed into the front seat beside her. "I'm sure he'll be thrilled."

Dr. Stone, Blossom's only veterinarian, had taken over the tiny downtown clinic from the retiring veterinarian who had been there forever, as far as Rachel knew. Born and raised in Colorado, he had specialized in large animal medicine, but now found his practice shifting more and more to a dog and cat clientele. Old Dr. Jarvis had failed to tell his young successor that Blossom residents all knew that the vet lived in the house behind the clinic and that, if you pounded on the door with a midnight emergency, you'd eventually wake someone up.

Stone had accepted this custom with good grace, although he had been heard to grumble on some bleary-eyed mornings that he was going to rent the house and move into an apartment in Hood River—one with an unlisted phone number and unknown address.

But he hadn't gotten around to it yet. As Rachel pulled up in front of the dark veterinary clinic just off Main Street, Jeff hopped out and hurried around the side of the building to the house at the rear. Rachel followed, giving the hunched and miserable dog behind the seat a cautious glance. The sound of pounding greeted her as she followed the narrow alley around to the tiny patch of grass that served Dr. Stone as a front yard.

Dr. Stone was obviously a sound sleeper, because Jeff was doing a vigorous job of pounding on the door's wooden panels. As she reached the steps of the narrow porch, a light finally came on behind one of the upstairs windows.

"I sure hope this is important." The vet stuck his head out and yawned. "I've got a pot of boiling oil all ready up here."

"I'm afraid it's important." Jeff stepped out from beneath the narrow porch roof. "Sorry, Doctor. I don't think this can wait until morning."

"Oh." The vet leaned farther. "Didn't recognize you without your uniform for a minute. What you got?"

"Dog went out of a pickup. Broken leg, I think. He's pretty badly shredded."

"Bring him in the front." Dr. Stone vanished back into his bedroom.

Rachel followed Jeff back to the truck. She held the door as he coaxed the reluctant dog out of the truck and through the clinic door that Dr. Stone was now holding open.

"In here." The vet spoke briskly, all traces of sleep banished by the necessity of the moment. He ushered them into a back room with a steel surgery table and spotless Formica counter with two steel sinks. Wood-and-glass-fronted cabinets lined the walls full of shiny steel instruments, bottles, and paper-wrapped packages with masking-tape labels. An ancient gas sterilizer hulked at the rear of the long room.

The vet handled the dog deftly, examining his injuries, manipulating the injured leg, which wrung a hoarse yelp from the dog. As Jeff held him, Dr. Stone clipped the medium-length hair from his injured side, exposing the raw red abrasions where the dog had slid across the pavement. Rachel was relieved that not once did it try to bite either of the men, not even when they cleaned the injuries with disinfectant. In the glare of harsh light here the dog looked even bigger than it had in the darkness of the empty lot. It could swallow Peter in about one gulp, she figured.

"I'm going to put him in a kennel in back." Dr. Stone gave the dog an injection and straightened. "In the morning, we'll put him under, get an X ray, and set that leg.

With luck it'll be a clean break and I can just cast it. You know who the owner is?"

"I don't have a clue." Jeff's eyes narrowed at the vet's frown. "Go ahead and do everything that needs to be done," he said slowly. "If the owner doesn't show up, I'll pay for it."

"Okay. If it's a really bad break, I'll give you a call though." He picked up the rope and chirped at the dog. "Come on, boy. Let's get you settled."

The dog followed him obediently, looking back at Jeff one more time as he left the room.

"I hope the owner shows up. That was nice of you— saying that you'd pay."

"The poor guy needs to get fixed up, that's all." Jeff shrugged, his expression hard. "If the owner does show, we're going to have a little talk about safety."

Rachel shook her head, wondering why this seemed to matter to him so much. "What breed do you think he is?" she asked lightly. "Part Angus steer, maybe?"

Jeff shrugged. "Rottweiler, from the markings, I'd guess."

"Rottweiler and shepherd, I'd say." Dr. Stone returned, drying his hands on a towel. "Nice dog. Didn't give us a bit of trouble."

"Too big for me," Rachel said. "Way too big."

"I'd better get back and see what Bert's up to." Jeff lifted a hand to the vet. "Sorry to get you up."

"Oh well." Stone shrugged and yawned widely. "At least it was for a good reason. Night!"

The lights winked out in the clinic before Rachel had time to start the engine. "Let me find out where Bert is." Jeff had his cell phone out. "You can drop me off. I'm going to cruise on foot tonight. I hope that jerk is still out there."

"Who do you think it is?" Rachel turned onto Blossom's main street and stopped at the single traffic signal, stifling a pang at Jeff's decision to keep looking for the vandal. "Some kid, do you think?"

"I don't know." Jeff was frowning at the windshield. "Maybe. Whoever it is has an agenda, and whoever it is also seems to have ESP. They do a pretty good job of being where we aren't. Bert? What's up?" He spoke into his cell phone. "Where are you?" He listened, his frown deepening. "I'll get off at the hardware store and work down to you," he said and folded up his phone.

The light turned green and Rachel pulled through the intersection. This time of night, Blossom's empty street had an eerie feel. The streetlights cast stark shadows into the doorways of the stores and gleamed on the glass windows. She pulled over to the curb in front of the hardware store with an involuntary shiver. "Hey, don't be out all night," she said as lightly as she could. "You work tomorrow."

"I do, don't I?" He leaned across the seat to kiss her, briefly and regretfully. "Our vandal is probably in bed by now, laughing at us." A hint of bitterness tinged his tone. "I'm just going to walk the downtown, that's all. I'm sorry. It started out to be a nice evening." He sighed and opened the door. "Can I sleep on your sofa tonight?"

"No," she said. "You have to sleep on the bed. The sofa is Peter's."

"Anything you say," he said meekly, but his smile warmed and his taut face relaxed for a moment as he leaned over to kiss her again. "I'm not going to stay out long, if we don't find anything."

"I heard that. It's a promise." She smiled for him and waited in the idling truck as he crossed the deserted street to vanish in the darkness between two buildings. This was his town. She stifled a sigh as she put the truck into gear and drove slowly back toward Mrs. Frey's house. So much for a romantic evening tonight.

There was no sign of Peter as she climbed the stairs to her apartment. He was out prowling the midnight jungle and would show up ravenous in the morning. Rachel let herself into the apartment hoping that the vandal had indeed gone to bed, hoping that Jeff wouldn't stay out all night. She poured herself a glass of water and checked her answering machine. The red light winked at her and she tapped the message key, sipping her water as the tape rewound.

"This is Madame DeRochers," the brisk voice emerged from the machine. "It is necessary to speak with you—tonight, if you find the time. If not, then tomorrow, as soon as you arrive, perhaps? It is very important, mademoiselle. Very important." The message ended and the tape rewound.

Rachel stared at the machine, frowning, those whispered syllables echoing in her head: *People are dying . . .*

Madame sounded . . . upset. Madame was never upset. What was going on here?

Stifling a sigh, realizing suddenly just how tired she was, and how late it was, Rachel finished her water and carried the glass to the sink She would tell Jeff about the call as soon as she had talked to Madame. Maybe Madame could shed some light on all these hints. Stripping out of her clothes, she wrapped herself in her cotton bathrobe and grabbed her newest gardening magazine, determined to wait up until Jeff arrived. Settling herself on the sofa, she managed to get partway through an article on new lilac cultivars before falling asleep.

The sound of the key woke her, and a moment later Jeff let himself into the apartment, looking tired. "I was right," he said ruefully as she tossed the magazine aside. "He went home to laugh at us, I'll bet. You weren't supposed to wait up for me."

"I wasn't waiting up," she said as she stepped into his arms. "I was reading about lilacs."

"Sure." He kissed her. "Do you always snore when you read?"

"I was not snoring." She tried to tickle him, but he laughed and caught her wrists.

"No fair," he said. "I'm falling asleep on my feet. Can I do that lying down instead?" he asked plaintively.

"You bet," Rachel said. "I think we could manage that."

CHAPTER

5

Jeff woke her as he slipped from beneath the covers and tiptoed across the room.

"If you'd just stomp around, I'd never wake up." Rachel sat up and yawned. "What time is it?" She glanced out the window at the bright morning. This time of year, morning came early.

"It's six-thirty." Jeff leaned down to kiss her lightly on the forehead. "I'm sorry. I really was trying to be quiet."

He looked like he hadn't slept well. Morning beard shadowed his jaw and accentuated the shadows beneath his eyes and his cheekbones. "I'll make us some coffee." Rachel tossed the covers aside. "You get the shower first. Anybody who wakes up on their own at this time of the morning gets shower privileges." She grabbed for her alarm as it began to buzz. "Time to get up anyway."

"I'll take you up on the shower." Jeff gave her a wink. "You make better coffee than I do anyway."

"I want that in writing." Rachel caught his hand as he headed for the bathroom. "Hey. You." She waited until he met her eyes. "It's just some kid. You'll catch him."

"Yeah." He gave her a crooked smile. "We will. That's true." He kissed her hard and briefly on the mouth, then went on into the bathroom. The rush of the shower sounded as Rachel belted on her robe and went through the apartment to open the front door.

Sure enough, Peter sat on the doormat glaring up at her.

"You're the one who wants to stay out all night." Rachel stood aside as he stalked past her. "Don't blame me if I don't get up with the sun. Do you know what time the sun comes up this time of year?"

Peter marched into the kitchen and took up position in front of the counter, his posture expectant and impatient.

"I should let you starve. Coffee first, cat." Rachel laughed and stepped around him to get the beans from the freezer. She scooped them into the grinder, buzzed them briefly, then poured them into the filter basket of the coffeemaker. The scent of dripping coffee filled the kitchen as she took a can of cat food down from the cupboard shelf and opened it. As she set the food on the floor for Peter, Jeff entered the kitchen, his hair damp, smelling of soap.

"Your turn." He put his arms around her from behind and rested his chin on the top of her head. "I left you a little hot water."

"Thank you so much." She tilted her head up and made a face at him. "If I run out, I'll share the cold water with you."

Jeff didn't answer. He was staring through her kitchen window, a bemused expression on his face. The window overlooked the small parking area at the side of the house. "You have company," he said after a pause. "Sitting in the back of your pickup, as a matter of fact."

"What?" Rachel leaned across the sink, peering down at the asphalt driveway. There was her truck, just as she'd left it. And indeed, a lanky figure sat on top of the big tool box mounted in the truck bed, leaning back against the cab as if he'd been there a long time. Straight black hair cut short and an Asian-flavored profile widened her eyes. "Spider," she said. "It's Spider."

"I thought so." Jeff raised his eyebrows. "Is he visiting?"

"I guess so, but he sure didn't tell me." Rachel started for the door, then stopped, realizing that she was still wearing her bathrobe. Letting out an exasperated breath, she stomped back into the bedroom to put on some clothes.

Spider had always been exasperating. While serving time at a controversial juvenile detention center that had been built in Blossom, Spider had been hired by Rachel through a community-work program. By the time he had finished his term at the Youth Farm and had been released, Rachel felt that they had achieved a measure of mutual trust. Julio had been mostly responsible for that, she thought as she threw on shirt and jeans. Julio had acted as older brother to the sixteen-year-old. When he had left The Farm, Rachel discovered that she missed him. Once in a while. When life got boring.

Tucking in her shirt, she dashed through the living room and down the stairs to the parking area.

"I thought you got up early." Spider Tranh didn't move from his languid sprawl against the back of her truck cab. "What is this? Sunday?"

"It *is* early." Rachel halted beside her truck, grinning up at him. He had grown in the two years since she had seen him last. Once in a while he sent her a letter, telling her about school and his job with a local landscaping service, but she remembered a sixteen-year-old. He was taller now, probably much taller than his half-Vietnamese father, with a lanky grace that hadn't been there before. His dark eyes were still very Asian, but his whatever-cool was very American teenager. "What are you *doing* here?" Rachel said. "I haven't heard from you in ages."

"I'm really crappy at writing letters." He made a face, looking briefly embarrassed. "I'm here to work for you. Julio says you need somebody, and I need a job. So what are we working on?" He levered himself off the truck box, landing in front of her with catlike grace.

He had earned the name "Spider" as a kid, he had told her once, in a rare moment of confidence. He had been little, and ran from the tough kids in his Lents neighborhood. They called him Spider because he could climb a wall faster than any big kid.

"Spider, I'm glad to see you." And without thought, she opened her arms and pulled him into a hug. She felt his momentary surprise, then his body relaxed and he hugged her back, lifting her briefly and gleefully from her feet.

"I'm taller than you. Hey, how 'bout that? So like I said, what are we working on?" His grin faltered just a bit, and for a moment he was that wary sixteen-year-old again. "I mean, you can hire me, right?"

"Yes, I can hire you." Rachel laughed. "Saves me from having to train somebody new. Julio has his own business now. He had to quit. We're doing a retirement home. Just don't call it a nursing home in front of the residents," she said.

"I won't." Spider rolled his eyes. "Old people scare me." He looked past her. "Hey, man. How're you doing?" He grinned. "Only cop I could ever stand." He stepped past Rachel as she turned, hand outstretched.

"You're looking good, Spider." Jeff clasped his hand. "You here for a visit?"

"Here for a job." He grinned. "She taught me how to work, anyway."

"Yeah, she did." Jeff gave Rachel a look filled with private amusement. "Life is never dull," he said. "The coffee's ready. You want some, Spider?"

"Sure, thanks."

They climbed the stairs together, and Spider gave them a brief and not-very-detailed account of his past two years. He had become a model citizen, he informed them. He had graduated high school with a 4.0 grade point average, and had worked hard for the landscaper who had hired him. "He wasn't like you," he informed Rachel loftily. "He just mowed lawns and trimmed bushes, and when people wanted, he planted a lot of cheap annuals. You know—pansies, marigolds, that kind of crap."

"Watch your language," Rachel said severely, which earned her amused glances from both men. Rolling her eyes, she finished her coffee. "Well, you'll probably wish you were planting annuals by the time we get the shrubs planted," she told him.

"Lyle's going to pick me up," Jeff told her as he rinsed his mug in the sink. "So you don't have to drive me downtown."

Lyle was another of Blossom's police officers. It was not a big department.

"Don't work too hard." Rachel kissed him, acutely aware of Spider's presence. "See you after work?"

"Give me a call when you're done for the day." He glanced out the window. "Lyle's here. That was fast." He lifted a hand to Spider. "See you later." And he was gone, footsteps pounding down the staircase. Rachel sighed as she heard Lyle rev his truck's engine, hoping they'd catch the vandal soon.

"So he gave you the ring?" Spider nodded at her left hand.

"Yep." She glanced at the narrow band of emeralds, annoyed at sudden heat in her cheeks. "He sure did. So let's get to work."

"I figured." Spider smiled.

"Did you." Rachel looked Spider up and down. He was indeed taller than she was now. He was still skinny, but now lean muscle wrapped those bones and rounded his once-thin shoulders into smooth curves of strength. "You look like you've been working out," she said as he followed her out onto the landing. "Lifting weights?"

"Yeah, sometimes." He ducked his head. "You work hard pushing those big Toro mowers around and pruning and stuff. Is there a gym in Blossom?"

" 'Fraid not." Rachel smothered a smile. "But I'll do my best to keep you in shape."

"Bet you will." Spider clattered down the steps after her.

"So he's with you?" Mrs. Frey stepped out from her side door as they reached the parking lot, her expression wary, verging on the hostile. "This boy? He was on your truck."

"Is there a law about that?" Spider bristled.

"This is private property," Mrs. Frey snapped. "If I see a stranger messing with my renter's vehicle, I call the police. Normal people come to the door before they start poking around."

"I wasn't poking around, lady." Spider returned the landlady's hostile stare. "I was sitting. Waiting for Rachel to get up."

So that's how come Lyle showed up so fast. "You remember Spider, don't you?" Rachel broke in hastily, mentally groaning. "He worked for me a couple of years ago," she said brightly. "I'm sure you met him. He's taking Julio's place for a while."

"I don't believe I have met him." Mrs. Frey's expression mollified slightly but refused to soften further. "Young man, there are two rules here. If you're waiting for Miss O'Connor, you come to the door and announce yourself to me. If I see someone skulking around in the bushes, I'll call the police. Naturally."

"Naturally," Spider echoed in a truly adult tone of irony. "And I was *sitting*. On her truck. Not skulking."

Mrs. Frey's weathered face flushed slightly. "The other rule," she said acerbically, "is that my garden is not a public place. You are permitted in the driveway and parking area and Miss O'Connor's apartment. You are not permitted in my rose garden."

Spider glanced slowly and deliberately at the neatly laid-out rose garden visible behind the house. "I saw the roses." He gave her a cool glance. "If you need some advice on how to prune them right, I'll be glad to help you out."

Mrs. Frey's sucked-in breath was as audible as a gasp. For a moment she merely stared wordlessly at Spider. Then her eyes shifted to Rachel and narrowed slightly. Her shoulders rose as she sucked in another deep breath. But instead of speaking, she turned on her heel and marched back into the house. Shutting the door. Not slamming it. Shutting it very gently.

This time, Rachel groaned out loud. "Nice going." She shook her head as she unlocked the truck. "You've done a very thorough job of pissing off my landlady."

"Is that who that was?" Spider looked back at the house and waved. "She's watching us through the curtains."

"She always does. And she wasn't kidding about her roses," Rachel said severely. "She's the local rose expert around here. Her pruning is just fine, by the way."

"No it isn't." Spider spoke with all the assurance of adolescence as he climbed into the cab. "She should cut the canes shorter in the winter. She'll get more bloom. The guy I worked for was a big expert," he answered Rachel's withering glance. "He used to be in charge of the Portland Rose Garden."

"Lots of people are experts." Rachel decided to abandon this course of discussion. "We're going to start plumbing today. I've got to stop at the hardware store on the way in and order some more parts though," she said ruefully.

"Julio said you were having trouble." Spider nodded sagely. "He said you guys hit a lot of rock. Tough break."

"Yeah." She glanced at him briefly. "Sounds as if you've been talking to Julio quite a bit," she said.

"Sure." He shrugged. "I guess he uses the computer down at the library and got onto one of those free e-mail systems—you know—the kind where you have to read a ton of ads, and you just get e-mail."

"I didn't know." Rachel hid her surprise. She hadn't realized that Julio was on the Internet, although why he shouldn't be when nearly every school kid in Blossom was, she wasn't sure. With a twinge of guilt, she wondered just how many of her Uncle Jack's attitudes had seeped into her subconscious during her childhood, coloring the way she thought. Too many, probably, she thought wryly. Well, she'd just had one of them shaken in her face. "So when did he tell you he was quitting?" she asked casually.

"Oh, last month, I guess." Spider shrugged. "I had to give my boss two weeks' notice. Good timing." He laughed. "My mom's got a boyfriend. He's okay—works for Freightliner and is a nice guy. But I was in the way, if you know what I mean. Mom's funny about that. Like I don't know, or something."

"I get the picture." Rachel firmly swallowed her brief irritation that Julio had shared his plans with Spider long before he'd shared them with her. Oh well. Pulling into a vacant parking space along the curb in front of the hardware store, she got out. "Be right back," she told Spider, then dug out her wallet. "Actually, why don't you run down to the Bread Box and buy us something for breakfast. I don't know about you, but I didn't eat anything yet."

"You bet." Spider hopped out, took the five she offered, and sprinted across the street.

Judging by his alacrity, he hadn't eaten yet either. Shaking her head, Rachel went into the hardware store to place her order for more fittings.

"How's it going?" Roth Glover, the store owner, pushed his reading glasses up onto his forehead and folded the newspaper he was reading behind the cash register. "What can I get for you this morning?"

"A few things, I'm afraid." Rachel handed him the list she'd made out yesterday.

Glover's eyebrows rose as he read it and he whistled. "That's for the Village job, isn't it?" He clucked his tongue at Rachel's nod. "You're putting in a lot more irrigation, huh?"

"I'm hitting rock, about every ten feet." Rachel sighed as she leaned her elbows on the ancient wooden countertop. "I'm going to end up spending my profit on extra irrigation lines."

"That's too bad. That darn rock is sneaky stuff." Glover raised his voice as he disappeared into the orderly chaos of his stock room. "I remember back when Josie and I were first married. She wanted a nice flower garden by the house. I swear every time I swung the grub hoe, I hit lava six inches down. I finally told her she could have a rock garden and grow rocks! We got everything." He re-emerged, lugging a large cardboard box filled with the parts she'd ordered. "You got enough pipe?"

"I think so. I always order extra." Rachel watched him write out the invoice in his slow, meticulous script, steeling herself not to wince at the total.

"Jeff catch those blame kids yet?" Glover peered over the top of his glasses at her. "They busted my front window. Just for the hell of it. Kids are going to hell these days. It's all that TV, those video games they play, and now the Internet. You don't know what your kid's up to. They can get into anything."

"Jeff thinks it's one kid." Rachel pulled out her checkbook. "They'll catch him."

"Hope so." Roth slid the invoice across the counter. "I can put that on your account. Hope they catch 'em. That window cost me six hundred bucks to replace. I got a five hundred deductible on my insurance, too. You know, that new guy came by the other day—Stanfield. He had some real good ideas about setting up a curfew like they got in the city, and making some ordinances against hanging around on the street after dark. I like the way he thinks." Glover nodded as he hefted the box. "We might ask him in to talk about his ideas at the next Council meeting. He's got some good ones."

More trouble for Jeff, if the City Council pitted the new officer against his boss. Rachel held the door for Glover as he carried the box of irrigation parts out to her truck. Joylinn and Earlene Guarnieri wouldn't back the kind of restrictions Stanfield wanted to impose. But the Council consisted of five members.

"Food." Spider leaned against the side of her truck. "Lots of food." He waved a large white bakery bag at her. "Five bucks buys you a lot there, boss lady." His eyes traveled to Glover, and he gave the hardware store owner a broad smile. "Hi, Mr. Glover. How're you doing?"

Roth looked startled, his expression wavering between scowl and smile. "Hello," he said finally, settling on a stiff and distant smile. He deposited the box in the bed of the pickup and gave Rachel a brief quizzical look. "I hope you don't run into any more rock." Wiping his hands on his jeans, he vanished into the store.

"He didn't remember me," Spider said in a mournful tone. "But I still don't think he likes me."

"Roth is not a fan of teenagers. And Joylinn gets carried away." Rachel sighed as she noted the heft of the bag. After last night's dinner she wasn't feeling awfully free to overindulge. "Help yourself and let's get going."

She had resolved to be very righteous about what she selected from that overloaded bag, but when Spider handed her a coil of rich pastry oozing cream cheese filling, she simply took it, enjoying every gooey, lemon-scented bite as she negotiated the county road that led to the Village.

"There's enough for lunch here." Spider peered into the bag. "That is some lady."

"She is indeed." Rachel took another bite of richness. "You ever hear of the food pyramid?"

"Yeah, in health class. Easy A. Don't remember a thing." Spider polished off his third or fourth cinnamon roll. "Julio told me that your boss is a real—"

"Yes, she is," Rachel cut in. "Spider, you're going to have to sit on the four-letter words." She gave him a serious stare. "This place is inhabited by older folk, who are going to take serious affront to things that you don't think twice about saying."

"Oh, great." He rolled his eyes skyward with such an expression of martyred suffering that Rachel nearly giggled.

Sternly, she squelched it. "And the director would just love to fire me, so don't give her the reason, okay?"

"How come she wants to fire you?" Spider sat up straight on the seat. "I can get somebody to whack her."

Sometimes, she wasn't sure when he was teasing and when he was serious. He had a rather rough history. She glanced at him and decided that this time he was kidding. "I've heard rumors that she wants to bring somebody in who's cheaper," she said slowly. "But whatever the reason, she's not happy with me. So we will not give her a legal reason to break the contract."

"I'll behave." Spider slumped on the seat, hands shoving deep into the pockets of his jeans. "I promise."

"I'm giving her a better reason than you could anyway," Rachel said slowly. "I'm way behind schedule."

"Not for long." Spider gave her a big grin. "Wait until you see what I can do on the end of a shovel."

He wasn't kidding. From the moment she parked the truck, he was an asset. He unloaded the tools without asking, and joined Eduardo's small crew with a brief greeting in orchard Spanish that earned him grins and nods. Julio had told Eduardo about Spider, Rachel figured as she started the men working. And she wondered just how long this exchange of employment had been in the works. Longer than twenty-four hours, she was willing to bet.

They were almost done with the digging. As Rachel joined in the shovel work, she estimated the remaining task and guessed that she could start laying pipe after lunch. She could let Eduardo and the crew go at that point. Which would take a big strain off the budget, right there. Of course, that schedule would fall apart the instant they hit another ridge of lava, she though grimly.

To her unbounded relief, they didn't hit another ridge of lava. Well before noon, the crew finished the last neat stretch of ditch, cleaned their shovels, and were finished. A precise network of narrow trenches divided the slope. Rachel wiped sweat from her face as the men put away the tools. The day had turned hot and a bitter hint of smoke tainted the dry east wind. Somewhere a fire was burning, but so distant that no plume was visible. Farther up the Gorge, Rachel thought, and hoped it wasn't big. Good weather for ripening fruit, but not so great for digging.

She paid the men and turned to Spider as Eduardo drove off with his crew in his battered car. "You sure have learned to work hard." She grinned at him, remembering the kid who had slacked off whenever possible, two years ago.

"Bill was a fair guy, but he figured if you couldn't work as hard as he did, why should he pay you?" Spider made a face. "That old guy could work like a son of a . . . Real hard," he amended quickly.

Rachel winked at him. "I don't think we have enough of Joylinn's goodies left for lunch, and besides, we both need something more than carbos for lunch. We can get some lunch at the dining room," Rachel said as she got a drink of water from the truck's big cooler. "Clean up. It's my treat."

"You mean up there with all those old people?" Spider looked uneasy.

"Only a few of them bite," Rachel said blandly. "Most of them just attack you with their canes."

"Ha ha, very funny." Spider put his shovel into the truck. "Okay, fine, let's go wherever."

He looked as if he were on his way to the dentist, Rachel thought as they climbed the path to the main building. Nobody was outside in the midday heat today. As they trudged along the asphalt path, Rachel remembered Madame's phone call with a stab of guilt. Spider's appearance this morning had driven the whole episode out of her head—including that warning on her phone.

Now, hearing those whispered syllables in her head again, she looked at the small groups of elderly men and women clustered in the main lobby as she and Spider came through the door. Who had called her? Someone here? Try as she might, she couldn't assign either gender or age to that hissing voice.

"There's a public rest room on the left where you can wash up." She gestured to Spider, noticing the tension in his posture. "You never spent time with grandparents, did you?"

"Didn't have any." He marched off, his back ramrod straight.

He did draw more than one stare. Rachel caught sight of Madame sitting in one of the armchairs that clustered in the wide space. The aid she had met yesterday perched casually on the arm of the chair, grinning and chatting with her. Jason. Rachel remembered his name as she hurried over.

"I'm so sorry," Rachel said as she reached them. "I didn't get your message until after midnight. This morning I forgot," she added sheepishly. "I guess I'm getting senile early."

"I've had that trouble since I was little." Jason winked at her, his blue eyes twinkling. "I write notes to myself about everything."

"You are very busy." Madame inclined her head in forgiveness. "I will not chide you."

"What's wrong?" Rachel cast a sideways glance at the smiling aid, deciding this was not the time to mention anonymous warnings. Rumors had wings here, and grew like zucchini wherever they landed. "Is something wrong with Harris?"

"Monsieur McLoughlin is well," Madame said with a trace of acerbity. "I was simply concerned." She didn't look at Jason. "One of our members was taken ill last night. I have heard that she is still unwell, and that perhaps she may go to the hospital."

"You mean Emily." Jason's open smile darkened to a look of concern. "She was feeling pretty crummy last night. Dr. Welsh came in this morning. An ambulance took her to Hood River to the hospital, early this morning."

"An ambulance?" Rachel blinked, trying to place the woman's name.

"At lunch yesterday, she had the look of health." Madame's Quebec accent had thickened slightly. "Her mind, it was clear."

Now she remembered. Emily was the woman with the pearls and the unhealthy complexion, the one who had complained that her statement contained extra charges. Rachel glanced curiously at Madame. Her accent directly reflected her state of mind. When she was upset, it got stronger. Rachel glanced at her smooth and unreadable face. Nothing there. But the skin of her knuckles gleamed on her hands, folded so demurely on her lap.

"Well, that's a rarity these days—Emily having a clear mind." Jason made a face. "She's really getting bad. Aliens were running the government last week." He shook his head. "I'm not sure that there's anything really wrong with her." He leaned forward confidentially. "With her, you can't tell. Remember that stomach flu she had two months ago? She was sure someone had poisoned her." Jason rolled his eyes. "I'd better be off. We aids are still waiting table." He gave Rachel a meaningful glance and departed in the direction of the dining room.

"I do remember that she made a few . . . accusations." Madame's eyes went briefly to Rachel's face. "Ah." Her glanced shifted. "*Bonjour,* my young one." She inclined her head regally. "I believe that we met some time ago. You were the young assistant to Mademoiselle O'Connor, yes?"

"Uh, yeah, I mean, yes, I was." Spider looked as if he'd rather be anywhere but here.

"You have grown well." Madame's eyes twinkled as she eyed the uncomfortable Spider. "You have the insect name, as I remember? Was it Beetle, perhaps?"

"Spider." He shifted on his feet as if he was about to flee.

"Ah, yes." She clucked her tongue with a hint of coquettishness. "Such a droll name for such a handsome young man. Ah, here is Monsieur Harris." She smiled as the retired detective wheeled up. "This is Monsieur Spider, *mon ami.* You remember him, yes?"

"You were working for Rachel." Harris extended a hand, but his smile was preoccupied. "Are you working for her again?"

"Yeah, yes," Spider mumbled.

Madame had risen gracefully to her feet and now slipped her arm through Spider's, before he could escape. "Shall we proceed to lunch?" Her eyes were full of mischief. "Such a strong young man. I asked Ricki to set an extra place for lunch, in hopes that I might tempt you here to eat. She will add another place for you, *mon petit.*" She smiled up at Spider. "It is no trouble, I am sure."

He managed to stammer out a thank-you, which made Madame's eyes sparkle even more.

She was enjoying herself immensely. Rachel smothered a smile, feeling a bit sorry for the trapped Spider, but not very much. She tried to catch Harris's eye to see if he was sharing her amusement at Madame's teasing, but his face wore an inward look, and he was frowning slightly as he wheeled after Madame and Spider. A finger of unease touched her and she dropped back to walk beside him. "Is something wrong?"

"Dr. Welsh just stopped by. I happened to be in the director's office when he arrived." He shook his head. "Emily Barnhart was diagnosed with acute kidney failure, he says. She's in intensive care at the moment. He says they don't think she'll make it."

Chilled, Rachel couldn't answer. Yesterday, the woman had sat within a few feet of her, alive and seemingly well, complaining about her bill.

Today, she lay dying.

Rachel shivered. "I think I need to talk to you," she told Harris in a low voice. "I got a strange phone call last night."

"After lunch," Harris said softly. "You know, *ma chère,*" he directed his words to Madame DeRochers. "You are way too experienced for this laddie. You'll overwhelm him."

"Ah, you underrate him, my love." Madame fluttered her eyelashes at him. "Or are you jealous?"

"I am always jealous." Harris took her hand and seated her at a table near the window. "Don't mind her." He gave Spider a wink. "She's not really dangerous."

Spider looked as if he seriously entertained that possibility. Stiffly he settled himself at the table, his hands beneath it, his posture suggesting that he was in school, facing a tough math test. Jason served them their lunch, flirting charmingly with Madame, and giving Rachel a warm grin and a touch on the shoulder that wasn't lost on Harris, Rachel noticed.

"Have you heard any more?" Madame asked as Jason deposited their plates of chicken salad and sliced tomatoes on the table. "How is Madame Barnhart?"

"I . . ." Jason looked around and lowered his voice. "She died," he murmured as he bent to place a basket of four rolls neatly in the center of the table. "I heard our director talking on the phone, just a few minutes ago when I went to take her lunch. I don't think she wants anyone to know yet."

Of course they would now. Rachel glanced at Harris, noticing the tight line of his lips as he reached for a roll. Madame was not a gossip, but if Jason had told her, he would tell others.

"She was not ready to die." Madame lifted her head, looking Rachel straight in the eye. "I tell you, *ma chérie.* I know when one has opened one's arms to death. She had not. This was not her time to die."

"You mean somebody murdered her?" Spider looked up from his plate suddenly.

"Enough." Harris spoke sharply.

A little to Rachel's surprise, Madame lowered her eyes, and a faint color touched her cheeks. Then she turned the conversation to the weather, and the state of the landscaping job, and Emily Barnhart's death did not come up again.

But judging from the hushed, intense murmurs at some of the tables around them, word was spreading fast. Death was a personal enemy here—a dark familiar who peeked from the depths of the mirror and lurked behind the infirmary door.

As they left the dining room, she sent Spider on ahead to unload the irrigation fittings she had bought. Harris paused and said something to Madame, then crossed the lobby swiftly to catch up with Rachel at the door. "So tell me about your phone call." He wheeled along beside her, his lean face growing grim as she recounted her anonymous message of the night before.

"Tell Jeff today." He halted at the edge of the paved walkway, a muscular and upright man above his ruined legs. "Ask him if he'd find a reason to drop by here. A casual reason." His gray eyes were on her face. "I haven't seen him for quite a while. I think we need to talk."

"Madame was right, then. Something's going on."

Harris's face softened. "Madame has a deeper heart than she admits to." He shook his head. "It would be good to talk to Jeff. That's all." His expression betrayed nothing. "I'm not sure that there's any hurry," he added. "I gather that he's busy."

So even here, the vandal was news. Rachel sighed. "I'll tell him," she said. "I'm sure he'll drop by soon."

Harris nodded, lifted a hand to her in farewell, and wheeled himself strongly back up the walkway to the main building.

If he wanted to talk to Jeff, something was indeed wrong here.

CHAPTER

6

Spider surprised Rachel. He had obviously learned how to assemble irrigation lines and did so neatly, efficiently, and with little supervision needed on her part. Considering that she hated all aspects of plumbing, she was delighted with this new talent of his. His former employer had trained him well.

"So how did you get a job with this landscaper?" she asked as they cleaned their tools at the end of the day. "No one ever called me about a reference."

"Really?" Spider looked surprised. "He said he was going to call. I gave him your name. I figured there was only one Rain Country Landscaping in the area, and he said he'd heard of you. He shrugged. "There was this program. For kids who had . . . gotten in trouble." He made a face. "I guess they've got some kind of connection to the Farm. Anyway, Mr. Bard—the head guy out at the Farm—he gave me their phone number. I guess it's kind of what you did. A business hires some kid and somebody pays part of the salary. It paid okay. Better than flipping burgers. Which I probably couldn't get anyway, since I got a record and they always ask you that on the application. But the program won't take you after you graduate high school," he said regretfully. "And he didn't need another regular employee, so I had to quit."

"Well, I'm glad you were free." Rachel eyed the neatly glued joints in the system. Maybe, for once, they'd get a good pressure test on the main lines the first time. "So are you going to college this fall?"

"No." Spider shrugged at her raised eyebrows. "Oh, I plan to go. I don't want to spend the rest of my life shoveling. Not that I don't really like working for you," he added quickly. "But if I get a degree, I can maybe be my own boss someday, you know?"

"So how come you're not going this year?" Rachel asked. "I thought you got a scholarship from a foundation for full tuition?"

"Yeah . . . I did." Spider tossed the last discarded scraps of PVC pipe onto the trash pile. "It's called the Deborah Foundation." His dark eyes fixed themselves on her face. "I got a Christmas card from your mom and dad last year. You know what? On the return address, I saw your mom's name is Deborah. Funny, huh?"

"Yes," Rachel said with a perfectly straight face. "One of those coincidences." Because, of course, Joshua probably *was* the "Deborah Foundation," even if he wouldn't admit it, and a lawyer handled all the details. "Does that matter?"

"No," Spider said slowly. "But you know, I thought . . . what I really want to do . . ." He trailed off, looking at her sideways, as if he half expected her to laugh. "I want to be a doctor," he said in a rush. "Not to make a lot of money, but because there aren't a lot of doctors around that you can go to if you're poor, you know? I remember when I was sick, we went to the hospital. And we waited in the ER forever. There were people moaning and some of them were pretty messed up, and it was awful. And it always cost a lot. Mom would wait till I was real bad." He frowned. "But medical school isn't cheap. I checked out some of the numbers. And I don't want some foundation to be stuck with that big a bill. I mean . . . what if I can't do it? So I figured I'd earn money for a couple of years before I get started." He gave her that half-defiant, half-embarrassed look again.

"You'd do just fine in medical school," Rachel said, a little startled by this totally unexpected revelation. "You're smart, Spider. And you know, foundations aren't run by dumb people. They don't throw their money away."

"Maybe." Spider shook his head. "I'm doing it my way, thanks." He looked around the site. "I think we're finished," he said. "Can you give me a ride to Julio's house? He's letting me stay there for now. And I left my stuff in a locker at the bus station last night. Do you think we could go get it?"

"Hop in." Rachel tossed her gloves into the truck box and climbed behind the wheel. At least the director had left them alone today. That had made it a good day, she decided as she backed the truck around. Actually, it *had* been a good day. Spider's new skills with pipe had really sped things along.

Instead of going directly to the train station, she swung by the Bread Box and parked in the lot. "Milk shake?" she asked Spider, and received a broad grin in reply. That had been their custom, when Julio and Spider had both worked for her, two years before. When they'd had a good day, they'd stopped for shakes on the way home.

Joylinn waved from the coffee bar, where she was making two iced cappuccinos. It was busy again this afternoon. Tourist season was in full swing, and even at this hour, the Bread Box was half full of patrons dressed in shorts, bright shirts, and sandals. In a few weeks, as the apple and pear crops began to come in, Hood River's famous Fruit Loop would draw even more people to its fruit stands, hay rides, and petting zoos among the orchards.

"What can I get you?" Celia, Joylinn's longtime assistant, paused by their table with a tray of dirty dishes. "Hiya, kid. Haven't seen you for a while," she said to Spider.

"Chocolate shake, right?" Rachel raised an eyebrow at Spider. "Iced tea for me. And maybe a couple of blueberry muffins? If you have any left?" Spider had finished the pastries from the morning, and she had a feeling that he was ready for more.

He proved her right, reaching for a muffin as soon as Celia returned with the piled plate and two dewy glasses. Whipped cream topped his shake and a slice of lemon decorated her tea. "You see the *Bee* today?" Celia asked conversationally as she set the glasses down in front of them. "You ought to take a look." Then she was gone, whisking off to take an order from a newly arrived couple in hiking clothes who had just taken a table by the window.

"At least she remembered me." Spider looked impressed as he finished his first muffin and started on his milk shake.

"Celia remembers everyone." Absently Rachel sipped at her tea. "Be right back." She made her way to the small table by the door where a couple of issues of the daily paper could usually be found, left by the breakfast patrons. Sure enough, a refolded copy lay there now. She carried it back to the table, scanning the contents.

Uh-oh. Frowning, she sat down again, reaching for a muffin as the page one story caught her eye. TEENS LAUGH AT BLOSSOM'S FINEST. The article took up a prominent chunk of the page and reported on the graffiti sprayed last night across the front of the kite shop next door. That was what he had been doing when Jeff had spotted him, Rachel thought. It was not a kind article, and managed to give the impression that the police had probably been napping most of the night. The story directed readers to an accompanying editorial by Hallie Sylvester, the editor and an old friend of the former mayor. He was an outspoken opponent of nearly anything Ventura, the current mayor, said or did. Usually he covered Council meetings and local events. She frowned, wondering if Jeff had seen this yet.

Most likely. She sighed and turned to the editorial page. The editorial was a little gentler, but it still questioned whether the addition of a new officer had been a good decision.

In other words, was it Jeff's incompetence that was the cause of the problem here?

Rachel managed not to crumple the paper into a ball, making herself fold it neatly.

"Uh-oh." Spider raised an eyebrow as he polished off his third muffin. "Not good, huh?"

"Not good at all," she said grimly. "Somebody is out doing damage just about every night and nobody can catch him. Or them."

"One person's hard to catch." Spider shrugged. "You see headlights, you got time to hide. If you're smart."

"This one's smart." She finished her iced tea. "You ready to go?"

She drove him down to the tiny train station, where he retrieved a battered backpack from the bank of aged lockers. "That's it?" she asked as he tossed it into the bed of her truck. She drove him through town and up the narrow road that curved, became gravel, and led to the mobile home where Julio lived with his sister and brother-in-law. Julio's truck was parked in front of the well-kept yard. He had bought a used pickup and had added a freshly painted wooden stake-bed. His tools were neatly racked in the back, next to two plastic garbage cans for lawn clippings and a battered lawn mower with a grass catcher. He came out of the house as they arrived, his shirt off in the afternoon heat, grinning, hand lifted in greeting.

"Where are you sleeping?" Rachel asked, because the mobile was already crowded, she knew.

"On the floor probably," Spider said cheerfully. "I got to look for a place to stay. Want to rent me your sofa?"

He was grinning, but there was an intense sparkle in those dark eyes that she had never noticed before. It made her face warm, and startled her. Spider had been a kid when he had worked for her two years ago. All day she had been thinking of him as a kid. He wasn't. Not anymore. "We'll find you something," she said quickly.

"Okay. Great." Spider shrugged. "See you in the morning." He leaped out of the truck, grabbed his pack from the bed, and went bounding across the yard to pound on Julio's arm and get pounded in return. Julio waved at her as she turned the truck around.

They had both turned into men sometime in the last two years. Julio was getting married. Shaking her head, she drove back to town. Well . . . that wasn't quite true. While Spider certainly wasn't a child, he wasn't really a grown-up either, not yet. And somehow, she seemed to have signed a contract to take care of him. She sure didn't remember doing so, but Spider seemed to take it for granted. Well, whatever happened, she'd have to find him a place to stay. He sure wasn't sleeping on her sofa.

With that resolve made, she turned into the parking lot behind City Hall. It was still quite light, and hot enough to make her leave the windows open in the truck. The side door was locked, so she went around to the front and climbed the broad steps to the big wooden doors. As she reached them, they swung open, and Mayor Ventura very nearly knocked her down.

"Sorry," he said brusquely, reaching for her arm to steady her. "I'm sorry." And he hurried past, pounding down the steps and marching briskly down the block.

She wasn't sure he'd even recognized her. Rachel went on into the cool dim well of City Hall. Moira Kellogg, the mayor's petite, gray-haired personal assistant, was on her way down the wide staircase from his upstairs office, a thin sheaf of letters in her hand.

"Hello, Rachel." She smiled wearily. "Any chance our good mayor didn't charge out of here?"

"By now he's three blocks away." Rachel lifted an eyebrow at the middle-aged woman. "What happened? He just about ran over me."

"Well, at least you're not likely to sue him," Moira said dryly. "I told him he needed to sign these letters for the mail pickup, but did he hear me?" Hands on her hips, she shook her head, looking like nothing so much as everyone's first grade teacher— an assumption that led many people to underestimate her shrewd intelligence, to their cost. "Honestly. I should buy the man a lance. Then he can take on his windmills in style at least."

"Let me guess." Rachel smiled in spite of herself. "The *Bee*."

"Of course. What else." Moira rolled her gray eyes skyward. "I told him it's just Hallie, sniping at him yet again, but does he listen to me? Hallie Sylvester has used his position as editor to go after everything Phil has done since he won this office. He's never going to change his opinion of our fair-haired young leader. I don't know why Phil is taking it so peronally this time." She let out an exasperated breath. "Now I'll have to change the date on these letters. And at least one of them is going to have to be rewritten, if it's going out tomorrow. Honestly." Shaking her head, she started back up the staircase. "Sometimes I think I should lock the office door on him."

Her heart sinking, Rachel went back along the hall that led to the police department. All four of Blossom's police officers were present, collected in a tight huddle around Jeff's cluttered desk. Jeff glanced up as she entered, gave her a brief, preoccupied wave, and went back to talking. A few minutes later, the foursome broke up. Lyle and Kelly Jones greeted her on the way out. They didn't look happy. The new officer, Stanfield, stalked past her with a bare nod, his expression positively grim.

"He doesn't like the way I'm handling this." Jeff came over to lean against the long counter that divided the room. He sighed. "I guess he got himself invited to speak to the Council."

"Roth Glover told me," Rachel said dryly. "He'd love a curfew."

"He'd love an all-out war against anybody under the age of twenty-five." Jeff massaged his eyes. "But then, he did lose a window to this bastard, after all. You know, I'm beginning to think that Bert has his eye on my job."

"You're kidding." Rachel bristled. "So fire him."

"Not that easy, sweetheart." Jeff leaned over and kissed her lightly. "Don't lose any sleep over it. If Phil loses the next election, I'm out anyway." He straightened as the phone behind him began to ring. "We're all going to be on the street tonight. Three on foot, one in the car. We're going to get our little vandal." He picked up the phone. "Blossom Police." Frowned, then rolled his eyes skyward. "No, I didn't know that. Nobody has had reason to tell me, I guess." He mimed a sigh. "If the doctors at the hospital in Hood River had any suspicions of the death, they'd report it. It's out of my hands." His frown deepened. "I'll make a note of what you're telling me, but I'm afraid I'll need reason to look into it. She was old, wasn't she?" He winced. "Yes, I understand. You're way too young at heart to die anytime soon, Madame. I'll drop by and we'll talk about it, okay?"

"Madame DeRochers," Rachel hazarded.

"Reporting a murder." Jeff set the phone back on its cradle. "Only nobody else seems to think it was a murder."

"Emily Barnhart. One of the aids told us she died." Rachel swallowed as Jeff nodded. "That's why I came by. To tell you that I got a . . . a warning phone call. About the Village." It was her turn to wince at the expression in his eyes. "I just forgot to tell you. It was too late last night, and then . . . I just forgot."

"Tell me." His tone was neutral, and whatever he was thinking, it didn't show on his face.

She told him about the call, and added that McLoughlin had asked if he'd drop by.

"You're sure you don't know if it was a man or a woman." He stared past her.

"I couldn't tell." She shook her head. "A couple of the aids have suggested that the director is siphoning off money. One of them—a man named Jason something—said she wanted to fire me so that she could hire someone cheap."

"Madame said that the director murdered this woman." Jeff sat down on the corner of his desk, idly picking up a chunk of pink agate they'd found on a backpacking trip in the Oregon high desert. "I'll drop by and talk to Harris. Meanwhile, I'll find out what the official report is on this woman's death last night."

Rachel hesitated. "I was sitting near Emily yesterday, at lunch at the Village." She shivered in spite of herself. "She was complaining that she had found fraudulent charges on her monthly statement, and that it had happened before."

"I'll see what I can find out." He glanced at his watch. "But it will have to be in the morning. I'll stop by to see how you're coming along on the project." He gave her a lopsided smile. "Maybe reminding your boss that your fiancé is the chief of police will give you a bit of breathing space, if nothing else."

"I haven't been complaining that much," Rachel protested.

"It shows." Jeff set the chunk of rock down and stood. "We're going to be out pretty late tonight, but I might just come by and catch a couple of hours of sleep at your place, after. If that's okay."

"Is it ever not?" She stood on tiptoe to kiss him firmly on the mouth. "Wake me up."

"I will," he said, and smiled, his eyes briefly warm and full of light. "I definitely will."

The sun was finally setting as Rachel left City Hall. She drove down to the Thriftway and did some shopping before going home. She figured she'd better pack a lunch for Spider, too—and remembered that she was supposedly finding him a place to stay. She thought of the orchard as she carried her sack of groceries up the stairs, but discarded that idea instantly. Yes, they had bedrooms, and Aunt Catherine would probably be happy to accommodate him and mother him at no charge. But then, there was Uncle Jack. She tried to decide just how long Spider would last before her uncle threw him out. Less than twenty-four hours, she guessed. This time of year, on the verge of harvest, he had no tolerance for anything or anyone who crossed him.

Next option?

"You got any suggestions, cat?" she asked as Peter appeared almost magically on the landing to rub against her ankles. "Know anybody who's got a room to rent?" She didn't really want him rooming with Jeff. Two was company up there, thank you.

Letting herself in, she fed Peter, then began to fix some dinner. Figuring that Jeff would grab a hamburger from the Homestyle Café—if he bothered with dinner at all—she unwrapped the chicken breast she'd bought, and started fixing a rosemary chicken and pasta dish. She called the police number and got Stanfield, instead of Jeff. He told her curtly that Jeff wasn't there, but that he'd be back later, and promised to give him the message that she was going to drop by. It was just getting dark when she drained the pasta, divided it into two plastic containers, topped it with the cooked chicken and a grating of fresh Parmesan, and packed the dinner containers into her canvas picnic hamper with a jug of iced tea and some grapes. Not a bad dinner for the spur of the moment, she decided as she walked the few short blocks to City Hall.

But when she arrived at the side door, it was locked. Jeff's Jeep was in the parking lot, but the black-and-white official car was missing. The main doors were locked, too, of course. It was full dark now, and she stood in the yellow glow of the streetlights searching deserted Main Street for any sign of Jeff. Either Stanfield hadn't given him the message, or he thought he'd be back before she showed up, or an emergency had called him away.

Feeling a bit miffed in spite of her reasoning, Rachel finally set the picnic hamper on the ground in front of the side door. They needed it more than she did, she figured, and told her growling stomach that there were plenty of salad fixings in the fridge. As she walked back along Main to the corner, the absolute emptiness of the downtown oppressed her. It might as well have been midnight, instead of eight forty-five. Glancing at her watch, she turned up Cedar, leaving the shops and stores behind. Ahead, houses with big yards fronted the street, their yards shored up with walls of rock or concrete. The streetlights ended, and it seemed very dark. Rachel found herself listening intently. Footsteps? A rustle of shrubbery. She laughed at herself, but it felt a little like whistling in the dark, and she wished fervently that she'd had the brains to bring her flashlight.

Somewhere, the vandal prowled.

He didn't attack people, Rachel reminded herself.

Not yet, anyway.

Up ahead, a slight figure turned onto Cedar from Second. The faint glow from a porch light revealed dark curly hair and a swinging stride. A woman, anyway, carrying a cloth shopping bag. The sight of her made Rachel feel better.

Without warning, a dark figure hurtled out of the darkness behind her. The black-clad stranger crashed into the woman, knocking her stumbling forward, grabbing at her bag as she lost her balance. The woman shrieked hoarsely, and began pounding at her attacker with her fists. With a gasp, Rachel halted, looking wildly around. "Help!" She screamed it as loudly as she could, fumbling her cell phone from her pocket, blessing herself for carrying it tonight. "I'm calling the police!" she yelled. "Somebody help us!" Touching the autodial, she clutched the phone, ready to run if the dark figure turned her way. He started to, but the woman had recovered herself, and was now pounding at his face and shoulders with one fist.

The man shoved her away, staggering backward. Someone answered her cell. Rachel babbled details into the phone, breathless. "He's running away," she cried as the mugger tried to wrench himself away from the woman. Shrieking like a banshee, his victim clutched him with one hand, while she clawed at the ski mask that covered his face with the other.

With an audible grunt, he flung her to the sidewalk and fled down the street into the darkness.

Blue-and-red light pulsed and headlights flooded her as Rachel ran up the street to where the woman was picking herself up from the sidewalk. The car screeched to a halt as Rachel reached her. "He went that way!" Rachel pointed wildly after the vanished attacker.

"You all right?" Lyle's crisp voice cut the air. As both women nodded, he was already backing the car around, to go roaring down the street in pursuit of the fugitive.

"Are you hurt?" Rachel took the woman by the arm, her eyes still dazzled by the headlights. "Celia!" she gasped. "Are you really all right?"

"I skinned my knee," the older woman said breathlessly. "If I'd have hung on another minute, I'd have given the SOB the black eye of his life. Guess I'm getting old. What the heck did he think he was up to."

Footsteps pounded up the block and a flashlight beam stabbed at them. In spite of the light, Rachel's stomach contracted. But it was Jeff who emerged from the darkness. "Rachel! Celia! Are you all right?"

"I am. I don't know about him." Celia tossed her head.

"Tell me," Jeff said urgently. "Lyle's on him. Bert was down below, so we'll get him. Do you want to sit down? Are you really all right?"

"He was wearing a ski mask. And dressed in black."

"You're sure he was a man."

"Oh, yeah." Celia gave him a look. "That I'm sure of. I guess he wanted my bag." She laughed. "Joke's on him." She looked around, then bent to retrieve it from the street, where it had landed next to the curb. "It's full of leftovers from the bakery. I carry my money in this." And she patted a small belt pack cinched tightly around her waist.

She couldn't remember anything more specific than that. Rachel volunteered the snapshot memory of a slender rather than bulky shape, who was maybe a little taller than Celia, but not much. Not a lot of help, she thought morosely. Not unless they caught the man tonight.

It wasn't a group of roving teens, anyway. Jeff had been right from the first.

"I'll take you home," Jeff was saying to Celia. "You, too, Rachel."

"I'm just going up the street a block." Celia nodded up the slope. "My boyfriend lives there. He borrowed my car today, because his is in for brake work."

"I'll walk you there." Jeff took her bag of bread and rolls. "Get him to pick you up tomorrow night, if he's still got your car." Jeff's tone was grim as the three of them walked up the block. "Unless we catch this guy tonight. You sure you're all right?" He took her elbow. "You're limping."

"Just my knee." Celia's laugh was a bit pained. "Just a scrape. I'd rather have Willy take care of it than a doctor, thank you very much. All it needs is iodine."

"Use some ice on it, too." Jeff walked with Celia up the concrete walk of a small frame house surrounded by dense shrubbery. A light was on inside. Celia unlocked the front door, called out to whoever was inside, and waved to Rachel. The warm summer night brought her the scents of leaves and dust and a whiff of flowers as Jeff rejoined her.

"I'll drive you over to your house. I need to head back downtown."

"They didn't catch him." Rachel walked beside him, keeping up with his fast pace. "Right?"

"They would have called me." He didn't say anything else as they reached the car, just helped her into the front seat, then drove her the long block and a half over to Mrs. Frey's tall house.

"Good thing she knows I'm engaged to a police officer," Rachel said lightly as he pulled up in the parking area. "She'd be scandalized."

"Rachel?" Jeff hesitated, his expression serious in the yellow glow of the floodlight mounted on the side of the house. "Celia has short dark hair, and she's built like you."

"She's taller." A tiny finger of apprehension brushed the back of Rachel's neck.

"And she was walking down Second. The way you might walk if you were heading downtown."

"Jeff, what are you saying?"

"It's not exactly a secret that we're engaged," he said gently. He turned to face her, touching her cheek with one fingertip. "This is beginning to feel like a personal contest," he said. "I don't know why. But it's something more than just a kid tipping over garbage cans and spray-painting dirty words on the walls. I don't want you to become a target." He leaned forward and kissed her on the mouth. "Be careful," he said softly. "For me, please? Don't go out by yourself after dark."

He was really asking her, and that chilled her. "I . . . I promise," she said and shivered in spite of herself.

He pulled her against him, hugging her fiercely for a moment. "This is something that I've thought about," he said slowly. "It's the one thing that made me . . . hesitate. That you might be in danger because somebody wants to get at me."

"Hey, it's part of the job description." Rachel made her voice light for him, suppressing another shiver. Because she hadn't thought of that at all. Not really. "He could just have been there, and so was Celia . . ."

"Maybe." Jeff opened the door, and came around to her side of the car. "Come on. I'll walk you up to the door."

Rachel found she was glad of his company on the stairs. Shadows filled the yard beneath and seemed to prowl like huge black cats. Peter met them on the landing, darting through the opening door and into the yawning darkness beyond. Rachel fumbled for the light switch, breathing a sigh of relief as the familiar shapes of sofa and bookshelves sprang to life. Peter sat on the sofa back, washing his face.

Even so, Jeff prowled restlessly through the apartment before kissing her once more at the door. "I'll stop here later if I can," he murmured, his arms tight around her. "Be safe, okay?"

"I will." She let him go and watched from the landing as he bounded down the steps and into his car. When the taillights had dwindled, she went inside and locked the door behind her.

For the first time in her life, she felt afraid in Blossom.

CHAPTER

7

Rachel was wakened by a combination of bright morning sun streaming through her bedroom window and the sound of voices raised beneath it. Sleepily she rolled out of bed and padded barefoot to the window. The summer sun that flooded the garden banished the last dark echoes of night. She peered through the screen.

Mrs. Frey stood in the middle of her neat rose beds, gloved fists on her hips, a loam-crusted trowel jutting up from one hand. Spider faced her, his chin up, his expression as stubborn as only a teenager's can be. Rachel sighed, and reached for a shirt and pair of jeans. Shower later. As she threw on her clothes, she realized that Jeff hadn't come by last night. At least, if he had, he hadn't wakened her and had left no sign of his visit.

It was early. Giving the clock a glower, wishing for another half-hour of peaceful sleep, she marched out the front door, nearly tripping over the outraged Peter. "In a minute, cat." Stomping down the stairs, she rounded the corner of the house and strode into the garden. "So what are you two arguing about at this hour?"

"We're not arguing," Mrs. Frey said loftily. "I was informing your young employee that this is a private garden and he is not welcome to simply march in here and trample my roses."

Sure enough, Spider had a perfect yellow rosebud in his hand, its half-furled petals spangled with dew. He waved it at Rachel's landlady.

"You're just ticked because I'm right about the pruning. What is it? Adults can't ever let themselves admit some kid might be right and they might be wrong, huh?"

"I'm perfectly willing to admit that I'm wrong when I am wrong." She waved the trowel at him, scattering crumbs of dark loam. "I was raising prize roses before you were born."

"Who gave 'em a prize?"

"I don't have time for this." Mrs. Frey turned her back on Spider. "I do hope you will speak to *all* your employees about trespassing." Her tone was frosty. "Personally, I don't see why you need a new employee. What happened to that nice Mexican young man who worked for you?"

"He has his own business now, Mrs. Frey." Rachel swallowed a sigh. "Spider won't bother your roses again."

"I certainly hope not," the older woman said distantly. "If you'll excuse me." She set her trowel neatly on a shelf beside the back door and vanished inside.

Rachel winced as the door slammed behind her. "Thanks, Spider." She glared at him. "Get me kicked out of my apartment, why don't you?"

Spider rolled his eyes. "What a crazy. You'd think I'd cut off one of her hands when she saw me with this." He regarded the rose in his hand. "What a nutcase. Why don't you move out?"

"Because the rent is cheap and I like the apartment."
Rachel stifled a yawn. "What are you doing here at this
hour?"

"It's not that early." Spider shrugged. "Julio had a job.
He dropped me off." He looked at her curiously. "You
look like you had a long night."

"Thank you very much." Swallowing another yawn,
Rachel started back around the side of the building.
"Come on up and make some coffee, will you? I need
to get a shower and we need to get going." It wasn't really that early. Spider was right. She didn't need to have
the director waiting for her and checking her watch this
morning.

As she showered and toweled in a rush, she wondered
what had happened to Jeff. Maybe they had caught the
man who had attacked Celia last night. Maybe he had
gone on home, thinking it was too late to stop in. As she
emerged from the bathroom toweling her still-damp hair,
the smell of fresh coffee and toast greeted her. Spider
perched on the corner of the counter, steaming mug in
hand, watching Peter devour a can of cat food.

"He really wasn't starving, you know." Rachel draped
the towel over the back of a chair and grabbed her travel
mug from the shelf. "Don't let him kid you."

"I think he was gonna bite me if I didn't feed him."
Spider grinned and hopped down from the counter. "I
toasted those English muffins that were on top of the
fridge." He nodded at the scatter of crumbs around the
toaster. "And I put some peanut butter on 'em. Since
we're late."

"Hey, I had a wild night." Rachel took the paper bag
he handed her. It was still warm and the scent of toasted
bread and warm peanut butter made her stomach growl.
"So bring your coffee and let's get moving. Since you're
in such a rush to dig."

"Yes, ma'am, Ms. Boss Lady, sir."

"Ha ha." Rachel let Peter out and followed Spider as he clattered down the stairs. She would have liked to drop by City Hall to find out what had happened, but Spider was right. It really was time to get moving. Considering the precarious state of affairs at the Village, showing up late wasn't going to improve the situation.

"Julio thinks a friend of his might rent me a room." Spider scrambled into the truck. "Here." He dug into the bag and handed her one of the warm muffin sandwiches.

"Good." Rachel bit into her breakfast as she started the truck and backed down the driveway. As she drove down toward Main, she glanced left down Second, to where the black-clad man had attacked Celia. What if Jeff was right, and he had been waiting for her? Had he followed her down to City Hall when she had tried to deliver dinner to Jeff? Rachel shivered.

"You really do look like it was a rough night." Spider was eyeing her. "What happened?"

She told him about the streak of vandalism and the events of last night. She didn't mention Jeff's theory.

Spider grunted. "How come nobody has seen this guy?" He rolled an eye at her. "I'll tell you, this town squeezes me. I walk down the street, and people stick their heads out the door to stare at me. What? They never seen a kid before? I feel like I oughta be carrying a passport."

There was a sticky grain of truth in what Spider was saying. Strangers got noticed. Which meant that their vandal wasn't a stranger?

"I bet Price is shitting," Spider said cheerfully. "He doesn't like to mess up, does he?"

Ouch. "Let's see if we can get the rest of the pipe in today." Time to change the subject. "Maybe we'll luck out and the system won't leak when we test."

"Hey, luck isn't part of it." Spider struck a pose. "All those joins are solid. Bet you five dollars. Not one drop leaks out."

"You're on." Rachel laughed. "If we get through with the plumbing that easily, it'll be worth five dollars."

It was going to be another scorching day. A solid high-pressure system had built up and dry wind was sweeping westward down the huge wind tunnel of the Gorge, bringing heat with it from Eastern Oregon and Idaho. None of the Village residents were outside, not even down in the thin shade of the young willows by the pond. A single mallard circled sullenly on the murky water, waiting for somebody to come feed it bread.

At first, things seemed to be going well. For once. Sweating, stopping often for water breaks, she and Spider worked to lay out the maze of lines that would water the shrubs and beds of the finished landscape. The rocks for the rock garden were to be delivered later in the week, and they could get those lines in. The necessary detours imposed by the basalt ridges had nearly doubled the amount of main line they had to lay, but by noon they had made good progress finishing this stage of the water system. Rachel consulted her plans, flagging the branch lines for the secondary drip lines that would be installed after the plants were in place. She had talked the director into going with drip irrigation with the promise of a much-reduced water bill. With the federal restrictions on river use because of the endangered salmon runs, water was suddenly on everyone's mind. The dry summer brought the point home, too. There would be very little grass in the final landscape. Green would be provided by drought-tolerant ground covers and perennial plantings. Paths and spaces between beds would be carpeted in rock or bark chips or gravel.

But that kind of watering system required a lot of drippers, and the detours required by the intrusive basalt had only complicated matters. Rachel thought of her deadline and winced. They hadn't even started planting yet. There was the rock garden. And the pond. Never mind the paths and the benches, and the final finishing touches. Too bad she couldn't just go out and hire about six workers.

"I think it's time for lunch." Spider stood up suddenly and stretched, wiping his face on his shirt, which he had removed long ago and tied around his waist. "I brought lunch today. Julio's sister made it for me. Okay? Mind if I go eat it? Can we test the line after?"

Rachel followed his gaze as he rattled this off, and found the source for the sudden urgency in his manner. Harris was on his way down from the buildings, wheeling his chair along the single concrete path that curved down to the pond below them. "Spider, get over it." She shook her head. "Age isn't contagious."

"Don't know what you mean. I'm taking my lunch break now. Union rules." He slung his damp shirt over his shoulder and headed briskly up to the parking lot, picking a trajectory that took him well clear of Harris.

"Is he scared of me personally, or old folks in general?" Harris nodded after the retreating Spider as Rachel approached.

"Old folks in general." She pulled her red bandanna from her jeans and wiped her face and neck, envying men and hating clothing taboos. "Did Jeff come see Madame yet?" She had watched for him, but he could have parked in the service lot behind the building.

"He's on his way. He's bringing pizza—just stopping by to visit old friends. Nothing official. I'd . . . like you to join us." Harris's tone was unexpectedly serious. "I want your perspective on what we've found out here."

"Sure." She walked with him as he wheeled back up the path to the parking lot. "Want a push?"

"No thanks." He wasn't even breathing hard, although his face and muscular arms gleamed with sweat. "I haven't had my run yet. I need some kind of exercise." He nodded as Jeff's Jeep passed them. "Lunch has arrived."

They reached the Jeep as Jeff was retrieving two white pizza boxes from it. "Hey, Price, haven't seen you for a while. Madame told me you might drop by one of these days."

"I knew Rachel would be out here, so I brought lunch. Have you and Madame eaten yet?"

This was an interesting little charade. Rachel smiled and joined in the bit of theatrics, wondering whom it was meant to impress. A couple of aids were taking a cigarette break by one of the side doors. Rachel recognized Jason, but not the older, dark-haired man with him. She went into the building with Jeff and Harris, wanting to sigh with pleasure at the cool touch of the air-conditioning.

"I'll call Madame," Harris said, and stepped to one of the house phones.

"How did last night go?" Rachel asked, not really needing his head shake to guess the answer. Jeff looked as if he hadn't slept. He had shaved, but his face looked gaunt and exhausted.

"Sorry I didn't make it by last night." He set the pizza boxes down on a corner of the information desk that gave the entry the air of a hotel lobby. "We scoured that damn town. I swear that guy has radar. Or maybe he can teleport."

"I figured you were out all night." She touched the back of his hand lightly. "Don't kill yourself?" It came out as a question, and he answered it with a small shake of his head.

Not an appropriate topic. "I'll catch a couple of hours this afternoon." He smiled for her, then turned to greet Madame, who had just swept into the lobby.

"Ah, Jeffrey." Her accent had thickened so that his name contained three syllables. "How marvelous to see you again." Madame stood on tiptoe, offering him her cheek. "What a surprise, this visit? Are you here to speak with our director?" she asked gaily.

They were entering the lobby now, and Rachel noticed at least four or five residents who were close enough to overhear this exchange.

"I just dropped by to see you and Harris." Jeff gave her a wide smile. "And I brought pizza. In case you're tired of dining room lunches?"

"I am always delighted to eat pizza." Madame twinkled up at him. "I am sure that we may find one of the card rooms empty. I will tell the kitchen that we will need some iced tea." She swept off with a flutter of her long, pale fingers.

They settled in one of the small rooms that had been furnished for card players with small square tables and a closet full of chess sets and other table games. Madame reappeared, followed by the aid Jason, who carried a laden tray. "You are so helpful," she murmured as he set out plates, glasses, and napkins on one of the tables.

"No problem," he told Madame, and gave Rachel a bright smile. "How's the job going? On days like today, I really can't wait for that shade!"

"We're making progress." Rachel returned his smile. "If the pressure test works this afternoon, I can get started on the rock garden. Harvey's going to dump the rock tomorrow. I'll get to rent a Bobcat to place them." She loved any excuse to use the quick and responsive little front-loader.

"It's so cool to watch this all coming together. I never really gave much thought to how those pretty yards got that way." He offered Jeff his hand. "Hi. I think I've met you before, but I can't remember when. Sorry."

His eyes widened ever so slightly as Madame made the introductions.

"Wow." He gave Jeff a crooked grin. "I hope this isn't an official visit."

"It isn't," Jeff said easily. "It's just lunch with friends. If I'm official, I'll wear my uniform."

"He is a nice young man." Madame looked thoughtfully at the door as the departing Jason closed it behind him. "I believe he knows much more than he appears to. He is not the one to speak gossip, so he is very quiet. But he watches. I see him watch."

Rachel thought of his conversation with her in the parking lot.

"So let us eat your pizza." Madame seated herself gracefully in the chair Harris pulled out for her. "We can chat while we eat, since I am sure you have many things to do this day," she said to Jeff.

They sat down, and Madame presided, praising Jeff's choice of toppings, and graciously distributing the thick slices of fragrant dough and sauce. The pizza came from Pizza House, a little storefront parlor with imaginative seasonal specialties that had successfully fended off the brief challenge of not one but two national chains. This time of year, the crisp dough was topped with a fresh tomato sauce, garlic, lightly sautéed summer squash, and mild spring onions, which had been scattered with Romano, Parmesan, and mozzarella cheese, along with a few kalamata olives.

For a space of time, nobody said much. Jeff finished a single slice and sat back with his glass of iced tea. Harris wiped his fingers on his napkin and set his uneaten crust neatly on it. "Thanks for coming out without much explanation." He glanced from Madame to Jeff. "Something has come up. We think you need to know about it. Since the Village is inside the city limits. Thanks to our mayor's annexation fest a couple of years ago."

Jeff nodded, waiting patiently as Harris and Madame exchanged another long glance.

"What *mon ami* is so politely not saying is that I have conducted myself in a manner which is, perhaps, less than the most law abiding." Madame made an airy, dismissive gesture. "But when one leaves one's office door open, and

the computer on, obviously one is not concerned about
the privacy of the files displayed on that screen." She
shrugged. "How can you protest if someone perhaps wanders into your office and happens to overlook them? Is
that so terrible? To look at something in plain sight?"

Harris cleared his throat and looked ceilingward.

"Well, if she did not wish someone to look at those
files, surely she would not have left them upon her
screen." Madame drew herself erect, her expression
mildly outraged. "I would never turn on a computer and
try to find a file. Besides, she certainly uses a password,
oui?"

"Madame, you never cease to amaze me," Harris murmured.

"My dear granddaughter keeps all her records on her
computer. One invoice looks very like another. It only
takes a moment to find a name and look for a particular
month. That is the beauty of it, although I warn her that
when her hard drive fails, she will regret all this convenience." Madame waggled a finger at Harris, then turned
a sweet smile on Jeff. "As you can see, he does not approve. But I did what I did."

"And just what did you do?" Jeff asked patiently.

"I simply looked up 'Barnhart, Emily,' and looked at
the last monthly statement we received for fees and services. On the day that she took ill, Emily Barnhart complained that she had been charged for services that she
had not utilized. She named these services, and informed
everyone within hearing that the director had apologized
and removed the offending charges. She also suggested
that this had happened before, although . . ." Madame
made that dismissive gesture again. "Her memory was not
the most . . . how shall we say . . . was not of the most
clear."

"She had been diagnosed with the early stages of Alzheimer's," Harris put in dryly.

"Perhaps." Madame gave him an arch look. "Her memory of that charge and its ensuing removal seemed to be quite clear. But my dear, when I looked up her name, I found on those statements the very same charges that were to have been removed."

Jeff's expression was thoughtful, but he said nothing.

"Then there are the printed statements, of course." Madame waved a triumphant finger at him. "Poor Emily has died. There seems to be no crime, so her room is locked, but no policeman sits there to watch over her possessions. The director has a key. Of course the printed statements will be there, and they will be the same as the files on the computer. Emily was very tidy and orderly. I have no doubt that those invoices were easy to find." Madame clucked her tongue. "She cannot protest those charges now. Who will ask about them? None of us listened carefully to Emily's complaints. She had many complaints. *Voilà.*" She shrugged. "The extra money will be collected from the estate, and who will question it? It is not an outrageous sum."

"Who, indeed." Jeff still wasn't giving anything away. "So you are suggesting that Director Bellingham is embezzling from some of the patients?"

"So many here are confused about many things." Madame's tone was thoughtful, but there was a grim light in her eyes. "It would be not difficult to add a few dollars here and there, yes? But no, that is not what I am saying. Not entirely."

Harris looked away.

"I am saying that Madame Barnhart was murdered. By our director."

Without warning, Harris flung his chair at the door. One wheel slammed into the plasterboard wall with a sharp thud as he grabbed the door handle. Jeff and Rachel bolted to their feet as Harris flung the door open. He lost his grip on it and it banged against the closet door, rebounding into his chair as he wrenched through the doorway.

Jeff reached his side as he halted in the middle of the pastel-walled corridor.

"Damn," Harris said in a matter-of-fact tone. "Whoever it was, they're quick."

"Someone was listening?" Jeff murmured.

Harris nodded, and spun his chair neatly around. "For a while now, I think."

They all returned to their places. Only Madame hadn't moved. Nobody said anything while Jeff closed the door and returned to the table.

"Murdered?" Rachel finally uttered the word. "What do you mean?"

"Poisoned, most probably." Madame shrugged again. "I am sure that the scientists will tell us. She was not ready to die. Yes, she was murdered."

"Madame DeRochers." Jeff's voice was very quiet. "Do you have any other reason to believe that Ms. Barnhart was poisoned?"

For a moment, Madame looked surprised. "No," she said decisively. "Of course not. That is your job, no?" But her eyes had narrowed as she regarded Jeff.

Harris, too, was watching Jeff closely.

"I hope you haven't said anything to anyone about this." Jeff stood, looking from one to the other. "If there are a hundred rumors floating around here, it's going to be impossible to sort any kind of truth from the guesses."

A gleam of triumph flashed in Madame's eyes. "If I wish to start a rumor, I do so," she said severely. "If I do not, I do not chatter idly. But perhaps, the horse has already been stolen from the barn. It will depend on who that was who listened at the door, *non?* Rachel, perhaps you would like to bring the remainder of our pizza to your young assistant?" She smiled a hostess's gracious smile, as if the talk of murder and embezzling had never happened. The luncheon was clearly at an end.

As Madame disposed of the paper plates and plastic glasses, Rachel piled the leftover slices into one of the boxes, anxious to leave. Madame, at last, seemed to be giving in to senility. The prospect horrified her. She wondered if that lunge at the door by Harris had been real, or if he was merely humoring Madame. Perhaps he couldn't face the prospect of Madame's intelligence failing, either. Mind spinning, Rachel sneaked a glance at Jeff and Harris, who were engaged in a quiet conversation in front of the window.

"Harris does not believe me." Madame regarded the two men with amusement. "It strains his belief that I can know when one is ready to die. It frightens him, I think. Although I tell him he is not ready yet."

"It would scare me, too." She *was* scared. Rachel watched as Harris shrugged sharply and wheeled back to the table to rejoin them.

The foursome broke up awkwardly. Jeff reminded Madame to be very careful about mentioning her suspicions to anyone, which earned him a frosty stare. "Can I carry this down to your truck for you?" he asked, Rachel, hefting the box.

"Thanks," she said, wanting a few minutes more with him. "Thanks for the lunch," she said to Harris and Madame—who reminded her that Jeff had brought the lunch.

She fled, with Jeff at her side. *Fled* was the only word for it. They crossed the lobby and left the cool for the furnace blast of the noon sun, without exchanging a single word. It wasn't until they had left the paved paths and were crossing the dry, hacked slope of the grounds that Rachel finally let the words erupt from her.

"I can't believe it. Madame! I mean, I know she's been upset with the director, but I never thought she'd . . . start losing it." The last words came out as a hushed whisper, too heavy to speak aloud.

"Rachel." Jeff halted beside her parked truck and set the pizza box down on the hood. "I want you to be very careful here." He took both her hands, his eyes on her face. "I know you can't just walk off the job, but . . . be careful."

"What are you saying?" Her mouth felt dry, and she heard once again the whispered warning that had rasped from her phone.

"Emily Barhart *was* poisoned. Possibly others." His fingers tightened briefly in hers. "You know, and Harris. Nobody else. We *are* talking murder here."

She swallowed, at a loss for words. "So there really was someone in the hall?" she whispered. "It's all true?"

"We've got no solid suspect yet." Worry narrowed Jeff's eyes. "I mean it about being careful, okay?" Reluctantly, he let go of her hands. "And . . . tell me anything you notice."

"I will," she said, still breathless. "I will."

The eavesdropper had been real. The voice on the phone had been speaking truth. Rachel shivered as Jeff retraced his steps to the parking lot. Suddenly, the summertime noon wasn't hot at all.

CHAPTER

8

Rachel walked back to the job site as Jeff's Jeep vanished in the direction of Blossom. Suddenly she seemed to feel someone watching her. Blinds shuttered the Village windows against the sun, giving them the look of half-closed, watchful eyes. She shivered again, and looked around for Spider.

He was down at the bottom of the slope, holding an armful of PVC pipe, chatting with one of the aids. Rachel recognized Ricki, the aide who had served them in the dining room yesterday. As Rachel watched, Ricki tossed her head and laughed at something Spider said. Even from this distance, Spider's grin was visible. Giving him a wave, Ricki turned away and hurried up one of the main paths that led to the buildings. Slowly, Spider walked up the slope.

His eyes were sparkling as he reached her. "I was talking to Ricki Gerren, one of the aids," he told her. "She lives with her great-uncle, who used to be a gardener. She asked me if I'd drop by and meet him. I guess he needs some help with things—he's eighty or something like that. And he won't ask for help, but Ricki figures if I just dropped by to visit her, I could pitch in and the old man wouldn't figure he was asking me." His mouth wanted to grin but he wouldn't let it. "I told her I could probably do it." The studied casualness of his tone made Rachel roll her eyes.

"I thought old people made you break out in hives," she said.

He looked genuinely puzzled for a moment, then shrugged. "It's okay," he said. "He's a gardener. Maybe I can learn something from him. Ricki told me he's into mushrooms, too. He used to make a lot of money hunting wild mushrooms up in the forest and selling them to fancy restaurants, back before everybody started doing it. She says you can make thousands of dollars. Just for stuff you find in the woods." Spider looked impressed. "He sounds cool to me."

"Well, good for you for helping," Rachel said dryly. She was willing to bet that it wasn't just the prospect of learning to identify mushrooms that brightened Spider's eyes. "So what have we got left to do? I'm sorry I took so long."

"Hey, you're the boss lady." He gave her a sly grin, then shrugged. "Let's test that line. I want that five bucks you're going to owe me."

"Okay, let's do it." She was relieved that he didn't ask her about the luncheon. Ricki's distraction had been timely.

"We were talking about college," Spider went on as they walked up to the head of the irrigation system, at the top of the slope. "She's going to go, too, but she figured she needed to make some money for a couple of years first. So she wouldn't have so many student loans. She's pretty cool," he said casually.

"Yeah, she is." Rachel kept her smile to herself. "Ready? I sure hope I owe you five bucks. One, two, three, go!"

Spider opened the valve. Narrow fountains of water leaped into the air, dozens of them, as if they had turned on a giant, branching soaker hose. Rachel leaped backward as cold spray hit her in the face. Farther down the slope, the spraying gushers lost height and force as the pressure fell.

"What the . . . !" Spider grabbed for the tap, twisting the valve closed.

Numbly, Rachel stared down at the leaks as they diminished into weak arches and then sank away to nothing, leaving behind only puddles and mud.

"Goddamnit!" Spider yelled as he charged to the nearest of the fading fountains.

For once, Rachel heartily agreed with him.

Slowly, heavily, she followed him. He crouched over a length of pipe a dozen yards from the valve. Wiping her wet face on the hem of her shirt, she looked over his shoulder. Slowly, very carefully, he touched the small holes that had been drilled into the pipe. It looked like somebody had used a battery-operated drill with a 1/8-inch bit. "Who did this?" His voice trembled with anger. "Who the hell would *do* something like this?"

"Watch your language," Rachel said wearily. "And I don't have a clue." The vandal? The ghost who threw paint and cracked expensive windows in town? She found herself shaking her head. Who would think of holing irrigation pipe?

An orchard kid. Heck, she thought, anyone who lived around here would know how much damage a ruined irrigation line could cause.

Well, Jeff had guessed that the vandal was local.

"When I find out who did this, they're gonna need a doctor." Spider stood with his feet a little apart, both fists clenched. "Somebody took a battery drill and did this so no one could hear them."

"I just might help you. It must have happened late last night, after we left." Spider was right—those little drills didn't make much noise. Neither of them had had any reason to look closely at the parts of the system that they'd already finished yesterday as they worked on the final segments today. She turned away from the ruined line, finding the slope nearly too steep to ascend. All that work. All that pipe. She winced, wondering if the vandal had damaged the expensive fittings, too.

"Who would do this? Look here. They smashed some of the valves, too." Spider's outraged voice rose as he followed the muddy traces of vandalism. "Why? Why mess up a bunch of pipe? Who hates you, Rachel?"

Good question. Rachel opened her eyes to find a tall, upright figure marching down the main path toward them. The director. Nice timing. Rachel drew a deep breath.

"I left a message on your machine that I wanted to speak to you this morning." Director Bellington's shoulders and ruler-straight posture conveyed her displeasure even without her frosty tone. "Did you get it?"

"No, I didn't." Rachel's shoulders wanted to slump. "I must have left already."

The director obviously doubted this. "You haven't even started on the rock garden. It was supposed to be finished by now. And what about the pond? I don't see any progress there at all." She looked around at the muddy slope. "The irrigation system is finished?"

"Oh, it's finished all right." Rachel drew a deep breath. "Somebody vandalized it last night. They used a drill of some sort to drill holes all along the lines. And they damaged some of the valves. Everything is going to have to be replaced."

"Why would anybody do that?" The director stared at her with chilly disbelief.

"Good question, lady." Spider came up beside Rachel, bristling. "We'd sure like to know that, too."

"Spider, that's enough," Rachel said with quiet intensity.

"This project is in full view of the building," Bellington went on as if Spider hadn't spoken. "I find it hard to believe that a stranger here wouldn't have been noticed."

"Meaning what? That Rachel did it herself?" Spider glared at the director.

"Start pulling out the pipe." Rachel turned to her assistant. "Save anything we can use. Get going," she snapped as Spider hesitated.

"I wouldn't tolerate that kind of behavior in an employee." The director looked briefly after the sullenly departing Spider. "I take it that you intend to bill the Village for the replacement parts?"

"No." Rachel met her stare. "I don't. I'll bill my insurance company for the damage." Although she wasn't entirely sure how much they would cover.

"You'll still meet your deadline." The director's stare didn't waver. "If the magazine has to postpone their article on the Village, they won't do another one," she said coldly. "Editors aren't happy when you ruin their schedules. So I've been informed. And muddy wastelands don't look good on the covers of magazines."

"I . . ." Rachel hesitated. She wanted to say that they would have everything perfect in time for the photo session, but would they? You could cover a lot with extra bark dust and close planting, but that would take a lot of money that wasn't budgeted in the contract. She'd have to sit down with the numbers, but Rachel had a feeling that the alterations to the system required by the sneaky basalt veins had already taken her over into the red on this job as it was. She simply didn't have the reserves to go farther into the loss column just to get this job finished on time. "I don't think it will be as finished as you wanted by the date of the photo session," she said slowly. "It will still look good, but some things won't be completed." She took a deep breath. "I'd better call the police and report this mess."

"I'll do it. You may keep on working." The director turned on her heel and marched back up the slope to the main entrance, the flat heels of her shoes clacking with an angry rhythm on the concrete walk.

Rachel felt as if she was about to burst into tears.

"Boss lady, she sure is some . . . Okay, I won't say it." Spider came up beside her, glowering after the departing director. "Maybe you know which car is hers, out in the lot?"

"No way." Rachel laughed wearily as she trudged back to her truck. "She'd guess in a minute."

"So?" Spider shrugged. "You want her to guess. You just don't want her to have any proof of anything."

"Knock it off." She said it more sharply than she'd meant to. "Let's get this damn pipe torn out and call it a day."

"Better watch your language out here," Spider said with a perfect expression of innocent concern. "Some of these old folk, they don't like those kind of words."

Rachel made as if to throw a spade at him. He ducked in feigned terror and she laughed. It helped—a little.

They spent the afternoon tearing out the pipe and salvaging what they could. The vandal hadn't done nearly as much damage to the expensive fittings as it had first appeared, to her vast relief. But it was still going to cost her time and money to replace everything. You had to glue a lot of pipe in order to cover that large an area. It was late in the day by the time they tossed the last piece of ruined pipe onto the pile beside her truck. She'd haul it away tomorrow, Rachel decided wearily. Stripping off her gloves, she filled her mug from the water jug in her truck bed and drank thirstily. Right now she was too tired and discouraged to deal with anything.

"Hey?"

She looked up to find the aid Jason surveying the ruins with his fists on his hips. "What happened here? Ricki said you had all the pipe laid, after lunch."

"Somebody wrecked it." Spider kicked the pile. "Any of that water left?" He began to fill the plastic cup he was using.

"You're kidding." Jason frowned at Rachel. "What did they do?"

"Drilled holes in the line." Rachel tossed her gloves into the truck box. "Last night. You weren't here last night, were you? I should find out who was, and ask them if anyone saw anything."

"Yeah," Jason said slowly. "Actually, I was here. Real late." He looked at the pile, his lips tight. "I came by to pick up a friend of mine who gets off at midnight. He needed a ride." He paused again, then gave Rachel a sideways look. "Maybe you should ask our director how come she was here at midnight last night."

"What?"

"Well . . . it probably wasn't her." Jason scuffed the drying mud with one foot, his shoulders hunched. "I saw someone as I was sitting out front waiting. They walked around the end of the building, and the outside door to her office is that way, and I didn't think anything about it. But when we were driving out, I sort of noticed that I didn't see her car and I wondered how she got up here, that's all." The words came out in a rush, and he looked at her unhappily. "Only, I couldn't swear that it was her, and if you say anything, she'll fire me. She'll find a reason."

The director? Or the vandal? The Village was a long way from Blossom, where the vandal had been working. Why?

A couple of reasons occurred to Rachel and they didn't make her happy. "Thanks, Jason," she said slowly. "Too bad you didn't get a better look at her, but if it was her, she was probably here for some good reason or other."

"Yeah." Jason nodded. "She probably got a cab from Hood River, or got a ride. Or something."

Maybe. They both looked away from each other, and Jason cleared his throat. "I'm really sorry about it," he said, jerking his head at the maze of now-empty trenches. "Hey, if I'm here at night again, I'll sure keep an eye on the place. It's so ugly here." He looked around. "It kind of depresses me sometimes. There's no place to dream here, you know?" His hazel eyes fixed on her face. "The people who live here need dreams," he said softly.

"I agree."

"I'd go nuts if I had to live here." He was staring across the slope now, his gaze fixed on the scummy pond. "There's no place for magic in a place like this, no place to escape."

Rachel understood. She had found a lot of private worlds in the trees of the orchard and the hillsides around them. They had been her escape from the orchard, her uncle's temper, and later, her mother's darkness. "Everyone needs their own private universe," she said.

"Yeah. That's it." He turned back to face her, his face alight. "I kind of thought you'd understand—when I saw the drawings you'd made of the garden. That's what you do, isn't it? You create magic places for people. So that they can dream, they walk into them and escape all the ugliness of the real world."

He sounded so *young*. "Yeah, I guess you could describe it that way." Rachel smiled. "I must admit that I did have my own private place when I was a kid. It was a doorway. I pretended it led to a different world." A door frame had stood in a neighbor's pasture, tilting crookedly among spring daffodils and summer daisies. The placid

Herefords grazed around it, ignoring it. Rachel had never seen one pass through it. "I used to pretend that I could walk through that doorway and into a magic world," she said, laughing. "I know it was probably the door to an old shed once, or maybe a house that got torn down. But back then, it really was a gateway."

"It still is," Jason said urgently. "Don't let your adult mind talk you out of it. That's why you're so good, don't you see? Because a part of you still believes you can step through that doorway and escape. That's why your gardens work."

"I . . . never thought of it quite like that," Rachel admitted, intrigued by Jason's intensity. "So did you have a magic doorway, too?"

"It was this well." He looked beyond her, no longer seeing the barren slope around them. "It was way back behind our house all covered in weeds. Nobody knew about it but me. It went way down, and you could hear water running. There's a river at the bottom. If you jump in, it will take you somewhere else. To the world you really belong in." He looked up suddenly, light and shadow moving in his hazel eyes. "You never went through your door," he said, and it wasn't a question.

"No." Rachel shook her head. "I didn't." Because she couldn't have come back. That was one of the rules. But she had stood in front of it one rainy, moonless night about a week after her father had died. And she had almost stepped through it then.

Jason nodded, his eyes dark with sympathy now, as if she'd spoken out loud. "Don't let her run you off," he said. "We need you. We need the magic places. This is too real. There's nowhere to escape."

"I won't let her."

"Good." Jason grinned at her, his eyes gilded with afternoon light. "I'm glad. And don't worry. I'll keep an eye on things." With a jaunty wave, he headed back up the path.

"Wow." Spider nodded after Jason. "You really got a fan."

"I guess so." Rachel smiled and shook her head. "Are we ready to get out of here?"

"Everything's put away." He swung himself up and into the cab. "Can I wash up at your place?" he asked as she pulled the truck onto the driveway. "I was going to walk over to Ricki's place. She only lives a few blocks away. I told her I'd drop by and meet her great-uncle. It's a long walk from Julio's," he said plaintively.

"Get mud in my shower, huh?" She glared at him.

"Just a little." His grin was bright and full of anticipation.

Young love. Rachel suppressed a smile. "Fine. Just clean up the bathroom when you're done, you hear me?"

"Yes, ma'am." His grin widened. "I sure will."

They stopped at Julio's home on the way into town so that Spider could get clean clothes. He came out swinging the backpack he'd retrieved from the locker on his first day, and Rachel had a feeling that he was bringing everything he owned with him. "I could talk to my aunt," she said as they turned onto Mrs. Frey's driveway. "You could maybe stay there for a while."

"Yeah, right." He gave her a sideways look. "I've heard you talk about your uncle. I don't think that's gonna work, huh?"

She didn't either.

"Don't worry." He shrugged. "Julio hasn't kicked me out yet. I can sleep there until I find something. I told you."

Maybe she'd have to ask Jeff after all, if he could find bed space for Spider. Rachel wondered once more just when she had signed on as this kid's caretaker. She went into the kitchen to survey the refrigerator and decide what she could make for dinner. Salad, maybe? She wasn't hungry. Leaving dinner decisions until later, she called up her job numbers on the computer and sat down to figure out how she was going to finish the job at the Village on time without emptying her bank account. In the bathroom, water ran and she heard Spider humming to himself. Giving up on the uncooperative numbers, she shut off her computer, realizing that she hadn't checked her answering machine yet.

She had three messages. The first was from her mother, informing her cheerfully that she was just saying hi, and that she'd seen a very nice dress in Hood River that would look great on Rachel and at a wedding. Hint, hint. Rachel smiled as she erased the message. Maybe she'd just take a day off and go shopping with her mother. If anyone could put his job in perspective, it was her irrepressible mother.

The second message was from Jeff. He was going home to get some sleep, he told her. But if she wanted to come over after work, they could do something for dinner. "I'm on my way," she announced to the whirring machine. "Soon as Spider takes off."

"Ms. O'Connor." The director's slightly nasal voice emerging from the machine banished Rachel's smile. "I believe that we have reached an impasse as regards our agreement for the Village grounds. As you may recall, a timely completion was of central importance when we signed our contract. Apparently that timely completion is no longer possible without a significant increase in the cost, or a final result that is not satisfactory. I do not for a minute believe that someone sneaked onto the grounds of the Village and sabotaged your irrigation line. Your attempts to defraud the Village are clumsy. If you cannot assure me of a timely completion, I will be conferring with my lawyer about a lawsuit designed to recover the costs of hiring an honest contractor to meet our deadline for the photo session."

The call ended. Numb, Rachel stabbed the delete button.

An *honest* contractor! A lawsuit! Against her.

Rachel's face felt clammy and she breathed hard, as if she'd just run up the steps, her heart pounding. A lawsuit. Where would she get the money to pay for a lawyer's court time? She closed her eyes, remembering a lawsuit that had been brought against the orchard by a former employee. Her uncle had taken the suit to court in spite of his lawyer's suggestion that he settle. He had eventually won, but the financial impact on the family had been felt for years.

"Hey, I'm clean." Spider emerged from the bathroom in a roiling cloud of steam. "You got a bag for these?" He brandished a roll of dirty clothes. "I'm gonna have to hit the Laundromat later this week."

"I've almost got a full load." Rachel opened her eyes, trying for a casual tone. "Give 'em to me and I'll wash them tonight." She snatched the soiled clothes, and busied herself with detergent and washing machine dials, glad of the chance to regain her composure. It wasn't really necessary. Spider's mind was obviously elsewhere.

But when she offered to give him a ride over to Ricki's house, he thanked her and said that he'd walk. It was only a couple of blocks away on Second, less than a block from where Rachel had witnessed the assault the night before. "I'll get Ricki to give me a ride over to Julio's after," he told her. "Don't worry about it."

"Keep your eyes open for our vandal." She watched him swing over the last few steps on the staircase, landing lightly on his feet. Young love indeed. She had a feeling Ricki's great-uncle might get quite a bit of help from Spider.

Rachel rummaged her refrigerator for salad makings and left to go wake Jeff up for dinner. Still in a dark mood, she drove up the slope from the river, turning onto the winding road that led to the overlook where Jeff's house stood. The sun was sinking into bands of orange and magenta, colors too vivid to be real. Streaks of moisture too thin and high to be called clouds banded the sky from west to east. Ocean air coming inland. Not enough moisture for rain, though. If it continued, she'd have to haul away the brush she'd piled up. She'd never be able to burn it . . .

Which didn't really matter, did it? Not if she was being sued? Not if the job wasn't hers anymore? Stop thinking about it, she told herself sternly as she turned onto Jeff's long, freshly graveled driveway. Maybe they were just threats. Maybe the director would apologize in the morning.

Yeah, sure. Try as she might, the word buzzed like an evil wasp at the back of her skull.

Lawsuit.

First thing in the morning, she'd have to call Gladys Killingsworth, her lawyer.

Stop. Thinking. About. It.

Think about Jeff instead, and the vandal, and Jeff's incredible news that the Barnhart woman had been murdered. She pulled off the gravel to park on the neatly mown grass behind Jeff's Jeep. Ahead, the house seemed to perch at the lip of the Gorge, although the slope below it wasn't really a cliff at all. He had replaced the rotted siding this summer and finished the front porch. With the new roof, the house barely resembled the abandoned "haunted house" that she and Jeff had dared each other to enter as kids. Rachel carried her bag of salad makings onto the front porch, walking quietly. He must be asleep. She eased the screen door open.

Sure enough, he lay on the sofa, head cradled on his arm, his face drowned in sleep.

Something huge, black, and white exploded with a bloodcurdling roar from the floor beside the sofa and charged her. Rachel shrieked, registering a snapshot vision of a giant dog lunging at her, its snarling mouth full of white teeth. She leaped backward, grabbing for the door, deafened by deep baying. Weight hit the door, slamming it closed against her, bruising her knuckles. Inside, Jeff was shouting something. The screen door slammed open as she reached the bottom of the porch steps.

"Rachel, wait!" Jeff bolted onto the porch, banging the door shut behind him. "It's okay. Wait!"

She halted on the walkway, trembling, clammy sweat sticking her shirt to her body. "What was *that*? Oh, my god, it's that dog. It went after me."

"I'm sorry. I didn't hear your truck." Jeff leaped down the steps, his arms going around her. "I figured I'd be awake by the time you got here. I'm really, really sorry. I guess he was asleep. I think you scared Ben about as much as he scared you, by the way."

"Ben?" she asked weakly. She looked past him. A big black shape stood inside the screen door, staring at her intently. "I think he wants to eat me."

"No, he doesn't. Come on. Please?" He tugged gently on her hand. "He didn't know you were supposed to come in. He was just trying to protect me. He's an awfully sweet dog. Really. He just doesn't know who his friends are yet."

"Don't worry. I'm not one of them!" But she reluctantly let him lead her back up the stairs, half expecting the enormous dog to start growling and showing its teeth.

"You be nice now," Jeff said sternly. "Or you'll get yourself kicked out of here."

The dog lowered its head, its short stub of a tail tucked close to its hindquarters, and slunk aside from the door with an air of guilt. Its broken leg had been encased in a cast that rose clear to its shoulder, and it moved awkwardly, the cast thumping heavily on the wood planks of the floor.

"He's trying to figure out what the rules are." Jeff pulled her down beside him on the sofa. "He really tries to do the right thing. Poor guy. Nobody has even bothered to look for him."

"How come . . . how come he's here?" Rachel tried not to flinch as the dog stumped over to her, tongue lolling, ears down.

"He's apologizing. Just hold your hand out. Like that." His fingers cradling her palm—which still wanted to tremble—he offered the back of her hand to the huge black muzzle. The dog sniffed, then gave her hand a grave lick, its stubby tail wiggling briefly. "Ben, meet Rachel. Rachel, meet Ben. You two going to get along now?"

Ben gave Jeff an adoring brown eyed look and waggled his tail stub even harder.

"No," Rachel said. "I'm not sure at all that we're going to get along."

"If he so much as gives you a hard look, I'll take him over to the pound in the morning," Jeff said penitently. "Can you give it a try tonight? Dr. Stone only has one big-dog kennel at the clinic, and he needed it. I didn't want to take the poor guy over to the pound right away. His owner might still show up, and you know they're not going to place a big rottweiler mix like this. They'd euthanize him in no time."

He was almost pleading. Rachel swallowed a mix of surprise and irritation. "I'll give it a try." She gave the dog a distrustful glance. He grinned at her, and the array of clean white teeth made her shiver. His jaws looked big enough to bite your hand off at the wrist. Or higher.

"Thanks." Jeff kissed her. "I won't let him bother you, and it's only for a day or two."

"Glad to hear it," Rachel murmured. And the dog was going to bother her just by being here, thank you. But she didn't say that out loud.

"Have you had dinner yet?" Jeff yawned, his fatigue revealed briefly and starkly. "I've got some cooked shrimp. We could make a salad, or something."

"That sounds good. I brought some peppers and stuff for salad. I figured you had lettuce." Rachel went outside to retrieve the bag she'd dropped when the dog attacked her. The dog poked his head through the screen door, his brow furrowed, as if he was worried. It would have been faintly comical if he wasn't so darned big. "Out of my way, you," she said, making no move to open the door. "Right now!"

Jeff whistled from inside, and the dog vanished immediately, his cast thumping on the wooden floor. Rachel carried her bag into the kitchen, skirting the dog, who sat like a small black mountain at the edge of the kitchen.

"I told him to sit." Jeff was taking things from the refrigerator. "He really minds well. Why would somebody just abandon a dog like that?"

She could think of a couple of reasons. Several, actually. Rachel dumped orange and red peppers and a bag of sliced almonds out on the counter and reached for the colander that hung on the wall.

"I picked some of that red oak-leaf lettuce." Jeff set a bronze leafy head in the sink beneath the stream of cold water she'd just turned on. "Lovely stuff, but it gets a lot of dirt deep in the heart. And there are some lemon cukes. They're early." He added the yellow globes of cucumber as well as a handful of baby carrots, still dusted with soil. "The garden is really taking off this year. Although if we don't catch this creep, the weeds are going to rule." His tone hardened. "Joylinn's going to have to sand the graffiti off her storefront. She wasn't real happy with me this morning."

"I didn't know." Rachel paused, her hands full of dripping lettuce leaves. "I haven't seen Joylinn today. How awful!"

"Sooner or later one of us is going to spot him." Jeff unwrapped a wedge of blue cheese and began to crumble it into chunks. "Tonight, maybe. He's only working downtown, and all four of us are going to be out there tonight." He looked grim. "It's not like we're marching around with red and blue lights flashing. Odds are that one of us will be in the same place as he is, one of these nights. This is definitely a war. I just wish I knew why."

Poor Joylinn. Rachel began to slice peppers with angry precision. Her landlord was notoriously slow about making any kind of repairs. So she would have to deal with the spray paint herself. "Jeff, what about the woman at the Village?" She looked up from the cutting board, frowning. "You scared me this afternoon."

"I hope so." He got a bowl full of pink shrimp from the refrigerator, set it down on the counter, and put his arms around her. "The toxicology report came back on her." He hesitated. "Nobody knows about this yet, and I don't want anyone to know. But she was certainly poisoned. I should have more details tomorrow."

"In the dining room?" Rachel swallowed. "She was sitting at the next table, at lunch that day."

"No," Jeff said slowly. "Probably not that day." He shook his head. "I'm sorry. I can't tell you any more than that right now, okay?"

"I understand." Rachel shivered again. "Do you have any idea who did it? You don't think Madame is right, do you? That the director killed her to cover up her thefts?"

"We don't have proof of any of that yet." Jeff's expression was serious. "And the last thing I need is to have a dozen rumors floating around out there. We don't have much to go on as is. And I'm not insulting you." He touched her cheek with a weary smile. "I know you don't talk about things I tell you. Let's just hope Madame is as discreet as you." He hesitated. "I don't want you to be involved in this, but . . . if you hear anything . . ."

"I'd let you know in a minute," she said automatically. That is, if she was still working there. Rachel frowned as she began to tear the lettuce into pieces and drop them into the salad bowl. "How did the vandal make it out to the Village if he hit the Bread Box last night? He must have wings."

"The Village?" Jeff looked blank. "What happened at the Village?"

"Didn't the director call you?" Rachel tossed a last handful of torn lettuce into the bowl. "Someone drilled holes in all my irrigation lines last night."

"Why didn't you call me right away?"

"The director told me she'd report it." Rachel bit her lip, remembering the message on her machine. "I think she believes I did it myself. Oh, Jeff. She really thinks I'm trying to cheat her."

Jeff put his arms around her, holding her tightly. Which brought Ben to his feet, his head tilted, expression worried.

"It's okay, boy," Jeff said, but Rachel pulled away from his embrace.

"Maybe she'll report it in the morning," she said. "It's okay." She shook her head at Jeff's worried expression. "I'll get it fixed. Let's eat, shall we?"

She didn't tell him about the phone call from the director as they finished making the shrimp salad and set the table. She told herself that he had enough to worry about without her troubles. But the truth was that she was still a bit angry about the dog, and that was part of it.

They ate dinner, but the meal lacked its usual warm intimacy. Jeff was clearly preoccupied with the upcoming night on the street, and Rachel found herself worrying about the director's threat and wondering what her lawyer would tell her in the morning. And then, there was the dog. Ben. He lay politely on the floor beside Jeff's chair, his casted leg sticking out at an awkward angle, his expression hopeful. He really was a polite dog, Rachel had to admit grudgingly. Their friends Sandy and Bill had recently acquired a poodle-Pomeranian mix puppy who was utterly annoying at mealtime. But this dog was just too big. And there were those teeth.

They washed up together, and afterward, Jeff walked with her out to the truck, letting Ben out to stump around the yard. "You're going straight home, right?" he asked, his lips against her cheek. "No roaming around the streets tonight, okay?"

"No way." Rachel's arms tightened around him, her heart squeezing her. "Be careful, please? Want to come by after? I'll keep the bed warm."

"I'm always careful." His lips brushed the line of her cheekbone. "I'd better come home afterward." His sigh tickled her cheek. "I don't want Ben to have to hold it too long. No point in testing his housebreaking."

Rachel sent the oblivious Ben a glare over Jeff's shoulder. Two days, she reminded herself. She left before Jeff, driving a little too fast down the narrow county road, angry, and not quite sure whom she was angriest at—the director, Jeff, or the damn dog. Or maybe herself. This had not been a good day.

CHAPTER
9

Pounding woke Rachel. And voices, confused and loud. Angry. Blinking, groggy, Rachel shoved the covers aside, groping for her bathrobe. One of the voices was Mrs. Frey's. The other was Spider's voice, she realized, and she felt a disconnected moment of shock, because he sounded like a man, not a boy, and she hadn't noticed that his voice had changed.

"What is going on here?" She yanked the front door open, grabbing for her robe as it threatened to fall open. Peter stalked in past her, his tail ramrod straight, obviously dissociating himself from this unseemly noise.

"Somebody broke into your truck." Spider's eyes were wide and angry. "Will you tell this . . . woman . . . that I didn't do it?"

"Well, what were you doing sneaking around here at this hour in the morning?" Dressed in an ankle-length chenille robe, Mrs. Frey plucked at his sleeve. "And you trampled my roses! How could you do that?"

"I didn't touch your roses. Jeeze. It was light enough to see. Why would I wade through a bunch of thorns, huh?" Impatiently, Spider shook her off. "Rachel, he busted your window and yanked out your tape deck. He didn't do a very good job either." Scorn tinged Spider's voice. "He really messed up your dashboard."

Rachel pushed past the two of them and ran down the steps to the yard. Bits of shattered glass, like fragments of ice, littered the gravel. Heart sinking, Rachel peered into the cab. The tape deck had indeed been removed. Roughly. Scratches marred the plastic of the dashboard and wires dangled like severed nerves from the gaping hole where it had been. The carved bead that her friend Beck had given her for luck was gone, too. "Oh, no!" Rachel pulled the door open, searching the seat and floor, hoping that the bead had simply fallen. But there was no sign of it. The thief had taken it.

"What a creep." Spider came up beside her. "Too bad I didn't come over when I first woke up," he said with genuine regret. "I might've caught the . . . the jerk." He glanced sideways at the still-glaring Mrs. Frey. "I would've liked that," he said thoughtfully. "A lot."

"I think I would have liked it a lot, too." Rachel let her breath out in a rush. "I guess I'd better tell Jeff."

It hadn't occurred to her before—not really—that someone might hate her, try to do harm to her, because of Jeff. Oh, she knew it was a possibility. Had accepted it, because after the attack on Celia, how could she not?

This wasn't just a possibility. This was broken glass, and it was her truck. Her skin felt tight between her shoulder blades as she turned to climb the stairs back to her apartment to call Jeff and to get dressed. Not even the strange warning call she'd received had bothered her this much. What had Jeff said last night? That this was a war.

Trying to shrug off her jagged thoughts, she slammed the door behind her, shedding her robe and pulling on clothes even as she dialed the Blossom Police. Bert Stanfield, the new officer, answered, sounding weary. "I'll come take a look." He didn't sound enthusiastic. "Don't touch anything until I get there." And he hung up.

Well, they'd already left their prints all over the truck. Rachel sighed and dressed, feeling unbelievably tired. What she wanted to do right now was to crawl back into bed and go back to sleep. To hell with the job and Director Jennifer Bellington and her damn lawsuit anyway. Gritting her teeth, she ran a comb through her hair and went down the stairs, just as the black-and-white Blossom Police car crawled up the driveway. The front doors opened and Stanfield climbed out, looking rumpled and irritable in spite of his freshly shaven face. A teenaged boy was climbing out of the passenger side. He had short-cropped blond hair, blue eyes, and a rectangular face that looked like a younger version of Stanfield.

"This is my son, Greg." Stanfield nodded at the young man, pride a bright gleam on his face. "He wants to be a cop. So I let him ride along. Help me out." He nodded approvingly at his son. "He's got good ideas—knows how kids think better than we do, huh?"

The boy shrugged, a little awkward, a little embarrassed. "I'm just learning stuff." He offered Rachel a hand. "I'm Greg. Like Dad said. Glad to meet you."

"I'm Rachel." She felt Spider's presence close behind her. But as she opened her mouth to introduce him, Greg turned abruptly away to prowl back over to the truck, where Stanfield was circling it, making notes on his pad.

"Doesn't look like whoever did it knew what they were doing." Greg peered through the broken window. "Looks like they used a pry bar to get it out."

"No duh," Spider said under his breath.

Greg didn't appear to have heard him. "You didn't hear anything?" He looked at Rachel. "You don't have a dog or anything? He must have walked right up the driveway from the street."

"There's a streetlight right by the driveway, in case you didn't notice. The creep came through the garden," Spider drawled. "Or else somebody walked through a lot of thorny roses for no good reason. Climbed over the back fence from the next yard over. They don't have a dog neither."

"Either." Mrs. Frey gave Spider a look. "They don't have a dog *either*. And whoever did it is going to owe me for a new Tropicana. That old rose is a favorite of mine, and they broke the main stem all to hell. Bought it the first year it was introduced, the year Robert died." She paused, her eyes on the trampled roses behind the house. "Nobody grows them anymore," she went on querulously. "Tropicanas never were all that popular. Where can I get another one?"

"You got to wonder how this guy keeps on getting away with this kind of thing." Greg's lip seemed to want to curl. "I mean, the chief's got four guys out prowling what—a handful of blocks? I mean, shoot. This kind of thing was going on in Portland, they wouldn't put more than one officer on it, and the guy would be waiting for trial right now."

"Oh, yeah?" Spider cocked a skeptical eye at him. "You know just how to do it, don't you?"

"Better than Price." Greg shrugged. "Guy's a bumbler. No wonder he's stuck out here in a loser town. Well, I guess he's good enough for a bunch of hicks, but—" He doubled over with a gasping cry as Spider's fist caught him just below the breastbone.

"Spider!" Rachel started forward, but it was Mrs. Frey who stepped up beside him and put a hand on his raised arm.

"I think you made your point," she said dryly, eyeing the gasping Greg, who was on his knees now, his arms wrapped around his midriff. "That's always the time to quit, for the best effect."

Spider gave her a sideways look as Stanfield strode over.

"What the hell?" Angry blotches showed on his face. "What happened?" He was speaking to his son, ignoring the rest of them as if they didn't exist.

"He . . . slugged me. For . . . no damn reason." Greg struggled to get the words out. His face had taken on a faint greenish pallor.

"Get up." His father's tone was cold and he stood with his hands on his hips, making no move to help his son as he struggled to his feet. "The way I see it," he drawled, "is that if you're slow enough to let somebody sucker punch you, then you deserve it."

"But . . ." Greg clamped his lips together. "Yes, sir," his said in a clipped, strangled voice. And shot Spider a single venomous look.

"I think we're done here." Stanfield's words were directed to Rachel, but his eyes were on Spider, ice-cold and contemplative. "Nothing much more to see, unless you noticed something else missing. You should get a light out here—one with a motion detector on it. Or you're just asking for this kind of activity. Get in the car," he told his son. Turning his back on them, Stanfield climbed behind the wheel as his son shuffled around to the passenger side, his head down, still clutching his midriff. Nobody said anything as the black-and-white car backed too fast down the driveway and swung out onto the street in a scatter of gravel.

"Good thing nobody was coming up the hill," Mrs. Frey said acerbically. "Would be kind of fresh, getting hit by a police car. Save you a phone call, I suppose."

"I'm sorry." Spider faced Rachel. "I didn't mean to make trouble for you."

"You didn't." Mrs. Frey spoke up. "You made trouble for that boy. And for yourself, if I read Dad right. I don't think he appreciated you putting his precious son on the ground, young man." She clucked her tongue. "Just don't go jaywalking downtown. Honestly, you boys remind me of a couple of male dogs meeting on the street corner, all hackled up and stiff-legged, ready to fight. At least you don't lift your legs on my roses." She snorted, started for the rear of the house, then paused to look back. "You got a nice left hook there. Have to admit, the prick sure had it coming. Well, I'd better get started cleaning up. See what I can salvage. That Tropicana's a loss, though. Never was a real vigorous plant. That awful person broke it off below the union. It'll come out to rootstock now. Nothing left to do but dig it up. I sure hope it scratched the heck out of him." Her grumbling monologue faded as she vanished around the corner in the direction of the small shed where she kept her tools.

Spider stared after her, stunned. "She called him a prick."

"Don't underestimate Amelia." Rachel went to get the broom that hung beneath the stairs. "She isn't quite the sweet addle-headed little old lady she lets on to be." She began to sweep up the glittering shards of glass from the driveway. "You know, it sounded to me as if you were defending Jeff."

"No way. He was just being a prick. That's all. Here, I'll do that." He took the broom from her and began sweeping meticulously, his attention focused on the job as if it were the most important thing he'd done in his life. "Besides, he called us all hicks."

"I guess he did." Rachel watched him a moment or two, then shrugged and opened her truck box. Scratches marred the paint around the lock, and she scowled. The vandal had tried to pick the lock? Looked like it. Everything inside was in place. She went back upstairs to pack a lunch and fill the water jug. She packed enough for two because she hadn't noticed any kind of lunch sack sitting around. As an afterthought, she grabbed the last four bagels from the bag on top of the refrigerator, added the jar of peanut butter from the cupboard, and tossed three oranges into the sack. She wasn't hungry. Anger still knotted her stomach, and more than anger—a thread of fear. Peter wasn't around. He tended to vanish when strangers showed up. She filled his bowl with dry food and left it on the landing beside the door. Gladys hadn't answered her call, but her office hours were a bit arbitrary.

Spider had swept up every tiny bit of glass and was dumping glass shards and gravel into the galvanized garbage can behind the house. Rachel stifled a sigh as she stowed the lunch sack in the truck box. For the first time she could remember, she didn't want to go to work. If the director really asked her to quit this morning, she thought grimly, she'd pack up and leave in a moment, never mind the lawsuit!

"Let's go," she said, and climbed into the truck. Spider had cleaned the glass from the inside, too. And put the broom and dustpan away, she noticed. No sign of the carved bead, even under the seat. It had meant a lot to her, that bit of wood. Beck, her crazy carpenter friend, had carved a single block of pale wood into an open spiral that caged a perfect polished sphere within it. How he had done it, she had no idea. But it was beautiful. She sighed as Spider piled in beside her. "Bagels." She handed him the paper sack as she finished backing out of the driveway. "And a jar of peanut butter. Do-it-yourself breakfast. And oranges. You have to eat at least one of them."

"Yes, ma'am," he drawled, but he opened the bag with alacrity. "You better do something about that window before it rains. Maybe Julio's brother-in-law would do it. He's really good with cars." He stopped talking to smear a chunk of bagel with peanut butter and wolf it down in one enormous bite.

"When *did* you eat last?" Rachel asked mildly.

"I had breakfast," he said quickly. "I guess I'm just hungry in the morning, is all." But he took a smaller bite of bagel. "Want me to fix you one?"

"I'm not hungry at all, thanks. They're all for you." They were speeding along the county road toward the Village. With every turn of the wheels, her stomach knotted tighter.

But when they finally reached the Village, the director's car wasn't in its parking space. Rachel breathed a sigh of relief. They went to work laying out and gluing the pipe all over again. It was slower than laying out the original system, since they had to clean the salvaged pieces before regluing them. As they worked, she kept a list of valves and fittings that would have to be replaced. It wasn't as bad as she had feared. Mostly, it would cost them time. Which was what she was most short of now.

It was nearly noon when a tall, lanky figure limped down the path from the buildings to where they were working. Rachel straightened up, her hands stained with mud, and shaded her eyes. He was tall and spare, his face weathered and lined, his shoulders straight in spite of the cane he leaned on lightly. In his free hand he carried a covered plastic pitcher and a stack of plastic glasses.

"Hi, Gus." Spider put down the spade he'd been using to clear out some feet of eroded trench. "What're you doing here?"

"Stopped in to see Ricki. She sent me out with some lemonade for you two." The lanky stranger handed pitcher and glasses to Spider, and offered Rachel a gnarled and knotted hand. "I'm Gus Van Dorn, Ricki's great-uncle. Nice to meet you. You got a nice eye for design. I can tell when you've worked on something around town."

"Thank you." Rachel hid her blush by wiping her sweating face on her sleeve. "Ricki told me you were one of Portland's top gardeners."

"Dunno about that. Mostly, I did yard work." He folded down a small seat that was attached to the handle of his cane and sat on it, balancing easily. "Hope you don't mind if I sit. The legs are getting old. You took off early this morning, young man. The young always sleep late. I figured on giving you coffee at least. You could have had a bed, you know. We got a guest room."

Rachel raised an eyebrow at Spider, whose face was turning a fascinating shade of cinnamon-red.

"I . . . I didn't want to bother anybody," he stammered. "I . . . Ricki loaned me a sleeping bag. I hope it was okay."

"It would have been okay if she'd asked you in, and then I would've had somebody to drink coffee with. Too bad. You missed my biscuits. I do good biscuits." He chuckled at Spider's obvious embarrassment. "You know, I didn't just come down here to harass your assistant. You got a good one, by the way, if he works as hard for you as he did for me. I figured I'd teach him the mushroom trade, come the rains this fall." He poured out a glass of icy lemonade and handed it to Rachel. "Anyhow, long as I was here, I figured I'd introduce myself and invite you to drop by." Handing Spider a glass, he filled one for himself. "Ricki made this out of real lemons. Kind of a special treat, I think. Cheers." He raised his glass in a brief salute.

"I'd planned to drop by and meet you." Rachel sipped at her lemonade, finding it tart and full of lemon flavor. "She told me you've got a lovely garden."

"Was once." Van Dorn nodded. "Could be again, but that takes a lot of work. Even if you got good help." He nodded at Spider. "Ricki, she works some pretty long hours out here. Too many, if you ask me, but I guess that's what you got to do these days. And she never was real keen on gardening, although she was always good about helping out when I asked." He sighed. "She wants the money for school, so who am I to say go slow?" He peered into the depths of his half-empty glass, his expression contemplative. "When you decide what you want, you got to take a leap for it, never mind if you think you'll grab it or not. You get too careful, you get too busy doing the right thing, and you wake up one day and realize it's too late for you. So you got to just jump for it, once you know what you want. And if you fall flat—well, at least you tried." He drained his glass and lifted the pitcher. "More?"

"Thanks." Rachel held out her glass, watching him divide the last of the lemonade meticulously among their three glasses, remembering suddenly that Doc had said something about Gus Van Dorn meaning to be a doctor before he quit school to help his family. "I'll definitely drop by."

"I was going to come over after work today and finish that pruning." Spider finished the last of his lemonade, ice tinkling against his teeth. "I think I got the hang of it. I thought maybe I'd tackle that last one by myself," he said casually.

"You do that." Van Dorn nodded. "I think you got a good feel for what you're doing. You make a mistake, the tree won't die. The place up there is buzzing." He was speaking to Rachel now, his faded eyes sharp on her face. "All kinds of rumors flying around. How some lady was murdered, and that she was getting cheated on her bill. Folk are pulling out all their receipts, I guess. I wouldn't want to be in the administration's shoes if there are mistakes on those monthly statements. I don't know, though." Those pale dry eyes pinned Rachel. "I worry about my niece. I've raised her since she was three. Guess I've got to thinking like a parent."

"I . . . don't know anything." Rachel's tongue wanted to stick to the roof of her mouth, as if she'd just eaten a big wad of peanut butter. "Why should I?"

"Dunno. Your name sort of comes up. But you know what this place is like. Ricki calls it the gossip mill." He took the glasses from them, emptying the melting remnants of ice onto the ground. "Just wondered if you knew anything."

"No." Rachel looked down at the ice, already soaking small dark patches of ice melt into the dry soil. "I don't know anything at all." And wondered where the rumors had come from. Madame? Harris? Who else would know these things? Or did they even know? Jeff had told her about the murder. Had he told them?

"Well, I'll be heading out. See you when you get over to do that pruning." Van Dorn levered himself to his feet, folding the small cane-seat back against the handle. "Plan on having dinner with us tonight." He was speaking to Spider, issuing something between an invitation and an order. "Gets boring, just the two of us." Carrying the empty glasses and pitcher, he made his way slowly back up the path to the Village's main building again.

"So you slept at Ricki's house last night?"

"Out in the yard, actually." Spider shrugged. "I got to talking with Gus. Time it got dark, I figured it was too late to call and ask Julio for a ride. The guy's up at dawn, goes to bed before it's full dark. Didn't feel like walking, so I asked Ricki if I could borrow a sleeping bag." He shrugged again. "I'm kind of in the way over there anyway." He didn't look at her. "They're being really nice about it, but it's crowded even without me, what with Chankina—you know, Anita—living there, too."

She'd have to ask Jeff. Rachel let her breath out in a silent sigh. Spider had to live *somewhere*. Just for a while, she told herself. She'd find something permanent for him. Surely. And right now, Jeff still had the dog, she reminded herself. She wasn't going to hang out there until it was gone anyway.

They went back to work. It was harder, doing it the second time. Or it seemed so, anyway. Not harder. Just frustrating. As she glued fittings, she wondered glumly if the vandal would sabotage this setup, too. No matter how she figured it, they couldn't complete the repairs and get the system covered up in one working day.

As the sun began to sink toward the horizon, the wind died. The heat lay still and thick as a blanket on the barren slope, and any dust they raised hung in the air. It clung tan to their faces and arms, gritty on their lips. The muscles between Rachel's shoulders ached hotly. She had set Spider to filling in the repaired lines, never mind the test. If they tested and something gave, they could dig up the spot. It would be muddy, but at least the buried lines were safe from the vandal. Unless he had a shovel with him.

"It's after six." Spider leaned on the long handle of his spade. "Considering that you told me this . . . uh . . . woman is suing you, I figure you don't owe her too much overtime."

"I guess I'm hoping she'll back off if we catch up." Rachel set the glue-wet fitting into place, made sure it was solid, and got to her feet. "All right. We're through for the day." She stretched, wincing, thinking that she needed a long hot soak, never mind the heat. "Let's get cleaned up and out of here. You're really going to go spend your evening pruning?" She raised a skeptical eyebrow as they began to clean the tools and stow them.

"Yeah, why not?" Spider shrugged. "It's not that much work—it's just summer pruning. Shaping, you know? Mostly, it's figuring out what to cut and what to leave. Gus is something—he snips out a few twigs and the tree looks like artwork or something. I think I'm getting an idea of how to do it."

"So does Ricki help, too?" she asked casually, and hid her smile as Spider's cheeks warmed briefly. He blushed about as easily as she did, she decided.

"Well, yeah, she pitches in, too." His tone was very, very casual. "But she works about a ten-hour day, and she's pretty tired. Last night she just hung around and talked for a while, and then made dinner. She says she'd rather cook than weed any day. Uh-oh." His eyes fixed on something up the slope behind her. "Trouble," he said softly.

Rachel turned to look and her stomach contracted. The director was striding down the path toward them, her mouth a thin hard line in her face, twin spots of color glowing on her cheeks.

"Take off. I'll say you went for more parts," Spider said quickly. "I'll get a ride home with Ricki." And he muttered something multisyllabic under his breath.

"No." Rachel sighed. "I really should talk to her." She straightened her shoulders "Something wrong?" she asked as the pale-faced director approached.

"You're behind these rumors." The director's voice was shrill, but hushed, as if she was afraid someone might overhear. "You started these . . . these *calumnies* about Emily being murdered and my cheating the residents! I know you did this!"

"Cal-lummys," Spider mused. "Now I can win my next hot Scrabble game."

"Shut up, you." The director spun to face him, her hands clenched to fists at her sides, her shoulders twin sharp lumps of tightness. "I'm not talking to you. Get out of here."

"I think I can sue you on some kind of federal harassment charge," Spider drawled. "You better watch it."

"Spider," Rachel said wearily. She really wanted to laugh at his hackled-up protective posture. It reminded her of Jeff's dog, in a way. But she didn't have the energy to either laugh or get angry. "Jennifer." She used the woman's given name, saw her nostrils flare slightly in surprise or outrage. "Jennifer, I didn't start any stories about you. I've been out here digging up the mess that jerk left for me since yesterday noon. I might have reason to be mad at you for that lawsuit threat." Understatement of the year. "But I didn't start these rumors." And felt a twinge of guilt, because she knew who could have started them.

"Don't give me that." The director's voice quivered with rage. "You're local. You could be in touch with these people when they get off work. You could have started all of this—pointing at me as an outsider, making me the enemy. I know how these small-town gossip things start. I got *stuck* with this damn loser project. Because I'm a woman, and I'm good. So they give me this misrun money sink of a nursing home and tell me to make it profitable. They wouldn't even let me fire the incompetent who ran it into the ground in the first place. I think she's their spy. They just snapped their fingers. Just like that." Her eyes had gone wide, fixed on Rachel, the pupils huge and black, irises rimmed with white. She seemed to have forgotten that Spider was there. "And now they're cutting the budget on me, after I've already hired contractors and ordered repairs. Where's the money going to come from? And so when I fail—as if anybody could turn this dump around—they'll fire me, nod over their martinis, and tell each other that women just don't make good administrators in tough situations. And then they'll hire some man in my place, and increase his budget. And he won't be nearly as good as me. I *will* turn it around. Do you hear me? And that article is going to put me over the top, because I'll get national publicity for what I'm doing with this place. And none of them are going to be able to touch me, or to say that I failed. None of them." She was speaking only to Rachel now, her pale, polished nails digging into her palms. "Never mind that they gave me an impossible job and then reduced the money. Never mind that they gave me a time limit. I'll pull this off for them, and they'll never be able to pass me over again, do you hear me? They'll have to admit that I'm good."

Rachel took a step back, stunned by the woman's passion. "So let me finish this job," she said with quiet intensity. "I can have this place looking good for your photo shoot, even if it's not exactly what we talked about. But it will look good. I'm promising you this."

The director blinked and peered at her as if she had forgotten that Rachel was even there, as if it surprised her that Rachel could speak. Turning on her heel, she marched back up the path without answering.

"Jeez," Spider said in a hushed voice. "She's really nuts."

"I don't know." Rachel shook her head. "Maybe." And she wondered again who had started the rumors about murder and embezzlement. She'd have to tell Jeff about this, she thought. As soon as she saw him. "Let's get out of here," she said absently.

"How 'bout for good?" Spider raised an eyebrow at her.

Not a bad idea. "Sorry, kid. We're staying till it's finished."

CHAPTER

10

Rachel took Spider home to shower, then dropped him off at Van Dorn's house. She thought guiltily that she should stop and tour the garden, but she simply wasn't in the mood. She told Spider she'd see him tomorrow and drove back downtown, past City Hall. She didn't stop there, even though Jeff's Jeep was parked in the lot. Right now, she didn't really feel like chatting with anybody. Not even Jeff.

She turned down the street that ended at the riverside shops, but for once, she didn't park in the Bread Box lot. Instead, she pulled over onto the strip of weedy vacant land that lay between the street and the Columbia. The river rolled along uncaring, blue in the end-of-day light. As she walked through the sunburned leaves and seed heads left from spring blossoms, she felt a faint breath of cooler air and smelled the river—a mix of mud, water, and long-dead fish. A blue heron rose up from a clump of willow scrub that grew at the edge of the water, its wings seemingly broad as a small plane's at this close distance. Rachel stood still, her heart full, as the huge bird soared out and over the river before circling back to land farther downstream. A small scum of twigs, leaves, and bits of plastic trash from upstream picnickers pooled in the eddies between the boulders that had been dumped at the water's edge to protect the boardwalk from flooding. Small birds hopped and pecked among the floating debris.

Riverside peace—the smell of decay and water . . . life.

Feeling oddly better, Rachel turned back to her truck. A figure leaned against the fender, waving briefly to her as she trudged back through the weeds. It was Gladys, her lawyer, dressed in her usual outfit of expensive slacks and tailored blazer. The motorcycle helmet beneath her arm spoiled the professional effect.

"You looked like Ophelia, ready to drown yourself in the stream," the stocky woman announced cheerfully as Rachel approached. "I thought I'd better hang around until you made up your mind. Having a bad day?"

"Did you get my message?" Rachel sighed and leaned against the sun-hot fender beside Gladys, wanting nothing so much right now as to take a long, cooling swim. Her lawyer's big Harley-Davidson motorcycle was nowhere to be seen. Probably parked over in the Bread Box lot, Rachel thought wearily.

"Yes, I got your message." Gladys studied the huge placid river. "I'm having a hard time figuring out just why your boss thinks she can sue you. Unless you've really messed up?"

"I'm behind schedule," Rachel said dully. "There's a photo session for an important magazine article scheduled for this fall, and I won't be able to do everything I promised before it happens. That's why. Especially if the summer stays this hot and dry. And it's supposed to."

"How come you're behind?"

"We . . . hit a lot of lava. I had to redesign the water

system." Rachel sighed. "And then somebody sabotaged the system, so now we have to do it all over again."

"I wrote the contract you use, remember?" Gladys gave her a sharp look. "Unless you crossed out a lot of stuff or signed a piece of toilet paper instead, you're quite well covered against unforeseen problems." She raised her eyebrows. "Including unexpected lava ridges and sabotage. I am rather good at writing contracts. Your boss's lawyer was not so good at crossing things out, I noticed."

"I know you're good." But Rachel blushed. "I didn't really think about whether she actually could win or not. I was just so spooked by the idea that somebody . . ."

"Somebody's gonna sue you. Oh, baby." Gladys rolled her eyes. "You don't know how many folk have parted with how much cash just because the threat of a lawsuit scared the crap out of them. That's the idea, sweetheart." She shrugged. "So how much does she want?"

"Want?" Rachel blinked.

"Want. Want. Like what's her price to settle?" Gladys snapped her short, thick, competent fingers. Her nails were blunt-cut, without polish, and impeccably groomed. "What is she really after here?"

"She wants me out of there, so that she can turn the job over to somebody who won't charge as much." Rachel enunciated each syllable carefully. "She can save money that way."

"If that's all she wants, bow out and count your blessings." Gladys shrugged. "Settle. Tell her she can have a few bucks and you'll pack up."

"What?" Rachel gaped at her stocky lawyer, feeling as if the older woman had just punched her in the chest.

"Look, dearie." Gladys put a hand on her shoulder, her expression a mix between big-sister sympathetic and irritation. "You can't afford to take this to court. Whether you win or lose. Trust me. Court time is expensive. If all she wants is for you to bow out—you're getting off cheaply. If she wants real money, too . . ." She shrugged. "Then we'll see."

"No!" The word exploded from Rachel without thought, without will.

"Why not?" Gladys raised an eyebrow. "They don't put you in jail for settling out of court."

Why not? Rachel struggled to settle the whirling maelstrom of thought and emotion in her head. "Because. . . because . . . Just because." Rachel drew a deep, slow breath, suddenly calm and certain. "I am not playing this kind of game. I didn't do anything wrong."

"Say hi to the old goat, your uncle, next time you're up there for a nice friendly family dinner," Gladys said crisply. "Maybe I should send the bill to him."

"This has nothing to do with my uncle!"

"Whatever you say." Gladys shook her head. "So okay, you don't want to play the game her way. Fine. We'll wait and see what develops, then we'll talk again."

"I know I'm being stupid, okay?" Rachel crossed her arms and glared at her lawyer. "But I'm not going to change my mind. I am not saying that I was incompetent if I wasn't. And . . . I promised the people at the Village that garden." She thought of Jason's words—that she would give them all a place for dreams. "And I don't care what Uncle Jack thinks. Just for the record."

"Just for the record," Gladys drawled. "Well, I'm off." She swung her helmet in one hand. "Let me know when you hear something." Still shaking her head, she marched through the weeds toward the Bread Box.

Blinking back tears, Rachel turned back to the river, hearing after a few minutes the throaty roar of her lawyer's powerful bike. Gladys was probably right. She should probably just settle. The hard yellow light of the sinking sun flooded the wrinkled surface of the wide river, edging each swell with brightness. It dazzled her eyes, making her vision swim. She closed her eyes briefly, wanting to drive up to Jeff's house, go sit out on the deck with him and tell him this. He would listen. He wouldn't be upset, no matter what he thought.

But he had the damn dog.

Shoving her hair back from her face, Rachel straightened her shoulders. Instead of going back to her truck, she headed back for the riverbank. No Ophelia, thank you. Grimly she picked her way through the weeds to where the ground dropped off to the water's edge. Underwater in winter, it was dry bank in the summer. A narrow path, barely visible, wound along the bank, down below the board walkway of the new shops, below the view of the tourists on the Bread Box deck with their iced teas and afternoon sandwiches. Smelling the river, her face bathed in the harsh glow of the lowering sun, she followed the narrow path between clumps of willow and tall, sunburned grass. A red-and-white bobber gleamed like strange fruit from a clump of willow, wound tight to the slender twigs by a knotted tangle of black fishing line.

It was hot, even down here by the water. The wind had died, leaving the air still and heavy. Rachel stopped near a jumble of branches and old roots that had been washed in by the winter's high water. Her shirt was sticking to her back between her shoulder blades, and she lifted her hair from her neck with both hands, wishing for a breeze. You always had wind along the river. Always. Time to go home and take a shower. Cook dinner, go to bed, don't think about the lawsuit, she told herself sternly.

Yeah, right.

As she started back along the path, the fading yellow light now at her back, she caught a glimpse of a figure ahead. For a moment Rachel hesitated, remembering that dark-clad attacker who had leaped out at Celia. But whoever this was, they didn't move like a stalker or an attacker. The man—she was close enough now to see that it was a man—veered erratically, seeming to stumble.

It was Dr. Welsh. Rachel recognized the town's only doctor with surprise as he neared. At first she thought he must be fishing, although as far as she knew, he was a trout fisherman first and foremost. But as he drew near, she saw that he was wearing his office clothes—plain white shirt and suit pants. The shirt was open at the neck, sleeves rolled up, and mud stained his shoes and the cuffs of his pants. His face looked slack and slightly flabby, and a stubble of silvery whiskers shadowed his jaw.

"Dr. Welsh? Hi. Are you okay?"

He squinted at her with bleary surprise, as if he hadn't until this moment noticed her ahead of him on the riverbank. "Rachel?" He slurred the word slightly. "What're you doin' here?"

He was drunk. She realized it a second before she caught the harsh reek of alcohol on his breath. Very drunk. He staggered suddenly, and she reached out automatically, needing both hands to keep him from falling. Dr. Welsh, at well over six feet tall, might be lean, but he was not a slight man. "Sit down." Rachel helped him as he sagged down onto the dry grass. "I was just out walking."

"Walking." The doctor sighed, his eyes on the fading daylight on the river. "I am not walking well." He enunciated the words with careful precision. "I am very drunk. But that's all right. I am *entitled* to be drunk. I used to fish at Trout Lake." He peered at her over the rims of the glasses, his expression very serious. "Back when it was a lake. There was a lodge. It was very famous. Do you know how long ago that was?"

"A long time?" Rachel looked up and down the empty riverbank, wondering just what she should do here.

"Before you were born, my dear. I am seventy-one years old." Dr. Welsh hiccoughed, and pushed his slipping glasses back onto the bridge of his nose. "Don't tell anyone. Nobody knows but you and I. Not that it matters."

His face drooped mournfully. "I am too old. I have been too old for a long time. I suspected it a long time ago, anyway. I was going to quit. But who is going to take my place? Can you tell me that?" He prodded her with one long, bony finger. "Hot young doctors don't want to live in the middle of nowhere. Hospitals are closing. You want a good doctor, you better live in a city, young lady. But it doesn't matter." He turned his gaze back to the river. "Time to quit. Time to quit when you let someone kill your patients and you don't even notice."

"Doctor! What do you mean? What are you saying?" Rachel seized him by the arm, wondering for a panicky moment if he was really just drunk or if the old man was going suddenly senile. "Nobody's killing your patients."

"Are they not?" He turned unexpectedly clear eyes on her. "Some person fed Emily Barnhart a meal of poison mushrooms. Galerinas, according to the toxicology report. Go look them up. They cause flulike symptoms and, later on, organ failure. Kidneys. Liver. It all shuts down and you die. Like Emily. And perhaps like Rosemary Forbes last year. And Robert Dearborn before her. Kidneys fail in us old folk. Systems wear out and stop functioning. Like me. Like my brain." He laughed a single harsh syllable. "Their kidneys and livers, my brain. All worn out. Only they weren't." His eyes pierced her once more, shadowed now with an agony of guilt. "Someone made them die. Someone took those last precious months or years from them. And I helped them. I stood back and let them get away with it. If a spectrograph shows orellanin in Rosemary or Robert, then . . . I'm guilty. I helped kill them."

Stunned by this flood of words, Rachel groped for a response. "I don't . . . I mean, are you sure?" She floundered.

"I don't know why." Slowly, unsteadily, Dr. Welsh hauled himself to his feet. "My dear, I was old when you were born." His expression weary and tender, he brushed a wisp of hair from her face. "I do not want to know why some madman killed old men and women. I do not think I want to be part of a world where I have to suspect murder each time I make out a death paper. It is time for me to quit."

More than a little frightened by his tone, Rachel took his arm in a firm grasp. "I'm going to take you home," she said. "Right now."

"I was not planning to commit suicide, dear." Cory Welsh laughed the warm rich laugh that she had heard so often at Joshua's house. "I will simply go fish. There are a lot of trout waiting for me."

But the undercurrent of pain beneath those words tainted his laugh. Rachel shook her head silently and tightened her grip on the doctor's arm. "Let's not fall in the river, okay? That's all I ask."

"I can't promise anything, my dear." Dr. Welsh began to make his way back down the path, lurching against her. "I haven't been this drunk for a long, long time. Not since the night my wife died, to be precise."

It was a long, slow trip back to where Rachel had parked her truck. Dr. Welsh stumbled against her with every other step, and she had to struggle to keep him on his feet, and keep both of them from falling into the shallow water along the bank. But they made it, finally, just as the dusk was thickening into full dark. Rachel managed to get the doctor into the front seat and clasp the shoulder harness across him. By the time she had turned the truck around, he was snoring stertorously, his head lolling against the back of the seat.

Fortunately, she knew where he lived—in a big square Queen Anne–style house at the top of Fir, only a couple of blocks up from the Van Dorn house. No lights were on in the house as she arrived. Leaving the doctor snoring peacefully in the cab, she climbed the porch steps to try

the door before she woke him up to ask for the keys. The
door swung open to her touch, pushed by a blessed whisper of breeze from the west. The unlocked door didn't
really surprise her. Locked doors were a recent thing. She
groped for a light switch, found two, and switched on
porch light, a pair of floods mounted on the porch eaves,
and the hall light.

She found herself in a hallway, facing the wide stairs
that led up to the second floor. A small Oriental rug added
rich tones of red and purple to the faded ribbon motif of
the wallpaper. Through an archway to her left, she spied
a shadowy clutter of dark wood furniture and magenta
upholstery. Heavy brocade drapes closed the big picture
window. Rachel left the heavy front door standing open.
By the time she had reached the truck again, Dr. Welsh
was awake and groggily fumbling with the door handle.

He thanked her as she helped him make his precarious
way up the porch steps and into the hall. Mumbling, he
started up the stairs, clutching the bannister, his other arm
around her shoulder, but seemingly unaware of her presence. At the top of the stairs, he turned left across the
wide hallway, stumbling into a narrow room at the rear
of the house furnished with a twin bed, plain pine dresser,
and a venerable teak desk cluttered with papers. Sitting
on the edge of the bed, he focused on Rachel as she took
his shoes off, his expression mildly surprised, as if he
wasn't quite sure why she was there.

"Thank you." His voice was polite, without the slightest
trace of a slur. "You have been very kind to me today. I
appreciate it."

"You have been very kind to this town." Rachel set his
muddy shoes by the closet. "You're not being kind to
yourself."

"You remind me of your mother." Dr. Welsh smiled at
her, his silver hair wisping around his face in an unkempt
halo. "That, my dear, is a very real compliment."

"It is. Thank you."

"I was in love with her once." Dr. Welsh began to unbutton his shirt.

"With my mother?"

"With Emily. I took her to the Spring Fling dance in our junior year in high school." He laughed softly. "I spent too much time studying, she said. Funny, that. She married a botany professor at University of Oregon. But he died, and she came back to Blossom, to live at home for a while. I was already married to Martha by then. I don't mean I would have traded Martha for Emily." He looked up at Rachel with faint anxiety, his shirt open to reveal a sleeveless undershirt beneath, never mind the summer heat. "Martha was . . . a friend. I loved her terribly." His voice caught slightly on the word. "I felt sorry for Emily." Taking off his shirt, he folded it neatly, laid it over the headboard, and lay down on his side. "She was never the same after the accident. How could you be the same, knowing that you had killed a mother and child, even if it was by accident?"

"I didn't know Emily was involved in a fatal accident."

"She had been drinking." Dr. Welsh's eyes closed. "Sherry. She always liked sweet sherry."

"How long ago was this?" Rachel asked.

A snore answered her. Rachel stood for a moment, looking down at the doctor. In sleep, the taut lines of his face relaxed and he looked no older than her uncle, except for his silver hair. She worked the light summer spread from beneath his trousered legs and covered him, leaving the bedroom window open. It wasn't too bad in the huge old house—cooler than her apartment. She found a wastebasket beneath the desk and put it near the head of the bed. Just in case. Then she turned out the light and tiptoed out into the upstairs hall. Across from this small room, a door led to a large front bedroom. Rachel peeked in, discovered a big four-poster bed, twin dressers, and a dressing table with mirror, all crafted from bird's-eye maple. A silver-backed set of brushes and a hand mirror lay on a lace doily on the dressing table. As if waiting for a hand to pick them up, run the brush through thick hair. Waiting.

Still tiptoing, Rachel descended the stairs, looking once more into the living room that a woman named Martha had decorated a long time ago. Softly she closed the front door behind her, leaving the hall light on, leaving the outside lights on. She didn't lock the door. The doctor wouldn't approve.

It was late now. She had to be up early, no matter what Gladys recommended. Rachel started the engine but instead of turning off onto her own street, she continued on down the hill into town, across Main, and on down beneath the freeway to the Bread Box.

Joylinn didn't serve dinner, and the Bread Box had been closed for hours, but she would be baking for tomorrow. As Rachel pulled into the parking area, it occurred to her that Joylinn spent most of her waking life at the little café and bakery. And for the first time she thought to wonder if it was only by necessity. Her headlights swept the lot, spotlighting the blue MG parked near the front door. Her mother's car. Rachel pulled in beside it, wondering what brought her mother down here at this hour. Locking the door—a new habit in this town—she made sure the tool box was also locked and went around to the kitchen entrance.

"I had a feeling it was you." Joylinn opened the door at the first rap of her knuckles. "Come on in and join the after-hours coffee klatch. Only you'll have to help glaze muffins. That is, if you want one."

"I'll work. Hi, Mom." She greeted her petite, dark-haired mother, who sat at the big wooden worktable, dipping muffins into a pan of sugary glaze. "So I'm not the only one who sneaks in here for a snack, huh?"

"Actually, I was looking for you, and figured that if you weren't home and you weren't with Jeff, you'd show up here eventually. The pay is good." She gestured at a half-eaten muffin on a plate at her elbow and grinned. "Very good, actually. Hazelnut."

"I guess I really am a creature of habit. Move over, I'm helping." Rachel took an apron from the several hanging on a hook by the door, tied it on, and went to wash her hands in the big steel sink. "Save some of them for me to do."

"Don't worry. There's plenty," Joylinn spoke up breezily. "I got a big order from a caterer over in Hood River. New business." She hummed as she opened the oven door, releasing a wave of heat and sweet baking smells. "So get to work. And Julio's looking for you, too, by the way. He and his girlfriend—what's her name?—were going to Fong's for dinner. He said he'd stop in later."

"Anita," Rachel said. "I'll see if he's still there when I leave. Gee, I'm popular tonight." She dipped one of the tender muffins into the glaze, careful not to let it pull apart as she set it upright on the cooling rack. "How come you were looking for me?" she asked her mother.

"Actually, I didn't start out to look for you." Her mother frowned as she set out another glazed muffin. "I ran into Jeff. He looks awful."

"I know." Sobering, Rachel worked silently for a while. "He's out all night," she said at last. "And not sleeping much. This vandal thing has really gotten to him. Especially since our esteemed editor ran that bit in the paper about how we spent money to hire another officer and they can't even catch a kid. Jeff's taking this pretty personally."

"I'm glad he is." Joylinn shook her head as she set the freshly baked trays of muffins out to cool briefly. "Celia was attacked by this guy last night. Did you hear?"

"Attacked?" Rachel's mother sat up straight. "Oh, my goodness, no, I hadn't heard that. Where?"

"Right down the block from Rachel's apartment." Joylinn looked grim. "She was on her way over to visit that boyfriend of hers. I told her I'd give her a ride next time she didn't have the car. You'd think he'd have picked her up, at least."

"Why? Celia walks everywhere, even when her car's sitting in the lot here." Rachel dipped two more muffins, concentrating on the task. "He just tried to grab her bag is all." Maybe. "Jeff will catch him sooner or later, and believe me, I know he looks awful. There's no way he's going to go easier on himself until he has the guy in jail."

"I'm not blaming you for Jeff, sweetheart." Her mother reached over and put her hand on Rachel's lightly. "I just worry about him. He's one of those people who is never going to take it easy, no matter what. There are a few people like that in this world. Cory Welsh is one of them." She sighed. "They're terribly good at what they do, but they pay a high price for it. So do their families." She gave Rachel a brief pointed look. "You haven't been over there much lately, have you?"

"I was over there for dinner the other night. I talk to him on the phone all the time." Rachel tried not to sound defensive and failed utterly. Maybe her mother had a personal spy satellite? "And he has this big ugly dog he took in. Honestly." The words burst out of her, surprising even her with their knife edge of irritation. "What does he want to keep that thing for? It's vicious."

"Oh, the stray. I heard about that." Rachel's mother eyed her, her expression thoughtful. "I hadn't heard that it's vicious."

"Well, maybe not really," Rachel conceded, but she still couldn't let go of her anger. "It still makes me nervous. I'm not going to hang around over there until he gets rid of it."

"I got a dog from the pound when I was a kid. A little black dog with a curly coat." She smiled a little sadly. "I called him Curley. I don't think he ever really got over being abandoned. He was always afraid, I think, that I was going to go away and leave him. And you know, I finally did. He died the week after I left for college."

"I . . . didn't know." Rachel blinked, because as far as she could recall, her mother had never mentioned a dog.

"Abandonment is a lasting wound," her mother went on slowly. "No matter what the circumstance."

Rachel kept her head down. "You mean Jeff's father leaving, don't you?" Not dying, as her father had done. That wasn't abandonment. He hadn't meant to leave. Stubbornly, she kept her eyes on the muffins in front of her. "So he rescued the dog because they were both abandoned, is that it?"

"I don't know if many things in life are quite that simple." Her mother glanced at her watch. "I really ought to get going," she said. "Poor Joshua is going to think I drove off the road into the river."

"Wonder why he'd worry about that?" Joylinn snickered. "I still think you've got a career on the racing circuit if you ever want it. Here." She handed Deborah a white bakery sack. "These aren't perfect, but they'll taste just fine."

"Ohh, such wages." Deborah peeked inside, inhaling deeply. "Maybe I'll share one with Joshua. If he's very good. Maybe."

"Mom?" Rachel set two more dripping muffins on the rack. "Have you seen Dr. Welsh lately?" she asked.

"Not since our dinner." Her mother looked surprised. "Why?"

"I think . . . he's taking it hard—about that woman dying at the Village. That's all." Her tongue felt clumsy, and she watched her mother's eyes narrow just a hair.

"Maybe I'll drop in and say hi tomorrow. If he's not out fishing." Deborah lifted a hand in farewell. "See you both."

She would check on Dr. Welsh tomorrow. Rachel knew her mother, and hoped that he would repeat what he had told her. Her mother would know what to say. She always did.

"I'm not going to ask," Joylinn said virtuously. "I'm just going to make you work your butt off for carrying on that cryptic little conversation right in front of me."

"It wasn't cryptic," Rachel protested. "I'm just worried about Dr. Welsh is all. Mom's good at getting people to talk to her."

"She is that." Joylinn opened the oven door. "Last batch, dear. And I saved a couple more blems just for you."

It took them less than an hour to finish glazing the muffins and clean up. They left together, each glad of company in the empty parking lot. As Rachel got into her truck, however, Blossom's black-and-white police car pulled into the lot and alongside her truck. Jeff Joylinn waved and honked but didn't stop as she left the lot and turned down the street toward the mooring where she lived on her houseboat.

"I've been looking for you." Jeff got out of the car to lean against her fender, grinning at her. "You're a hard lady to find tonight." He looked exhausted.

"Jeff, you need to sleep." Rachel got out of the truck and put her arms around him. "You can't just keep on like this forever."

His arms tightened briefly around her, hard enough to leave her breathless. Then he released her and moved slightly away. "I know." He leaned down to kiss her lightly and softly on the forehead. "But I can't quit yet. I got that report back on that death at the Village."

"I saw Doc tonight. He said it was poisonous mushrooms." The words tumbled out. "He told me there were *three* murders."

"I hope to hell he didn't tell anyone else."

"I don't think he did." Her voice caught. "Jeff, he was right? Three people?"

"We got an exhumation order after we got the toxicology report back." He let his breath out in a long, slow sigh. "We've been waiting for the results on the other two bodies. I'm on my way over to the director's office right now with a search warrant. Bert is on his way to her apartment in Hood River."

"The director? You think she did it?"

"It looks as if the people who died could have been victims of embezzlement. They were all confused, in the early stages of Alzheimer's. None of them had family looking over their accounts. We've been working on this ever since Madame first called me. We're getting a lot of cooperation from the assistant director, and none whatsoever from Ms. Bellington. It fits." He shook his head. "Theft and then murder to keep it from being discovered. Cold-blooded," he said and his tone was flat. "We're talking about less than twenty thousand dollars, total. Is that the price of three human lives?"

Mute, Rachel shook her head. Twenty thousand dollars? It made sense, but still . . . "I just don't think she could kill anyone," Rachel said slowly. "And for so little."

"Maybe she was simply afraid of discovery, no matter what the amount." Jeff held her close for a long moment, then released her reluctantly. "I need to ask you a favor," he said with uncharacteristic hesitation. "I haven't been home since noon and it's likely to be a long night. Could you go let Ben out for me?"

Ben. Rachel swallowed, her stomach clenching

"Never mind." Jeff hugged her again. "It's okay. He'll be fine. And I'll take him back to the pound in the morning. As soon as they open. I promise."

"No." Rachel drew a deep breath. "I'll go let him out. It's fine. As long as you promise he won't eat me." She managed to make the words sound almost casual.

Jeff looked at her for a moment. "Thanks." He kissed her again, a light brush of his lips, gentle with longing. "I meant it about tomorrow," he said. Then he let go of her, and got into his car. "Be careful," he said. "Remember what I told you."

She had a feeling that Bert hadn't told him about her truck yet. Maybe he wouldn't have asked her to take care of the dog if he had known. Why had she insisted on doing this? He was waiting for her to get into her truck, she realized, and so she slid quickly behind the wheel. She'd go by Fong's, she decided. Find Julio and get him to come with her out to Jeff's. It wouldn't take long. She drove out of the lot with Jeff behind her, and turned eastward toward Fong's. He drove on toward the Village as she turned into the restaurant lot, and she wondered what he would find.

Nothing, she hoped. Jennifer Bellington might be a bitch, but Rachel didn't want her to be a murderer.

Rachel cruised the scatter of cars in the lot. Not too many late-night diners and drinkers here tonight. Most of the trucks and cars were parked near the lounge entrance. Julio's pickup was not among them. She went inside to look for him, but he and Anita must have left.

Feeling suddenly very alone, Rachel went back out to her truck.

With both hands clenched tight on the wheel, she left Fong's and drove up through town, taking the road that curved up above the town, driving slowly and carefully up to Jeff's house.

CHAPTER

11

The drive to Jeff's house up on the rim of the Gorge seemed longer than usual. Dark shadows lurked beneath the trees like skulking dogs. Crossly, Rachel reminded herself that Jeff wouldn't have asked her to do this if the dog was dangerous.

But maybe he would be the last to know, like the parents of child criminals who protest to the end that their child was wonderful and would never ever do anything wrong.

By the time she pulled—slowly—into the graveled parking space in front of Jeff's house, her heart was pounding. Wiping her palms on her jeans, she sat for a few moments, drawing deep breaths of the cooling summer night, listening to crickets and the whisper of the wind through the big cedars that stood beside the small house. No lights were on in the house and there was no sound. Jeff must have expected to be home before dark. Not even the porch light was on, and shadows walked the front of the house. The dog hadn't barked. Maybe it had escaped and was gone. Rachel sighed at her brief spasm of hope. The dog was in there. Silent. Maybe watching her through the window. Waiting.

Rachel hesitated, then thrust the door open and got out. "You are being silly," she announced to the night. "Hi, dog. I'm here to let you out."

Only a horned owl answered, to-whooing softly in the distance. It was such a lonely sound.

"Hey boy, are you in there?" For the life of her, she couldn't remember what Jeff had named it. "So, dog, do you need to go out? Guess what? You get to move out tomorrow, so let's get this over with." Amazingly enough, her voice didn't quaver at all. Standing straight, she marched up the front steps and unlocked the front door. Still no barking. "Some watch dog." She opened the door, tensing in spite of her brave tone.

A black shape thrust against the door, knocking it out of her hand so hard that it banged against the wall. Rachel froze as a huge black muzzle shoved at her, pushing her backward with damp, snuffling violence. Through her brief terror, she realized dimly that the dog's docked-short tail was wriggling a mile a minute and the wet, slobbery thrusts from the big head were . . . a greeting.

"Well, hey, whoa." In spite of herself, Rachel reached down, her hands encountering a dervish of wiggling, excited dog, his cast thumping as he tried to chase his nearly nonexistent tail. "Calm down, for heaven's sake!" Laughing now—more at her own fear than at the dog—she reached inside the door and flipped the light switch. The porch light came on, flooding the planks of the porch and the wide wooden steps with warm welcome light. The dog thumped back and forth in front of her, every tooth gleaming in what even she could recognize as a grin. "All right, come on out and pee, and then you go back in before you wreck that leg, you idiot. Jeff doesn't need any more vet bills." She went down the steps and out into the yard with the dog right on her heels, bumping along valiantly in spite of the cumbersome cast. She waited while he circled the yard, lifting his leg against her tires, propped awkwardly on his casted limb. When he seemed to have finished, he followed her back into the house, straining his way three-legged up the steps, the cast on his front leg banging the riser. Inside he prodded her again with his broad muzzle, looking up hopefully, wagging his entire back end.

"Let me guess." Rachel patted him a little hesitantly. "You're telling me it's dinnertime?" She went into the kitchen, discovering that she possessed a canine shadow. "Jeff didn't say anything about feeding you." She eyed the dog, noticing that in spite of its broad build, she could see the shadow of ribs and the jut of hipbones beneath the rough coat. At least Jeff had given him a bath. "I don't think food is going to hurt you any." She opened cupboards looking for dog food and finally discovered a forty-pound sack stashed in the narrow closet where Jeff stored his cleaning supplies. "Why do I think he wasn't planning on taking you to the pound in the morning?" Shaking her head, Rachel picked up the big salad bowl on the floor next to a pail filled with water and scooped what she hoped was a reasonable amount of kibble into the dish. She recognized the bowl. Jeff had bought it at an old farm sale out near The Dalles. It was painted with cherries, the blue-bordered rim chipped in spots, the glaze yellow with age. "This is a nice bowl, dog." She set the dish of food on the floor. "You need a dog dish."

The dog waited politely until she straightened up, then shoved his face into the bowl and did a credible imitation of a vacuum cleaner. Rachel steeled herself against the heartfelt expression of imminent starvation on his face when he finished, filled his pail with fresh water, and went back to the living room. "I think I'll wait for him, dog," she said as he padded into the room after her. "Ben," she said as he curled up on the rug in front of the sofa. "That's your name, I remember. Ben?"

Ben looked up at her, waggled his pathetic excuse for a tail, then laid his head on his paws with a sigh.

"You are an ugly dog." Rachel reached down and scratched his ears, not hesitant this time. His coat had been clipped short in patches and the healing abrasions made him look as if he suffered from some terrible skin disease. The casted leg stuck out awkwardly. "Why did somebody cut your tail off when you're not a purebred?" she wondered out loud. "I guess you looked like one when you were born. You're really not so bad, are you, Ben?"

He lifted his head to nudge her hand. Smiling, Rachel pulled the afghan from the end of the futon sofa and tucked it around her, curling up against the arm of the sofa. "Wake me up when Jeff gets here," she murmured, her eyelids drooping. A little later she roused enough to feel a warm weight against her side. She groped with a sleepy hand expecting to touch Jeff. She felt thick, soft fur instead. Too comfortable to wake up, she smiled and drifted back into slumber.

Wild barking jolted her from sleep. With a gasp of terror, she bolted upright, blinking in dim light, trying to remember where she was. Not home.

"Knock it off, you idiot. It's me!"

Jeff's voice. Rachel blinked the sleep from her eyes, remembering, recognizing the familiar furniture. Jeff stood in the doorway, rubbing the dog's ears as he thumped about delightedly, all toothy grin and wriggling backside. "You two made a cute picture, all cuddled up on the sofa." He smiled at her, his eyebrows in a somewhat quizzical arch. "I take it you're not so scared of Ben anymore?"

"I guess not." Rachel got to her feet and waded past the dog to put her arms around him. He still looked tired, but without the grimness that had marked him in the last few days. "What happened?" She touched the stubble on his jaw.

"Bellington took off." He stroked her face, one hand on the dog's head to quiet him. "We found dried mushrooms hidden in the back of a file drawer. They're off to the lab. When we got to her apartment with a warrant, she was long gone." He shook his head grimly. "Place was a shambles. Looks like she packed a few things anyway. Somebody called her—probably while we were at the Village. My fault."

"The director." In spite of the evidence, his announcement still shocked her a little "I don't know," she said slowly. "It's just . . . hard to believe. And it's not your fault," she said fiercely. "You didn't have enough evidence to arrest her before you found the mushrooms."

Jeff grunted. "It makes ugly sense." He collapsed onto the sofa with a sigh, fending off Ben's efforts to lick his face. "Enough, dog! I am tired," he said with feeling. "We'll get her. She's not going to get too far. When this is all over, can you take a few days off?" He tugged her gently down beside him. "I feel like we've barely spoken to each other for the last week. Maybe we could go out to Steen's Mountain and camp for a few days? Take a little time to remember that we're getting married in a couple of months?"

"I'm not about to forget that." Rachel settled herself against him. "Not for a moment. We've both been under a lot of stress this last week." She looked up at him from the corner of her eye. "I'm going to go buy Ben a real food bowl tomorrow," she said. "And a collar and leash. You don't have *anything* for him, do you?"

He gave her a slow smile, his eyes filled with warmth, and a thanks that didn't need to be spoken out loud. "You're sure?" he said.

"He really is a nice dog." Rachel reached to scratch the dog's broad head, which caused him to instantly shift it from Jeff's thigh to hers.

"You're easy, dog," Jeff said, and laughed.

He had wanted this dog a lot. And he would have taken him to the animal shelter tomorrow, just as he'd promised. Rachel sighed, because Ben really was *big*. "Welcome to the family, Ben," she said, earning herself a damp grin from Ben.

"You scared me a little tonight." Jeff touched her cheek gently. "I went by the apartment when I got done and you weren't there. I . . ." He paused, and looked away. "I sure was relieved to find your truck parked here," he said after a moment. "I worry about you. Like I told you . . . I've put you at risk. Because of my job." He lifted her chin gently, so that she met his eyes. "What about moving in here now? At least I'll know you're safe when I wake up in the middle of the night."

"With Ben to protect me?" She gave him a mischievous smile. "Or are you promising to quit staying out all night looking for our vandal?"

"We'll catch him. And Ben did a pretty good imitation of a watch dog when I opened the door just now. Not that I was all that quiet coming in here, you lazy mutt." He grinned, although a shadow lurked in his eyes. "Is that a yes? Or would it upset your aunt and uncle too much?"

"You didn't ask if it would upset my mother," Rachel said archly. "Nothing is going to upset Uncle Jack more than my refusing to run the orchard for him. As to my aunt . . ." She pursed her lips thoughtfully. "She's about as sharp as my mother, for all she pretends otherwise. How else could she have lived with Uncle Jack all these years? No, it's Peter I worry about. How he and Ben will get along."

"I think he'll run Ben out of the house." Jeff patted the dog. "Mrs. Frey is going to be glad to have him out from under her chickadee feeder."

"No, she won't. She'll miss him." Rachel took his face in her hands, her heart aching for the fatigue she saw there. "I'll pick up some things in the morning. Then I'll talk to Mrs. Frey. We haven't really discussed my moving out, although she knows I'm going to."

"Thank you," he said and kissed her. His arms slid around her, and the kiss deepened.

Ben barked and gave them each a sharp prod from his nose, his ears up, tail stub wagging.

"You weren't invited to this party. Out, dog." Jeff laughed and untangled himself from Rachel. "You can have the sofa, big guy. Three's a crowd."

They shut the bedroom door in Ben's disappointed face, but after a scratch or two, he didn't bother them anymore. Through the window, Rachel could see the first telltale gray in the eastern sky. Jeff wasn't going to get any sleep tonight either, she thought. Somehow, she didn't think it bothered him much at the moment.

She was right.

CHAPTER
12

It was nearly midmorning by the time Rachel pulled into the parking area beside Mrs. Frey's house. Jeff had left early. He had been gone when the alarm had wakened her that morning, and she wondered if he had slept at all. He had left her a pot of coffee and a note, saying that she looked too peaceful to waken. Rachel had called to ask Mrs. Frey to tell Spider she'd be late. There had been no answer, and Mrs. Frey didn't have an answering machine. She hoped Spider had waited, but saw no sign of him as she parked beside Mrs. Frey's car and turned off the ignition.

Peter was sitting on the steps giving her a reproachful glare. "You got fed last night, cat," she informed him. "You're not starving. I'll let you in in a minute." She peeked around the corner of the house and halted.

Spider and Mrs. Frey were huddled over one of her precious roses, arguing. Not *fighting* arguing, but arguing with the amiability of friends. Spider pointed to branches, Mrs. Frey shook her head vigorously, so that the dried seed pods decorating today's garden hat clacked and clattered.

"I grant you it might work," Rachel overheard her landlady announce as she tiptoed closer. "On one of those vigorous floribundas. But you take a less-than-vigorous hybrid tea that needs nursing along and it's just going to sulk. You won't get a blossom off it, pruning it like that."

"You try it and see." Spider tossed his head. "You try it on that lavender cultivar over there at the north end of the bed. I mean, you want a spindly tea that needs nursing, you can't beat the lavenders. You try it. If you don't get better bloom next year, I'll buy you any cultivar you want."

"Done, young man. I will go get my camera and take a picture of it right now. And one year from now, after you have pruned it your way, I will take another picture. And we will find an objective judge to decide which version is better. I'm going to want the new ARS rose of the year, you know. Just to see if I like it." Mrs. Frey thrust out one gloved, dirt-stained hand. "And if you think you can weasel out of paying by leaving town, just you forget it. You can find anyone these days."

"You think so, huh?"

"More than you guess, boy. So you be here to pay for my new rose when you lose."

"I'm not going to lose."

"We'll see." She tossed her head in a gesture that was so much like Spider's that Rachel barely stifled a laugh.

"Hey, look who finally showed up." Spider waved.

Mrs. Frey turned, her seed pods clacking. "I fed Peter this morning. So he wouldn't breakfast on my chickadees."

"So what is this discussion all about?" Fascinated, Rachel looked from one to the other. "This is a bit of a turnaround in attitude, isn't it?"

"I don't know what you mean." Mrs. Frey straightened her hat with enormous dignity. "We were just discussing pruning techniques for roses. John has some rather shaky theories . . ."

"Shaky my . . . eye!"

"Shaky theories about pruning, but we've made a small wager on the outcome of a little experiment. I shall enjoy owning a new rose at its first offering."

"Not a chance, lady." Spider rolled his eyes. "Say, what do I get out of this when I win?"

"Enormous satisfaction, I would assume," she said acerbically.

John? John Tranh was Spider's legal name, but he never told anyone that. No one called him John except his mother, as far as she knew. Rachel peered at the twosome, feeling as if she had fallen asleep in one universe and awakened in another. "Uh, shall we go to work?" she asked lamely.

"I figure we're a little late." Spider gave her a look as he headed toward the truck. "Hope the Dragon Lady doesn't catch us sneaking in."

"She won't bother us," Rachel said with a certainty that earned her a skeptical look from Spider. "We'll stay a little late tonight. Since we're getting a late start."

"I want overtime." He managed a credible straight face.

"How about a free lunch instead? Let's get going. So how are your evenings at Ricki's house?" she asked casually as they left Blossom and headed east toward the Village.

"Nice," he said. "Ricki wasn't there last night. She had to work an extra shift because somebody got sick." He shrugged. "Gus and I worked on some of his bonsai. He has some really neat trees that he started when he was real young. There's one maple that's really cool. He said it turns color in the fall."

It occurred to Rachel that maybe it wasn't just Ricki who enticed Spider over there in the evenings after all. "Mr. Van Dorn is a mushroom expert, isn't he?"

"Yeah." Spider nodded. "He's gonna teach me to hunt for the buyers this fall, remember? Why?"

"I just wondered. Have you had breakfast?" Rachel changed the subject, thinking that Jeff might need some information on gallerinas and where to find them.

Spider told her that Gus had made them pancakes, and the conversation languished. Rachel kept thinking about the director's arrest, and the mushrooms found in a file drawer. She wondered what Harris would make of this when he found out.

At the Village, they went right to work. To her vast relief, the system was undamaged. The saboteur seemed to be content with a single act of destruction. They could start on the soil amendments, and begin readying the beds for planting. Things were looking up, and a few high clouds from the west even promised a somewhat cooler day for working. However, they had barely begun when a couple of aids interrupted them, hurrying down the path from the Village. Rachel recognized Jason. "Hi." She straightened, leaning on her digging fork as he left his companion and hurried over. "What's up?"

"Oh, I'm on break, and I figured I'd see how things were shaping up down here." His eyes wandered over the piles of compost Spider had dumped into the nascent beds. "You're really coming along, huh? No more sabotage?" He smiled at her. "I've been keeping a close eye out when you're not here. Haven't seen anyone."

"Thanks." Rachel went to the truck to get herself some water.

"So have you heard the news?" Jason followed her, leaning one elbow against the side of the truck. "About our esteemed director?"

"No." Rachel gave him an innocent look, although her stomach contracted slightly. "What news is that?"

"I guess she skipped. The police searched her office last night." He spoke in a hushed tone, but his eyes sparkled with excitement. "I hear that they found the mushrooms she used right in her desk. She poisoned three people. Three! I mean, can you believe it?"

Rachel straightened, not having to fake her surprise. "Where did you hear this?" she asked sharply. "When did this happen?"

"Last night, like I said." Jason shrugged. "It's just going around. Noble—the assistant—took over, and she's sure not talking, but she looks pretty smug." He rolled his eyes. "She hates Bellington. Always has. I should give Ricki a call. She was on late shift last night. Maybe she heard something."

"What's up?" Spider pushed the rumbling wheelbarrow up, on his way for the next load of compost. "What's this about murder?"

"You have sharp ears," Rachel murmured. Frowning, she listened to Jason recite the news over again.

"You know," he told them as he finished this second recital, "I could believe that the assistant did it and framed Bellington. Almost, anyway." He laughed, excused himself, and hurried back up to the main building. Spider's eyes were glittering.

"Mushrooms!" He nodded. "What a bitch. Sorry." He wasn't at all repentant. "You knew already," he accused. "Jeff told you. That's why you asked about Gus, huh?"

"Well, yeah." She put her water cup away. "Let's get back to work."

"He knows about edible mushrooms, but I don't know about poisonous ones. Except how not to pick 'em." He scowled thoughtfully. "You could check the Internet."

That was a thought.

"So the Dragon Lady did it. Or do you think Jason meant it—about her assistant framing her?"

"He was kidding." Rachel picked up her fork. "The woman got demoted. You don't kill three people for that." But Joylinn had said something about her, too. "Let's get back to work, okay?"

"More company." Spider jerked his head toward the path. "I bet the place is buzzing up there. All right, all right, I'm working." Doing a credible job of visibly suffering, he hefted the handles of the wheelbarrow and trundled it off.

Harris was wheeling crisply down the concrete path. Rachel sighed and set her digging fork aside. So much for working hard today. "Hi," she said as he approached.

"Come take a walk with me." His expression was grim, and he wheeled his chair around without waiting for her reply, heading down for the sterile pond.

Rachel followed, having to stretch her legs to keep up with the powerful thrusts of his muscular arms. He kept up the pace, neither looking back nor speaking, until they had reached the barren little overlook above the naked pond. It had probably been intended to be shaded by trees, but the aborted landscaping had left nothing but a bare stone bench on a narrow terrace, without shelter from the summer sun. In spite of the wispy high clouds, the sun beat down mercilessly on the pale gravel of the terrace, and again today, there was no breeze at all. Rachel pulled her bandanna from her pocket and blotted the sweat from her face. Harris seemed unaffected by the heat. Certainly, nobody was capable of eavesdropping at this barren site. Rachel collapsed onto the bench, wishing she'd brought some water with her.

"Everybody seems to know that the director took off last night," she said as she fanned herself with the bandanna. It didn't help.

"You noticed." Harris's grim expression didn't alter. "It's like a kicked beehive up there." He jerked his head toward the buildings. "According to rumor, our esteemed director was embezzling from the more confused residents, and killed the three who found her out, using poisonous mushrooms to do so. Pretty impressive accuracy, considering that Jeff showed up here pretty late last night, and he sure wasn't explaining the situation to anyone." He cocked his head. "All I actually know is that she hasn't been here today, and that Jeff was apparently here in the early hours of the morning. Aside from those two facts, the rest is gossip."

She should admit to nothing, give nothing away unless she checked with Jeff.

"Jeff found mushrooms and Bellington took off," is what came out of her mouth instead. "How did everybody find out?"

"That, my dear, is an excellent question," Harris said dryly. He spun his chair abruptly so that he looked down at the surface of the still, murky pond. "Possibly Jeff planted the rumors for a reason." He looked back over her shoulder at her, nodded as Rachel shook her head.

"I didn't think so. It would be a stupid move." He let his breath out in a slow sigh. "I've spent the morning trying to pin down the source of all these so-very-accurate rumors. They *are* accurate, right?" He smiled grimly at Rachel's nod. "Whoever started them was clever. A resident heard it from an aid, who heard it from a resident, who heard it from an aid. It's like the snake that eats its own tail. Very nice job, I must say."

"Why?" Rachel got up to squat in front of Harris on the hot gravel. He wasn't angry, she realized. He was afraid. "Why start the rumors?"

"I have already heard ten different eyewitness accounts of our director's suspicious activities. By tomorrow, you'll have at least three people who will swear in court that they saw her delivering mushroom omelettes to our victims on the sly. Although I doubt that there's any question about the embezzlement," he said thoughtfully. "Mrs. Noble, her assistant, has been checking accounts. I gather that she has found quite a few . . . discrepancies."

"I hear she's being very helpful," Rachel said slowly.

"Oh, yes." Harris gave her a grim smile. "You heard right. She is delighted. She is not a fan of our esteemed director. Jennifer was very open about her opinion of Ms. Noble's performance. Our director is very clever in a sly, petty sort of way." Harris stared thoughtfully down at the still, dirty-looking pond. "I can see her firing you, hiring somebody cheaper, and pocketing the difference. I can see her overcharging the forgetful here—and there are a number of them—and keeping a double set of books. But . . ." He frowned, lifting his eyes to meet Rachel's. "To kill for that kind of money? How much can she have slipped past people here? Enough to kill for? And she does not have easy access to individuals. She holds the public eye when she is here. If she offered a nice plate of mushroom lasagna to someone, they would make sure their friends knew that they'd been singled out for attention. She would have a hard time being invisible here. She doesn't exactly mingle."

"Who does mingle?" Rachel asked softly. "And why kill these three people?"

"The person who started the rumors is the *who*." Harris nodded sharply. "Sooner or later I'll be able to triangulate the origin. Whoever started them is either a resident or an employee here. These stories went around too fast to have begun from an outside source. As to the *why* . . ." He shrugged, his expression cold. "Serial killer? Mercy killing? There are a lot of reasons for murder, I've found."

"What does Madame think?" Rachel asked. Harris gave her a long look, and the glint of fear in his eyes was clearly visible now.

"She believes that Bellington is a murderess as well as a thief." He held Rachel's gaze, his gray eyes murky with sudden shadow. "I agree with her." He enunciated each word clearly. "If Jennifer Bellington did not commit these crimes, then someone else here did. As long as Anne-Marie believes in our director's guilt, she is safe. Do you understand me?"

"Yes," Rachel said in a small voice. "I'm not about to say anything otherwise in front of her, Harris. I promise."

"I was not threatening you." Harris's expression softened, and he reached out to take her hand. "You speak the truth that you believe in." He smiled at her, his weathered face crinkling, the shadow banished from his eyes. "That's a rare and admirable thing. But sometimes it's dangerous. For you and for the ones you love."

"I'll watch what I say," Rachel murmured as he released her hand. He was talking about Jeff, not just Madame. About her life with him. And she hadn't thought about it before this last week—how his job would change her—would have to change her. "I won't say anything," she said. "And I'll remember."

"Good." He lifted her hand and bent his head to kiss the back of it, the way he often kissed Madame's hand. Then he released her, smiling, as if their conversation had been of nothing more important than her choice of plantings for the overlook here. "Tell Jeff that if I find anything out, I'll let him know immediately. I have his cell phone number."

"I will."

Harris spun his chair deftly and together they crossed the slope to the site where Spider was still wheeling compost into the new beds. There he gave her a terse nod, and headed back up the sun-baked path toward the buildings.

"So what was that all about?" Spider hurried up, his eyes full of surmise.

"Nothing." Rachel poured herself another mug full of water.

"There was a murder last night. Ricki told me. She just got here. She said she'd heard that they've already dug up two people who died here last year, and sure enough, they'd been poisoned. By mushrooms. *Which* Jeff found in the Dragon Lady's office."

"Harris told me." Rachel drank her water. "I guess it's a sure thing all right."

Spider was studying her face, his eyes narrowed. "I bet the Dragon Lady didn't do it. Why would she leave the mushrooms in her office? I bet it was one of the aids. And they framed Dragon Lady. Because she *was* stealing."

"I think you've been watching too much TV." Rachel tried for nonchalance, although Spider's guesses frightened her. Feigning indifference, she stowed her empty cup.

"Okay. Sure." Spider shrugged. "Whatever. And I guess I'd better get back to work. Ricki was really pissed, too. I guess that jerk showed up out here last night—the one who busted into your truck. He broke the window on her car and stole her jacket. She was really ticked about that."

So maybe the vandal had been the one to sabotage the irrigation lines after all. "I'm sorry for Ricki," Rachel said, and grabbed her second wheelbarrow, relieved to be able to put an end to the conversation. If Harris was right—if the director wasn't the murderer—Spider's curiosity could be seriously dangerous.

They worked hard until noon, and nobody else came down to interrupt them. Rachel told Spider that they'd go buy lunch at the convenience store down the road toward Hood River. She had no intention of showing up in the dining room where Madame could quiz her about Jeff and the director. If Spider had guessed that she was holding back, Madame would know in an instant. But as they were washing up, who should come marching down the path but Madame, her stride purposeful, her cane tapping a steady counterpoint to her brisk gait, dressed in a two-piece dress of summery printed cotton.

Rachel groaned to herself.

"I have come to invite you to lunch," Madame said as she reached them.

"Um. I can't." Rachel fumbled for an easy, confident manner and failed utterly. "I need to feed Spider, and—"

"Monsieur Spider will be pleased to keep Harris company, I am sure." Madame turned to Spider with an iron smile that brooked no argument. "Perhaps you would convey my regrets to him, and tell him that I found myself in need of a particular book that has arrived at the bookstore in Hood River. So I seized the opportunity to invite Mademoiselle to lunch so that I might bribe her to drive me to the bookstore." Her smile softened into charm. "I have already told your friend Ricki that you are my guest today. She was quite pleased. Perhaps she will join you. Harris will merely believe that I wish to hear the latest details of last night's excitement."

He certainly would. And he'd worry. For good reason. Rachel stifled a groan. Spider was looking at her questioningly. "I really can't take the time," she began, but Madame cut her off with a quick hand on her arm.

"Rachel, I am asking you to do this for me." She spoke quietly, her eyes on Rachel's face. "It is important. Please."

Madame commanded. She did not beg. Rachel found herself at a loss for words. "All right," she said, wishing she could tell Spider to reassure Harris. "You'll have to ride in my truck, I'm afraid."

"I will manage," Madame said with a small smile. "I'm sure I will survive the effort." Her smile revealed a dimple at the corner of her mouth. "You do not, after all, drive like your mother."

"No, I don't." Rachel nodded at Spider. "You don't mind having lunch with Harris, do you?"

"I'll survive." Spider's eyes gleamed.

Rachel wondered if he was thinking of Ricki, or of the opportunity to pump Harris about the murder. If the latter, he was about to learn a few things about Harris. "Well, let's go get your book," she told Madame.

Having prepared herself for questions about the murder, Madame's silence during the short drive into downtown Hood River filled Rachel with equal parts of relief and unease. Madame stared out the window at the slope of the Gorge, her expression preoccupied as rows of pear trees marched past, laden with ripening fruit. Downtown Hood River was busy on this sunny summer day, full of tourists and sail boarders. Cars lined the sidewalk in front of the brewery and brightly dressed families strolled the sidewalks. Rachel was lucky enough to spot a park on Oak Street, just around the corner from Waucoma Books. Madame really did pick up a book at the bookstore, greeting the young owner with the familiarity of a regular client. The book had a French title. "The author is from Quebec," Madame told her as she tucked the wrapped book beneath her arm. "This is her second work. I enjoy her voice. It is quite fresh." They had reached the corner of Oak, and Madame nodded at an iron-railed stairway that descended to a doorway below the street level. "Would you wish to lunch here?" she asked Rachel. "They have an excellent house soup and the food is very fresh, very well prepared. A young husband and wife own it. She does the cooking, I believe."

"Certainly," Rachel said absently, still trying to figure out the reason for this invitation. She accompanied Madame down to the entrance and into the small and intimate North Oak Brasserie. It had been decorated informally, with brown paper covering the woven green tablecloths and samples of customer art adorning the walls. Grape vines twined support pillars, and candles glowed in glasses on each table.

Harris would not be able to deal with the stairs, Rachel realized, and wondered if Madame had chosen this restaurant in order to assure herself that he would not unexpectedly join them. Her unease increasing, she sat down at one of the small tables across from Madame.

"The house soup is of Brie and roasted garlic," Madame informed her. "And the salad offerings are all excellent. They believe in using interesting greens for salad, instead of that terrible iceberg lettuce."

They gave their orders to the young waitress who arrived at their table. Madame requested a glass of local Pinot Noir, but Rachel stuck with iced tea. "Wine, hot sun, and using a spade don't mix," she informed Madame.

"You must never move to Provence, then," Madame informed her with a twinkling smile. "Everyone drinks wine with their lunch. How not, when you are surrounded by grapes?"

Their soup came, and their salads. Rachel was delighted with the creamy soup rich with cheese and mellow roasted garlic. She dipped a chunk of baguette into the saucer of olive oil that the waitress had set on the table, and decided that she wasn't about to worry about calories today. Her salad lived up to the soup, full of feta, pine nuts, sweet tomatoes, and kalamata olives. They did indeed use tender young greens instead of iceberg lettuce. Madame picked at her Caesar salad and nibbled her bread before setting her folk down. She leaned forward and stroked the cane that was resting against the table beside her. Its rich wood gleamed like satin beneath her long, elegant fingers.

"Harris carved and polished this for me. A gift of labor and love is a precious thing." She straightened. "I wish to speak to you of marriage."

Rachel set her fork down, surprised. "What about marriage?"

"Harris wishes to marry me."

"Congratulations." Rachel forked up a bit of curly endive, not sure where this conversation was going. "I don't think anyone will be too surprised. You and Harris make a wonderful couple."

"I said no." Madame lifted her glass of wine, and peered into its ruby depths. Deliberately she took a sip and set the glass down.

"Why?" Rachel finally managed to get the word out. "You seem so . . . in love."

"Of course." Madame's eyebrows rose slightly. "I have never loved anyone in my life in the way I love Harris. That is not the issue."

"Your age?" Rachel leaned forward, her food forgotten. "Is that it?"

"Let me tell you of my life." Madame sipped more wine, her eyes alive with memory. "I was sixteen when I married. My husband had a dairy. It was his father's. Later, we had an orchard. I raised six children. I worked very hard. In those days, everyone who lived by the soil worked very hard." She swirled her glass, watching the red wine climb the crystal curve of the bowl. "I was a faithful wife to the day that my husband died. And not once, not for one day, was I ever anything but Monsieur DeRocher's wife. Not even to him." She set her glass down and raised her eyes to meet Rachel's. "Do you understand?" she asked quietly.

Rachel looked away, remembering the dark years after her father died, when her mother had seemed to have vanished with him. "I think it's something like that that scared me," she said slowly. "About getting married. I think we're talking about the same thing." Sort of.

Madame was nodding. "And now?" she asked gently. "You are getting married. Have you changed what you think? I cannot see you as wife only."

"I don't think I can be wife only." Rachel drew a deep breath, realizing that these were things she had been thinking about for a long time. Only she hadn't thought about them in so many words. And she hadn't uttered them out loud—not even to her mother. Especially not to her mother. "Jeff . . . knows this. He . . . has said it. That I am myself. I don't . . . belong to him. Sometimes he hates it. Sometimes he loves it. Is that what you mean?"

Madame frowned, her expression gravely thoughtful. "Perhaps you are more fortunate than you know." She shook her head. "I cannot see you as anything other than who you are. That is why I am having this conversation with you."

"But you aren't going to be anyone but yourself either," Rachel burst out. "How could you be? And Harris doesn't want that. He's in love with you. He's not looking for a wife to raise children, milk cows, and cook meals for him."

"Well put." Madame laughed, humor twinkling in her eyes. "He is not. But he can have everything he wants without the ceremony. Why does he want that? I do not understand."

"I think . . . maybe . . . he needs you to say it out loud. For everyone. What you are to each other." Rachel groped for words, not sure that this had anything to do at all, really, with what Harris might be thinking. "I think he's afraid of losing you." She thought of the fear in his eyes this afternoon—fear for Madame. "Maybe that's it."

"Marriage will not save me from death." Madame laughed and picked up her fork again. "But then, I am not ready to die yet. Perhaps you are right, and for him it is like a magic spell, to make our days together last longer. He told me that life is too short. Sometimes he is such a little boy." Her smile filled her eyes with warmth.

"So you'll marry him?" Rachel drank the last of her iced tea.

Madame's smile faded, and she shook her head. "There is no need. I will make him understand." But she looked faintly troubled as she folded her napkin and laid it neatly on the table beside her plate.

She insisted on paying for the lunch, and chatted pleasantly about the job and Rachel's plant choices for the garden as they drove back to the Village. Madame's mind wasn't really on the conversation, Rachel reflected as she turned off onto the Village's winding driveway. But at least it kept her from probing about the director and the murder. When Rachel pulled up in front of the main doors, she caught a glimpse of a wheelchair inside the lobby. Harris. Worried that Rachel had revealed his doubts about the murderer's identity.

"Ah, la." Madame nodded as she climbed gracefully down from the cab of the truck, politely acknowledging but not really needing Rachel's assistance. "He worries so. I cannot even eat lunch with a friend without his worry." She waved to Rachel and walked lightly to the door where he waited, her cane seemingly more an accessory than a necessity.

They put in a good afternoon, and Rachel called it quits promptly at five. Harvey Glisan had showed up with his truck full of the rock she'd ordered for the rock garden. He backed the big truck effortlessly, dumping the rock precisely where he wanted it. His three-year-old granddaughter rode with him, dressed in a frilly pink blouse and small overalls, perched regally on the truck's big seat. She beamed at Rachel and waved. "My daughter's working part time," Harvey explained as he latched the dump truck's rear gate. "They're saving for a house. Katy's gonna take over for me one day, aren't you, sweetie?"

The child grinned, her blue eyes sparkling.

"So how was lunch with Harris?" Rachel asked as she drove Spider back to her apartment to use her shower.

"He's cool." Spider bestowed the accolade with dignity. "Smart guy. You can't get anything past him. Too bad he got shot. I bet he was a good detective."

"I think he was." She pulled over at the foot of Mrs. Frey's driveway. "I'm going to head out to Rhinehoffer's," she told him. "I'll see you later. Feed Peter for me, will you?"

"He'd kill me if I didn't. I'll be over at Gus's." Spider hopped out. "See you later."

Rachel drove through town and on out to Rhinehoffer's small nursery. It was doing well, offering specialty items and native plants to upscale Portland landscapers mostly. Daren had been talking about getting into retail catalog sales and maybe even doing the big home and garden show in Portland. Fortunately, she had made her selections for the Village early. They were all in stock, waiting for her. Daren was very nice about holding stuff for her, even in the summer like this.

Daren Rhinehoffer was glad to see her, if too busy to visit much. Iko, his wife, was in Japan visiting her parents. Although this wasn't a tremendously busy time of year for sales, the watering and plant care for their extensive specialty nursery was a big job for a single person. But he showed her where he'd put the plants she had picked out—native currants, tall blue and red elderberries, staghorn sumac for color, groundcovers of lingonberry and wintergreen, salal and various varieties of Mahonia, as well as witchhazels, red-twig dogwood, and hellebores for winter color. Any resident could eat these plants and not suffer.

She helped Daren with some of the watering and chatted with him about the new cultivars of Mahonia coming from England, so it was after six by the time she left the nursery and drove back through town. As she drove down Main, she saw Spider coming out of the public library. Surprised, she pulled over to the curb, tapping the horn to get his attention. He actually jumped and gave her a brief, guilty glance, as if she'd caught him stealing apples from a neighbor's tree. Then he straightened, and strolled over, his manner now as casual as any teenager on the street.

"Hey, what's up?" He leaned in the open passenger-side window.

"Want a ride?"

"I'm just heading back to Mrs. Frey's house. Sure. I'll save myself three blocks." He slid into the front seat with a sigh.

"So didn't they let you take out any books?" Rachel pulled back onto Main, signaling for the turn onto her street. "You can give them my address as a residence."

Spider gave her a brief, blank look, then shrugged. "Oh, I got a card already. I just didn't find anything I wanted to take out."

He said it a little too casually. Rachel sneaked another look at him, wondering what he thought he had to cover up here. She certainly wasn't going to give him grief for spending time at the library. And she knew both the librarians—had known them since she'd gotten her own library card in grade school. If he'd been up to anything, Mrs. Fullerton or Mrs. Montgomery would make sure that she knew about it. Rachel suppressed a smile. Spider had a lot to learn about small towns and personal privacy.

As they parked in the driveway, Mrs. Frey emerged, a purposeful expression on her face. Rachel's heart sank and she wondered just what Spider had done this time.

"Dinner's about ready, John." She nodded at Spider. "You just have time to wash up. I put some clean towels in the bathroom for you. They're the blue ones. The green ones are mine."

"Yes, ma'am," Spider said meekly.

"He's renting the downstairs bedroom from me." Mrs. Frey answered Rachel's blank look. "It's empty. Why not? I figure you'll leave him enough time to do a little garden work for me as payment. Meals are part of the deal. Move it, boy. Chicken-fried steak doesn't hold well." She tossed her gray head and vanished into the house.

Wordless, Rachel looked at Spider. Who shrugged.

"She said I could rent the room for six hours of work a week," he said. "I have to be in by ten but she threw in dinner." He shrugged again. "Why not?"

How things had changed. Mrs. Frey continued to surprise her. She went upstairs to check her machine and let Peter out for the night. Locking the door behind her, she realized that tomorrow she'd have to tell Mrs. Frey that she would be sleeping at Jeff's from now on. She had enjoyed her quirky landlady. She would miss living here.

It was full dark, and she drove over to City Hall instead of walking, searching the quiet streets for any sign of a lurker. She saw nothing, although she passed Bert Stanfield out on patrol in the Blossom car. His son wasn't with him tonight. Sure enough, Jeff was at his desk, working on some kind of paperwork. "You need a night off," she said as he looked up. She tilted her head, studying him. He had lost weight. Jeff did not need to lose weight. She sighed. "You definitely need a night off. Will you take it, please? Let's eat dinner at Fong's, go home, and go to bed early."

He was about to say no, but he hesitated, and grinned crookedly. "You're right. I admit it. I'm tired. And it doesn't seem to matter how many people we put out on the street. Maybe I'd make better decisions with a little more sleep." He rubbed his hand across his face and gave her a rueful smile. "Let me call Bert and tell him. Maybe he'll get lucky tonight. I'm not kidding about that guy having telepathy."

She waited in the hall while he phoned Bert on his cell phone, thinking about what Harris had told her. Not tonight, she decided firmly. She was not going to say another word about police business tonight. Not one.

CHAPTER

13

Rachel woke early and left Jeff sleeping, letting the enthusiastic Ben out, then warning him sternly not to wake Jeff. It was a sign of how exhausted he was that he didn't wake as she moved quietly around the small house. Normally, he was a hair-trigger sleeper, awake at the slightest noise. His alarm was set, she reasoned. No point in depriving him of any precious sleep. She'd tell him about Harris's suspicions later. Or Harris himself would probably call. She drove into Blossom, stopping at the not-yet-opened Bread Box for coffee, because she hadn't wanted to grind the beans at the house and risk waking Jeff. She rapped on the glass window in front, squinting through the fogged pane.

Joylinn pulled the door open, releasing a fragrant wave of yeasty baking scents that made Rachel's stomach growl. "What has you wandering at this hour?"

"I didn't want to wake Jeff this morning." She came inside, breathing deeply. "There have to be calories in these smells."

"Oh, I can provide a few calories, never fear. I've got a pan of pecan rolls coming out of the oven in a minute." She handed Rachel a white mug. "Coffee's on the stand. And I've got some cinnamon rolls already out, if you don't want to wait for a pecan roll."

"I'll wait, thank you very much!" Rachel looked around the café. She wasn't the only early riser waiting for the pecan rolls. Gus Van Dorn raised his own coffee mug in a smiling salute from a corner table. Rachel carried her coffee over to his table. "I've been hearing about your great pancakes. You impressed Spider."

"I only do that kind of thing when I have company. Ricki's not a breakfast eater, so I come down here a lot." He nodded at the other chair. "Spider told me somebody ruined your irrigation pipe. I'm sorry. That kind of thing is new around here." He shook his head. "Wrecking something just to wreck it—that's a city thing. I guess we're on our way to becoming a city, eh?"

"I hope that's not the definition of a city." Rachel sat down across from him, resting her elbows on the table as she sipped Joylinn's strong Viennese Roast coffee. "I think our mayor would disagree with you anyway."

"Probably." Gus smiled gently, his weathered face haloed by his wispy white hair. "I'm glad Spider found a place to live, but I must say I'm sorry, too. I'd have been happy to have him move in. There's a kid who gives you hope for the next generation. I hope he keeps on stopping by."

"I don't think you have to worry about that." Rachel smiled. "I thought at first that it was Ricki who attracted him, but I don't think she's the whole story. Not anymore."

"Ricki." Gus sighed. "She's . . . we'll . . . let's say she's real friendly to everybody, and some folk take it too serious." He shook his head. "But your boy's got his head on straighter than a lot. That's a bright kid."

"Wild about mushrooms, too." Rachel laughed. "He'll drag you all over the woods come fall."

"Yeah, he's interested all right." Gus nodded thoughtfully. "I knew a local kid once who reminded me a lot of Spider. Real bright boy. I was doing a lot of mushroom hunting in those days. It wasn't a big thing yet—mostly folk gathered for their own table. I used to sell to a couple of fancy Portland chefs. It was kind of a private arrangement, but they paid good money, and it was a nice little bit of extra income." His eyes held a look of old and familiar sorrow. "I'd just retired, and we'd moved back here. Melinda had always wanted to come back. I met her in Portland, back when I was working for the Franks. She grew up on an orchard east of here and always missed the country. So when the back really started to trouble me, and I retired, we found this house, and I worked around here until she died." He shook his head, a well-worn look of grief fading into simple nostalgia. "Picking mushrooms in the spring and fall kind of helped round out the social security check later on." He shrugged, smiling. "Like Spider, Jerry turned into my shadow. I felt sorry for the boy. His dad and mom had divorced and he and his little brother lived with her. Things were tough for them. I used to pay him to help me with the mushrooming. He was worse off than me, that's for sure. And he had a sharp eye, that boy. Smart, too. Always asking what each one was, taking spore prints and looking 'em up if I didn't know. I was learning from *him* after a while." He chuckled. "Yeah, Spider reminds me of him a lot."

"What happened to him?" she asked.

"I don't know." A shadow crossed Gus's face. "I feel bad about that. His mother and little brother got killed in an accident and his dad showed up to take him. He'd just turned thirteen, I remember. Jerry came to me that night— when his dad showed up. He asked me to adopt him, told me his dad didn't really want him, was going to leave him with his grandparents. I guess they hadn't liked his mom much. Way he told it, they were hard-line Christian types. Pretty strict." Gus looked away. "I guess I was still kind of hurting from Melinda's being taken so quick like that." He shook his head. "I didn't want anybody in my life right then. I told him I couldn't get between a father and a son, that the state wouldn't let me. But you know . . ." He looked at her, his eyes full of sadness. "I never asked the man. I could have offered to just keep Jerry, you know? I didn't have to adopt him. He might even have gone for that. But I didn't." He shrugged. "Jerry knew I was abandoning him, too, I guess. Anyhow, I never heard from him again. Not one letter, ever. I wondered sometimes what happened to him. He took his mom's death hard, never mind that he was quiet about it. Jeremiah was quiet about everything."

Abandonment, Rachel thought. It was a terrible thing. Glancing at her watch, she rose, picking up her empty cup. "Speaking of Spider, I'd better go pick him up. He'll think I ran off the road."

"Tell him he's invited to dinner, if he's interested. Cory Welsh is coming over tonight, and he'll bring fish. He can find fish willing to bite where nobody else can."

"I'll tell him," Rachel said.

"Don't go yet." Joylinn emerged from the kitchen with a platter of fragrant rolls in one hand and a couple of plates in the other. "These are just cool enough to eat now. At least take a couple for you and Spider." She set the plate on the table.

"Worth getting up for, gal." Gus reached for one of the sticky pecan rolls. "You beat anyone I've ever known for baking."

"You've twisted my arm." Grinning, Rachel took two of the huge rolls, dropping them into the white bakery bag Joylinn held out.

"Take three. Spider's a teenager, remember?" Joylinn selected another and added it to the bag. "Tell Jeff not to be such a stranger, will you? He hasn't been in here in ages. I'm sure not blaming him for that graffiti!"

"I will," Rachel promised, thinking that Jeff was maybe keeping a low profile in town until he caught the vandal.

Thinking about Jeff and the growing outrage over the vandal's continued rampage, Rachel didn't notice the figure lounging against the wall near her truck until she had pulled her keys from her pocket. As the man stepped suddenly toward her, she gasped and recoiled, dropping her keys.

"Julio! You scared me."

"I am sorry." He scooped the keys from the asphalt and handed them to her. "I have tried to find you, but you are never where I look." He smiled. "I knew you would be out soon. So I waited." He fumbled something from his pocket and held it out. "This is yours."

The bead Beck had given her! Rachel's eyes widened as she recognized the intricately carved sphere. The tiny ball inside rattled against the spirals of its cage as she took it onto her palm. "Julio! How wonderful!" Its loss had hurt. Beck invested a bit of his soul in each piece he created. "Where did you find it?" she asked breathlessly.

"Spider told me that it was stolen." Julio shuffled his feet, looking slightly uncomfortable. "I found it. I return it to you." He made as if to leave.

"Wait! Where did you find it?" She put a hand on his arm. "Where was it?"

"At . . . a market. You know." He halted, his expression unhappy. "One that sells old things. Clothes. Tools. Those things."

"A flea market?" Rachel prodded. "Is that what you mean? A junk store? Julio, the thief must have given it to someone, or sold it! Maybe that person saw him!"

Julio was clearly uncomfortable now. "*Señorita,* he is a friend. He . . . sells things. Old things, like I say. He buys them from other people. He does not buy things that are stolen." He pronounced the words clearly and emphatically. "When I see him buy this, I tell my friend that it was stolen. He will not buy from this man, next time he comes with things to sell."

"So this man sells his stolen goods to your friend? He's sold things before?" Jubilant, Rachel nearly danced. "Julio, this is just what Jeff needs."

"No." Alarmed, Julio recoiled, his dark eyes full of worry. "You do not understand. I cannot . . . my friend . . . he will not speak with the police. Do you understand?" "He cannot. I cannot ask him to."

An illegal? Rachel bit her lip. Was that what Julio was delicately telling her? That his friend was in the country illegally, and involving him with police was not something Julio would do? "Julio, will you come talk to Jeff? Please?" She spread her hands. "He's only interested in catching this man." She drew a deep breath. "He attacked Celia, who works here." She nodded at the Bread Box. "It was only a block from my house. Jeff thinks . . . that he believed he was attacking me. Because I'm friends with Jeff."

Julio's face tightened, and he looked away. "I trust Jeff," he said at last. "I will talk to him." But he didn't look happy. "I cannot say that my friend will also talk to him." He shrugged. "I can try."

"Thanks, Julio!" Rachel suppressed a twinge of guilt for using Julio's loyalty as a lever. But this was important, and Jeff was no threat to Julio's friend. "Can you come to City Hall right now? Do you have time?" She glanced at her watch. Jeff should be there by now. She'd have to call Mrs. Frey and have her tell Spider she'd be late. Julio was nodding, his manner still reluctant.

His truck, with its tools neatly racked, was parked near the entrance to the lot. Rachel got into her own truck and pulled out after him as he left the lot and drove back up toward Main Street and City Hall. She went in with him, into the quiet bustle of a business day morning. A copy machine hummed and phones rang as they went through the main lobby to the doorway marked BLOSSOM POLICE. Jeff was indeed there, drinking black coffee at his desk.

"You should have woken me up," he said to Rachel, then set down his coffee and got to his feet. "Hi, Julio. Haven't run into you for a while." He held out his hand. "I hear good things about your business."

"Thank you." Gravely, his eyes flicking once in Rachel's direction, Julio shook hands with Jeff.

"Can I help you with something?" Jeff looked from Julio to Rachel and back to Julio, his eyebrows rising.

With another brief glance at Rachel, Julio began to explain about the carving and about his friend who operated a flea market. He dropped intermittently into rapid Spanish and, with an apologetic glance at Rachel, finally dropped the English altogether. Jeff's fluency always impressed Rachel. He had had less Spanish than she when he had left Blossom, had learned it during his years with the Los Angeles Police Department, when he was paired with a Hispanic partner. Finally, the two men nodded, and Julio left. He still didn't look happy, but his expression was purposeful.

"He's going to talk his friend into letting us stake out his operation." Jeff's eyes gleamed with suppressed excitement. "I gather that this guy has sold goods to him more than once. It's just about a sure thing that sooner or later he'll show up again. Julio's going to ask his friend to put aside everything that the guy sold him. I told Julio we'd pay him back for what he spent. Since he didn't know the goods were stolen."

Rachel guessed that Jeff would repay the flea market vendor back out of his own pocket. Just to keep things simple. "I hope he's willing to help," she said slowly. "He's an illegal, isn't he?"

"I wouldn't know." Jeff studied the ceiling. "I didn't ask to see his birth certificate. No reason for it."

"Oh," Rachel said. "Of course. Silly of me to wonder."

"Thanks." Jeff took her face between his hands and kissed her lightly. "For bringing Julio by." He rested his cheek lightly against the top of her head for a moment. "I may have to ask you to take care of Ben again," he said huskily. "We're going to be stretched pretty thin if we stake this guy out round the clock. But at least you'll have the dog up there. You won't be alone."

"Hey, I'd have Spider if I was at the apartment," Rachel said lightly. "Mrs. Frey is renting a room to him. For a few hours of work and a fistful of rules, I gather."

"I thought they were feuding." Jeff straightened, laughing. "You know, I'm not surprised. They're two of a kind, those two."

"Spider and Mrs. Frey?" Rachel blinked. "You're kidding."

"No." Jeff shook his head, grinning. "Not at all. So have you quit the Village job?"

"No. Oh!" Rachel sucked in her breath. "I was going to call Mrs. Frey and tell her I'd be late to pick up Spider." She glanced at her watch and groaned. "I hope she isn't worrying. I'd better get moving. And you need to talk to Harris, by the way. He's not satisfied that the director's guilty."

"It's not a sure thing." Jeff's expression sobered. "But we do have means, motive, and opportunity. Not to mention her taking off like she did. If he's got someone else in mind, I'd like to hear who it is. I'll go talk to him." He put his arms around her, pulling her tightly against him. "Sometimes it's going to be like this. I'm sorry. I

wish I could say that this is the only time." A roughness
marred his voice. "You can still change your mind."

"If I wanted to, I sure could." She kissed him, never
mind where they were or who might come in the door.

The soft sound of a cleared throat broke them apart.
Rachel looked over Jeff's shoulder, found Moira Kellogg,
Mayor Ventura's receptionist-cum-assistant, smiling in
the doorway.

"Good morning to you both." She beamed through her
glasses, her waved gray hair and unassuming clothes making her look like a generic grandmother.

"It's so nice to see a little humanity on display down
here." She smiled, a dimple winking at the corner of her
mouth. "I thought I'd better remind you about the City
Council meeting at nine, Jeff. Since you're on the hot
seat."

"Don't worry." He gave her a rueful grin. "I couldn't
forget if I tried, and believe me, I have. It's about Bert's
suggestions," he answered Rachel's questioning look. "I
guess he handed the Council a nicely written proposal for
a curfew and an anticruising regulation." Anger thickened
his tone. "Basically it would banish anyone under twenty-
one from the downtown area after dark unless they were
on an errand for their parents. Talk about sending the kids
out into the woods to drink and smoke dope." He made
a disgusted sound in his throat.

"Well, he's from the city," Mrs. Kellogg said thoughtfully. "They have more problems there. I guess our little
vandalism spree seems pretty usual to him. Unfortu-
nately . . ." She raised her eyebrows. "You've got a few
folk on the Council who think all teens should be neither
seen nor heard from."

"Do tell," Jeff said dryly.

"Bet my newly elected uncle is one of them." Rachel
sighed.

"Bert hasn't ever lived in a small town." Jeff paced the office, scowling. "What might work there—if it does, which I doubt—isn't going to work here. I'm not going to stand by and watch this happen."

"You know, the mayor is worried that you're going to do something rash." Mrs. Kellogg examined the immaculate polish on her nails. "Just between you and me, the thought of running Blossom without you scares the piss out of him."

"My my, Mrs. Kellogg, such language." Jeff smiled, but the smile didn't quite reach his eyes. "Our mayor does just fine on his own and always has."

"You don't reassure me, Jeffrey." Mrs. Kellogg pinned him with the look a third-grade teacher might give a student who showed up claiming that the dog ate his homework. "You think about what's good for Blossom, and if you've got any false modesty floating around in that handsome head of yours, kick it the hell out. Do you hear me?" She marched out of the room without waiting for an answer, her back ramrod straight.

Rachel gaped after her. "I have never in my life heard Moira Kellogg use any word that could remotely be thought of as an expletive," she murmured. "Unless my ears deceive me, I just heard her use two."

"She's pretty protective of the mayor."

"Jeff, was she serious?" Rachel turned to face him. "I didn't know there was a Council meeting today. She was hinting that you might resign. You aren't thinking about it, are you?"

Jeff looked over at his cluttered desk, his expression uncertain. Then he straightened and reached for her hand, his fingers twining with hers. "I don't think it will go that far. I should have talked about it with you, but the meeting didn't get scheduled until yesterday and . . . I didn't want to even think about it last night." He shook his head. "I have to put my foot down or the Council gets to make me dance like a puppet. If they want it done Bert's way, I'm not the one to do it. If a curfew and restrictions on kids are more important than how I do my job, then they're telling me something, and I might as well go now as later."

"Oh, Jeff," Rachel whispered.

"We don't have a problem." Anger flickered beneath Jeff's words. "We've had a couple of skateboarding incidents, and some petty graffiti. That's all. We do have one very smart, very slippery vandal who's proving God knows what to us and himself, and is working hard to achieve a very high profile. If we adopt these measures, we *will* have a problem. We'll have kids out of sight drinking and doing drugs, driving and dying on the roads. Roth may not like the teenagers hanging around smoking on the corner, but they don't hurt his business. I want Blossom to be open to *all* its citizens. Not just the middle-aged taxpayers."

Rachel reached for him, hugged him tightly. "Call me," she whispered. "On my cell. Let me know what happened. Please?"

"I will," he said gently. "Now go get Spider before Mrs. Frey calls up to report you missing."

"I'm going." But she paused at the door, because there were a thousand things to say and this was neither the time nor the place. "Whatever you have to do at the meeting . . . we'll make it work."

"Thanks," he said softly. "That means a lot to me."

She left then, hurrying through the main entry, her head down, afraid that she might run into her uncle, afraid he might say something negative about Jeff. The words were there, just waiting to burst out. She knew her limits. And her Uncle Jack shared her Irish temper. All they needed was a reporter from the *Blossom Bee* and they could probably entertain the town for a week, she thought with irony.

But she was fortunate. She managed to escape from City Hall without running into any of the Council members at all. Very late now, she drove the few blocks to Mrs. Frey's house. Peter was sitting on the landing at her door, washing himself. He protested that she hadn't fed him yet, but his protests were halfhearted. "I know they fed you. You're bulging."

"About time you showed up." Spider was standing at the bottom of the steps. "We figured you two, uh . . . slept late." The glint in his eye and the sense of suppressed laughter made her wonder just what that conversation had included.

"For your information, I was up early." She sniffed. "I stopped in at the Bread Box and then I ran into Julio and he had some information that Jeff needed to hear on that vandal."

"Yeah, Julio was here earlier." Spider swung himself up onto the railing and slid a couple of feet to the bottom. "I told him you'd be along, but he didn't stick around. What did he want?"

"He got my carving back for me." Rachel pulled Beck's piece from her pocket and dangled it triumphantly. "So have you had breakfast?"

"Are you kidding?" Spider rolled his eyes. "You think Amelia's going to let me out the door without stuffing me with food? Although she does a pretty good biscuit, I got to say. Even better than Gus's. But don't say I said that."

Amelia? Rachel shook her head, wondering what the universe would offer up next.

CHAPTER

14

The few high clouds visible to the west at dawn had thickened ominously by the time Rachel and Spider pulled onto the Village grounds. Rachel turned the radio on and listened, frowning, to the weather report. An unexpected shift in the jet stream had brought a big low-pressure front onshore well south of its expected course. Rain was predicted for the Gorge, heavy at times. She thought of the orchard pear trees, heavy with fruit. High winds and heavy rain could play havoc with the nearly ready fruit. There was always something to worry about—frost, hail, heavy summer rain, or drought. Something. She had a feeling that her uncle wouldn't have his mind entirely on the Council meeting this morning.

One eye on the sky, she checked their work from yesterday, regretting the lost time this morning. No new sign of vandalism marred the amended beds. At least the irrigation lines were covered. "I'm going to go get the trailer and pick up some of the plants from Rhinehoffer's," she told Spider. "You can start work on the beds down by the pond." They had dumped half of the compost down there, so it wouldn't be a long wheelbarrow trip to the beds. "I should be back in a couple of hours." She hauled the plastic water cooler out of the truck bed and set it in the meager shade of a struggling juniper, which had been badly placed by the first landscaper. "Drink a lot of water," she told Spider. He already had his shirt off and his rapidly bronzing shoulders gleamed with sweat. "Don't forget, huh?"

"Yes, Boss Lady." He thrust a shovel into the pile of compost. "You taught me about water when I worked for you before, remember?"

"Glad to hear it." Rachel glanced at the thickening clouds to the west. "Looks like a good time to transplant," she said dryly. "I wouldn't mind working in the rain right now."

"Speak for yourself." Spider grunted as he tilted the very full wheelbarrow onto its wheel and trundled off for the bed he was working on.

Leaving their plastic water mugs upside down on the cooler, Rachel drove back into town, her windows rolled all the way down. The breeze felt cool and delicious. The air today was heavy with moisture that had come in from the ocean, ahead of the front. Rain would be welcome, even if it cost a few pears. The summer had been so dry. Not drought-dry, but dry enough to make global warming a popular topic of conversation at barbecues and picnics. She pulled around behind the Blossom Feed and Seed, to the back lot where she stored the flat-bed trailer she used for hauling plants.

Sweat stung her eyes as she backed the truck into position, dropped the hitch onto the truck's ball, and connected the safety chains. As she was plugging the trailer lights into the truck's receptacle, Brian Ferrel, owner of the feed store, came out onto the back loading dock, pushing a handtruck stacked with big salt blocks for livestock.

"You got everything squared away?" he called as he righted the hand truck. "Want me to check your lights?"

"Thanks, Brian." She pulled the trailer forward, then ran through turn signals, brake, and taillights, eliciting a stiff thumbs-up each time from Brian. Gray frosted his temples, she noticed, and lines around his mouth gave him an aged look. Rachel felt briefly sorry for him. He was her age. They had been friends in high school. But his father's murder of a city councilman and his subsequent suicide had turned once easygoing and extroverted Brian inward, causing him to withdraw from everyone. His wife had left him, Rachel had heard. He didn't participate much in social or political events in town. Although he had offered her the use of his lot for her trailer, his manner with her was a trifle formal. She had a feeling that he'd never really forgiven her for helping to reveal that his father was a murderer. The light check finished, he had turned back to his load of salt blocks and was stacking them neatly against the wall, where they would be safe from rain.

"Thanks," she called to him. Brian lifted a hand in response, but didn't pause the rhythm of his stacking.

Rachel pulled the trailer out the back entrance and onto Pine Street, meaning to turn back onto Main and head out of town to Rhinehoffer's nursery. Restlessly, she glanced at her watch, then peered down the street, trying to get a glimpse of City Hall. It was after ten. How long would this meeting last anyway? Rachel found herself chewing at a fingernail—a habit she had broken years ago. Angrily, she clamped her hands onto the wheel, flicking the turn signal lever as she braked at the stop sign.

Motion caught her eye and she looked left to discover Mrs. Frey waving vigorously from the far corner, her canvas shopping bag swinging from one hand. "Pull over a minute." She cupped her hands around her mouth, hollering as if Rachel were across a football field, instead of across the street. "I want to talk to you."

With a sigh, Rachel pulled onto Main, drove past the feed store's front driveway, and pulled over along the fortunately empty curb. The truck cab immediately threatened to become an oven with the morning sun slanting in through the windshield. Rachel got out, suppressing another sigh, as Mrs. Frey marched up. "What is it?" she asked, trying not to sound too irritable.

"I wanted to talk to you when John wasn't with you." She clucked her tongue. "That boy might as well be your shadow. Did he tell you about his mother?"

"I met his mother." Rachel glanced at her watch again. "A couple of years ago. Spider told me she had a new boyfriend."

"You can spare a minute," Mrs. Frey said with asperity. "You need to make some decision about that boy. He's on his own. Did you know that?"

"What do you mean?" Startled, Rachel dragged her thoughts away from Jeff and the Council meeting. "He's just working here for the summer."

"I mean that he has no idea where his mother even is."

"He can't reach her?" Puzzled, Rachel tried to follow the conversation. "Did he call her?"

"She moved out. Before he ever came out here. Didn't he *tell* you? Didn't you *ask*?"

"Ask *what*?" Sweaty, worried, Rachel felt her temper fraying. "He asked for a summer job and he told me his mother had a boyfriend and he said he was in the way. What was I supposed to ask?"

"Anything about him would probably have been nice." Mrs. Frey drew herself to her full height, which put their eyes on a level. "He told me that his mother moved out of her rented house and into the house of her new boyfriend. John was staying with friends and sleeping in parks. I don't get the impression that he was too popular with the boyfriend. Then one day he went over there to see his mother, and that house was empty. I . . . gather that it had been a few weeks since he had last visited." She cleared her throat. "In any case, they had moved. He doesn't know where. What are you going to do about that boy?"

"Moved? Without telling him? How could she *do* that?" First his father, then his mother. Rachel drew back, stunned, a dozen questions churning in her mind. All of a sudden, some things made more sense—such as his few possessions. "He . . . he's eighteen. He's legally an adult." She stifled a moment of panic as she met Amelia Frey's steely glare. "What do you mean, what am *I* going to do about him?"

"Rachel O'Connor, I don't want to hear that kind of talk from you." Mrs. Frey shook her finger at Rachel. "That's the kind of talk I'd expect to hear from some city person, somebody who didn't even know the name of the neighbor next door."

"I'm sorry." Rachel's shoulders slumped. "I don't mean it like that. But he is a legal adult. He gets to be part of any decisions anyone makes." She drew a deep breath. "He wants to work for a couple of years to earn money for school." She started to say that he could rent her apartment since she was moving in with Jeff, but paused. Mrs. Frey was very careful with her money. Her husband hadn't left her much, and he had died a long time ago. It occurred to Rachel that the money from the apartment might be an important part of her income.

"You know, I was thinking about asking you if I could keep the apartment." Rachel spoke slowly, doing some very rapid calculations in her head. "I can't move all my stuff into Jeff's house, and some of it I'd like to keep. Maybe I could leave stuff there and Spider could rent it from you. Perfect." She snapped her fingers, as if the thought had just occurred to her. "I don't mind if he uses the furniture. He can pay for part of the apartment, and I can pay for the rest. That way it won't be too expensive for him." And she'd better pick up a couple of new clients, she thought ruefully. She hadn't counted on this continuing expense.

"That would work." Mrs. Frey seemed to be doing her own calculations, too. "I hate to take money he's saving for school. And it will be nice to have a strong pair of arms around here come wood-cutting season." She nodded, her eyes sharp on Rachel's face. "Done, dear. I think we can both manage this without going broke."

So much for subterfuge. Rachel grinned and offered her landlady a ceremonious hand. Which Mrs. Frey shook with equal ceremony. "Besides, you can't take Peter to Jeff's. Not with that dog there." Mrs. Frey nodded with decision. "He might hurt the poor thing."

"Well, we can see how it works out," Rachel said diplomatically. "Ben is a pretty easygoing dog."

"I wasn't worried about the *dog* hurting *Peter*." Mrs. Frey sniffed. "I've watched that cat run a dozen dogs off the property. That husky mix from down the street thought he was tough. Ha. Well, I'd better get this milk into the refrigerator before it sours." She hefted her shopping bag. "You tell John when he can move upstairs." Waving cheerfully, Mrs. Frey turned and marched back toward Pine and her house.

Shaking her head, Rachel climbed back into her truck. "Well, Jeff, you brought a dog to this marriage. I guess I'm bringing a teenager." Her laugh stuck in her throat. How did it feel to have both your parents simply walk out of your life? She put the truck into gear and headed for Rhinehoffer's to pick up her plants.

Daren was busy checking the plastic greenhouse coverings, and getting the nursery ready for wind. He had a radio playing, and as she loaded plants, Rachel heard the ominous squawk of the emergency broadcasting system.

Pausing, her skin prickling, she listened to the tinny voice announce a thunderstorm cell with high-velocity winds moving across the Willamette Valley floor. Miles away, perhaps, but it promised a nasty storm to come. Every last trace of breeze had died and her skin prickled with the sense of storm coming. Falling pressure, she told herself, but the breathless uneasy feel of the air lent an urgency to her loading. Making sure that the pots were secured, she waved at Daren and headed back for the Village, forcing herself to drive slowly so that the heavily laden trailer wouldn't start swaying.

Spider had accomplished a lot in the hours she had been absent. Pleased, Rachel told him to take a break. Worried because she hadn't heard from Jeff, she called his number. Bert Stanfield answered.

"He went off with some Mexican kid." Bert's tone held a hint of disdain. "I don't know when he'll be back."

Julio, Rachel thought. He must have gone to see his friend right away. She thanked Bert, liking the man less than she had before. Dialing her own number, she found a message from Jeff on her machine. "The Council backed down—a little ways," he said, his tone hurried. "Julio and I are off to talk to his friend. I tried your cell but couldn't get you. I'll drop by the Village later."

Damn. Rachel tossed her cell phone onto the truck seat. He must have called while she was at the Rhinehoffer nursery. Once or twice she had had trouble with her cell phone in that area.

Nothing she could do about it now. But his phone message had sounded positive. He hadn't quit anyway. A wave of relief swept over her. She hadn't realized quite how much she had feared his resignation. Although if Mayor Ventura lost the next election, he'd be looking for a new job anyway. Suddenly the future seemed a lot less settled than it had seemed a short year ago.

They got to work on the plantings along the pond first, setting the blue and red elderberry along the bank where they would provide a sun and wind screen for strollers. Grassy bamboo would provide a nice screen to hide the sprawling Village buildings. Flag iris and cattails went into the pond itself. Spider volunteered to plant those, wading joyfully out into the still water, whooping when he caught a startled frog. She had seeded the pond with gambusia fish obtained from the state in order to keep down the mosquitos. The frogs delighted her, too. At least there were a few creatures living here. The habitat she was creating would hopefully draw more. She left Spider to his splashing and started planting young pussy willow along the shallow end of the pond. Eventually, they would screen and shade the benches there. "There are some water lilies still on the trailer," she called to Spider. "As long as you're wet, you can get them in, too. They're the plants in the buckets of water," she told him.

"So." She straightened finally, watching him wade back to shore, the empty lily pots in his hands. "How's your mom these days? Have you heard from her?"

"Amelia talked to you." Spider turned an unsurprised face up to her as he climbed out of the pond. "I figured she would." He smelled of scummy pond water.

"Yeah, she talked to me." Rachel sighed. "Spider, I'm sorry."

"Why?" He looked genuinely surprised. "You didn't do anything."

"I know." She shrugged, feeling enormously awkward. "It's just . . . it's hard when a parent is gone. That's all."

"She's not dead." Spider set the pots down and wrung some water from his soggy jeans. "I mean, she's with this guy she really likes. We were just done with each other, that's all. It was no big deal." He stared at the pots, his head tilted, as if listening to something far away. "It's not like it was with my dad," he said at last.

Spider had told her long ago about his father, the left-behind child of an American soldier and the daughter of a Vietnamese shopkeeper. When his unit left her village, that soldier had promised to bring his lover to America and marry her. She had never heard from him again. When Spider's father had finally made it to this country, he had searched war memorials all over the country for his own father's name, searching for the death that would justify that broken promise. After Spider was born, he took Spider along with him, searching more and more often. One day he went off searching and never returned. Spider had been eight. She sighed. "You get to move into my apartment," she said. "Since I'm moving in with Jeff. The price is, you have to feed Peter."

"He's a tough-guy cat." Spider nodded approvingly. "That'll work," he said. "Amelia's pretty cool, but I think we'd bug each other real fast, with me living down there."

The wind began to gust as they worked, riffling the still water and bending the potted bamboo so that the stems whispered together. In spite of the overcast sky and the wind, the rain held off. Rachel had already walked the bank, flagging the sites for the various plants, marking them according to her notes with different-colored flags. Spider dug the holes, leaving the flags stuck in the mounds of dirt he removed. She had already tagged the various plants with knots of surveyor's tape that corresponded to the flag color. So once she began planting, Spider could ferry the correct plant to the correct hole from the trailer. They worked fast and comfortably, exchanging a little banter, but mainly getting plants into the ground. Rachel sprinkled a handful of time-release fertilizer granules around each plant. They'd apply a barkdust mulch around the finished plantings, to keep the soil from eroding into the pond with the winter rains and to improve the look of the newly planted landscape. Rachel mentally noted spots where she would have to build small barriers to keep

water from following already established erosion troughs
into the pond. After the first hard rain she'd come back
out here to make sure that the newly planted banks
weren't eroding. She squinted, blinking windblown dust
from her eyes as a car wound up the driveway and into
the parking lot at the top of the slope.

Sure enough, it was Jeff's black Jeep. Rachel straightened, stretching her back, looking for Spider. He was
around the far curve of the pond, way ahead of her, de-
positing two three-gallon pots beside their respective
holes. "Break time," she called, and glanced at her watch.
Nearly two o'clock! "Make that lunch and break time."
She stuck her spade into the ground and hiked up the
slope to meet him as he came around the far end of the
pond. "Why didn't you tell me it was lunchtime?"

"We were really moving." Spider shrugged, wiping
grimy hands on his jeans. "And I wasn't all that hungry.
Mrs. Frey wouldn't let me out the door until I ate a pile
of biscuits this morning. I think she gets up at about three
A.M."

"Well, it's lunchtime now. Better late than never," Rachel said absently. For once, she wasn't hungry. As Spider
headed for the truck to get his lunch cooler from the bed,
she hiked up the path to where Jeff had parked the Jeep.
He came down to meet her, an arm out to scoop her close.

"Did you get my message?" Worry squeezed the corners of his eyes as he ducked a sudden fierce gust of wind
and dust. "I tried to get you, but your cell didn't answer."

"I got it. So it went well?" She searched his face as he
shrugged. "You said they backed down."

"They did." Jeff gave her a lopsided smile. "I was . . .
surprised. I guess they're not ready to can me yet." He
laughed shortly. "But they're going to invite Bert to present his proposal at the next formal meeting. I think I've
been given a deadline—catch our vandal by then, or
they'll vote for Bert's plan. We'll have him." His grin

held a hint of triumph. "We've got him now."

"Julio's friend?"

"His name is Ramon Valdez. I convinced him that we're not the Immigration and Naturalization Service and not interested in working with them. I left Kelly staked out where he has a clear view of Ramon's house. I'll relieve him later tonight, and Bert will take over after me. Ramon said our boy hasn't been back since he sold him your carving. He's pretty reluctant, but I think he'll cooperate okay." Jeff grimaced. "Apparently our little thief has hit a couple of cars out here at the Village. So maybe he'll try to unload the things he took."

"Ricki told me she lost a jacket." Rachel hugged him. "I hope you get him tonight."

"Me, too," Jeff said soberly. "I wouldn't mind living a regular schedule again. None of us would mind it. Have you had lunch yet?" Jeff twined his fingers through hers. "Can I buy you something here?"

"I think the dining room is closed by now," Rachel said ruefully. "Although from what Ricki told me, nobody wants to eat there anyway. She said they were going to bring in catered box lunches." They had reached the main entrance and pushed through the tall glass doors, releasing a breath of cool conditioned air. Dusty wind swirled in behind them, making the door close with a sharp thud.

Heads turned as the residents lounging on the chairs and sofas looked up to see who had entered. Four women playing cards at a small wooden table set their hands down to peer at Jeff. Already some of the residents were getting to their feet, heading in Jeff's direction with determined faces.

"Uh-oh," Rachel said under her breath. "Your cover's blown."

"I should have sneaked in the back way." Jeff turned to greet a wizened man crouching over a walker who threatened to stand the metal legs directly on Jeff's feet.

"What's being done about these murders?" His cracked and wavering voice could have carried to the far corners of the Notre Dame Cathedral. "I want to know what's being done to keep us from being murdered in our beds?"

"I've heard you haven't caught her yet. What's to stop her from coming back here?" A woman with a footed cane flanked him with her companion, a bony woman Rachel had noticed before in the dining room.

"What's being done to protect us?" The companion pushed at waves of lavender hair that appeared to have been varnished in place. "You can't trust anyone here."

"Why can't we have copies of our accounts?" Two more men wearing identical striped shirts and hearing aids closed in behind Jeff. He was trapped. Rachel found herself outside a circle of elderly residents whose worried complaining voices rose in decibel level as they pressed closer and closer.

"Hold on just a minute." Jeff raised his voice to be heard, his hands out, palms down in a quieting gesture. "I'll answer all the questions I have an answer for. But I can only answer one at a time. Yes." He nodded to the woman who had first spoken. "Director Bellington has not been apprehended, but every officer in the state is watching for her. She won't come back here. Your assistant director is in charge. Any questions you have about your accounts should be brought up with her."

"She won't do anything." Lavender-hair raised her voice querulously. "She says she doesn't have the authority to change anything. And she's never in her office. I think she's hiding from us."

"She never did anything anyway," one of the twins in the striped shirts muttered under his breath, giving Rachel a wink. "She always said she had chronic fatigue syndrome. Chronic fatigue syndrome, my eye." His snort riffled his bristly gray mustache. "Chronic booze syndrome, I'd call it. You could smell her coming. Fräulein Director liked it that way, I bet. She could cook the books all she wanted. Noble was too busy drinking wine with lunch and feeling sorry for herself to add two and two, most days."

Jeff was busy reassuring residents, repeating answers as the same questions were asked over and over, explaining that there should be no danger, that if anyone had any concerns or any information, they could certainly contact him. With a face of suppressed resignation, he began handing out cards with his telephone number on them.

His answering machine was going to be busy. Rachel was willing to bet money on it. She caught a glimpse of Harris appearing from the hallway that led to Madame's room. Rachel waved. Harris waved back and wheeled over, his expression a mix of amusement and sympathy as he regarded the small mob scene around Jeff.

"He's doing awfully well," Harris murmured as he wheeled up alongside her. "He could go into public relations if he gets tired of being a cop."

"I think he's about ready to take a job as a fire spotter up in a Forest Service tower," Rachel whispered back. "Or volunteer for duty in Antarctica."

"I should have warned him." Harris shook his head. "I'm amazed we haven't had a dozen heart attacks this week. Actually, all this excitement might be just what a few of these folk needed. I haven't heard so much lively conversation in years." He chuckled. "I'll see if I can't extricate our poor chief of police. I appreciate him coming out here." Harris shrugged. "Not that I have much to tell him. I've heard an interesting bit of rumor." He wheeled back from the slowly diminishing crowd around Jeff. "Seems that Emily was seeing quite a bit of our assistant director. Noble was spotted by more than one person leaving Emily's room late at night. A few interesting rumors were in circulation about what was going on in there."

"Interesting." Rachel chewed her lip thoughtfully. "I keep hearing that she hated Bellington. Did she spend time with the other two residents who were murdered?"

"I don't know." Harris's expression was grim. "Unlike our director, Noble wanders around here all the time. Nobody pays much attention to her."

Before Rachel could reply, Harris touched her hand lightly and wheeled forward. Jeff had managed to extricate himself from the last of his questioners. Harris greeted him with surprise and delight, exclaiming on this unexpected pleasure. The two men moved off, chatting about sports and the weather, heading toward the hall where the director's office was located.

Rachel headed for the door. Time to get back to work. She could indulge herself at the Bread Box after work since she'd managed to leave her lunch on the counter this morning. By now, Ben had probably eaten it.

"Hey, Rachel." Ricki emerged from the dining room, waving. "I thought I saw you. Hang on a minute." She vanished inside to reappear a few moments later with a paper bag. "Chocolate chip cookies." She handed the bag over. "I drew baking duty this morning. They came out good."

"You're not only waiting tables but cooking, too?" Rachel opened the bag and sniffed. "Mmmm," she said. Lunch after all. Not healthy, but then, she was stuck, wasn't she?

"Our cook quit at dinner last night, after about the thirtieth person accused her of poisoning folk. The rest of the staff left with her. In protest, I guess." Ricki sighed. "Ms. Noble isn't very decisive as an assistant director," she said. "She says she'll get somebody in. Maybe tomorrow. I sure hope so." She made a face. "We did tuna sandwiches for lunch and we'll have canned soup and spaghetti for dinner. Boy." She shook her head. "If people thought they were in danger of being poisoned before . . ." She laughed.

"Well, the cookies won't hurt anybody." Rachel took a bite of one and made appreciative noises.

"So is Spider's name really Spider?" Ricki tilted her head to one side.

"It's John Tranh, actually." Rachel finished the cookie and wiped her fingers on her jeans. "Why?"

"Oh, I had a bet with someone." Ricki waved a hand airily. "I told him Spider had to have a nice normal first name. I mean, nobody names their kid Spider, no matter how weird names get. And they're pretty weird sometimes. I had a friend named Amarantha. She was named for some kind of plant or something. Her parents were kind of New Age types. You know—they were vegans and did meditation and yoga and called God 'she.' That kind of thing. They weren't from around here. See you around." And Ricki tripped back to the dining room, her bright hair flashing in the dim light.

Ricki left her feeling out of breath. Shaking her head, Rachel looked around. No sign of Jeff or Harris. She ate another cookie as she headed back to the truck, thinking of Harris's words. Did he suspect the assistant? She was the one who had been scandalized by his behavior with Madame. Outside, the clouds had thinned a bit and it no longer looked as if it was going to rain. But the wind still gusted from the west, kicking up twisting dust devils where they were working.

Jeff came by about an hour later, looking thoughtful. "The assistant director has done a very fast and thorough job of auditing the resident accounts." He eyed the clouds streaking the sky. "In fact, it's so good that one would think she began this little project some time ago." He lowered his gaze, made a face, and shrugged. "Whatever the motive and time frame, it appears that Bellington put away a nice tidy sum with her fake expenses—if Noble's figures are accurate. An independent auditor will have to confirm it, but it looks bad for her."

"You think Noble knew about the embezzlement?" Rachel glanced at Spider, who was wheeling several large potted witch hazel trees. Their winter's bloom in yellow and orange would provide some color for the slope just above the pond.

"Maybe." Jeff shook his head. "We're keeping an eye on Assistant Director Noble. Somebody has sure leaked a lot of details about this murder, and she's very involved in the daily activities. I'd give a lot to know just where they got their information, whoever it is."

"Harris thinks it's the murderer."

"The director is still our main suspect." Jeff met her eyes, worry darkening his own. "But as I've said before, I want you to be careful here. Okay? Very careful."

"I am." She meant it, too. It scared her to think that the murderer might pass her in the hall here, or come down to comment on a plant. What if it was the assistant director? "Will you have time for dinner before you take over the stakeout?" she asked him.

"I can take a couple of hours." He leaned over to kiss her lightly. "How about if I pick up a couple of steaks on the way home? We can grill them. I'm not taking over until dark, so that gives us a little while."

"It's a deal." She grinned. "See you at the house." She waved and watched him climb the slope to his parked car. He still walked tired. Maybe—with luck—they'd catch the vandal tonight. Thoughtfully she reached through the truck window to touch the wooden carving with her finger, set it swinging. "What do you think about quitting this job?" she asked as she heard Spider trundling the empty wheelbarrow back for another load. "I'm not sure I want to be out here anymore."

"Weren't you just telling people how we're not quitting no matter what? So how come you want to quit? What's to be scared of?"

"I didn't say I was scared." She drew herself up, trying for indignation. "I don't know if we're even going to get paid for this. For all I know, the people who own the place will put it on the market tomorrow. Or declare bankruptcy."

Spider grunted and gave her a doubting look. "Whatever you say." He shrugged and heaved another potted witch hazel onto the barrow.

By quitting time, Rachel had decided that they'd resign after getting the rest of the plants in. Let somebody else finish the job. They would get out of there. Safely. Harris would watch out for Madame, and Jeff was watching out for Harris.

But as they were cleaning and stowing their tools, a small, mousy woman in a green linen suit that was a little too bright picked her way down the path. Her ruddy face gleamed with perspiration, and her limp ginger hair clung damply to her forehead and neck. "I'm sorry to bother you," she said awkwardly. "I don't think we've been introduced. Every time you were with Jennifer, I think I was busy somewhere else. I'm Ms. Noble. I was . . . am . . . uh . . ." She blinked, as if she had suddenly run out of script. "I'm the acting director," she said with the barest trace of defiance. "I . . . a lot of the residents have been asking me about the landscaping project. I just wanted to say that what you're doing is so very important to us. And if you have any questions about being paid, I'm sure that nothing has changed. I mean, your contract was with the parent company. Jennifer's . . . aberrations . . . don't affect that." A small triumph gleamed in her dull hazel eyes. "I checked. You're to go ahead and finish the job. And I just got a call from the woman who's doing the magazine article. I . . . she doesn't know about . . . about our troubles yet." Again that flash of sly triumph brightened her eyes. "I . . . just wanted to be able to reassure the residents that you'll continue to finish our lovely garden." She straightened herself slightly. "I have to be honest and say that Jen . . . the director was less than satisfied." Her voice firmed. "And I also want you to know that as far as I can tell, you are doing an excellent job. The residents are very excited about having a pleasant place to stroll at last. I . . . we . . . are asking you to remain." Lips parted, her eyes gleaming, she waited expectantly for Rachel's reply.

"Of course." Rachel refused to look at Spider, who was making very small noises that might just be snickers. "Of course we'll finish the job."

"Oh, I'm so glad." Acting Director Noble looked as if she had just won a nice fat bet. "I can't tell you how happy I am. All of us are. I just don't know what I'd have done if you quit. Well, I'll go tell everyone the happy, happy news. Life must go on, mustn't it? Even in the face of such terrible, awful events." Turning, she marched back up the path, her flat-soled shoes clacking on the concrete, her suit flapping in the gusty wind.

"So how could I say no, huh?" Rachel racked her shovel, refusing to look at Spider.

"Just don't eat any mushroom pastries," Spider said gaily. "Wanna bet she goes back up and tells everybody how you were gonna quit, but she, Superlady, saved the day?"

"You're about to walk home." Rachel scanned the site for any forgotten equipment.

"That's probably against some kind of labor law or other."

"It probably is." Rachel glared at him. "Get in the truck, okay?"

"Yes, Boss Lady, ma'am," Spider said meekly and climbed into the truck, still grinning.

Noble was certainly pleased by the turn of events. Triumphant, not pleased, Rachel thought. A couple of aids were taking a cigarette break out beside the buildings, where they were protected from the wind. She didn't recognize either of them. If Noble had exposed the embezzlement earlier, would Emily have died? Or was Harris right? "Ricki asked me what your real name was," she said absently. "I told her. I hope that was okay."

"How come?"

Rachel turned to look at Spider. "A bet or something. I'm sorry. I didn't think . . ."

"It's fine." He frowned through the windshield. "Who was the bet with?"

"She didn't say." Rachel braked at the end of the driveway, waiting while a flatbed piled with stacked apple boxes roared by. Harvest was beginning to pick up. Soon it would be in full swing as the main crop varieties were harvested. "You could ask her."

"I will."

Spider was uncharacteristically quiet after that, staring out through the window as they drove back to town beneath the threatening sky. A few raindrops splatted against the windscreen as she turned in to Mrs. Frey's driveway. "Are you going over to Ricki's house tonight?" Rachel asked as she parked.

"For a little while. Gus has been teaching me chess." Spider hopped out of the truck and slammed the door. "I better tell Amelia where I'm going." He took his empty lunch cooler and vanished through the side door into the main part of the house.

Rachel climbed the steps to her apartment. His new relationship with her landlady still amazed her. Peter was waiting on the landing, the tip of his tail twitching, his gaze inscrutable. Rachel opened the door and he stalked past her, heading straight for the kitchen. Of course. "Okay, okay." She checked her answering machine, found one message waiting, and hit the play button on her way into the kitchen. As she took down a can of cat food from the cupboard, she heard Jeff's voice on the machine.

". . . I picked up a couple of nice steaks and some local corn on the cob for tonight. I'm going to catch some sleep, but how about it I pick you up later . . . say, around seven? I was going to drop in at City Hall anyway, and I can give you a ride in, in the morning."

"Sounds good, Jeff." Rachel smiled as she opened the can, pinned by an impatient feline stare. "I don't have any other plans, cat, do I?" She emptied the can onto a plate and set it down for Peter. "I'm glad he's at least getting some sleep." The kitchen overlooked the driveway. Spider appeared, saying something over his shoulder as he headed down the drive. As she rinsed the can beneath the kitchen tap, Rachel watched him turn left at the end of the driveway. Which was odd, she thought as she tossed the clean can into the recycle bin. If he was going to Ricki's, it would be shorter to turn right and take the narrow, unpaved Fourth Avenue. It led almost directly to Gus Van Dorn's house.

She shrugged and turned away from the window. He was probably doing an errand for Mrs. Frey. She glanced at the clock and headed for the shower. As she passed the drafting table that served as her desk, pink caught her eye. It was a pink Post-it note with Jeff's mother's phone number on it. She had stuck it there months ago, meaning to call her and personally invite her to the wedding. She hadn't. She'd let Jeff do it. Rachel paused, picked it up. For a moment she hesitated, then reached for the phone.

Before she could lose her nerve, she had punched in the number. It wasn't until the phone on the other end shrilled for the second time that the butterflies all took off at once in her stomach.

Jeff's mother had always intimidated her. Tall and almost coldly formal, she always seemed impatient and displeased when Rachel called on Jeff. Not that she had reason to go to his small house often. He bicycled out to the orchard to swap books or work on school projects or just to sit in the family kitchen and eat Aunt Catherine's cookies. Jeff's mother had never invited any of them into her kitchen for cookies. It was from her that Jeff had inherited his Paiute blood, and her dark eyes had always seemed to hold a shadow of hostility. At the beginning of Jeff's junior year in high school, she had simply taken him away, announcing that they were moving to Los Angeles on a Monday, and making Jeff load the U-Haul van every day after school. They had driven away from Blossom early on Saturday morning. The rented house had stood empty for two weeks, and then another family had moved in.

Rachel swallowed the rush of memories as someone picked up the phone.

"Hello?" The voice sounded distant and tinny, with that hint of impatience that had always seemed to color her tone.

"Mrs. P—" Oh, God, she'd remarried. What was her new name? Her first name was Miranda, but Rachel found she couldn't call this cold, distant woman by her first name. "Uh, hi. This is Rachel O'Connor." Her cheeks were burning. "How are you?"

"Is something wrong with Jeff?" Guarded alarm.

"No, no, he's fine." Rachel swallowed, struggling for words that had all flown south for some reason. "I just . . . I hope I'm not disturbing you."

"It's not late." Her voice had become even more guarded.

Just do it. "I . . . I'm calling because Jeff told me that you didn't think you could come up here for our wedding. And he didn't say anything else, but I know it bothers him. That you won't be here. And it occurred to me that . . . that I never asked you. And I'm sorry. I don't mean to be rude. I just . . . I guess I've just been shy. No, that's not true. You scared me a little. But it's just because I never really got to know you. And that wasn't your fault.

And I should have called you and talked to you. Before now." The words ran out and she clutched the phone, her heart pounding, breathing as if she'd just dug fifty feet of ditch in ten minutes. *What* had she just said to this woman who was a veritable stranger? Where had these crazy words come from? Numb, she tensed for the click of a hang-up.

Silence hummed on the line.

"It's just that I don't think I can get time off." Miranda spoke at last. A thread of amusement colored her tone. Or perhaps it was just her imagination, Rachel thought.

"I hope you can." Rachel drew a deep breath. "I think it matters to Jeff."

"Does it?" No clues now, in her tone. None at all. "I'll do my best. Thank you for calling. I'll let you go now. Good-bye."

"Good-bye," Rachel said, but the dial tone was already buzzing in her ear.

Slowly, she replaced the receiver. So. What had she just done?

She wasn't sure. Probably nothing at all. Letting her breath out in a rush, she went to take her shower.

CHAPTER
15

Jeff arrived just before seven to pick her up. Although the strain of the past few days still showed in his face, his eyes glittered with energy. "We've got this guy," he told Rachel as they went down the stairs to his Jeep. "According to our flea market friend, this guy has been a regular, selling a radio here, briefcase there. We got a description, but it's not too clear." His triumph dimmed slightly as he backed the Jeep down Mrs. Frey's driveway. "It does sound as though he's in his late teens. That's going to throw a lot of weight behind Bert's curfew proposal." His brief frown evaporated and he shrugged. "To be honest, I don't care what age he is. I just want to get this guy." He shook his head as they drove up the slope away from the river, heading up to the house. "I want to know why he's doing this."

"Me, too." Rachel leaned back against the seat, enjoying the cool wash of the wind in her face. It was cool tonight, almost cool enough to raise goose bumps on her bare arms. The clouds had thinned to reveal a hazy

glimpse of the crescent moon. The big front that had troubled the southern Willamette Valley had stalled for now.
The weather report had warned that it would move in
strongly tomorrow, though. They would be picking the
last of the Gravensteins at the orchard, Rachel thought
soberly. The pears weren't quite ready yet. A bad bout of
wind and rain would cause a lot of fruit loss. A storm this
time of year wasn't usual at all, but they happened. A
freak storm had brought hail just as the pears were ready
to pick one year. She had looked at pictures in the family
album of leaves, twigs, and bruised fruit littering the
ground beneath the orchard trees. She crossed her fingers
that the storm would bring rain only, and not much wind.
Her uncle wouldn't be sleeping tonight, she guessed.
When weather threatened, he paced the floor.

"I started the coals in the grill right before I left." Jeff
interrupted her thoughts. "They should be just about ready
by the time we get back. I thought I'd put the corn on the
grill instead of boiling it. Sound okay?"

"Sounds great." Rachel shook her head and let the hint
of moisture in the air caress her face. "This is when we
really get to test Ben's table manners, huh?"

"He's learning that he has to lie down on his rug while
I'm eating." Jeff grinned. "He's not thrilled, but he's willing to behave. You have to remind him once in a while."
He negotiated the sharp curve that led to the crest of the
hill, where the house stood on its bench of level land. As
he slowed to turn into the narrow gravel drive that led
back to the house, his cell phone shrilled. "Hang on a
minute." He braked to a halt and answered the phone.

"Price." He listened for a moment. "What?" The ex-
plosive syllable startled Rachel and sent a roosting bird
twittering from a young alder. "What the hell is going on?
Who brought them into this? No. Tell whoever the *hell* is
in charge that I want to talk to him. I'll be there in ten
minutes." He had already put the Jeep into gear and was

backing fast down the track, dust rising up from beneath the churning wheels. Swinging the Jeep out onto the asphalt, he floored the accelerator, heading downhill the way they'd come at a speed considerably above the legal limit. Never mind the limits of safety.

Rachel hung on to the door, heart pounding, glad she trusted Jeff's driving. "What happened?" she yelled over the roar of engine and speed.

"The damn INS showed up. They busted our guy." Jeff's profile was hard and grim as he swung the Jeep around the curves, centripetal force pulling at Rachel. "Why tonight? Why this guy?" He slowed as he reached town, jaw clenched as he negotiated his way though town. On the far edge he turned westward, his speed increasing again. They turned off a short distance beyond the Thriftway, dropping down toward the distant interstate highway to where a cluster of modest cabins stood in a small grove of firs. An ancient weathered sign that had once advertised tourist cabins had faded to illegible traces of red paint. The cabins—in nearly as bad a state of repair as the sign—were rented to orchard workers, along with a handful of battered travel trailers. The mayor had grumbled about the condition of the property and had predicted that the state would come in and close it down, sooner or later. But it was outside the Blossom city limits, and there was nothing he could do but grumble. The owner—a taciturn man who ran a small messy equipment repair shop on his equally run-down place—didn't seem concerned.

Strings of laundry crisscrossed the space between cabins and trees. Tables made of plywood on sawhorses surrounded the end cabin, as if awaiting weekend flea market merchandise. A homemade sheet-metal cookstove stood on a patch of beaten earth where one of the cabins had burned years ago. The stove pipe fed into the still-standing chimney of the vanished cabin, and smoke seeped from the top. Rachel caught its resiny scent mixed with the

smell of food cooking as they pulled into the bare trampled ground around the cabins. Several older cars were
parked here and there. This time of year, the small en-
campment would be full of pickers and their families, Rachel knew. Children's clothes fluttered on the lines like
pale flags in the gusty wind. The owners should be running through the trees, playing hide-and-seek, yelling and
laughing as the adults cooked, and did laundry, and rested
for another day picking.

Not tonight.

Tonight, a white van and a car stood in the center of
the semicircle of cabins. Uniformed officers of the Immigration and Naturalization Service were loading several
handcuffed men and women into the van. Children peeked
from the cabins, and a small boy sobbed quietly, his face
pressed against the skirt of a young woman who held a
baby in one arm while she comforted the weeping boy.
She didn't look at the newcomers, kept her eyes fixed on
the van. More pickers stood silently watching, hands at
their sides, their sun-darkened faces unreadable in the fading light. Rachel spotted Kelly Jones, the officer who was
on the stakeout, standing to one side of the group, dressed
in jeans and a faded khaki shirt. He nodded and strode
over to the Jeep as Jeff pulled up behind the van, raising
a fresh drift of dust.

"Good luck," Jones said under his breath. He looked
angry, his usually cheerful face flushed, his brown eyes
hard in the dusk. "We don't seem to count for a whole
lot here."

"As I told your officer, this isn't your jurisdiction." The
heavyset man with dark hair and a square face who
marched over was apparently the officer in charge. "These
people are illegals. I'm sorry if we got in the way of one
of your operations." He shrugged, his expression suggesting that he wasn't sorry at all. "Next time, pick a
better informant."

Jeff leaped out of the Jeep to confront the man. "What the hell is this? How come you decide to raid this place tonight, huh?"

"Who are you?" The INS officer held out a hand, looked at Jeff's ID. Handed it back. "This is outside city limits," he drawled. He turned to look back at the van. "All set? Let's get out of here."

"Why now? Why tonight?" Jeff stepped in front of him as the man turned back toward the van. "It's just too much of a coincidence."

For a moment, the INS officer studied him silently. "We got a tip," he said at last. For a moment, he looked slightly uncomfortable. "We got told that a truck full of Mexicans straight from the border was due in here tonight. The info sounded good. It fit with some stuff we got from down south." He hesitated another moment. "Sorry we messed up your operation." Stepping deliberately around Jeff, he marched back to his officers, who had finished loading the last of the residents. Silently, they climbed into their vehicles and pulled away from the camp, headlights creating cones of yellow light in the haze of dust.

Jones met Jeff's eyes and shrugged. "Guess we're through here," he said. "Unless you think he might show up anyway."

"No. He won't show." Jeff drew a deep breath, let it out slowly. "Go on home." His glance strayed around the ring of silent faces watching them. Nobody had moved. The small boy still sobbed, his face against the young woman's skirt. She stood with her head down, her eyes on the dust at her feet, her baby asleep in the crook of her arm. No one made a sound.

Jeff's shoulders jerked. He turned abruptly and followed Jones across the trampled dust where the INS van had parked. Without a word he got into the Jeep. He waited until Jones had gotten into his own blue Chevy that he'd left parked off in the weeds, then followed his officer back out to the main road. It wasn't until they had almost reached the Thriftway on the way back into town that he finally spoke.

"Damn." He struck the steering wheel a single blow with his fist. "Damn, damn, damn." He spoke softly, almost under his breath.

Rachel didn't speak. There was nothing to say. This kind of thing happened—the INS raided a camp, rounded up any of the workers who lacked proper documentation. Why tonight? Why this camp?

When they reached City Hall, Jeff slammed the Jeep into a parking space and got out, his posture taut and angry in the yellow glow of the street lamps. It was nearly full dark now. The western horizon was dark, the moon lost behind thickening clouds. A warm wind gusted suddenly, swirling scraps of litter into a twisting, miniature cyclone that vanished after only an instant. This wind felt different, Rachel thought absently. That storm was finally getting here. Jeff didn't protest as she followed him into the building, through the after-hours side door that led directly into the police offices.

Bert Stanfield was at the desk. He looked up as Jeff shoved through the door, his eyebrows rising. "You look like it's been a bad evening."

"Damn right. Who knew about the stakeout? Besides you, me, Kelly, and Lyle?"

Stanfield rose slowly, his palms flat on the desk top. "Nobody. Not as far as I'm concerned."

"Somebody else knew. Somebody talked. The INS just happened to get a call from a concerned citizen who claimed that a truck full of illegals was due in tonight." Jeff's eyes glittered with anger. "Kind of a coincidence, isn't it? Our boy has an inside line into this office."

Very deliberately, Stanfield's eyes fixed themselves on Rachel.

Rachel felt her cheeks pale as she thought back over the afternoon's conversation with Jeff. Was it possible? "No," she said hesitantly, then more strongly, "No. I only talked to Jeff about it. Spider wasn't around, and nobody from the Village was within earshot." She shrugged. "I didn't talk about it to anyone else, so it wasn't me."

Stanfield arched one eyebrow. His expression suggested that he'd heard better lines.

"If she says she didn't, then she didn't." Jeff spoke flatly. "I'll talk to Lyle and Kelly. Somebody said something. To someone." He turned on his heel, nearly colliding with the mayor in the doorway.

"I thought I heard voices down here." The young mayor eyed Jeff's grim face. "I was going to ask how the stake-out went." He grimaced. "I'm not sure I need to."

"Somebody sent the INS down to the camp. They took Valdez."

"Great." Ventura ran a hand through his thinning hair. "Back to square one?"

"Back a little farther, I think." Jeff shook his head. "Sorry, Phil. Looked like we had him."

"Me, too." Ventura sighed. "Me, too." He opened his mouth as if to say something, glanced at Stanfield, then shrugged. "Well, I guess we can all get some sleep to-night, anyway. Why don't you drop by in the morning, and we'll see if we can brainstorm something else clever."

He was making light of this night's disaster, speaking cheerfully, as if it were just a minor setback. But was it? This would swing the Council behind Stanfield.

"Sure." Jeff lifted a hand, not meeting the mayor's eyes. "Good night, Phil. You, too, Bert."

Outside, he slipped his arm around Rachel and pulled her close, saying nothing.

"Thanks for standing up for me," she said softly.

"Of course." He stroked the hair back from her face with both palms, tilting her face up to his. "When you say something, you tell the truth. I'm sorry," he said. "I thought we had this guy's ass."

"Maybe the Council won't pass the curfew. After all . . ." Rachel broke off. Jeff was staring over her shoulder, his body suddenly wire-tight.

"Shit," he said softly.

She turned, his arms falling away from her. The bright red scrawl covered the side of the Blossom Pharmacy building, directly across the parking lot from City Hall. *Ha Ha!* had been calligraphed in a tall, looping scrawl. Had it been there when they had pulled in? Rachel tried to think, but she had been focused on Jeff and hadn't really looked at the building. Together they walked across the lot. The vandal had carried sweeping loops of paint around the corner and on to the brick front. The loops sprawled across the front of the building, and the door had been liberally sprayed, as if the vandal had simply tried to do as much damage as possible. It would take a lot of work to clean that off.

"This is now very personal," Jeff said very softly. "I am going to get this guy."

They were silent on the drive back up to the house. It was late now, and the wind had picked up. The tops of the firs swayed, and once they had to stop to pull a huge limb from their lane in the road. It took both of them to move it. Ben was hysterically delighted to see them when they finally reached the house. He bounded around them, panting and wriggling his stub tail, obviously distressed by the stormy weather. Rachel glanced at the barometer as she went through the house to the kitchen. It had dropped a lot since this morning. The front was definitely coming in.

Jeff had slumped onto the sofa and was stroking the delighted Ben. "I'm going to broil those steaks," she told him. "We both need some dinner."

"I'm not hungry," he said and sighed. "But go ahead. If you want the corn, it's in the fridge."

She hadn't been hungry either, but once she got the corn into the steamer and ran the two thick steaks under the broiler, the scent of cooking meat made her stomach growl. Ben certainly thought it smelled good. He appeared in the kitchen door, plopping his butt down instantly on her stern command to sit, then turning into a doggy statue as she cooked. A statue that drooled. She hid a smile as she turned the steaks, refusing to be beguiled by his piteous expression.

Her smile faded instantly. Jeff had been so close to catching their ghostly vandal. And who was behind this? she wondered as she turned the steaks and checked the corn. Jeff was right. She eyed the wooden wine rack next to the counter, finally selecting a bottle of Oregon cabernet. This entire string of petty crimes seemed awfully personal. She forked the sizzling steaks onto two warm plates, added the corn, then filled two wineglasses with the ruby cabernet and managed to crowd everything including silverware onto a tray.

Jeff looked up as she shuffled into the room with Ben drooling at her side. "What's all this?"

"Dinner. Assuming Ben doesn't leap onto it the moment I put it on the table."

"Down," Jeff said sharply. Ben sank to the floor, his expression fervently hopeful. "I'm really not hungry."

"That's fine. Ben will eat yours, I bet." Rachel set the plates on the low table in front of them and handed Jeff the full glass of wine. "Drink it. That's an order."

"Yes, ma'am." He managed something that was almost a smile, but he did take a solid gulp of wine. And another. "Who talked?" he said, staring at the plate in front of him. "Somebody said something and the person who heard it said something . . . That's Blossom." Absently, he picked up his knife and fork and cut into the richly browned steak. "Whispers put the speed of light to shame." He put the steak in his mouth, chewed, swallowed, and looked at Rachel. "I was hungry." He sounded mildly surprised. "How'd you know that?"

"ESP," she said dryly, suppressing a smile as he dove into his steak in earnest. Too bad, Ben. You lose.

For a few minutes Jeff ate with a single-minded intensity that made Rachel suspect that lunch had been omitted from the day's schedule. When he sat back finally, he hadn't left much for Ben. "Thank you." He gave her a slightly crooked smile. "For putting up with me."

"Any time." She set her plate on the coffee table and moved over to the sofa to sit beside him. "You'll catch him," she said. "He's getting too cocky now. Sooner or later somebody is going to see him."

Jeff didn't answer right away, Instead, his lifted her chin with the tip of one finger so that he could look into her eyes. "I told you I was planning to quit if the Council went ahead with the curfew." His dark eyes held hers, enigmatic, full of shadow. "You need to know that it might well happen. That I resign."

"Why?" Rachel wanted to look away, but she couldn't. "They backed down. They were behind you."

"I've got a political job." He touched her cheekbone with one fingertip, ran it very slowly down the side of her jaw. "I had a long talk with Phil. He's coming up for reelection next year. If I'm unpopular around here, if I'm perceived as doing a poor job, I'm a liability."

He said the words so calmly. No, Rachel wanted to shout. Phil would never say that.

"Did he ask you to quit?" she whispered.

"Not yet." He leaned down slightly to kiss her slowly and gently. "He let me know that he might have to." He straightened, those dark eyes giving nothing away. "You need to think about that."

"Before we're married, you mean?"

He nodded, the flash of pain in his eyes vanishing so fast that she could almost believe that she'd imagined it. Rachel drew a deep breath. "I have thought quite a bit about this," she said slowly. "Ever since you said you were thinking about resigning. I don't . . . want to leave Blossom." Her voice wavered for a beat, then steadied. "But you know—I can run a landscape business nearly anywhere. I'd have to start over, but I know how to do that. I might even find something else I want to do." It was she who was holding his gaze now. "I thought about it and . . . I cried about it." She paused, swallowed. "And it's something I can do, Jeff. It's something I'm willing to do. I'm not kidding. Okay?"

"Okay," he murmured, his lips against hers now, his arms going around her as they sank back onto the sofa together.

Ben whined and nudged Jeff in the ribs.

"Go lie down," Jeff said.

Ben did as he was told.

CHAPTER

16

The sound of the phone woke Rachel. She kicked free of the tangled sheets and sat up, yawning, feeling as if it were just minutes ago that they had stumbled from where they had fallen asleep on the sofa to bed. But sun poured through the window and she winced when she saw the time on the bedside clock. Late. The call would be from Spider, wanting to know where she was. Sniffing at the scent of brewing coffee, she grabbed her cotton robe and headed for the kitchen to apologize.

But it wasn't Spider on the phone.

Grim-faced, a thick stoneware mug steaming unnoticed beside him, Jeff spoke into the phone. "Somebody called them in. Why the hell would I want to bust pickers, Jack? You know me better than that. I don't care what stories are going around." He slammed down the receiver, picked up his mug, and took a long swallow. "Better and better." He laughed shortly. "The INS got a taste of blood and went on a rampage yesterday. They hit a couple of camps hard. All of a sudden a couple of orchards are hurting for pickers. Your uncle's included."

"That *was* Uncle Jack." Rachel groaned. "Why would he blame you? And he doesn't hire illegals. He's really tough about green cards."

"I get the feeling that the INS wasn't being awfully picky last night." Jeff sighed. "The story making the rounds is that I called them in."

"You? That's crazy." Julio. She bit her lip. "I should have gone to see him last night," she said slowly. "I wasn't thinking."

"Julio." He nodded, sighed again. "I'm the one at fault. I should have gone over there." He shook his head, ran a hand through his tousled hair. "I had too much on my mind, I guess. Stupid." He swallowed the last of his coffee. "I'll drop you at the apartment and get over there first thing. I don't know if he'll still be home."

"I'll come with you." Rachel poured herself a cup of coffee and headed for the bedroom. "I persuaded him to talk to you in the first place. Five minutes," she said as she tossed her robe onto the bed and began to fish underwear from the dresser drawer she'd claimed temporarily.

There was plenty of work this time of year, and never enough pickers. If word went around that the INS was sweeping the camps, some workers would pack up and simply go elsewhere, even if they were in the country legally. Stories of unfair treatment at the hands of the INS abounded. True or not, they had their effect.

In a very few minutes they were in Jeff's Jeep and on their way down to Blossom. Julio's new pickup stood in front of the home Julio shared with his sister and brother-in-law. But when Jeff and Rachel knocked on the door, no one answered.

"Julio, I know you're there." Jeff leaned close to the door. "I came over to tell you what happened. I'm sorry about Ramon. I don't know who called the INS. It sure wasn't me. It was somebody who didn't want him to help us. Julio? Do you hear me?" Jeff banged on the door, again to no effect. "I'm sorry, Julio." He turned away, his face unreadable. "I guess that's it." He walked past Rachel, his shoulders tight.

Rachel hesitated a moment, looking back at the curtained windows of the house, hoping for some sign. No curtain twitched. Nothing moved. She followed Jeff back to the Jeep and they drove in silence to Mrs. Frey's house. She suppressed a twinge of guilt as Jeff pulled into the driveway. She had completely forgotten about calling Spider to let him know why she was late. Oh well. This was the morning for apologies. She climbed out of the Jeep and went around to the driver's side. There was nothing to say. She kissed Jeff lightly. He hugged her briefly, hard, then backed the Jeep swiftly down the driveway and into the street.

So who had leaked the information about the stakeout? Shaking her head, she looked around for Spider. No sign of him. Neither he nor Mrs. Frey were in the garden. She went to the side door and knocked. Mrs. Frey opened the door, a look of surprise on her face, a mop in her hand. "I thought you were at work already." Alarm raised her eyebrows. "Did something happen to John?"

"Why, no." Taken aback, Rachel hesitated. "I was late this morning, and I didn't call. I guess he gave up waiting for me."

"Really?" Mrs. Frey peered past her, as if Rachel might simply have overlooked Spider. "That's funny. I didn't even realize you hadn't come. This is my day to wax the kitchen floor." She made a face. "I hate the job. I suppose I should have one of those no-wax floors installed, but I like the old tile. So I suppose I have nobody but myself to blame."

"He's probably up in the apartment, listening to music or something. I gave him a key. Sorry to bother you."

"Oh, any interruption is welcome." The alarm hadn't quite faded from Mrs. Frey's face. "I'm sure he's up there. I can't think where else he'd get to. He wouldn't leave if he knew you were coming, certainly." She followed Rachel up the steep stairs to the apartment, clutching the railing with one freckled hand, her mop in the other. Peter sat on the railing, washing his face. He jumped down immediately, twining himself around Rachel's ankles as she unlocked the door. Rachel bent down to scratch his ears, which earned her one of his motorboat purrs.

Mrs. Frey stood close behind Rachel as she unlocked the apartment, peering over her shoulder as the door swung open. Peter stalked inside and claimed the back of his sofa, returning to the engrossing task of cleaning every hair in his glossy coat. Silence greeted her. The light on her answering machine burned steadily and no note lay on her office table, the kitchen counter, or anywhere else in the apartment. "I guess he got tired of waiting and went somewhere." Frowning, Rachel turned to Mrs. Frey. "My fault for not calling, I guess." But she wished he'd waited, or left her a note. They'd have to work out a system for this kind of thing.

"Maybe he went to the library," Mrs. Frey offered. "To surf."

"Surf?" Rachel blinked at her.

"He uses their Internet access." She chuckled. "He was pretty disgusted to find out that my modem's broken. I've got to get a new one. Next time my nephew is out from Portland, he's going to install one. He keeps telling me I could do it myself, but I'm not touching the inside of that thing. All those circuits! I just know I'll get electrocuted! So he uses the public access at the library."

"Oh," Rachel said faintly. So that was why he was at the library. She frowned. Why hadn't he said he was using the Internet that night she gave him a ride home? No reason, and that small silence felt wrong to her. "Well, I'll swing by the library. If he shows up in the meantime, have him give me a call on my cell phone, okay? If I don't hear from him, I'll just have to do without him."

"Oh, I'm sure he'll be back in a minute." Mrs. Frey regarded her mop with mild surprise, as if it had just materialized in her hand. "I guess I'd better get back to work. At least it will be done for another month." She tripped down the stairs with the agility of a mountain goat. "I'll have him call you the moment I see him."

Filled with vague disquiet—which had no basis whatsoever in any reality, Rachel reminded herself—she made a quick lunch from the meager supplies in the kitchen— a cup of strawberry yoghurt, a handful of carrot sticks, a slightly stale bagel and the last of the chocolate chip cookies from the bag in the cupboard. Crumpling the empty cookie bag, she tossed it into the trash beneath the sink. Spider was fine. It was broad daylight. Why in heaven's name worry about the kid?

But she did.

She watered the Persian violet that drooped thirstily in the kitchen window, apologizing silently for her recent neglect. "Okay, cat." She scooped Peter from the sofa. "Time to go back to terrorizing Mrs. Frey's chickadees." He was in one of his rare cuddly moods, purring and wrapping velvet paws around her head as she buried her face in his fur. "What are we going to do with you, cat?" she murmured as she carried him out onto the landing. "Do you want to stay here? That's what Joylinn thinks. Or do you want to come live with Jeff and me? And Ben. Oh, lordy, cat. How is this going to work out?"

Peter purred loudly, batted her nose with one paw, then twisted in her arms and leaped with acrobatic accuracy to the railing.

"One day you're going to fall to your death, you know."

He gave her an unwinking stare that told her just what she could do with *that* comment, then returned to the seemingly never-ending task of coat cleaning.

Shaking her head, seized by an unexpected threat of tears, Rachel hurried down the steps to her truck. Fine. She'd check the library and then she was off to the Village. She'd wasted enough time already. This day was not going well. Not at all. She tossed her lunch into the truck's box and backed down the driveway. Midmorning on a weekday during harvest season, Blossom's Main Street wasn't awfully busy. Rachel kept an eye out for Spider on the sidewalk as she turned onto it at the bottom of Pine and cruised along the block to park in front of the square brick library with its skinny columns and brick face. The huge gray concrete planter in front of it brimmed over with blue-gray fescue clumps, low-growing penstemon, and the spiky and colorful mounds of jovibarba and sempirvivums. A chunk of pitted lava rock added interest to the center of the thriving plants. The heat and drought-tolerant planters had been her first city contract for the brand-new Mayor Ventura. Rachel parked, suppressing a brief shiver at the memory of Death's intrusion into that project. Spider had just started to work for her back then. She took the concrete steps two at a time, pushing through the double doors into the cool musty atmosphere of the library.

Books en masse seemed to have an exhalation of their own. Rachel tried to identify the components as she scanned the aisles of tall wooden shelves closely filled with ranked books in all subjects. An old man drowsed over a newspaper skewered on a wooden rod in one of the armchairs in the center of the room. The long wooden tables, bearing scratches and scars as testament to years of doodling students looking up Egypt and alligators for school papers, were empty. On the bright new rug just in front of the closed stack area, a woman sat on the floor amid a circle of young children, reading aloud from a picture book, holding it up so that the children could see the pictures.

"Rachel, how are you?" A short, heavyset woman wearing a blue flower print dress, a pair of reading glasses dangling around her neck on a chain, bustled up. "I haven't seen you in ages." She ran a hand across her pinned-back, carefully tinted auburn hair, managing to dislodge an extra strand or two as she did so. The gray roots were just beginning to show. "I just saw Catherine the other day. Your aunt told me you're getting married. Congratulations, dear." Head librarian Amy Fullerton gave Rachel a hug. "I hear the lucky man is that young chief of police our mayor hired. How exciting for you. Aren't you going to have a big wedding?"

Amy Fullerton and her Aunt Catherine had played Bingo at the Grange Hall every Thursday evening for as long as Rachel could remember. Not even harvest season got in the way of those Thursday night games. Her uncle used to joke that if something happened on Wednesday, everybody in town would know about it by nine o'clock on Thursday night.

"We're just going to have a quiet family affair," Rachel said. "Neither of us goes in much for big parties."

"Oh, I know Catherine's so disappointed." Amy clucked at her reprovingly. "She doesn't have any daughters to do a wedding for, dear. You were her only hope."

"Oh, I'm sure she'll be glad at the end that she doesn't have to deal with a thousand details," Rachel said lightly. She peered into the dim recesses between two of the long stacks. Neither Amy nor Elinore Montgomery, her assistant, thought much of the Internet. They had stuck the public-access computer between two stacks, isolated on a small desk against the wall. Rachel could just make out the monitor and desk. Nobody there. "I'm looking for my assistant. He's about eighteen, with black hair."

"Oh, the Asian boy? He's in here every evening." Amy made her clucking noise again. "All these children spend too much time on the Internet. We won't have any readers at all in another generation." Cluck cluck.

She sounded a bit like one of her aunt's fat Rhode Island hens, Rachel thought. Even the color was right. She folded her lips tightly to suppress her smile. "Was he in here this morning?"

"Oh yes, yes he was. About an hour ago. He was using the computer." She followed the disappointed Rachel to the door. "At least he reads. He took out every book on mushrooms in the library and read all the encyclopedias. I asked him if he was doing something for college. But he told me he was just interested."

"Mushrooms?" Rachel halted at the doorway.

"Oh, yes. Not that we have many, but we probably have as many as a Portland branch library. I suppose he's going to go running off into the woods this fall, trying to make a thousand dollars picking mushrooms for those buyers that come through here."

"Probably." Rachel glanced at her watch. Homework for Gus? "We probably passed each other and he's waiting for me." She said a hasty good-bye to Mrs. Fullerton and hurried down the steps to her truck. Today's behavior wasn't like Spider. He had always been punctual. Mushrooms. Well, that was understandable, but why not just tell her he was on the Internet? A suspicion was growing in her mind, and she said a brief fervent prayer that she was wrong.

Instead of returning to the house, she detoured over to Fir and up to Gus Van Dorn's house. Unlike most yards in Blossom, with their neat junipers, camellias, or rhododendrons, and maybe a few annuals in a bed along the walk, Gus Van Dorn's front yard overflowed with per-

ennials. Rhododendrons created shady nooks that were
filled with astilbes, cyclamens, hellebores, and a variety
of primulas in spring. This time of year hostas glowed in
shades of emerald, chartreuse, and ivory in the dappled
shade. Thalyctrum offered foamy stalks of white and
lavender, sheltered from the wind by the tall shrubs. Rachel followed the stone-flagged walk up to the wide steps
leading to the front porch that ran the width of the house.
Honeysuckle curtained the east-facing porch, trained onto
a bamboo lattice, to provide a well of cool shade on a
hot summer morning. A few scarlet runner beans twined
through the lush green honeysuckle, the bright blossoms
contrasting vividly with the pink-and-white trumpets of
the honeysuckle. A hummingbird with a green-and-scarlet
throat withdrew its long beak from a honeysuckle blossom
and darted over to hang in front of her face like a flashing
jewel. As Rachel sucked in her breath at the nearness of
this beauty, it chittered at her shrilly, then dove straight
at her face. Instinctively she ducked, gasping, then
flinched as it darted around her, wasplike, still scolding
her in its tiny voice. With a final tirade, it waggled itself
in midair as if to say "so there" and darted away into the
neighboring yard.

"That was Earnest." Gus Van Dorn's voice came from
the shady porch. "I named him that because he reminds
me of a neighbor I once had. When I put up the back
fence, damned if he wasn't out there with a tape measure,
checking property lines right down to the inch. Always
feuding with the folk up the street who let their Lab run.
Every time that dog set foot in his yard, he was out there
screamin'. Territorial, kind of." He emerged from the cool
shadows, grinning. "Come on up and set with us," he said.
"I've got a pitcher of lemonade. None of that frozen stuff
either. Come and visit for a while. You're always running,
seems like."

"I was looking for Spider," she said, hope leaping at that "us." "Is he here?"

"I haven't seen him today." Gus shook his head. "Usually he comes by in the evening."

"Is that you, Rachel?" Doc Welsh appeared at Gus's shoulder, his face flaccid and frighteningly old. "We were just talking about the old days."

She almost thanked them and declined, but something held her, some whisper from the back of her brain. "Sure," she said, climbing the sagging steps. "I'd love a glass of lemonade."

Gus ushered her with charming formality over to the wooden swing, hung by heavy chains from the porch ceiling. Faded, flowered cushions covered it. A couple of wooden folding chairs with similar cushions flanked it. A glass pitcher full of cloudy yellow liquid, ice, and sliced lemons occupied the top of a wooden folding table, crowded by two glasses half full of ice and lemonade. Gus vanished into the house as she seated herself gingerly on the swing. As a child she'd always longed for a porch swing, had wheedled her uncle to build one to no effect.

"Gus tells me your new kid is quite a help around here." Dr. Welsh picked up his lemonade glass. "Good to see the young actually putting a little muscle into their work. So many of these kids seem to think that taking out the garbage is a major effort."

"Maybe nobody has asked them to do anything," Rachel said. She looked up as Gus emerged from the house with a clean glass filled with ice and a plate of ginger snaps.

"I use fresh ginger, so they're spicy," he warned as he squeezed the plate onto the table. The pitcher tottered precariously for a moment, then apparently decided to remain in place. "So how come Spider is missing?" He filled her glass, handed it to her. "That doesn't sound like him." In spite of his mild tone, worry creased the corners of his eyes.

"It isn't." She sipped her lemonade, approving of its icy tartness. "I was late this morning and didn't call. He probably went off to do an errand, and he's probably back at the apartment waiting for me." She winked. "But it's a good excuse to visit."

"You're still working out at the Village?" Dr. Welsh was eyeing his lemonade as if it were medicine.

"I am." Rachel nodded. "I don't want to see the company that bought it dump it. The magazine article that's scheduled to appear is pretty important, I gather. So I'll have the place looking good for the camera. Hey, it's a chance to grandstand for edible and drought-tolerant landscaping." She took a cookie as Gus offered her the plate. Ginger permeated the molasses-fragrant cookies, biting her tongue fragrantly. "Wonderful," she said with her mouth full. Swallowed. "Spider has been checking out all the books in the library on mushrooms," she told Gus. "Is this homework?"

"From me?" Gus looked surprised. "No. I guess he's just trying hard. He's that kind of a kid."

Her earlier sense of disquiet grew stronger. She needed to find Spider now. Not later. Now. "I'd better get to work." She rose, emptying her glass. "Thank you so much for the lemonade. I'll remember it fondly this afternoon." She insisted on carrying her glass into the kitchen. Doc and Gus followed her, exchanging words about runs and lures that undoubtedly meant a lot but not to her. As she passed through the dim, cluttered living room, she paused.

It seemed that every horizontal surface in the crowded space was covered with photographs in various grades of metal and wooden frames. Young children, family groups, very old people in stiff poses, the photos tinted sepia. One picture had stopped Rachel, hooked her like one of Doc's trout. The photograph stood alone at the very end of the

fireplace mantel, a little apart from the thickly clustered
family shots, as if it didn't quite belong. A woman with
laughing blue eyes and short blond hair grinned at the
camera, a toddler on her lap, one bare arm hugging the
towheaded young boy. She wore shorts and a sleeveless
shirt, and a basket of blackberries stood in front of the
trio. The boy grinned at the camera from beneath ragged
bangs, his eyes bright and full of life. He was about eight,
Rachel guessed. He looked familiar. Frowning, she
crossed the faded and carefully vacuumed rug to stand in
front of the picture. The memory wouldn't come. The
harder she tried, the more it eluded her. "Gus, who is
this?"

"Oh, that's Jerry." Gus came up beside her. "He was
the kid I was telling you about. The one who hunted
mushrooms with me. He knew more than I did." Gus
chuckled, but there was a sad note in his voice. "I always
figured he'd get a Ph.D. in mycology. I hope he has a
good life."

"Jerry." Rachel tried to remember. "His mother was
killed in an accident, right?"

"And his little brother there." Gus shook his head. "Terrible tragedy. I hope he finally managed to forgive that
woman. He'll find no peace if he doesn't."

"What kind of accident?" Rachel asked.

"Oh my God." Doc's voice interrupted. "I know that
picture. Gus, where'd you get it? Emily had it in her
room." Doc stepped a bit unsteadily into the stuffy room,
his face pasty in the dim light, like the translucent skin
of a cave creature. "That's the family Emily hit that night.
She said it was raining and she didn't see them until too
late. She hit the brakes and hydroplaned."

"Huh?" Gus turned perplexed eyes on Doc.

Doc was saying something about remorse and peni-
tence, but Rachel barely heard him. That boy, the older
one, with the bright smile and blond hair . . . Waves of

heat and cold rippled across her skin. She closed her eyes, reliving that afternoon when Jason had told her about his magical gateway. "What's his name, Gus?" Her voice trembled. "Jerry what?"

"Jerry Gainer." Gus gave her a troubled look. "Are you all right?"

Gainer. Jerry. She shook her head.

It had to be him. "What was her name before she married? Jerry's mother?" Rachel held her breath.

"It was Marl. She told me once, I don't remember why. She wasn't from around here. I should have tried a lot harder to keep him." He shook his head. "Hindsight is a great thing. Something to keep us awake at night, awed by our own stupidity."

Jerry Marl. Look at that kid, think how he'd look at twenty. Oh, yes. It was him. Rachel sucked in a quick breath, feeling as if someone had punched her in the stomach. "Jason Marl," she whispered.

"Who?" Gus peered at her.

Doc's perplexed expression matched Gus's.

"Jason Marl." She drew in a quick breath. "He's an aid at the Village. Him. The kid in the picture. Jerry. I'm sure it's him." And Emily had his picture in her room. Had she recognized him? "Gus, I need to use your phone."

He took her into the kitchen. She seized the antiquated rotary phone and dialed the police number, silently cursing the twirl of the dial.

Bert Stanfield answered.

He didn't know where Jeff was. He sounded tired and irritable. She hung up, tried Jeff's cell phone. It was off. Damn. Why would he do that?

"What's going on?" Gus seized her by the arm, his fingers squeezing her with surprising strength.

"The boy whose family was killed by Emily—he works at the Village. Where she was poisoned," Rachel gasped.

Gus released Rachel, his face ashen. "No." His voice trembled. "He wouldn't kill anyone. Not Jerry."

"Gus, come with me." It was her turn to take his arm. "Right now. Let's go see Jason. You can tell me if he's Jerry."

"I've been there to see Ricki." Gus hung back, his face closed and resistant. "I never saw Jerry there."

Maybe Jerry had been careful to stay out of Gus's way. Rachel released him. Stupid thing to do anyway, she thought. Gus's face would give him away if he saw Jason and recognized him. Jason could be gone before Jeff had a chance to get out there to arrest him. Stupid, girl. Think. Before you blow this for Jeff. "Can I borrow this photo?" She hurried back into the living room and snatched up the photo. "I'll take good care of it."

"It isn't Jerry." Gus followed her, but the stubborn expression on his face was eroding. "I mean, he was angry at her, sure. He said he hated her, but what's any kid going to say about the driver who killed his family?" The words ended feebly. "Damn." His voice trembled. "I should have kept him. I should have."

Doc put a hand on his friend's shoulder.

Hindsight could gut you. Rachel thanked Gus as she left, but he was staring at the small clean space on the dusty mantel where the photograph had stood and he didn't answer. She ran down the walk to her truck. She had to find Jeff. And she had to find Spider. Mushrooms. Fresh fear squeezed her. Jason—Jerry—was a mushroom hunter. Spider had been on the Internet a lot, but hadn't told her about it. He had been researching mushrooms. What was the connection here? He had listened to Harris, who didn't believe that the director was the murderer.

Whatever Spider had been up to, Jason Marl was very possibly a cold-blooded killer. And Spider didn't know.

She flung herself behind the wheel and started the engine. Her rear wheels spun on the dry pavement as she pulled away from the curb. Easy, easy, she told herself as she accelerated down the street. All you need to do is find Jeff and tell him. He'll take it from there.

Find him where? Her hindbrain kept insisting that it was too late for calm. Way too late.

She hoped she was wrong. Swinging by City Hall, she checked for Jeff's Jeep but it wasn't there. She'd have to try and convince Stanfield that she wasn't crazy. She had a feeling that it wasn't going to be easy. But she went on past the driveway and turned onto Pine. First she would go back to the house and make sure Spider had returned. Surely he had. By now.

But when she reached the house, Mrs. Frey's car wasn't in the driveway. The house was locked and nobody answered downstairs when she knocked. Peter, sunning himself beneath Mrs. Frey's bird feeder, eyed her warily as she pounded up the stairs to her apartment. She burst through the door, holding her breath as she checked kitchen, desk, and bedroom. Nothing. No note. No message on the machine, no sign that Spider had been there. Peter met her on the landing, giving her a quizzical *mrrrp.* "You tell me, cat." She leaned against the door frame, a headache beginning to pulse behind her eyes. "Is he playing hooky, ticked at me because I was late? Is he with Mrs. Frey doing the shopping? Or . . ." She shook her head, unwilling to give voice to that possibility. Jason Marl would be at work, right? She dashed back into the house and grabbed the phone book, looking up the phone number for the Village office. "Is Jason Marl there?" she asked when the receptionist answered.

"Just a moment," a pleasant-voiced woman said.

He was there, safely at work. He wasn't out murdering Spider or doing anything else crazy, and she felt like an idiot. She'd hang up as soon as she heard his voice, she told herself. And hoped they didn't use caller ID at the desk!

"I'm sorry to be so long." The woman on the other end sounded genuinely regretful. "I had to take another call. Jason is off today. I'm afraid I can't give out his home number. Can I take a message?"

"No. No, thank you." Numbly, Rachel replaced the phone. Spider was missing. Jason was off.

She bolted through the apartment and past the perplexed Peter, taking the stairs two at a time, not even bothering to lock the door behind her.

Time to call in the cavalry. Even if the cavalry was Bert Stanfield.

CHAPTER

17

"Let me get this straight." Stanfield faced Rachel across his neatly ordered desk, his expression cool. "You think that an aid at the Village has a relationship to one of the murder victims?"

"Yes. I mean, it's almost certain. Gus Van Dorn would have to identify him, I guess. He's going by the name of Jason Marl, but he's really Jerry Gainer, and Emily Barnhart killed his mother and brother in a car accident, back when he was a child."

Stanfield laced his fingers together and said nothing

He reminded her of the principal of the grade school, Rachel thought distractedly. He would do the same thing when one of the teachers marched her up to the office with a complaint about her behavior. Listen to her indignant explanations, then sit staring, his fingers laced, letting the thickening silence somehow confirm her guilt.

"He's off today and my assistant is missing. There might be a connection." The thick sticky silence made her words sound thin. Rachel let her breath out in a slow sigh.

They were getting nowhere fast. "I think Spider guessed that one of the aids was involved." She didn't know that at all, but she had to say something. "He might be in danger."

"You're talking about the boy who works for you? The half-Asian kid? He was a resident at the Youth Farm. I checked up on him." Stanfield's eyes pinned her. "I was going to drop by and have a talk with him. Can you verify his whereabouts after dark?"

"What?" Rachel blinked, then flushed, as his meaning sank in. "He wasn't even in town when the vandalism started." Her voice was rising and she forced herself to get hold of her temper. "I'm not talking about spray paint and broken windows here. I'm talking about three dead people."

"Sometimes we forget to check our own backyard." Stanfield leaned back in his chair. "So you don't know what he's up to at night then?"

"He was staying with my former assistant's family. And then with Gus Van Dorn. And now he's renting a room from my landlady. He's not out roaming the streets, okay?"

"So where is he now?" Stanfield raised his eyebrows, miming an expression of innocent confusion.

Rachel closed her eyes and drew two slow breaths, reciting several sentences in her head that would not improve the situation at all, were she to actually utter them. "So you are refusing to look into this complaint?" she asked in her sweetest voice.

"Complaint?" Stanfield's eyebrows rose. "What complaint?"

"That my assistant is missing. That I have information that leads me to believe that the family of one of the Village's aids was killed by one of the murdered residents. That this same aid is also connected to my assistant and may have kidnapped him." She enunciated each syllable clearly and distinctly.

"What the hell is this?"

Rachel and Stanfield turned in such perfect unison that she would have thought it comical, if she hadn't been so furious. Jeff stood in the doorway, frowning, his eyes moving from Stanfield to Rachel. "What about an aid?"

"Jason Marl." Rachel gave Stanfield a single searing look. "Is probably the son of a woman who was killed in a hit-and-run accident by Emily Barnhart. His younger brother died, too. Gus Van Dorn says he hated her. His real name is Jerry Gainer. And Spider is missing." She drew a shuddering breath. "I think he found out somehow that Jason had something to do with mushrooms and guessed he might be the murderer."

"Shit," Jeff said softly. He gave Stanfield a look.

"Sounded pretty far-fetched to me." The older officer shrugged.

"How long has Spider been gone?" Jeff said sharply. "And has Gus identified this aid for sure?"

"Spider disappeared this morning. Mrs. Frey thought he went to the library when I was late," Rachel said reluctantly. "And Gus says he never saw Jerry at the Village. But he had a photo of him as a boy." She handed him the photograph. "His mother's maiden name was Marl."

Jeff took the photo and looked at it. His face tightened. "Emily Barnhart had this same photograph in her room," he said quietly. "We'd better check it out." He handed the photo back and rubbed his hand across his face. "I know you're worried about Spider, but he could just be off somewhere. He'll probably show up this evening with a good story about why he didn't work today."

"Jason Marl has the day off today." Rachel swallowed, because her fears were rising like ghosts from a shallow grave. Jeff wasn't going to do anything either.

"I'll go talk to Marl." Jeff nodded. "Gus can come along with me."

"What about Spider?"

"Sweetheart." Jeff took her lightly by the shoulders, his dark eyes compassionate. "He's been missing a few hours. He could have played hooky and gone to Hood River to see a movie. If he doesn't show up by this evening, we'll worry about him. If Marl is Jerry Gainer, and he has done something to Spider, then Jerry is still our shortest route to him."

Rachel nodded mutely, because it didn't seem to be enough. Out in the hall, a lanky figure approached the open door, then hesitated, and started to turn away.

"Julio!" Rachel recognized him, and stepped past Jeff.

He stopped short, paused for a moment as if undecided about whether to answer or not. Straightening his shoulders, he returned, his hat in his hand. "*Señorita,*" he said formally, his eyes low, not meeting hers. He flicked a brief glance at Jeff, then straightened fully, his head back, his lean profile stark in the dim light of the hallway. "*Señor* Price," he said with immense dignity. "You are an honest man. Always. If you tell me that you did not call the Immigration men to take Ramon to jail, then I believe you." His eyes met Jeff's and he lifted his chin. "This is my town, as it is your town. I am a citizen of Blossom. I do not want this man who is a thief to do harm here. I saw him. I remember what he looks like. I will help you find him."

Bless you, Julio, Rachel thought, and wanted to dance a jig right there. But she kept her mouth shut.

"Thank you," Jeff said gravely. He held out his hand. "I am sorry about your friend. Truly. I will do whatever I can for him."

Julio returned the handshake without speaking.

"Have you seen this man since the time he visited Ramon?" Jeff ushered Julio into the office.

"Yes." Julio nodded. "That is why I came here." He gave Stanfield a wary look and a nod, which Stanfield returned stiffly.

"I saw him come out of the food store on Main." Julio turned back to Jeff. "He was walking." Julio shrugged. "I was on my way to a job. I did not see where he went."

"That's a start." Jeff's eyes glittered. "If he was walking, maybe he lives down that way. There are a couple of rental houses up on first, back behind the library."

"We're renting just up above there, on Second." Stanfield spoke up. "If we can get a good description, I can have my son keep an eye out for him." Stanfield snorted. "It'll give him something to do besides sit in front of his damn video games all day."

"What did he look like?" Jeff walked around behind Stanfield's desk to pick up a notepad from his own cluttered desk top.

Julio followed, then halted, his posture stiff.

"What's wrong?" Jeff looked up at him as he dropped into his chair. "Have a seat." He pushed a chair an inch toward Julio.

But Julio shook his head. "That is him," he said simply. And pointed to a small, framed photograph on Stanfield's desk. "That is the man who visited Ramon. He had the carving from *la señorita's* truck."

"The hell you say." Stanfield rose, his face flushing. "That's my son."

Rachel craned her neck. Sure enough, the photograph was of the young man who had accompanied Stanfield when he had responded to her report on her vandalized truck. Blond, with cropped hair and his father's rectangular face, he grinned at the camera, his expression confident, almost cocky.

Jeff was also staring at the photograph. A tiny muscle leaped in his jaw as he raised his eyes to Julio's face. "You're sure?" he asked quietly.

Julio nodded.

"That's crap," Stanfield exploded. "You're going to take the word of this—"

"Enough!" The word cracked in the air.

Stanfield glared, his face flushed, eyes glittering. "Look, Jeff, he saw some blond kid. We probably all look alike to him. We're talking about my son here. I can tell you for sure that he isn't involved in this shit."

"Can you?" Jeff's voice was dangerously quiet.

"Yes."

For a moment, the two men stared at each other, and a thick, taut silence filled the office. Julio looked away, his eyes fixed on the battered copier in the corner. Finally, Stanfield's eyes shifted just the tiniest bit.

"Julio and I are going to go visit your son." Jeff spoke quietly. "Do you have time, Julio?"

Julio nodded, not looking at Stanfield.

"I'm coming along, too." Stanfield's voice was thick and his gray eyes were flat and angry.

Jeff shrugged. "Transfer incoming calls to your cell," was all he said.

He didn't invite her, but Rachel decided that she wasn't going to miss this. Not for the world. Still jumpy with worry about Spider, she got into her truck and pulled out onto Main, following Jeff and Julio in Blossom's single cruiser. They parked on the quiet street, just down from Stanfield's house. Julio and Jeff walked together. Stanfield followed, his thick body rigid with anger, distancing himself from them. Rachel hung well back, not wanting to get in the way. She had learned her lesson about getting in the way one dark night on the steps of Beck's cabin. Once was enough.

The house was a single-story Craftsman-style dwelling. It sat back from the sidewalk with a sloping front yard, divided by concrete steps that led to the front porch. Low green mounds of juniper bordered the steps and the porch, backed by a couple of well-grown rhododendrons. Boring landscape, Rachel thought. Rental-house landscape. Easy to maintain. A new Samurai was parked at the curb, its metal-flake blue paint gleaming in the sun.

"Your son's car?" Jeff asked as they reached it.

"I gave it to him for his birthday." Stanfield's voice was stiff.

Jeff looked through the window without touching the vehicle. "Wonder what he's got under the blanket in back?"

Stanfield shrugged and didn't answer. Julio stood a little apart from the two men, his eyes on the house.

The door opened, and a blond young man hurried out, a blue nylon pack in his hands. He hadn't seen them yet. Rachel recognized him from the morning of the truck break-in. He trotted across the porch, then halted abruptly, taking in the threesome standing below him on the sidewalk. "Hey, Dad?" He grinned. "What's up?"

"*Sí.*" Julio turned to Jeff, speaking quietly. "That is the man."

"Crap!" Stanfield took one step toward Julio, halted at Jeff's look. "Greg, this . . . this man claims you're the one who's been responsible for all the damage in town lately. He's got his head up his butt, but I want to know where you were every evening for the last two weeks, who you talked to, and what you did. We need to stuff this idiocy right now."

"How could I go anywhere, Dad?" Greg Stanfield stood at the top of the steps, his posture relaxed and easy, the grin still on his face. "You don't let me go anywhere. We moved out to this shitty little dump because you didn't want me doing the music scene in Portland, or hanging out with my friends. My friends, Dad. They weren't good enough for you. Well, the hicks here aren't good enough for me. So I got nothing to do. Is that better than hanging out, huh?"

"What?" Stanfield rocked slightly back on his heels, as if his son's words had weight and force, like thrown rocks. "What the hell are you saying?"

"It took you long enough is what I'm saying. What a bunch of hicks. I knew right where you were, every night. You'd tell me right where you were going to be all night, all of you. What a joke. I'd hit some place, and laugh all the way home." He looked at his father. "You're so full of shit." He threw the pack at his father's head, spun on his heel, and bolted around the side of the house.

Jeff flung himself up the slope of the yard, hot on his heels. Julio raced after him.

Stanfield stood on the sidewalk, staring down at the pack, which had hit him in the chest. A fake-leather portfolio, two cell phones, and a handful of CDs had spilled onto the sidewalk. The silver CD disks shimmered with rainbows in the sunlight. A crash from the back of the house and the sounds of a scuffle finally brought Stanfield's head up. Slowly, stiffly, he circled around the spilled items and climbed the steps. As he reached the foot of the porch steps, Jeff came around the side of the house, propelling a handcuffed Greg in front of him. A fresh scrape marred the side of the youth's sullen face. Julio followed closely and watchfully at their heels.

Bright blood streaked Jeff's left arm and Rachel caught her breath.

Stanfield stopped in front of his son, his eyes on Greg's face. His lips moved slightly, as if he were going to speak. Instead, he shifted his gaze to Jeff's face. "I'll take him in," he croaked.

"I will." Jeff shook his head. "Go on back, Bert," he said quietly. "I'll be along."

Stanfield looked as if he was about to protest, then his glance shifted to his son and his shoulders slumped. Moving like an old man, he descended the steps, walked past the spilled disks and cell phones, and climbed into his car.

Rachel felt a small twinge of pity for the man as he pulled away from the curb. But not much. Jeff was putting the teenager into the back of the cruiser, hand on his head to protect it as the youth slumped onto the seat. Spots of bright blood gleamed on the sidewalk.

Rachel ran back to her truck and fumbled the box open. Grabbing the first aid kit, she hurried back to the car. Already a small cluster of people had gathered down the block, an elderly man and a gray-haired woman in slacks and a heavyset young mother with a baby on her hip. They watched and murmured, staying well back. "What happened?" Rachel reached the cruiser. "Jeff, you're bleeding."

"He swung a board at me." Jeff rotated his arm, grimaced at the slick of blood on his forearm. "I guess it had a nail in it. I don't think it's bad." He flinched as she swabbed at the blood with an antiseptic pad from her kit. "Ouch, what is that? Alcohol?"

"No. Hold still." The gash on his arm was deep but not very large. "You're going to need a couple of stitches in this, I bet," she said as she wiped it clean. Fresh blood welled instantly into the ragged tear. "Hold it until it stops bleeding." She pressed a gauze pad over the wound.

"Thanks, Rachel." He pressed on the pad, turned to Julio. "Thank you for helping me out, Julio. Glad you were there."

Julio nodded soberly. "Do you need me longer?"

Jeff shook his head. "I know you have clients. I'll need a statement, but we can do that later. Do you want a ride back to City Hall?"

"I can walk to my truck." Julio lifted a hand to Rachel, then hurried down the block toward the center of town.

"I'm going to get a warrant and search the house now." Jeff sighed as he leaned against the car. "You never know." He shook his head, the weariness of the past week

showing in the slope of his shoulders and spine. "I feel
sorry for Bert."

"I don't," Rachel said crisply. "He wanted your job,
and his son has been giving you hell."

"Bert thought he could do it better." Jeff straightened,
frowning at the items that had spilled from the pack. "I'd
better bag this stuff." The pad on his arm was soaked red,
but the bleeding had slowed. He let Rachel put a fresh
pad in place and bandage the cut temporarily, promising
to get it looked at later. Crouching, he began to pick up
the CDs and cell phones, using a handkerchief, and deposited them in a plastic bag.

The cheap portfolio had burst open as it fell and a
paperclipped wad of papers spilled out onto the sidewalk. They looked like printouts of e-mail messages.
Shroomer@fastmail.com, she read in the heading.
Shroomer. Mushrooms? Squatting, she scanned the top
page.

"What is it?" Jeff scooped the last of the CDs into the
bag. "Looks like he busted into somebody's car."

"Jeff, can I read these?" The hair on the back of Rachel's neck began to prickle. "Whoever this is, he's talking about galerina mushrooms." She swallowed. "In this
message he's answering somebody's question about poisoning an old woman with them."

Without a word, Jeff slipped the papers from the portfolio, careful to avoid handling the leather. "Paper doesn't
hold prints well," he said, although he handled the dis-
arranged sheets by the edge. Together they began to look
over the pages. Apparently, the owner of the portfolio had
kept a chronological record of his e-mail conversation
with someone called JT. As Rachel sorted through the
messages, reading quoted e-mails from Shroomer as well
as JT's replies, she found herself holding her breath.

so let's pretend I want to off this old lady it's for the
book i'm writing not for real, ha hah she's in a nursing

home and i don't want anyone to find out i poisoned her so what kind of mushroom would you use, huh

Shroomer had answered that although there were a lot of toxic varieties, they could be detected in a toxicology screen. *what about something like galerinas?* The next message from JT read: *by the time the old gal died of organ failure, could you still detect the chemical? and what if you pinned the murder on the director? say she was embezzling patient money, so you plant a bag of dry galerinas in her office, and hey—if anyone finds mushroom in a screen, they check her office and you're home free pretty smart huh?*

"You little idiot," Rachel said softly. Cold in spite of the growing midday heat, she hunted for the next message in the sequence. *Pretty good plot,* Shroomer had responded. *Let me know when the book comes out and I'll buy a copy.*

oh, it gets better, JT wrote in his next message. *just wait till you read it the bad guy kills two other old timers that the director was stealing from, just so nobody figures why hes doing it, only he doesn't know that somebody found out the real reason hes doing it, and how and who he really is hey, Shroomer, can you show me some of those galerinas? i need to get the description right we could talk about my plot, huh? i think you might like it a lot i think you might want to buy into it, if you get me*

"Son of a bitch," Jeff said softly. He looked over at Rachel. "You think this JT is Spider, don't you? Rachel, this is the Internet. JT could be typing this in from Germany."

"Oh, sure, and get all the details right? It's Spider." Rachel spoke through stiff lips. "John Tranh. That's his real name. It has to be him. That's why he didn't tell me he was on the Internet. That's what he was doing at the library. He went fishing." She sucked in a quick breath. "And Ricki asked me what his real name was. She said

she had a bet with someone." Her heart began to pound.
"I didn't ask her who made the bet. I bet it was Jason."
She pounded her fist against her thigh. "I'm so *stupid*."

"Not hardly. You could be wrong," Jeff said thoughtfully.

She merely looked at him.

"I didn't say that I thought you were." He rose to his
feet as Rachel began to hunt for the next message.

"Too bad you stole that portfolio and those CDs from
that lady's car in Hood River when you mugged her." Jeff
leaned into the cruiser, his posture casual. "Attempted
rape sends you down bigtime."

"Don't give me that shit." Greg leaned forward, sneer-
ing, but the corner of his left eye twitched. "I wasn't anywhere near Hood River. You prove it."

"The stuff proves it." Jeff shrugged. "It's all on the list
of items stolen from her car. We're heading into Hood
River. She can ID you there. The description fits." He
sauntered around to the front of the car and opened the
driver's side door. "You'd be surprised how many people
pick somebody out of a lineup, even if the real perp isn't
there. They feel that they have to pick somebody. I just
read a report on it." He grinned coldly at Greg. "Can't
say I'd grieve one bit if you went down for a rape you
didn't try. Keep you out of my hair."

"I wasn't there, I tell you." Hatred and fear flared bright
and ugly in Greg's flat blue eyes. "I grabbed this junk out
at that old folks' home. Where she works." He jerked his
head at Rachel. "I was gonna grab that stupid wood carving again, because I thought she'd be dumb enough to
stick it back in her truck. It would've been a neat trick.
But she wasn't there, so I busted into one of the cars. It
was a gray Toyota. A beat-up old Corolla. That's where
I picked up the briefcase thing and CDs. Ask the damn
owner."

"Jeff." Rachel had been listening as she shuffled through the papers. "The last one in the stack is from this morning." Her voice quavered as she handed him the sheet.

The quoted message from Shroomer read: *I know where there are plenty of galerinas. You really want to kill someone, don't you? Ok, hotshot. I'll put death in your hands. Meet me at ten and I'll show you. Go to that road I told you about—the one where you can get back into the forest and find a lot of chanterelles. I'll be parked up there a ways, waiting for you. We'll go find you your killer mushrooms.*

JT had replied: *see you there and we can talk plot i expect i'm going to get a big advance for this book*

According to the header, JT had sent it this morning at 8:45.

He had indeed been at the library. For a while. Rachel glanced at her watch. It was after noon now. "That little idiot." She spoke between clenched teeth. "Why didn't he tell me? What was he trying to do?"

Jeff frowned at the page. "Do you have any idea what road this guy is talking about?"

Rachel shook her head. They could be anywhere—in the Gorge, up in the Mount Hood National Forest. Hundreds of miles of roads and tracks crisscrossed the terrain. "Gus." She looked at Jeff. "He might know. He was really close to Jason, or Jerry." She shrugged impatiently. "They used to hunt mushrooms together. Maybe he'd know where he might go to pick chanterelles."

"Let's hope so. It's worth a try." Jeff's face was grim. "I'll take our boy in and notify the sheriff. You don't know Marl's license plate, do you?"

Rachel shook her head, swallowing fear. "I'll go see if Spider's back yet. Maybe everything's fine. If he isn't, I'll go talk to Gus."

"I'll be downtown." Jeff put an arm around her and hugged her briefly and hard. But he didn't reassure her that they would find Spider, or that everything would be all right.

That frightened her most of all. She ran back to her truck, flinging herself behind the wheel and driving the few blocks to Mrs. Frey's house too fast. Mrs. Frey's car was in its usual place, and her landlady was out in the rose garden, trowel in hand, shaded by one of her many fantastic hats, this one wreathed and fringed with dried red rose hips.

"Well, hello, dear. You're home early." Mrs. Frey looked up, the red pods swinging and rattling around the brim. "Have you eaten yet? I made a batch of chicken salad and there's plenty left. I thought John might want it for sandwiches tomorrow."

"He's not here?" Rachel swallowed, her throat thick and dry. "You haven't seen him since I was here this morning?"

"My dear, what's wrong?" Mrs. Frey got to her feet, tilting her head to peer up into Rachel's face. "What happened to John?"

"We . . . we don't know." Rachel's tongue felt stiff. It was hard to get the words out. "I need to find him. You didn't give him a ride anywhere?"

"No. Not this morning." Worried now, Mrs. Frey tossed her trowel into her gardening basket. "I suppose he could have taken my bike, if he wanted to go somewhere. I told him he could borrow it." She marched over to the neat shed at the side of the garden and pulled the door open. "It's gone." She frowned. "I guess he borrowed it, since it was there last night. What is going on? You look pale."

Rachel shook her head. "I just need to find Spider." She could hear a clock ticking in her head, measuring off the seconds until . . . what? "If you see him, will you call me on my cell phone? You have the number, right?"

"Rachel, what's wrong?" Mrs. Frey followed her to the truck, stripping off her soiled gloves. "What happened to John? Is he all right?"

"We don't know." Maybe Gus would have the answer. "I hope so." She slammed the door and backed the truck down the driveway before Mrs. Frey could say anything else. Gus, she thought. Don't fail us. She looped through town as she drove up to the Van Dorn house, searching the quiet early-afternoon street for a lanky dark-haired figure.

No Spider.

Rachel said a small prayer that Gus would have some kind of answer for her.

CHAPTER

18

Nobody answered Rachel's knock. She looked around the vine-shaded porch. No trace of Doc, or their earlier chat, remained. She cupped her hands around her face and peered through the front window, squinting to penetrate the gloom inside. Maybe he was out back, in the garden. She knocked again, pounding hard on the wooden panels this time. Still no answer. She turned away, was on her way down the steps to go around back when the door opened behind her.

"I'm sorry." Bleary-eyed, his white hair standing in rumpled tufts, Gus yawned. "I was asleep. Got into the habit of an after-lunch nap a couple of years ago when I got the flu. Now I can't seem to shake it. Come in, come in." He stood aside to usher her inside. "Cooler inside than out, still. You look in a hurry." He peered at her face as she crossed the threshold, absently fingering the suspenders that supported his loose khaki pants. "I apologize for the underwear." He glanced down at his worn-thin T-shirt. "I don't think too fast when I first wake up."

"Gus, that's fine." Rachel drew a deep breath, not sure where to begin. "Did Jerry have a favorite place to go? To hunt chanterelles?"

"Jerry?" Gus blinked at her. "I can't stop thinking about him. About him maybe killing that woman."

"Yes." Rachel struggled to control her impatience. "Where would he go in the woods?"

"It depended on what we were after." Gus shuffled into the kitchen. "Want some tea? I don't know that he had one favorite place to pick, if that's what you're asking." He set a teakettle on the ancient gas stove and lit the burner beneath it with a thick kitchen match. "Depends on what you're looking for, you know. When the oysters were on, we went where we knew we'd find oysters—way up this canyon west and south of Hood River. It was full of alders, seems like you'd find ten pounds on every tree. Right down low, a lot of 'em." His eyes glazed with gentle sorrow. "Great place. Haven't been back there for a few years now. Lot of 'em blew down in the last few years. Trees got to be dying before the oysters grow on 'em. Did he kill that woman?" He took two china mugs from the cupboard, not looking at her.

"Yes," she said. It hadn't been proven in court, but . . . "Yes." The words tumbled out. "I think he's going to kill Spider, Gus. They were going to meet on some road. He said something about picking chanterelles there. I don't know which road or where, but Spider's been gone for hours. Where would he go?"

The teakettle began to whistle. Gus stared at the furious jet of steam, unhearing, his eyes fixed on a distant vision. "I wonder," he said finally, softly. "I wonder if it would've turned out different. Too late for anything but regret now, huh? That's all we have left at the end. Regret." Gus shook himself, reached for the kettle, and lifted it from the flame, its shriek dying instantly to blessed silence. "We went to a couple of places for chanterelles.

They like it high. They don't do so good at lower elevations. There were two real good places we'd always go."

"*Where*, Gus?" Rachel's voice trembled.

"Let me get a map. One's pretty close. You take the cutoff that leads over to Highway 30, only you turn off south before you get there. You cross a creek and turn off onto this forest service road right after." He set the kettle down. "I'll see if I can find it." He left the mugs on the counter and shuffled into a small room off the kitchen. Rachel followed.

The tiny room—probably a back bedroom once—clearly served as combination office and storage space. Yellowed stacks of newspapers and dusty magazines crowded the floor. Papers and receipts cluttered a heavy wooden desk, along with a disorderly pile of nursery catalogs. Dust coated a metal desk lamp and rose in a small cloud as Gus shoved piles of paper aside. He opened one of the desk's deep drawers and began to root inside, muttering to himself. A moment later, he straightened with a grunt of triumph, unfolding a brittle map across the desk top. "Forest Service map," he announced as he fumbled a pair of reading glasses from his pocket. "Shows all the service roads. There." His finger stabbed down. "That's the creek. This has to be it. It's been a while, though." He stared at the map, his brow furrowed. "The other place is way up here, off Highway 30." He touched a second point. "It was private land, I remember. Don't know what's there now."

Rachel's heart sank. The two points were miles apart, and the map was old. If the roads hadn't been maintained, you'd have to hike in for miles from the nearest paved county road.

Then again, if the the roads hadn't been maintained, then that probably *wasn't* where Jason was headed. "Can I take this with me?" she asked Gus.

He nodded, raised his head to look at her. "Why Spider?" he asked huskily. "Why would he hurt the boy?"

"Spider guessed that he'd poisoned Emily. I think Jerry knows that he guessed."

Wordlessly, Gus shook his head. "Hindsight and regrets." His voice creaked as he straightened slowly. "The legacy of old age."

"Gus, if you remember anything more, will you call me?" Rachel pulled one of her business cards from her wallet and wrote her cell phone number on it.

Gus nodded as he took it, his shoulders drooping. He didn't say anything more.

Rachel drove quickly down to City Hall. No call from Mrs. Frey. 2:30 P.M. The clock ticked louder in her head.

Her cell phone rang as she climbed out of the truck. Rachel grabbed it, her heart leaping, but the voice on the phone wasn't Spider's.

"Mademoiselle." Madame DeRochers spoke crisply, her voice undiminished by the cell connection. "Monsieur McLoughlin has disappeared."

"What?" Rachel leaned against the sun-hot metal of her truck's door. "What do you mean?"

"He is not here. He is not at the Village. Something is very wrong."

"Maybe he . . . maybe he got a ride into town, or into Hood River." Rachel's thoughts scattered like a flock of frightened birds, refusing to settle. "Maybe he's doing an errand, or wanted to surprise you or something?"

"Non." The single syllable was emphatic. "He is not here. He did not leave here with a ride to do shopping. He did not take his run this morning. He took my cane with him last night—the one he made. He wished to carve my initials in it. When he did not come to breakfast, I went to his room. His bed has been slept him, but he is gone. So is my cane. There is . . . blood on the pillow.

Not a lot, but it is there." Her voice had faded to a whisper.

"Did you call the police?" Rachel asked breathlessly. "Did you tell Jeff?"

"*Oui.* And now I tell you." The line went dead.

First Spider and now Harris. Rachel snapped off her phone and took the steps to City Hall two at a time. She didn't quite run across the main lobby, aware of the receptionist's surprised look as she burst through the door into the police offices. Bert was there, his face angry. So was Jeff. He looked up as she entered, worry dark in his eyes.

"Madame just called me."

Jeff nodded once, tersely. "She saw Harris last night. Nobody has seen him this morning. He is not in his room. She told me there were bloodstains on the pillow."

"He cut himself shaving yesterday." Stanfield's tone was flat and without emotion. "I'd say he's out shopping."

"Maybe," Jeff agreed. "For now, I'm going to believe her." His tone chilled Rachel. "Harris has been keeping an eye on the aids for me."

The phone rang and Stanfield reached for it, his movements jerky, like an automaton in need of repair. He listened briefly, thanked the caller, then hung up. "That was the assistant director at the Village." He enunciated the syllables precisely. "According to her, two of the aids on break just discovered Harris's chair. It was hidden in a pile of brush behind the buildings."

Her burning pile. Rachel felt the color draining from her face. Harris hadn't left the Village without his chair. Not voluntarily.

"What did you find out from Van Dorn?" Jeff asked.

"They hunted chanterelles in two places." She unfolded the old map and laid it carefully out on Jeff's desk. "He said it was either here or here." Her finger touched the two points Gus had indicated.

"I'll talk to the sheriff's people." He frowned at the map as he reached for the phone. "They're already watching for Marl's car, and for Spider." He dialed, asked for a deputy named Rogers, and then began to describe the locations Gus had pinpointed.

Rachel's cell phone rang again. She answered it, stepping out into the hallway so as not to disturb Jeff's conversation with the deputy.

"Rachel? Can you come get me?"

Spider's voice. Rachel nearly dropped the phone. "Spider! Where are you? Are you all right?" She clutched the instrument so tightly that her knuckles gleamed white. "We thought . . ."

"I've got a sprained ankle." His voice sounded thin and distant. "I crashed Mrs. Frey's bike. Bent the wheel. This guy stopped and he's letting me call you. I got pictures for you. You got to come get me. I'm on the old highway. There's a bunch of cabins and trailers and stuff—like a camp. You know where I mean? It's just down from the freeway."

The pickers' camp. The county road that led to the closer chanterelle site took off not far from there. "I know where you are," she said. "We'll be right there, and Spider, if you see Jason, the aid?"

"I got pictures of him. He's the one. If I see him, he won't see me. I got to give the phone back."

She heard him thanking somebody and then the call ended. Hand shaking, she slipped her phone into the clip on her belt. "Jeff, that was Spider."

"I heard. Let's go get him." Jeff had come around the desk, already had his keys out. "Where?" he asked as they took the rear door to the parking lot.

"He's at the camp where Valdez was living. Let's take the Jeep." She climbed into the front seat. "He said he sprained his ankle." She swallowed. "He says he got pictures of Jason. He . . . he didn't say anything about Harris." She grabbed for the door as the Jeep leaped forward.

They didn't say anything more as they cut through town and took the highway west. The broken weather of the past few days had moved on and the wide Columbia sparkled blue in the sun. The bright sails of Windsurfers danced across the water like wind-blown petals, crimson and orange and yellow.

Where was Harris?

Rachel leaned forward as they neared the pickers' camp, searching for a sign of Spider. The roadway was empty. An empty delivery truck from the lumberyard passed them, then a battered brown-and-white Chevy pickup. Jeff braked and pulled off the road onto the rutted track that led down into the camp. In daylight, it looked shabby and unkempt. Moss greened the sides of the old trailers and furred the roofs of the cabins. White shirts, jeans, and a few pieces of children's clothing swayed from a couple of clotheslines strung between trees. This time of day, the camp seemed deserted, although Rachel guessed that a few pairs of eyes watched them.

Still no sign of Spider. Jeff pulled off onto the dusty grass at the side of the track. As he did, a familiar figure rose from the tall weeds and brush at the edge of the road. Spider! Rachel sucked in a gasp of relief. He leaned down to stand a blue ten-speed bike on its wheels, then began pushing it toward them, limping badly, using the bike as a crutch. His right arm was scraped raw and filthy with road dust. One cheek was also scraped, and he was grimy from head to toe.

"Spider!" Rachel flung herself out of the Jeep and raced to meet him. "I was so damn worried. I ought to beat you!"

"Watch your language, lady." He managed a ghost of a smile, his face grimy and tight with pain. "Never know who might be listening."

"I should smack you." She slipped her arm beneath his free one and around his waist. "Lean on me, will you?"

"I think you break all kinds of labor laws, hitting your employees." The grin widened for an instant, then crumpled. "I got a picture of him. Jason. I started hanging around this chat room with a bunch of these mushroom pickers and woods crafters—that's what they call themselves. And I started saying as how I was this mystery author writing a book, and I told 'em I had this dynamite plot about how this guy gets revenge on this old lady for something she did years ago, and he poisons her with galerinas, and this guy, Shroomer, started being way nice to me, and *really* helpful, and—"

"We know," Rachel interrupted him gently. "Why do you think I was so scared."

Spider gave her a blank look.

"You owe it all to our vandal." Jeff leaned the bike against a hawthorn and slung Spider's arm over his shoulder. "Let's go, kid. So you got a picture of Jason?"

"You guys know all about this?" Spider glowered at him. "Fine. I guess I don't have to tell you anything then. Yeah, I did. Get a picture." Sobered by Jeff's expression, Spider dropped his flippant tone. "I took Mrs. Frey's camera. It's a thirty-five-millimeter. She keeps it in the back entry with all her garden stuff. She'll probably kill me for that, and for the bike." He glanced at it regretfully. "The chain came off when I was really moving and I went down hard. And have you ever noticed that there aren't a whole lot of pay phones nailed to the trees around here? Somebody oughta complain." He stumbled, and Jeff's arm tightened around him.

"You okay, guy?"

"Banged up. I don't know." Spider looked over at the bike. "It was so weird. I mean, I didn't really know who was gonna show. I thought maybe it was the Dragon Lady after all, or that crazy boozer who's her assistant. I think

Harris figured it was her, too. Then this car drives up the
road and the door opens and . . . it's Jason." His voice was
hushed. "I mean . . . he did it. He killed that woman. I
guess he was going to kill me, too. I mean, there aren't
any galerinas growing this time of year. And I was just
talking to him yesterday. We . . . we were talking about
music and . . . our dads. He's . . . he was . . ." He stopped,
swallowing. "He got out of the car and looked around for
me," he said in a small voice.

"You are so lucky," Rachel said between clenched
teeth. "Why didn't you tell me?"

"What was to tell?" Spider gave her a sideways look.
"It could have been somebody playing a game. People do
that kind of thing."

"Was there anyone else in the car?" Jeff leaned the bike
against the Jeep. "Sit down and let's get that shoe off.
Your ankle's pretty swollen."

Harris. Rachel bit her lip. She had managed to forget
about him in her relief to find Spider.

"No." Spider eased himself down onto the Jeep's floor
as Jeff knelt in front of him. "I didn't see anybody. Oh . . .
sh . . ." He sucked in a breath and clenched his teeth as
Jeff pulled off the running shoe he was wearing.

His ankle was a dusky red, thick and swollen from his
foot to well above the ankle. The skin looked tight and
almost shiny. Jeff ran his hands over it, flexing it gently,
eliciting a strangled groan from Spider. It was a bad
sprain, if not a break. Beads of sweat gleamed on Spider's
forehead and his face had turned the color of old ivory.

"I don't think anything is broken, but we need to get
some ice on it. You take the passenger side. We'll stick
Rachel in the back." Jeff half lifted Spider, and helped
him around to the far side of the Jeep. Spider kept his
foot off the ground, his face gleaming with sweat now.
"Nobody was in the car? You're sure?"

"I don't think so." Spider sagged onto the car seat, breathing hard, his face pale. "We were supposed to meet on this trail—it takes off from this road about five miles from here. He gave me directions. You can drive back a ways, and then the road ends, and there's kind of a trail. Anyway, I was flat on the ground under a bunch of bushes. When I took a picture, it sounded like a firecracker going off. But he didn't hear me, thank God. Actually, when he got back in, just as he started the car, I thought I heard some kind of thumping. This kind of thud-thud noise—not real loud. I just figured it was something wrong with the car."

"Maybe in the trunk." Jeff looked across the seat at Rachel. "I wonder if Deputy Rogers is having any luck."

"Who?" Spider leaned forward, winced as he moved his ankle. "Who are you talking about? Who was in the trunk?"

"Maybe Harris," Rachel said, turning toward Spider, whose eyes grew wide. She faced forward again. Please be Harris thumping. In the trunk and not dead. She closed her eyes briefly, remembering her luncheon with Madame. *Life is too short, he told me. He is such a boy still.*

She said a small quiet prayer for Harris McLoughlin. And for Madame.

Jeff's cell phone rang. He stood, snapping it from his belt. "Price here."

Rachel held her breath as he replied to the caller in monosyllables and grunts. "Thanks," he said finally. "I'll let you know if we find anything more. That was Rogers." He answered Rachel's unspoken question. "The other site is impassable by car. You'd have to get in on foot or by horse."

"Now what?" She clenched her teeth in frustration.

"We go talk to the man," Jeff said grimly.

"I want to come—but I can't leave Mrs. Frey's bike here." Spider leaned forward anxiously. "She'll kill me."

"I've got a chain." Jeff went around to a tool box in the back of the Jeep, fished out a cable chain and a heavy padlock, locked the ten speed to a young fir. "We're not leaving you here. This will have to do," he said.

Rachel clung to the door handle as the Jeep hurtled back toward Blossom. The sun was sliding down toward the horizon and the clock-tick had become a shrill frenzy in her head. On the way in, Jeff called Lyle Waters and told him to meet them at Jason Marl's apartment complex. Marl lived over in Hood River, Jeff told her. Out on the western edge.

Lyle was waiting for them when they arrived, sitting behind the wheel of the Blossom police cruiser, listening to country music on the radio. He turned the music down as Jeff pulled beside the car. "No sign of his car, or of him. Don't think he's there, but I got the warrant. Hood River is giving us backup. They're up the street, waiting for a yell."

"Let's hope he shows up." Jeff pulled over to the curb and got out, walking back to speak to Lyle briefly. Then he returned and they continued on down the street. This was a neighborhood where residential Hood River had petered out into one-time small farms and family orchards. An old motel, long and low and ugly, offered phones in the rooms and TV in faded letters outlined in neon tubing. Three cars waited outside of rooms. A mangy yellow dog lifted its leg on the straggling arbor vitae planted outside the office, regarding the Jeep with a mildly interested stare. Thirsty geraniums and the remnants of pansies straggled in peeling white boxes in front of each room. The apartment complex—two fourplexes set side by side—had been built at the end of the motel. Their stark new shape contrasted sharply with the shabby motel and the old lopsided frame house beyond it. A dozen unpruned fruit trees filled the lot between the apartments and the house. Jeff slowed the Jeep.

"What's out back?" he asked.

Rachel craned her neck.

"There's a parking lot." Spider spoke up. "There's one of those Dumpster things, then a fence and a field behind that."

Jeff grunted and drove on down the street, out of sight of the apartment. He turned the Jeep around in the driveway to a sagging dairy barn and parked, far enough from the plexes to be inconspicuous, but with a clear line of sight to the front doors. "If our boy heads out the back, Lyle will spot him. He's covering the back." Jeff turned off the ignition and looked sideways at Rachel.

"I'll stay put." Rachel said quickly. "So will Spider."

"Hey." Spider gave her a scowl.

"Sit still," she told him and took a firm hold on the back of his shirt.

Jeff leaned back over the seat to kiss her lightly. "Thanks." He got out.

The sun had become an orange-yellow ball of fire hovering on the horizon. A car pulled up and parked in front of the plexes—a gray Toyota.

"Well, look who just showed up," Jeff said softly.

Jason got out, apparently oblivious to their presence, and went around to his trunk to retrieve two bags of groceries. As Jeff stepped up beside him to peer into the trunk, he looked up, eyebrows arching into an expression of innocent surprise. "Hi." He closed the trunk with a thump. "Are you looking for me?"

"Jason Marl?"

The young aid nodded. "Aren't you the police officer who was out about poor Emily's death?" He set down the bulging plastic bags. "What can I do for you?"

"Where is Harris McLoughlin?" Jeff kept his eyes on Jason's face. "What did you do with him?"

"Who?" Jason shrugged and reached for his grocery bags. "I don't know who you're talking about."

"I think you do." Jeff seized him by the arm. "You are under arrest for the murder of Emily Barnhart." He spun Jason around and shoved him against the side of his car, handcuffs glittering in his hand.

"This is crazy," Marl shrilled as Jeff cuffed him. "You're crazy. I never killed anyone. Never in my life."

Jeff pulled him erect again. "Anything you say may be used against you . . ." Jeff recited Miranda as Lyle came up behind the wild-eyed Marl. "Where is Harris McLoughlin?" Jeff's voice cracked hard and cold. "What did you do with him?"

"McLoughlin who?"

"If he's dead, you're going up for the death penalty." Jeff stared into Jason's eyes, leaning slightly forward, weight on the balls of his feet. "If he's still alive, if we find him, you might be able to cut a deal with the DA. I might put in a word for you for cooperating."

"I don't know what you're talking about." Jason didn't move his feet, but his body drew back a hair, as if it was shrinking in on itself. "McLoughlin who?"

"If he's dead, that brings the count to four murders." Jeff leaned closer, his voice pleasant now, as if they were having a casual conversation. "You're dead."

"McLoughlin? You mean Harris? Out at the Village?" Jason tried for a laugh that sputtered. "What are you talking about? I wasn't even out there today! This was my day off."

"Let's talk about last night. Let's talk about how you knocked Harris unconscious with the cane in his room, put him into his chair, and wheeled him out to your car. You hid his chair in the brush pile out near the parking lot and you left with him. This morning you drove out through Blossom to Forest Service Road 22, where you intended to meet John Tranh. We have photos of you there. We know everything you did, Jerry. So where is McLoughlin?"

Rachel barely breathed, her eyes on Jason's face as Jeff's words hammered at him. When he said the name "Jerry," she thought she saw his eyelids twitch.

"My name is Jason." He seemed to gather himself, his earlier fear vanishing, his face seeming to age before their eyes. "I don't know what you're getting at with this story about hitting people with canes and Forest Service roads, but I sure hope you have some proof." Calm words, but his eyes gave him away, darting here and there, never once fixing on Jeff's face.

"We have proof. We'll find more in your car," Jeff said pleasantly. "McLoughlin was bleeding. You didn't get rid of all of it, and we'll find the traces. Never underestimate science."

Jason shrugged. "I work at the Village. I took his wheelchair into Portland once when it needed fixing. If you find hair or DNA or whatever in my trunk, it's from that." But a muscle jumped in the angle of his jaw. "I've been home all day. Until about an hour ago when I went to do some shopping. Ask my neighbor next door, Angela. She's home all day. She's disabled. She'll tell you I was here." He glanced sideways at Lyle, his body briefly tensing. Then he visibly relaxed, straightening his shoulders and giving Jeff a thin smile. "You're making a mistake. Why would I kill anyone?"

"Emily Barnhart killed your mother and little brother," Jeff said quietly. "She was drunk."

"Yeah." Light flared and died in Marl's eyes. "But *I* don't kill." He stared into Jeff's eyes. "When people are guilty, their own sins condemn them. They *choose* to die." His voice had dropped to a breathy whisper and his eyes gleamed like chips of polished agate. "I might hand them the means of death, but it is their own evil that kills them. I am merely a tool. God's hand holds me. If they are innocent, God's hand will pass over them. My hands are clean. What about yours?"

The voice. Rachel put her hand over mouth. The voice on her machine! That cold breathy whisper warning her that people were getting hurt at the Village.

Jeff nodded to Lyle, who stepped forward to lead Marl away. As he reached the street, Marl seemed to notice Rachel for the first time. "Harris is your friend, isn't he?" he said to her, his eyes seeming to pulse with golden light. "Don't worry. He's fine. He's just not in this world anymore. I guess I should have gone with him. You know, I thought about going. I guess I should have. I guess it was time." And he laughed softly as Lyle walked him to the cruiser, which he'd double-parked at the curb.

Rachel shivered. "He's crazy," she said softly. "Jeff, he left that warning on my machine." She closed her eyes against the pang of grief that stabbed her. *He's not in this world anymore.*

Jeff put a hand on her shoulder, her grief mirrored in his eyes. "Let's go take a look. You, Sit." He put a hand on the door as Spider started to shove it open. "You need to stay off that ankle, and two people are enough."

"He said stuff in the trunk was from him taking the chair in to be fixed." Spider leaned forward, his eyes wide. "You never said you thought he put Harris in the trunk."

"You noticed that, did you?" Jeff nodded, approving. "While we're in there, think, will you? Think back over your e-mail conversations with Jason. Did he say anything that might suggest where he'd have taken Harris?"

"I don't think he did." Spider eased his swollen foot, frowning. "I'll try. And I'll stay here." He looked up into Jeff's face. "He killed Harris, didn't he? That's what he was saying."

"I don't know." Jeff turned quickly away from the car.

Rachel followed Jeff across the arid front yard, her heart heavy. Planted lawn grass struggled and died in the sun-baked soil. The builder hadn't bothered to bring in topsoil and hadn't put in an irrigation system either. Grass

survived in patchy green clumps along the sidewalk and
in the shade of the straggling arbor vitae, but most of the
lawn resembled a dirt school yard. A dusty plastic kiddie
trike and a couple of orange-and-yellow dump trucks littered the front walk of the next unit over. Jason's neighbor
had planted large pots with white lobelia and blue ager-
atum.

Jeff had taken Marl's keys. He opened the door and for
a moment or two simply stood on the threshold, looking
around. Rachel peered over his shoulder. The unit was
long and narrow. Stairs rose to a second floor on their
right. Ahead, a cheap living room suite—sofa, one chair,
matching coffee table and end table were arranged in front
of the gas fireplace set into the wall beside the stairs. No
magazines, papers, or books cluttered the table. The walls
were bare of pictures.

"Looks like a furniture showroom," Jeff said.

Rachel followed him into the room, not touching anything. No dust showed on the cheap maple veneer of the
tables. A partial wall divided the kitchen–dining area from
the front room, with a bathroom and small bedroom beyond it. A large-screen TV occupied a corner of the dining
room, on the far side of a wood veneer table with four
matching chairs. The kitchen counters were spotless, as
was the stove. A new microwave stood on the narrow
counter and a single glass, a bowl, and a spoon occupied
a blue plastic dish drainer beside the sink. Rachel opened
the cupboards with a fingertip on the edge, found ramen
noodles, pancake mix, a few cans of fruit and chili, and
a box of soda crackers. A coffee mug filled with packets
of Parmesan cheese, soy sauce, Chinese mustard, and taco
sauce stood beside an open bag of potato chips. A mela-
mine dish set with what were probably matching glasses
and a few pots and pans occupied the other shelves. A
teakettle stood on the stove.

Jeff was checking out the rear bedroom. It had been used as storage, mostly. A few yard tools leaned against the wall, along with a pile of winter clothes. An exercise bike took up the center of the room, and a small TV stood on a battered desk that was piled with old mail. A mountain bike leaned beneath the window. Boxes labeled with the name of a storage company filled the twin closets. Jeff pried up one of their lids. "Books." He picked one up. *"Comprehensive Mycology,"* he read the title. *"The Mushroom Hunter."* He put the books back, sneezed as dust drifted into the air. The miniblinds on the two windows were closed and filmed with dust. They hid a view of the parking lot and Dumpster. "He didn't dust back here much." Jeff drew a line in the white film on the blinds, leaving a clear track.

"This place reminds me of one of those furnished cabins you can rent for vacation." Rachel looked around the downstairs. "You wouldn't have a clue who lived here. There aren't any pictures, any magazines. Nothing."

"Let's take a look at the bedroom."

The upstairs contained one large bedroom, a bathroom, and a washer and dryer crammed into a narrow hallway behind the bedroom closet. The room smelled closed, as if the windows were never opened. Blue sheets covered the unmade bed and a summer comforter lay tumbled at the foot, half on the floor. A glass stood on the bedside table. Jeff picked it up carefully and sniffed it. "Whiskey," he said. The bottle stood in the closet, on the floor beneath the sparse array of slacks and shirts arranged on hangers. The computer was up there, on one of those computer desks that come as a kit. While Rachel looked through the drawers, Jeff opened his e-mail account. "Nothing here but today's dose of spam." He clicked through files, swearing softly under his breath. "Everything is passworded. The trash file's empty." Growling, Jeff shut off the system. "I'll have to get that computer whizz kid over from Hood River. You find anything?"

"I think so." Rachel nodded at the file drawer she'd pulled open. A scrapbook lay there, a cheap item from a discount store with a maroon fiber cover. Jeff pulled on a pair of gloves and picked it up. Inside, neatly glued to the white pages, were newspaper clippings. Some were copies and some were genuine, yellowed and old. A blurry twin to the photo on Gus's mantel headed a front-page article from the *Blossom Bee*. MOTHER AND CHILD DIE IN TRAGIC ACCIDENT. More newspaper reports, letters to the editor, and finally, an obituary notice had been aligned neatly on the pages. Three obituaries from the past year were each centered on its own page. Rachel swallowed as she recognized the names of the murdered Village residents.

"Maybe that's why he printed out the e-mail," Rachel whispered. A second scrapbook, its plastic shrink-wrap still intact from the store, lay at the bottom of the drawer. Rachel looked around the bedroom. The blinds were closed, and in the dim light, it had the look of a hotel room after the occupant has checked out, just before the housekeeper arrives. "Jeff, what now?" She looked up at him. "Where do we go from here?"

"I'll drop you off at the apartment, okay?" He spoke harshly. "Why don't you take Spider over to get his foot looked at. I'm going to go have a long heart-to-heart talk with our boy."

Despair and rage lurked in those dark eyes. Harris had been a friend. Rachel reached over to touch Jeff's arm. Harris, Harris. Rachel found herself mourning the gray-haired man with the indomitable will and the steel-muscled arms who did his daily ten miles in his wheelchair and rarely needed anyone's help—the man who was Madame's lover, openly, and with joyful abandon. The man who wanted to marry her, because life was too short, and it didn't matter than she was twenty years older than he and he was sixty.

Spider was sitting upright in the Jeep, his face expectant. Waiting for them to take off—the cavalry on the way to rescue Harris, Rachel thought. If only there were a cavalry.

His face stiffened slowly, expectation modifying into neutrality. No cavalry. He looked away.

"How're you doing?" Jeff waited until Rachel had squeezed herself into the rear seat and then slid behind the wheel. "Hurting?"

"Some." Spider didn't say anything as they pulled away from the curb and headed back toward Blossom.

"You didn't think of anything?" Jeff kept his eyes on the road.

"No." Spider shook his head. "I talked mushrooms and he talked mushrooms and we were both talking about that lady at the Village. Then we left the chatroom and we went to e-mail, but we never talked about anything except the poisoning, really."

"It's all right," Jeff said, although Spider hadn't been apologizing.

He turned off toward Mrs. Frey's house. Rachel hadn't said anything since she had climbed into the car. Something . . . something was there. In the back of her brain. Something about another world. He's fine, Jason had said. Not dead, just in another world. Almost. She almost had it. Rachel wanted to pound on her skull, and shake that elusive connection loose. Jeff braked and turned into the driveway. His cell phone rang.

"Price." He pulled up behind Rachel's truck and parked. Nodded. "Thanks, Emory." He sighed. "The guy drives a Toyota. He couldn't have made it back there anyway, but I appreciate you checking it out. We picked up the guy, but he doesn't have McLoughlin, and he's not talking." Frustration edged his tone, and his knuckles gleamed as he clutched the phone. "No, we've got nothing to go on."

"The gateway! The well," Rachel yelled, bumping her head on the Jeep's canvas top. "He said it was a gateway to another world. So he can say he didn't kill Harris!"

"Hold on, Emory. What about a well?"

"We had this weird conversation about magical gateways to another world and he told me about this well behind his house with water running at the bottom. And it was a gateway to another world and that's what he meant when he told me that Harris wasn't in this world, don't you see? It has to be." She ran out of breath, gulping for air.

"That could be it." Jeff's eyes gleamed. "Emory, McLoughlin might be down a well behind an old house. Yeah, I know where I can find out. I'll get back to you as soon as I've got a location." Jeff hung up and handed her the cell phone. "Call Gus," he said.

She did, and listened to the phone ring five times, six, ten. After twenty rings she hung up. "He's not answering, Jeff."

They were on the outskirts of Blossom by now. Jeff grunted, and turned off onto her street, pulling up in Mrs. Frey's driveway in a cloud of dust. "You take care of Spider. I'll go find Gus."

"He's out in the garden," Spider said. "Look out back. He turns his hearing aid off when he's working and doesn't answer the phone." He let Jeff help him out of the Jeep, stifling a groan as he put weight on his injured foot. "He never forgets anything, Jeff."

Rachel put her arm around Spider, helping him as he limped to the door. Jeff backed the Jeep down the driveway, scattering more gravel, and disappeared around the corner toward Gus's house.

"Mrs. Frey is going to have a fit," Spider said soberly.

That, Rachel figured, was probably the understatement of the year.

CHAPTER

19

"Oh, my lord, boy, what happened to you." Mrs. Frey opened the door at Rachel's knock, then flung it wide. "Is it broken or sprained? What did you do? Take a header off my bike?" She hustled them inside, shepherding them through the hallway with its woven rag mud-rugs and into the spacious kitchen with its yellow-and-white painted cupboards. "Sit down right there, and let's get that foot up on a chair. Rachel, why didn't you take him straight to the ER?"

"I wasn't thinking," Rachel said meekly. "I'll take him over there right now."

"Don't be in a rush." Mrs. Frey clucked and arched a brow skeptically. "Let me see. Well, it's swollen enough. Goodness."

Spider bit down on a yelp as she stripped off his sock. His foot looked worse. Muttering to herself, Mrs. Frey pried plastic ice-cube trays from her freezer, twisted the cubes out into a big steel bread bowl, and ran cold water to cover them. "There." She set the huge bowl down on the floor in front of him. "Put it in there. Ten minutes. Then out for ten minutes."

Spider poked his foot gingerly into the ice and water, and yanked it out, howling. "My toes will freeze off!"

"Be quiet and put that foot right back in there. You're a mess. You could have at least cleaned him up a bit." She shot Rachel an accusing glare as she went back to the sink to wring out a clean cotton dish towel under the faucet and collect various ominous-looking bottles and vials from a box on the top shelf of the cupboard beside the stove.

"I can't keep my foot in this any longer," Spider gasped. He yanked his foot from the bowl, ice water spattering the spotless green-and-white linoleum tiles. "I'm not kidding. My toes are gonna fall off."

"Well, keep it in as much as you can." She put her fists on her narrow hips and gave him an even sterner glare. "You'll hate yourself if you don't. That's a bad sprain. If you don't keep it iced, you won't be able to walk on it at all by tomorrow. Gee, you're a wimp."

"All right, all right," Spider growled. He levered his foot back into the bowl, sloshing small frigid lakes onto the glossy tile. "So I'll get frostbite. Fine."

"That's right," Mrs. Frey said cheerfully. "You probably will. Look up at me." She seized his chin and began to clean the dirt from the raw scrape on his cheek with the clean wet towel. Not gently. Blood and grime stained the white cotton and Spider was breathing fast and hard by the time she was satisfied, but he never made a sound. She finally gave him permission to take his foot out of the ice water, propped it on a towel, and went to work on the deeper scrape on his arm.

"So what happened?" She tossed the stained towel into the sink and wet a fresh one. "We were worried sick about you."

"I know." He sucked in his breath and tensed as she scrubbed grit from a particularly bad spot near his elbow. "I'm sorry. I . . . didn't have time to call anyone. I . . . had to go find a phone and tell Jeff. Ow! What, were you a veterinarian or something?"

"A school nurse. Many years ago." She stopped scrubbing, stood holding his arm. "Tell Jeff what?" Her eyes went to Rachel, eyebrows rising.

"He found out who killed the woman at the Village," Rachel said.

"I'm sorry. I took your camera. I got a picture of him." Spider nodded at the pocket of his khaki pants. "And we had to leave your bike. Jeff chained it to a tree. If somebody steals it, I'll pay for it. I didn't have time to ask you if it was okay. The chain came off—that's how I dumped. But I don't think it's too badly wrecked."

"If somebody wants to waste a pair of bolt cutters on that piece of junk, they're welcome to it. I've been wanting to buy a mountain bike for years now. John," Mrs. Frey said quietly, "did it occur to you that if this man killed one person, he might not be too worried about killing another?"

"I wasn't planning on letting him see me." Spider met her eyes briefly, then looked away. "I know. It was stupid. But he showed up." He gave them both a stubborn stare.

"Yeah, he did." Rachel sighed.

Mrs. Frey shook her head, rolled her eyes, and dropped the second towel into the sink. She returned a moment later with bottles, a wad of cotton, and a couple of thick, pointed, cactus-like leaves she had snipped from the spiny-looking plant growing on the sunny counter.

"What're those?" Spider leaned hard against the back of the chair, his expression far from trusting. "I bet they sting like heck."

"Not too bad," she said. "Liniment for the ankle. Peroxide for your scrapes." She moistened cotton with the peroxide and blotted the injuries. The cotton turned faintly pink as the peroxide foamed. "Okay. Not too bad," Spider said. "What's that?" He made a face as she split one of the thick leaves with a deft thumbnail. Juice flowed from the cut, thick and clear. "Looks like slug slime," he said. "Yuck."

"It's aloe. You don't want a scar on your face, do you? If you're going to have a scar on your face, it should at least be interesting, like a nice sword cut or some kind of cryptic mark." She began to smear the thick sticky plant juice on Spider's face and then his arm.

"That feels good," he admitted as she finished. He flexed his arm and winced. "Whew." He wrinkled his nose as she began to rub the liquid liniment on his swollen ankle. "That smells like turpentine."

"It might be," Mrs. Frey said with equanimity. "My old friend Carl Humphries makes it for his Percherons. He's been winning pulling contests with his teams since I was in pigtails."

"You got any pictures of that?"

"Of what? The Percherons?"

"No. You in pigtails." Spider's grin was almost normal.

"Huh. I guess you'll live." Mrs. Frey got to her feet. "If you took pictures of a criminal with my camera, you better give the film to Rachel right now. She can get it to Jeff. Didn't he just drop you off here?" She carried her collection of bottles back to the sink. "I thought that was his Jeep I heard." She tilted her head. "And here he comes again. What is going on? He's going to rip my driveway to pieces, tearing in and out like that!" Mrs. Frey began washing her hands. "Ask him in. I've got some soup I'll heat up. Think you could eat?" she asked Spider.

Outside, tires crunched on the gravel and an engine idled. Rachel opened the door just as Jeff reached it.

"Let's go." His eyes blazed in the fading orange light of evening. "Gus gave me the address, and I called Emory. He called some hiking buddy of his, and the guy knows the spot. The house burned down at least ten years ago, he says. The place is overgrown, but he remembers the well. He thought it was part of an old lava tube and covered it with branches so nobody would fall in. Emory called in a search and rescue team. They're on the way out there."

"I'll be back," Rachel called down the hall. She bolted through the door, ignoring Spider's yell from the kitchen. Running around the side of the Jeep, she levered herself onto the seat as Jeff let the clutch out and accelerated backward down the driveway.

The sun sank below the horizon as they drove south from Blossom, winding up onto the shoulders of Mount Hood, west of Hood River's fertile valley. The road rose steadily, leaving the neat rows of trees with their burden of pears and apples behind. Tall firs closed in along the road, second growth, dense and mature. They passed a recent clear cut, raw clay, piles of black stumps and brush, softened by spikes of pink fireweed and the bright purple of Russian thistle. "That thistle will take over in another year," Rachel said absently. "Where is this place we're headed to?"

"Not too much farther if I've got my directions right." Jeff turned right, onto a gravel forest service road, rutted by recent log-truck traffic. They passed the last of the clear cut and entered mature timber once more. It was as if someone had dropped a curtain on the day. They drove from sunset's last glow into dusk. Rachel leaned forward, peering down the twilight corridor of the road as it wound back and forth across the rising shoulder of the mountain. "Watch for two huge old chestnut trees," Jeff called out over the road noise. "They mark the driveway."

"There!" She pointed. They were American chestnut, amazingly, huge and thick trunked. Trampled and broken underbrush marked the place where more than one vehicle had turned off. Jeff twisted the wheel and they bumped down the overgrown track, twigs scrabbling at the sides of the Jeep. The spindly, light-starved stems of an old lilac and a scraggly rosebush marked the remains of the old home site. A few earthenware foundation blocks suggested the building that had burned. Moss-covered, fungus-ridden plums and apples struggled with blackberry and shade for survival. Rachel felt a moment of pity for the men and women who had tried to farm this place.

"There!" She pointed again. A white pickup with a police light bar parked between young firs, along with a van and a Jeep Cherokee with a county sheriff's department logo on the door. Small saplings and huckleberry brush had been broken down and crushed beyond the parked cars. The ground was rocky and uneven. Thick fir roots writhed across jutting outcrops of ancient lava. Sometimes the mountain reminded you that it was an old volcano— layers of rock had poured out across a prehistoric plain millennia ago, the same layers that had devastated her irrigation ditches. There was no sign of anyone.

They climbed out of the Jeep, hearing at first only the tick of cooling metal from the engine and the evening song of summer birds. Then, off to their right, they heard a shout. A faint light glimmered in the thick dusk. Jeff grabbed her hand and they ran toward it, crashing through the huckleberry brush.

Rachel stepped into soft mud, and Jeff caught her, hauling her to her feet. An old spring. A tumble of rocks suggested that the homesteaders had built a spring house here. The water trickled on in the direction they were traveling, the ground soft even this late in a dry summer. Jeff pulled a flashlight from his belt, clicked it on. Following the welcome yellow beam, they moved toward the glimmering light ahead. Another big truck had made its way in this far.

"Hey!" A man stepped away from the several figures gathered in a small clearing. Dressed in a Sheriff's Department uniform, he had a young face and a football player's husky build. "That you, Price?" He offered a calloused hand. "We got someone down there. Good call. We've got a team working."

"Is he alive?" Rachel gasped. Oh, please . . .

"We don't know yet." Rogers turned grave eyes on her. "We'll know pretty quick." Jeff stepped past him, toward a depression near the center of the clearing. A pile of limbs had been tossed to one side. Heavy ropes were tied off to sturdy firs. They disappeared into an overgrown and nearly hidden opening in the ground. Six members of the search and rescue team worked at the brink of the opening, tending the ropes, talking down to the invisible climbers below.

"Whoever brought him in here drove right in. We found this where he parked." The deputy held out what seemed to be a broken stick, bagged loosely in plastic.

"That's Madame's cane," Rachel gasped, recognizing it. "Part of it. I recognize the handle."

"Maybe he meant to throw it down there with your friend. He's lucky. I'm told there's a sheer drop, then a narrow ledge, then another long drop around fifty feet or so, down into water. He could have gone all the way down, but he caught the ledge."

"Harris wouldn't die easily," Jeff said.

Seventy feet down into cold water. Rachel shivered.

"Emory, this is Rachel," Jeff said. "She's been part of this investigation. She's a friend of Harris's."

Rogers nodded, gave her a brief searching look. "Let's hope," he said. "They should get down to him any minute now."

One of the men at the lip of the well shouted something down into the invisible shaft, then looked toward the deputy and pumped a fist.

"He's alive." Rogers spoke into his cell phone as he hurried over to join the pair at the rim. The team was working fast and efficiently, attaching a lightweight stretcher to the ropes with webbing, sending it down the opening to the waiting team below.

"Stay back." The deputy put a hand out as Rachel started forward. "We've got an ambulance on the way. I hope we don't need to fly him out. There's no close landing site."

Rachel stepped hastily back. She and Jeff watched, enforced spectators, as the search and rescue team worked crisply and efficiently. It seemed to take forever. Overhead, the moon showed in a clear patch of sky between fir tops, a crisp white crescent, oblivious to the goings-on beneath. Pulleys creaked and the topside team answered inaudible comments from the rescuers below. Finally, the lip of the stretcher appeared at the mouth of the narrow opening. The members of the team worked to keep it steady and level as they hoisted it up and out of the well.

Harris, white faced, his eyes closed, was strapped securely into the aluminum frame, his head taped into place. The team who had climbed down to him—a man and a woman—followed him out. Slowly, afraid, Rachel stepped over to where they worked on him, her heart pulsing at the base of her throat. The ambulance had arrived. A man in a blue paramedic's uniform crouched beside the stretcher and slipped a needle into Harris's arm while one of the search team members held a bag of clear fluid in the air. Dirt smeared Harris's face and blood matted his gray hair, streaking his pale face. Not good, Rachel thought with a clutch of fear. Not good at all.

"Guy's tough." The woman who had come up behind the stretcher looked up at her, her own face equally smeared with dirt. "He caught himself going down, grabbed a branch or something that had hung up in a crevice. Got himself wedged on a little ledge sticking out. Lucky he didn't go clear down. There's not much level down there, till you hit the water."

Tough. Yes. The paramedic was stabilizing one arm, wrapping it in a foam splint.

"How is he?" Jeff squatted by the stretcher, across from the paramedic. The man looked up and eyed Jeff's uniform. "Shock. Broken ribs. One might have nicked a lung. Broken arm. More than that . . ." He shrugged and checked the blood pressure cuff on Harris's arm. "He could have a mild concussion. I hope I'm that tough when I'm his age."

A second paramedic had appeared with a padded stretcher. They shifted Harris over onto this one with a smooth teamwork that barely jostled his unconscious body. Strapping him down, with one of the search team carrying the IV bag, they picked it up and headed in the direction of the track at a fast clip, never mind the rough terrain and darkness.

Emory Rogers joined them. "Glad we found your friend in time," he said.

"Thanks go to you." Jeff clasped his hand, hard. "I owe you."

"Like I said, we was lucky." The deputy slapped him on the arm. "Dan there—on the ambulance—he's my cousin. He'll get your buddy to the hospital okay. Don't worry."

"Thanks," Jeff said again.

"Me, too." Rachel stepped forward to offer Emory her hand. "I'm sure glad you were there." His handshake was hard, and she returned his grip. He grinned, then nodded at Jeff. "Look forward to working with you again."

"Me, too."

The search and rescue team were sorting their ropes, unhooking webbing and hardware as they made their way back to the Jeep, following the yellow splash of Jeff's flashlight beam. When they reached it, he clicked off the light, stowed it carefully beneath the seat, then paused for a moment, his palms on the Jeep's top, his face turned up to the cold sliver of moon riding high above the treetops. "He's quite a man. He was twice the cop I'll ever be."

Rachel put her hands on his shoulders, kneading the tight muscles beneath her palms. Slowly, slowly, they softened. Jeff turned, put his arms around her, and buried his face against her shoulder. For a slow succession of heartbeats he stood still, not speaking, just breathing deep and slow, her body pressed against his. Then he raised his head and looked down at her. "Thanks," he said.

"Lets go see how he's doing." Rachel drew a slow breath. "And then we need to tell Madame."

The drive to Hood River seemed to take forever. The hospital, when they arrived, had that midnight-crisis feel—bright fluorescent lights, hunched and distracted people in the ER waiting room, briskly moving staff—a mix of adrenalin, fear, and caffeine blended with the distinctive smell of disinfectant and illness. Hospitals were bad enough in the daylight, during visitor hours, Rachel thought as they approached the reception desk. At night they were fearful.

They were told to wait. Jeff spoke at length to the woman at the reception desk, but it got him no farther than the chrome-and-plastic chairs of the green-carpeted, green-walled room. So they waited. It occurred to Rachel as she stared numbly at the stack of out-of-date copies of *Time, Field and Stream,* and *Good Housekeeping* that she hadn't eaten anything since her hurried breakfast with Jeff this morning. Neither had he, she was willing to bet. Not hungry at all, she left him sitting tautly in a chair and went in search of vending machines.

When she asked a woman in green garb wheeling a trolley full of folded sheets, the woman directed her down to the basement. There, in a concrete-floored corridor, she found a bank of machines offering coffee, pop, juice, and an assortment of sandwiches, yoghurt, and even fruit. She purchased two sandwiches, a couple of apples, a can of grape juice for Jeff, and a French vanilla latte for herself. Carrying her booty in a precarious stack, she took the elevator back to the main floor. Jeff was staring blankly at an open copy of *Field and Stream* in his hands. He looked up and blinked as she dropped into the seat beside him.

"Calories." She handed him one of the apples and the bottle of grape juice. "Limited selection." She peered at the plastic containers that held the sandwiches. "Ham and cheese or roast beef?"

"Roast beef." Jeff took the container from her and managed a smile. "You mean they had real fruit in a vending machine?"

"They had hard-boiled eggs, too." She opened her own sandwich, tore a corner off the packet of mustard that came with it. "And yoghurt. Very impressive."

"I guess."

She squeezed the mustard—which turned out to be a blend of mustard and mayonnaise—onto her pale tan ham and very yellow cheese. The iceberg lettuce shreds were limp, but at least there was lettuce. She closed it up and took a bite. Pure heaven. When she took a sip of her latte, the sugar in the dense, sweet drink nearly made her dizzy.

"I was hungry." Jeff wolfed his sandwich in about two bites, started in on his apple. "I hadn't noticed."

"Me neither." Plastic cheese and ham out of a can had never tasted so good. Why waste money on a fancy restaurant? Just wait until you're starving and then everything tastes wonderful.

They finished eating. Jeff gathered up the trash and carried it over to the waste basket in the corner of the room. Then they waited. People came in—an old couple who held hands, clutching each other as if for support, tears running down the woman's face, the man's face stark and stony—a young man with bleached hair, many rings in his ear, and a tongue stud that clicked against his teeth. Doctors came out, called their names, beckoned them aside to talk and, eventually, to leave.

Jeff went to the desk, came back with a shrug. Nothing yet.

Rachel didn't look at the clock on the wall above the reception desk. The hands wouldn't move if she did. Finally, after an eternity, a middle-aged man in green surgical scrubs appeared behind the reception desk, then rounded it to step into the waiting area. "You're the police officer here for Mr. McLoughlin?"

"Yeah." Jeff was on his feet. "I'm the police officer, but Harris is my friend."

"Your friend is going to be okay. One rib perforated a lung slightly, and he's got a simple fracture of both tibia and fibula—clean break, shouldn't be any problem. There's no sign of concussion. He's out of recovery. You can see him for a minute if you'd like."

"Thank you," Jeff said.

The doctor directed them to the second floor and down a hall to a small room that held two beds. The curtains were drawn about one bed, but in the other, Harris lay flat, an IV in his arm, wires everywhere, a catheter snaking from beneath the sheets to disappear beneath the bed. His eyes were open.

"So how are you doing?" Jeff stepped up to the bedside, his hands on the metal rail.

Harris's lips twitched into a faint smile. "Long day," he whispered. "Jason Marl admitted it. That he gave Emily mushrooms. That he poisoned the other two who died last year. You want to get a tape recorder?"

"Nah." Jeff put a hand on Harris's shoulder. "They tell me you're going to live. I'll come back in the morning."

"Is the kid all right?" Harris made a movement as if to push himself erect. "The one working for Rachel. Jason said he was going to kill him, too."

"He's fine, he's fine." Jeff pushed Harris gently flat again.

"He is." Rachel stepped up beside Jeff. "Harris, I'm so glad . . ." Her voice failed her, and she realized with horror that she was about to burst into tears.

"Will you tell Anne-Marie? That I am all right? She'll worry."

"I'm going over there right now." Rachel took his hand—the one without the IV drip in it. "I just wanted to make sure you were okay."

"Tell her . . . tell her I'm fine." His eyelids fluttered.

Jeff pulled her gently away from the bed and they tip-toed out of the room, passing the young, dark-haired nurse who was on her way in. She gave them a smile and a thumbs-up. "Your friend is doing fine," she said. "Don't worry."

"I need to go tell her." Rachel looked up at Jeff as they retraced their steps down the corridor. "Madame. She'll want to come here."

"Do you want me to come along?"

"No." They were in the elevator, along with a young male aid in green who looked as if he was about sixteen. "This is girl stuff."

"Plotting, are you?" Jeff gave her a crooked smile.

"Damn right." The aid exited and they followed him out onto the main floor. "Drop me off and I'll get my truck. I hope I'll get home by morning."

"I'm going to be dealing with our vandal and Marl," Jeff said regretfully. "You'll probably get home before I do."

Home. She had said the word. So had he. And it was. "I'll wait up for you," she said.

Another ambulance had pulled into the semicircular driveway, laden with its burden of tragedy. Rachel looked away, shoulders hunching a bit as they hurried across the parking lot to the Jeep. "I am so glad." She stopped short as they reached it, looking up at Jeff. "I am so glad that he is okay." She stepped into Jeff's embrace and the tears finally won.

CHAPTER
20

Jeff had no sooner pulled up behind Rachel's truck in Mrs. Frey's driveway than Spider and Mrs. Frey both burst from the house. Spider was using a battered aluminum crutch as he limped across to the Jeep, his sprained ankle swathed in elastic bandages.

"Did you find him?" Spider leaned into the Jeep window. "Did you find Harris? Is he okay?"

"Yeah. He is." Jeff gripped Spider's arm. "He's in the hospital and he'll be fine."

"Oh, good." Mrs. Frey, crowding close behind Spider, let her breath out in a long sigh. "I was so afraid that he wouldn't be, and that man would get away with what he did."

"He wouldn't have," Jeff said grimly.

"I'm heading over to the Village, to tell Madame DeRochers about Harris." Rachel slammed the Jeep's door. "Did you by any chance feed poor Peter?" she asked Mrs. Frey.

"Of course, dear." Mrs. Frey clucked her tongue. "Really. I couldn't let him go hungry. He'd be after my chickadees in no time."

"You're wonderful." Rachel took Jeff's hand, their fingers gripping hard. "See you later," she said. "Go be police chief and then let poor Ben out."

"You're sure you're going to be okay?" he asked softly.

Rachel nodded, went to her truck.

"You be careful." Mrs Frey followed her as Jeff backed down the driveway. "It's very late, honey. You've had an emotional day. I could drive you, you know?"

"I'll be fine. Really." She smiled at her landlady. "I've got so much adrenalin in my blood that I couldn't fall asleep if I tried."

"Well, if you don't feel up to driving your friend back, you call me. You hear?" Mrs. Frey was using the same tone she used on Spider.

"Yes, ma'am," Rachel said, and got into her truck.

It was long past midnight. She decided not to look at her watch as she drove up the winding drive to the silent Village. In the wan light of the moon and stars, the rutted landscape of the grounds made her think of a battlefield, or the surface of an alien and deserted planet. Big halogen lamps shed sickly yellow light on the parking lot, reflecting back from the dark windows of sleeping residents. Rachel pulled up in front of the main entry. The doors were locked after all the residents had gone to bed. She would have to ring a bell to summon the person on night duty. But as she walked up to the big glass doors, she saw a single figure sitting up very straight on the sofa that faced the door, alone in the vast, dim lobby.

Madame DeRochers.

Rachel rapped softly on the locked doors, but Madame was already rising to her feet, picking up the small black purse at her side and an aluminum cane, her expression

serene as she crossed to the door and opened it. "I am
ready," she said. "Let us go to him."

"He's at the hospital in Hood River." Rachel closed the
big doors behind Madame. They latched automatically,
closing on the empty lobby full of shadows. A flicker
caught Rachel's eye. It was nothing more than a trick of
reflection as the doors closed, she told herself, but for a
moment the hair on the back of her neck rose, and she
felt as if someone was watching her, just out of sight,
perhaps behind one of the pillars. "It's over," she whispered to that invisible presence. Had Emily paid for those
deaths all her life? Kept that photograph to remind her of
what she had ended? Had she known why she was dying
at the end? "It's over," she said softly. "All over."

Nothing moved in the shadows, and she turned away
to find Madame regarding her. She nodded, did not speak,
walking quickly around the truck to climb into the passenger's side. Eighty years old, she moved with the agility of someone twenty-five years younger, her back as
straight as a ruler, the ugly aluminum cane seeming no
more than an accessory as she wrapped her skirt primly
about her blue-veined, still-slender legs. She said nothing
until Rachel had started the truck, and was driving down
the long driveway once more.

"Tell me," she said, her voice as composed as her face.

So Rachel told her the whole story of the long, fright-
ening day, from Spider's disappearance, to the dark cli-
max at Jason's well. Madame said nothing, listened with
her head tilted, hands folded in her lap, her slender body
swaying to the movement of the truck. She finished as
they reached the hospital. Madame was silent as Rachel
pulled into a parking space. She got out, still silent, and
accompanied Rachel through the hospital lobby and onto
the elevator. One of the nurses intercepted them at the
brightly lit station. The patient rooms were dark, their oc-

cupants sleeping, or at least lying in the darkness waiting
for pain medication or morning or both.

"I'm sorry," she began.

"I am his wife," Madame announced with dignity. She
marched past the young woman, leaving her no chance to
say another word, and as if guided by ESP, went directly
to the room where Harris lay. A night-light burned near
the tiny wash basin. The other bed was still empty. Harris
turned his head as they entered. He lifted his free hand as
Madame crossed swiftly to him. She lifted it to her lips,
kissed the back of it lightly, then turned it to press his
palm against her cheek. Still holding his hand, she sat in
the small chrome-and-plastic chair by his bedside, her
back still straight, both feet on the floor. "You may go
home now," she said to Rachel. "And sleep. I will be fine.
I thank you for the ride."

"You're welcome," Rachel said, and left the room, tiptoing down the quiet hallway. Machines hummed softly
and invisibly from the darkened rooms. Amber and green
lights glowed like strange eyes in the darkness. Signaling
life or the struggle for life, Rachel thought. She felt over-
whelmingly tired suddenly, her whole body aching with
a weariness that seemed greater than mere physical ex-
haustion. The young nurse at the bright island of the nursing station raised her eyebrows.

"Is your friend staying? We can give her a bed."

"I don't think she'll sleep," Rachel said. "She'll tell you
if she needs something."

"I'm sure she will." The nurse laughed. "I'm not about
to cross her, don't worry."

The eastern sky was just beginning to pale where it met
the forest as Rachel drove out of the parking lot. The drive
home seemed to take no time. As the truck climbed the
long winding road to Jeff's house, she realized, with a
start of guilt, that she had been driving on autopilot for
most of the trip.

The porch light was on, and Ben greeted her at the door, giving her a welcoming shove with his broad muzzle. Jeff was home. He had fallen asleep sitting up on the sofa, but he woke instantly as the door opened, got up to come put his arms around her. "He'll be fine," she murmured, her face against his shoulder. "She's there. She won't let anything happen to him." Not even Death could touch him now, she thought. Not even that.

"Go lie down, Ben," Jeff said.

Arms around each other, Rachel and Jeff went into the bedroom and closed the door behind them. They made love, long and slow, and it was an affirmation of life and a rejection of the death and echos of dark yesterdays that had tainted the day. They fell asleep, still twined together, as the sun edged above the distant horizon.

They were awakened what seemed to be minutes later by Ben, rooting at them with a remarkably cold nose, wriggling with delight because he'd managed to push the door open.

"Ouch." Jeff shoved his grinning head away, wincing as Ben rammed his muzzle into the small of his back. "I guess you're healthy enough. That nose of yours is like ice. Okay, okay, we're up."

Rachel laughed, then shrieked as Ben took this as an invitation and leaped gaily into the center of the bed. "Off, idiot dog, before the whole thing collapses." Laughing, she shoved at him, which caused him to plant his huge body flat in the middle of the quilt and grin at her, exposing every one of his white teeth. "You could scare anyone to death doing that, you silly dog. Off!" She pointed to the floor.

He put his ears down, gave her a mournful look, then slunk off the bed.

"Oh, don't give me the wounded-feelings look. No way are you going to start sleeping on the bed, dog." She sat up, stretching, feeling, if not rested, at least awake.

"You can go back to sleep if you want." Sitting on the edge of the bed, Jeff ran his hand through her hair. "No reason you have to be up."

"You're going over to the hospital, aren't you?" Rachel reached for her robe. "I'll come along. I want to see how Madame is doing."

"I'm glad to have the company." He ran his finger along her jaw, then got up abruptly. "I'll go get the coffee started, if you want to grab the bathroom first."

"It's a deal." Rachel padded barefoot to the front door to let Ben out, then on to the bathroom and the newly tiled shower stall. They had talked about adding a greenhouse sun room on the south side of the house and putting a Jacuzzi in it. Until then, it was shower only. Rachel stepped out, shaking water from her hair as she groped for the towel. The scent of coffee enticed her. She dried off and pulled on her clothes quickly. By the time she was pouring coffee for herself, Jeff was out of the shower, too.

Rachel drove to the apartment to see how Spider's ankle was doing and say hello to Peter. She found Spider sitting in the garden with a pair of crutches beside him and his bandaged ankle propped up on an upturned plastic bucket. Mrs. Frey was weeding and he had a book open on his lap. They were arguing about whether the news was ever unbiased.

"You show me somebody without bias and I'll show you that they're just more subtle about their prejudices than the average person," Mrs. Frey said crisply. "You can't write objectively. Period."

"Yeah, you can. If you know your own prejudices, then you catch yourself and you don't put them in."

"Show me a man who knows himself and I'll show you a liar." Mrs. Frey snorted.

"This is an erudite discussion." Rachel said. "How's the ankle this morning?"

"Feels like it's broken," Spider grumbled. "Amelia says it's gonna be six weeks before it's better. That's as bad as a real break!"

"That's how long sprains take to heal." Mrs. Frey pulled a sly little dandelion that had managed to insinuate itself among her marigolds. "And if you start using it too soon, you'll just sprain it again, worse. And the conversation was merely about the fact that nothing you read in the paper is objective." She glanced up at Rachel. "Have you looked at this week's *Bee*? It's hot off the press. My friend Rosemary Burbank brought it by first thing this morning."

Uh-oh. Rachel took it as Spider silently handed it to her. SON OF BLOSSOM POLICE OFFICER VANDALIZES TOWN, the huge black letters blared across the top of the page, beneath the logo of a tough-looking bumble bee flexing its muscles astride a sprig of apple blossoms. AID AT GARDEN VIEW RETIREMENT VILLAGE ARRESTED IN MURDER INVESTIGATION. The type wasn't quite banner, but it wasn't a whole lot smaller than the headline. Rachel sighed. *The people of Blossom, acceding to the mayor's request for more law enforcement for your growing town, has expanded our police department by twenty percent during this past year.* "He could just say that they added one person." Rachel rolled her eyes. *Not only has our increased number of officers been unable to stop the mysterious vandal who has been plaguing the hardworking businesses and citizens of Blossom, but now it appears that the criminal is none other than the son of one of the officers* . . . "I take it that this wasn't your example of subtle bias," Rachel said dryly. "Honestly, what's got Hallie's hackles up these days? He's worse than usual."

"We'd gotten beyond the *Bee*, actually." Mrs. Frey excavated another luckless dandelion. "Are you going to see that poor man at the hospital today?"

"Yes. Jeff is picking me up on the way. Damn, Hallie," she said with feeling.

"Well, you know what he's like when he gets on a crusade." Mrs. Frey was searching through the flowers, eyes sharp for more offending weeds. "He'll simmer down shortly."

"Ditto what you said." Spider looked up at her. "He's making it sound like Jeff's fault. There's the Jeep," he said, pointing out to the street.

She walked down to meet him, hoping he hadn't seen the *Bee* yet. After yesterday, this seemed doubly unfair. But he had. A copy lay on the seat. "Thanks," she said. "I already had my morning dose of editorial bile."

"Well, we sure don't look good." He turned around in the street and headed toward Hood River. "I think it's Lyle who is feeding him his inside info, but I don't have any proof. And Lyle's too good to fire. He hasn't given Hallie anything he shouldn't have anyway."

Rachel grunted. Her opinion was much less charitable.

At the hospital, as she had expected, Madame had established herself. Harris was sitting up in bed, looking almost normal again. "I'm going to have to get out of here soon." He gave Madame a sly look and reached for her hand. "She's got the nurses terrified."

Madame just lifted one precise eyebrow and said nothing.

"You want a statement?" Harris's expression sobered. "You feel up to it?"

"I feel pretty good, actually." Harris nodded. "I want to make sure this guy goes down and stays there. I never really suspected him. He's good." He licked his lips, reached for a container of cranberry juice, and sipped a little of the vivid liquid. "He played the sweetheart to the wealthier residents of the Village—you know. He flirted with the women, was respectful to the men, knew the names of the grandkids, and who was in which grade. He never seemed to have much backbone." Harris tried to laugh, winced, and stopped. "So much for my analysis of criminal ability. Actually, I suspected our assistant director. I ran into her coming out of Emily's room one night, and she was pretty flustered. I dropped a couple of hints that I knew more than the police were admitting. That got around pretty fast, so I figured someone would try something." Harris gave Jeff a wry smile. "I didn't expect the result I got."

Jason had let himself into Harris's room in the middle of the night with a master key that he must have copied or stolen at some time. Harris was a light sleeper and had put up as much fight as he could. The last thing he remembered was Jason swinging Madame's cane at his head. He had come to in the trunk of Jason's car. "We drove for a while." Harris's eyes narrowed as he remembered. "Then he parked for a long time. The sun must have come up, because it got hot. I had a hard time breathing." He drew a deep breath, as if his body remembered that sense of suffocation. "He'd tied my hands and I couldn't do much, but I finally managed to get loose and I started pounding on the trunk with my fist, but we were moving again by then and I think I passed out. The next thing I remember was him opening the trunk. We were in the woods. He was angry that I'd gotten loose and tied my hands again." The bruises on Harris's face testified to Jason's anger that he had freed himself. "He dragged me through the woods for a little way. He hadn't said much, but when he stopped dragging me, he leaned over me." Harris drank more juice, and Rachel noticed the gleam of sweat on his forehead in spite of the air-conditioning. Madame noticed it, too. She reached over to take his hand. His fingers closed around hers, and he looked at her. Smiled, then looked back to them.

"He . . . said some strange things. He was very earnest, as if I was a student and he was trying to explain a difficult lesson to me. He talked about God and how He was the only power to decide life or death. He told me that he, Jason, would never harm anyone, that it was God's decision that a chicken should die to feed us. He told me that when humans sinned, God did the punishing. He was only a tool to provide a means for God to punish a sinner. That if God chose to forgive, he would forgive, and not even poisonous mushrooms would harm the forgiven."

"Didn't they throw accused people into lakes once? God was supposed to save them if they were innocent." Rachel said.

"Trial by water." Jeff nodded.

"I think that was the idea," Harris said dryly. "He told me very seriously that Emily had murdered and God had punished her. If she had been innocent, then she would not have died. I asked him about the other two people who died. He didn't answer for a while. Then he repeated that God never let the innocent die. He picked up the cane I made for Anne-Marie. I guess it broke when he hit me with it. He tossed it into the weeds beside me and I realized . . . they covered the opening of an old well. I . . . heard the cane fall." He wiped his face on his sleeve. "He rolled me over, untied my wrists, and . . . pushed." Harris swallowed, eyes closing briefly, his knuckles whitening as he gripped Madame's hand. "I was falling, clawing at the sides, and then I grabbed something. I slammed the wall so hard that I nearly blacked out, and I thought my wrists were going to break. I remember dirt in my mouth and darkness, and I wasn't falling anymore. I got an elbow over the branch or stick that I'd caught hold of, and it wasn't straight, was kind of a ledge right there. I just . . . hung on. That was all I could do. I don't know how long it was." He shrugged. "I woke up here." He looked up at Jeff, gave him a crooked grin. "I am damn glad you showed up."

"Me, too." Jeff clicked off the recorder and reached over to grip the older man's arm. "I've got it," he said. "I'll bring it by for you to sign later." He stood up. "That branch you caught? It was the broken piece of Madame's cane. It jammed in a crevice."

Harris's eyes widened slightly. "I'll have to make you a new one, Anne-Marie."

"I expect it, *mon chér*. This one is cold and ugly." Madame rose and joined Rachel. Her eyes were the color of late-autumn leaves, sparked with flecks of gold. She took Rachel's hand and smiled gently at her. "I wish you to know that Harris and I will be married. He is such a boy." She looked over at him, her smile soft as spring. "I wish to be his wife, as well as his lover."

"Congratulations," Jeff said.

Rachel said nothing, merely squeezed Anne-Marie Celestine DeRocher's hand. She received a firm squeeze in return.

Jeff looked strained as they left the hospital. "Jason admitted giving the galerinas to Emily and the other two residents of the Village," he told her as they crossed the quiet lobby. "He told me that he'd discovered the director's embezzling because he routinely snooped through the residents' desks, and he had picked his first two victims from the residents who were being overcharged. Those first two were cover, so that we would suspect the director. Which we did." He shrugged. "Noble admitted to those midnight visits, by the way. She was conspiring with Emily to expose the director. But Emily was getting senile, and forgot she wasn't supposed to go around complaining about her overcharges. Marl gave her a larger dose of galerinas than he had used on his first two victims, because he wanted to make sure that her death was recognized as a murder."

Rachel shivered, remembering Jason's bright face as he assured her that Harris was fine. "Is he sane?" she asked hesitantly.

"They'll have to determine that, I guess. When we were questioning him, Jason went on and on about how he was merely a tool of vengeance in God's hands. That if God didn't want these people to die, they would be alive. He quoted all kinds of Biblical miracles to me to prove that God could do whatever the hell He—"

"Or She," Rachel said sweetly.

"Or She, wanted to do." Jeff gave her a look. "Is that better?"

"Of course." She tucked her hand into his elbow. "Please proceed. You know, Gus told me that the grandparents he went to live with were pretty rigid fundamentalist-type Christians. He thought they disapproved of his mother."

"Maybe that plays a role. Maybe he's just setting the scene for an insanity plea. This is a smart boy. He didn't make too many mistakes. And I heard from the State Police this morning. They picked up Bellington down in Coos Bay, heading for California apparently. I guess she was staying in a cheap motel down there. She may not be a murderer, but she certainly is an embezzler."

"I feel sorry for her," Rachel said slowly. "I think she got kind of a bad deal."

Jeff grunted, and didn't answer. They had reached the Jeep, and stood now with their backs against the shaded side of the vehicle. The Columbia rolled on below, blue today, blue as the sky, flecked with white and spangled with the bright water-bound butterfly wings of the wind surfers. "Do we ever really get away from the past?" His eyes were on the water. "Is there ever a moment when we say *that's over,* and finish it?"

"I don't know." She thought of Spider's father, lost in the seeking of his own past. "Maybe the best we can do is come to terms?"

"Maybe." He pulled her into his arms. "Maybe that really is the best." He kissed her. "So we'll leave the door open, huh?"

"Unless Ben is going to come in and jump on the bed," she said, and he laughed, which was what she wanted, and the reflected light from the river drove the yesterdays away.

CHAPTER

21

The apples and pears were picked, the big wooden crates
hauled off to the processor. The profits were being
counted. The losses calculated. Harvest was over. The
tourists had flooded in to buy fruit, cider, candy, pies, to
eat and drink at the restaurants, and ride in hay-filled wag-
ons pulled by sleek Belgian horses at the Hood River
orchards that participated in the Harvest Festival. Pump-
kins were ripening and hay mazes were being planned for
the wave of Halloween visitors later on. It was no longer
hot, but it wasn't really fall yet either. Indian summer. It
was the breathing space between harvest and winter
chores. You weren't ready to start getting the equipment
in shape for spring spraying and cultivation yet, but the
tomatoes and pears were canned, and the sauerkraut stored
for those winter dinners. You weren't ready yet to tackle
all those little chores that you didn't have time for during
harvest. You took a deep breath, enjoyed the weather that
still wasn't too bad, although the tomato plants had gotten
nailed by the last frost, and that was okay, because you

had plenty of jars in the panty, and you were tired of picking, drying, and canning, thank you.

The Village landscaping was finished. Julio had showed up with Anita and Eduardo, and they had worked with her while Spider's ankle healed. The grounds weren't perfect, but they would look good for the photographer. To Rachel's surprise, Brian Ferrel, the young owner of the Blossom Feed and Seed, donated a thousand assorted spring bulbs to the Village. After all her worries about finishing the landscape, the magazine had postponed the photo session until spring. So drifts of crocus and early daffodil would decorate the slopes around the pond for the camera. Most importantly, the grounds were now a lovely place to be. There were magic places there to be found. A cranky white swan had even appeared in the pond one day, much to everyone's surprise.

It was a good time for a party.

The party happened in the lobby of City Hall. It had been decorated with marigolds, chrysanthemums, boughs of scarlet and gold crab apples, their leaves still crisp, because they had been cut and hung only hours ago. There were no chairs here. A wooden table had been placed in the center of the lobby, covered with a lace cloth that had been crocheted by Madame DeRocher's grandmother, more than a century ago. Two tall candles burned on it, next to a bowl of local fruit: apples, pears, Asian pears, grapes, plums, and even kiwi fruit. More garlands of marigolds and chrysanthemums spiced the air and a lot of people crowded the space.

A childhood friend of Rachel and Jeff's played a flute softly, the music as breathy as the human voice. At the lace-covered table stood Blossom's mayor, and Judge Barret, a man who had served on the bench for nearly three decades and had grown up playing baseball with Rachel's uncle and father.

The flute segued into a cheerful version of the wedding processional. Rachel looked over at Anne-Marie Celestine DeRocher, dressed in an elegant and understated suit of linen that might have come straight from Paris, and very likely had, and she smiled. Her own dress was simple, a pale green brocade, calf length, that suited her stocky figure. She had looked at herself in the mirror and had been pleased. She looked *great.* She never looked great. But today she did. Joshua had pinned a corsage of white orchids on both her shoulder and Madame's. He had kissed Madame's hand and she had actually blushed.

Her Uncle Jack took her arm. The mayor took Anne-Marie Celestine's. They walked down an aisle that opened through the crowd as they moved forward, then closed in behind them. Sandy waved, bright and cheerful in a very pink, flouncy dress. Spider winked and grinned. Standing next to Mrs. Frey, who wore a scarlet sheath dress with a single white rose at her shoulder, he looked amazingly at ease in the suit that she had bought him. He could go a long way, Rachel thought. The double-pierced ear—one ring and one stud—which had appeared at the same time as the suit, looked good. Mrs. Frey refused to admit complicity, and officially clucked about it. But not very seriously.

At the table, they met up with Jeff and Harris in his chair. The ceremony was short. Spider had written it. They had discussed and proposed possible texts. Then, one afternoon, Spider had handed her a printed page.

We are here, they recited Spider's words together, *to put yesterday behind us but not to forget it, and to begin forever.*

The judge pronounced the official words. The mayor handed Harris and Jeff the rings. Silver, she and Jeff had decided, because it went with emeralds. Jeff slipped it onto her finger and his eyes held hers, dark as night, clear as water. "Forever," he said.

"Forever." The words overlaid each other, unanimous.

A flicker of motion near the doorway caught Rachel's eye. A tall woman stood there. For an instant, Rachel didn't recognize her. Her hair was a bright auburn, and she looked a little uncomfortable, as if she had perhaps wandered into City Hall by mistake. But then the dark eyes and the profile connected and she stifled a gasp of recognition. Jeff's mother. Rachel's heart leaped. The mayor was speaking the last words—"Bless this union. It joins like souls, and gives back to our community. So kiss, folks. That's what we're all waiting for!"

They did, both pairs, with enthusiasm. "This is madness," Madame said, cradled in Harris's lap, her eyes the laughing eyes of a young girl, never mind her aged skin and white hair. "But I will be mad with you," she murmured, looking into Harris's eyes. He swept her into a second, lengthy embrace. Everybody cheered, and crowded in to congratulate, shake hands, and generally celebrate.

"The party is at the Bread Box," the mayor announced, as if the whole town didn't know. Joylinn had been decorating all week, and her hints about what would be served had everyone in the town salivating. She was celebrating this wedding with all her might.

Slowly, the throng began to thin as people trickled out of the building for the short walk down to the Bread Box.

Deborah O'Connor embraced her daughter. She didn't say anything, but her face was wet with tears, and she held tightly to Joshua's hand. Uncle Jack threw his arms around her and lifted her off the floor, smelling of bourbon and sweat. "I'm proud of you," he yelled into her ear. "If you never graft another damn tree, I'm still proud of you, and always will be." He threw his arms around Jeff and thumped him on the back, while Aunt Catherine congratulated Rachel, and shared a brief eye roll at her husband's antics.

Jeff's mother stepped up behind them, dark-haired, her tawny oval face familiar and at the same time strange, as if Rachel had never really looked at her before.

"Congratulations," she said, reaching with both hands for Rachel's hands, pulling her close, kissing her on the cheek—not a society peck, but a real kiss. A relative's kiss.

"Mom." Jeff sounded stunned. "I thought you couldn't come."

"I decided I couldn't not come." She smiled at her son, a trace of sadness in her dark eyes. "Sometimes you have to step back and take a good look at your priorities." She smiled a little shyly at Rachel, then threw her arms around her son. "Congratulations," she murmured. "I'm proud of you, you know."

They walked over to the Bread Box under a clear fall sky. Daren and Iko Rhinehoffer walked beside them. Daren's small son rode his shoulders, both chubby fists clutching Daren's hair. "I think we should do a display at the big Portland Home and Garden Show next year," he told Rachel. "I think it's time."

"Don't talk business today!" Iko rapped him sharply on the arm. "Shame on you."

"This is a great day to talk business." Daren laughed and winked at Rachel. "How could she say no today?"

"All right, all right, we'll do it." Rachel laughed with him, her arm firmly linked through Jeff's. "Next year."

"Sounds like a good business move to me." Jeff smiled down at her. "As long as nobody gets murdered there."

"At a garden show?" Rachel laughed.

"It's a deal then. I've got you on tape, you know. You're committed." Daren laughed and ducked as Iko pretended to swat him and then yelped as his son yanked at his hair.

The crowd had filled the Bread Box and spilled over onto the decks. Joylinn had loaded long buffet tables along the sides of the room, offering smoked salmon, cheeses, and dozens of tiny pastries topped with goat cheese, fresh vegetables, and smoked meats. She had made the wedding cake, decorated with sprays of apple and pear blossoms. Tiny marzipan fruits clustered on the layers. Joylinn had tinted the fruits to represent the varieties grown in the local orchards—Gravenstein, Delicious, Fuji, Bosc.

Madame and Harris cut the first piece. Rachel and Jeff cut a second slice. The party began in earnest. Children shrieked and played tag outside, and a few tourists even wandered in to join the throng.

Together, holding glasses of champagne that Joylinn had poured, they moved slowly through the crowd, chatting, smiling, greeting friends and neighbors. It was indeed a fine party. Joshua and her mother were chatting with Jeff's mother, and they seemed to be having a wonderful time. Spider was perched on the railing of the deck outside, talking animatedly with a blond-haired girl who was a distant cousin of Rachel's. He was certainly no kid anymore. Rachel realized with a start that he was an awfully good-looking man, and the earrings set off his lean face perfectly. Julio and Anita came up to congratulate her. Anita offered her hand to Jeff with a shy smile.

People now knew that Bert Stanfield's son had called the INS after his father had told him about the plan to stake out Julio's friend. Stanfield had quit the Blossom Police. To Jeff's surprise, the Council had urged him to replace Stanfield as quickly as possible. And they had voted down the curfew proposal. Hallie had even—finally—run an editorial praising Jeff for his handling of the murder investigation. Rachel was threatening to frame it.

Hallie himself was over at the table, filling a plate with food, his sharp gray eyes missing nothing, in spite of his jovial manner. Rachel wondered briefly how he would describe this citywide party.

Finally, she and Jeff managed to sneak through the doors and out onto the deck that overlooked the river. This time of year, the sun was already sinking, gilding the water with the slanting beams of golden light. It was getting cool and the hint of fall in the air had driven the other guests back inside. Deborah O'Connor stuck her head through the open French doors and came to join them. She took her daughter's hand. "Congratulations to you both," she said, and her voice caught.

Rachel took her mother's hand and kissed it. Deborah gave her daughter a hug and slipped back inside. It was going to be chilly tonight—maybe even frost. Rachel rubbed her bare arms as a breeze gusted, riffling the Columbia's surface. Jeff stepped up close behind her and put his arms around her. "Want to slip out of here?" he asked. "As I recall, we were going to have something small and quiet, weren't we?" He was grinning at her, his eyes reflecting the river light.

"I seem to remember that was our plan. I'm not sure how this all happened." She answered his grin, feeling as if the golden river light was filling her to overflowing. "I think we can blame Joylinn and my mother, mostly. And Madame, and Harris, of course." She took his hand, her fingers laced through his. "They'll all do fine without us."

They ran down the steps together and up the street toward City Hall. Jeff's Jeep was parked there. They would go back to the house above the Columbia and let Ben out. There was a bottle of champagne and a platter of food in the refrigerator—delivered by Joylinn last night. It would be cold enough tonight to make a fire welcome. Tomorrow they would leave for a week of camping in the Oregon desert—a honeymoon that had made her mother shake her head, but which would be wonderful.

But that was tomorrow.

Nobody called to them as they ran hand in hand through the empty streets. It was not always going to be easy, Rachel thought as they reached City Hall. But it was going to be good.